THE BANNERS OF WAR

THE BANNERS
OF WAR

Sacha Carnegie

PETER DAVIES : LONDON

Peter Davies Limited
15 Queen Street, Mayfair, London W1X 8BE
LONDON MELBOURNE TORONTO
JOHANNESBURG AUCKLAND

432 02073 X

Printed in Great Britain by
Redwood Burn Limited
Trowbridge & Esher

My grateful thanks to Don Pottinger,
my collaborator in planning and research.

THE BANNERS OF WAR

Dramatis Personae

Henryk Barinski

Son of a noble Polish family, the friend and lover of Kasia Radienska during their youth in the Ukraine; separated from her by Turkish marauders, he was drawn into political intrigue in Rome and Paris, and fought at the Battle of Rossbach. His reunion with Kasia in St Petersburg was short-lived. Arrested as a spy, he was sentenced to imprisonment in Siberia.

Ewen Cameron

Cousin of Donald Cameron, 19th Chief of Clan Cameron. Escaped to France after Culloden. Returned to Scotland eight years later. Arrested and condemned to the Thames hulks until taken for service in the Royal Navy.

IN RUSSIA

Kasia Radienska

Henryk's childhood companion and lover. Parted from him nine years before when Turks destroyed her home, killed her family and took her off with them to the Crimea. After years of captivity and adventure she reached St. Petersburg where she became lady-in-waiting to the Grand Duchess Catherine, friend of their youth. Briefly reunited with Henryk until his arrest.

Grand Duchess Catherine of Russia ('Figgy')

The small German Princess who had known both Kasia and Henryk as children, and who, on the latter's arrival in St Petersburg, had chosen him as one of her lovers.

Count Stanislas Poniatowski

Cousin to Kasïa. Catherine's lover. The man who was one day to become the last King of Poland.

Count Lev Bubin

The Russian nobleman who found Kasia after her departure from the Don Cossacks and brought her to St Petersburg as his mistress.

Count Alexander Shuvalov
Head of the dreaded Secret Chancellery. The most powerful man in Russia.

Alexei Orlov
The second of five Orlov brothers who were to play a major part in Catherine's seizure of the throne. Thinking Henryk dead, Kasia became Orlov's mistress and was happy with him until his departure for the Seven Years' War.

Karzel
Polish dwarf, once the servant to Orlov, then to Kasia whom he worshipped. Dangerously jealous of Henryk.

Pavel and Uliana Tuntsev
Fur-trappers living in a small hut on the shores of the Dvina river, north-east of St Petersburg.

IN FRANCE

The Chevalier D'Eon
Friend of Henryk's from their time in Paris. The famous diplomat, spy, swordsman who was thought by many to be a woman.

The Prince de Conti
The man responsible for sending Henryk to St Petersburg the first time—on the business of the 'King's Secret'—to gain Catherine's sympathy and support for France.

Louis de Valfons
Professional soldier of France and Henryk's Regimental Commander at the Battle of Rossbach the year before.

Amande de Valfons
The girl who brought Henryk to Paris from Rome, lived with him, then married his friend, Louis de Valfons.

Toinon
The Marquise de la Ferte d'Imbault. Daughter of Madame Geoffrin, the greatest of the salonnières. A close friend of Henryk's during his time in Paris.

Madame Geoffrin
The great Salonnière.

OFFICERS AND CREW OF H.M.S. HUNTRESS

Thomas Primrose	Captain
William Stodart	First Lieutenant
Charles Wood	Second Lieutenant
Hon. Richard Gore	Third Lieutenant
Frobisher	Fourth Lieutenant
Francis Columbine	Purser
Ebenezer Boosey	Surgeon
Rev. Dunsterville	Chaplain
Lloyd	Midshipman
Tregotha	Midshipman
Prendergast	Midshipman
Mr. Hay	Gunner
Mr. Cromer	Master
Jem Pike	Boatswain
Yorston	Captain of the Afterguard
Mat Swaine	Quarter-gunner
Gazard	Ship's carpenter
Fitch	Seaman gunner
Gammon	Seaman gunner
Mendel	Seaman gunner
Croaker	Seaman gunner
Elmquist	Seaman gunner
Bunch	Purser's clerk

PART ONE

ON a bitter night in 1758 the wind blew from the east, from out of Siberia; the cruel winter wind, sweeping across four thousand miles of frozen wilderness, turned the night into a raging demon in which nothing could live.

But something did live, moving unseen, unheard and utterly alone.

Here and there the wind had cleared open patches on the river ice and across one of these a man was crawling with dogged slowness, pressed close to the black ice by the cruel force of the blizzard. He hauled himself forward painfully like a crushed slug and, from the iron band round his left wrist, a short length of chain slithered over the ice, inch by inch.

Since his escape from the *prut*—that shuffling procession of the damned, chained to long iron bars, on their terrible journey to Siberia—the blizzard had been at his back. Which was as well, for no living creature, least of all a human one could face that storm—his very skin would be stripped from the flesh in an instant by the red-hot kiss of the wind.

But now the snow swirled in his face; freezing white dust choked his nostrils and burnt his lungs. His eyes froze in sockets packed with the whirling drift and he felt the first numbness in his limbs, the first dread ache of his finger-nails. Soon he would feel nothing, the whiteness striking the nose and fingers, and ears peeling from the skull like withered white leaves. His hands and feet would harden and become brittle as wine-glass stems. He knew enough about frost-bite from his youth in Poland. And he knew also what the cold could do to the mind.

So simple to stop, to lower his head to the ice and sleep. No more effort, nor more pain. Lie down and sleep forever. The smoothness of the ice gave way to deep snow as he reached the low bank and, hauling himself upwards, he abandoned the bitter struggle and laid his head on a soft powdered cushion, and a voice he supposed was his own gave hoarse thanks to God for such exquisite relief.

Now I shall die, he thought, and his mind, for the first time since they came for him—was it days ago, or weeks?—was at peace. He knew a moment of complete contentment such as he had never experienced before, not even with Kasia, his woman. I shall drift into eternity, into nothingness, as the snow covers me softly, gently, without trace, and that will be the end. Drowsiness flooded his suffering body and death summoned him in a languorous whisper.

Then, as he lay slowly dying, another voice came to him on the wind, louder than the call of death: 'Is this the way a man dies?' There was contempt in his grandfather's words, a biting scorn. . . . 'You were born to fight, never forget that . . . not to give up like a miserable old woman in bed. . . . Get up and go on—on —on. . . .' The voice faded and the fugitive staggered to his feet, shaking off the pall of snow, forcing himself up the bank. Left foot—right foot. . . .

The storm held a different note now as it roared among the tall, swaying trees but he did not notice. On he went, dragging his frozen feet through snow as heavy as wet sand, left foot—right foot. Now and then he whimpered like a frightened child. Faces appeared in his mind, coming and going like will-o'-the-wisps, and he saw them with amazing clarity and knew that they heralded the final stage of the white death. Everything *was* clear to him now: he would not stop again: he would go on, and then when his feet in their rags broke off he would crawl and would not stop. The faces pleased him for they were company in this icy, swirling, twilit world . . . the handsome features of Poniatowski, smiling with all his suspect charm . . . the Grand Duchess Catherine, her beautiful eyes inviting. . . . But she had gone and in her place he saw Lev Bubin, 'May God damn him to eternal hell', gloating at the whistle of the knout in the dungeon of the Secret Chancellery . . . Alexander Shuvalov, the master of that place of terror, most powerful man in Russia, with his cold eyes and twitching face. . . . Left foot—right foot—left foot: the pause was lengthening between each tortured step and he moved in the utter darkness of the blind, groping among the trees, stumbling, falling to his knees, hauling himself forward with his last remaining strength. . . . The voice of Shuvalov in the swooping rush of the wind: 'Once again, who are you? Why did they send you to Petersburg?' Why? Who? ... The cut of the leather across his naked back, his muffled groans falling on deaf ears ... Now he was crawling, almost dead, and he saw the haunted face of the young man who had died beside him on the *prut*. A stranger had died so that another could live. If they had not severed two chains in the darkness by mistake ... Suddenly the ground went from under him and he was falling through the darkness. He landed in deep snow, rolled over and fell again a few feet further and this time lay still, unable to struggle any longer.

*　　*　　*

A man and a woman sat by the stove in the trapper's hut staring at each other in startled silence.

'Holy Mother, what was it, Pavel?' The woman's lower lip trembled as she glanced first at the smoky ceiling, then at the door. 'It sounded like—' She stopped and crossed herself to the ikon on the timber wall.

'A bear,' said her husband in an extra loud voice, but following her example all the same. 'That's all it was, a bear.'

Pavel Tuntsev was a fur-trapper. A grizzled, broad-shouldered man in his forty-sixth year, he had been employed for the last five years trapping beaver, ermine and silver fox for the Counts Stroganov, whose trading empire stretched from St Petersburg to far beyond the mountains of the Ural; he had built his cabin in a deep gully leading down to the marshy shores of the Dvina river, close beneath a high bank for protection against the blizzards.

'Yes,' he said even more firmly, having heard nothing further through the dull roar of the wind in the trees, 'it must have been a bear. Lost his way, probably and fell off the roof.' But his words did little to reassure either himself or his wife, and her dark eyes lingered in the shadows beyond the lamplight as if expecting the Devil himself to emerge from the pile of furs in the corner.

'You're a foolish woman, Uliana,' he growled, not unkindly. 'Always imagining things.'

13

But even so a certain uneasiness lurked in his small eyes as he went on scraping the skin stretched on the table before him.

'Is that imagination, then?' Uliana's hand went to her mouth. Through the sound of the storm they could hear the weak cry. Pavel got up and laid his ear to the door.

'No, Pavel, no. Don't—'

The wind rushed through the open door, filling the room with a flurry of snow; the flakes hissed on the stove as Pavel dragged the man inside and laid him on the floor by the heat. Then the couple sat and watched in silence as the mask of snow melted from the face of the unconscious stranger; thin steam rose from his clothes and with it the powerful stench of unwashed flesh; water ran from his beard and trickled out of the corners of his melting eyes. The thin high-cheekboned faced resembled a grey, hairy skull, across which a terrible scar ran diagonally from forehead to chin.

'Dear God,' exclaimed Uliana. 'Look, Pavel. Chains!' She began to moan softly, rocking herself to and fro. 'They'll come for him. They'll follow him here.'

'In a storm like this?' Her husband snorted. But Uliana went on obstinately.

'He can't stay here. They'll find him and—'

'And then you can hold your stupid tongue, woman.' He bent down, holding the flickering light closer, and drew in his breath sharply.

'Get some water heated, hurry. Look at his hands. And get the vodka.' She did not move.

'Go on,' he shouted angrily. 'Get it, we've enough. Besides, Osip will bring us more from Archangel. Hurry.'

As his wife fetched the pitcher of vodka Pavel brought in a tub of snow.

'Now help me with his clothes.'

With swift strokes of his hunting-knife, he cut the rotting material from the man's thin arms, then the filthy lumps of rags from his feet. Pouring the spirit into the palm of his hand, he began to rub furiously at the waxen arms.

'Go on, dolt, you do the feet.'

'Why waste good vodka?' Uliana asked sullenly. 'He'll die anyway.' But she rubbed the swollen feet.

'Would God have guided him to us if He wanted him to die?' The sweat gleamed on Pavel's broad face. 'Don't get in such a fret, woman,' he added more gently. 'They won't come here. Let 'em go, the snow'll finish 'em, or the wolves, that's what they say when a man escapes the *prut*. Anyway, who in hell comes here in the winter?'

'Supposing the agent—' she began doubtfully.

'Supposing the agent—' he mimicked. 'That fat swine. He's too damned busy swindling their Excellencies of Stroganov in Petersburg, like he swindles the lot of us. One day I hope I'll find his greasy carcass in one of my traps. Oh no, we shan't see Mister-precious-Davidov till the snows have gone.'

He paused in his labours and sat back on his heels, holding up a tattered remnant of cloth.

'This was once fancy stuff,' he said thoughtfully. Uliana glanced up, brushing the hair from her face.

'He'll likely be a noble,' she said, and Pavel saw the sudden little gleam in her slanting eyes. 'If we were to look after him well, perhaps—'

'Do they send nobles to the East with their pockets stuffed with gold?' His voice was scornful but in his own eyes there was an answering gleam.

'But he won't be a poor man like us,' she insisted.

'If we don't get the blood going he won't be a man at all.'

As they worked to bring life to the dead limbs Uliana asked, 'Why d'you think they were sending him to the East?'

'How should I know? Maybe he annoyed the Empress or tried to kiss the Grand Duchess, I don't know.' He chuckled. 'They say that German Catherine knows how to please a man.' Pavel helped himself to a swig of vodka. 'He'll stay with us till he's strong, then we'll see.'

'But how can we manage? There's no room. And the food, Pavel. We can never feed another mouth.'

'What's the use of being a trapper if you can't lay your hands on a bit of extra meat? If he recovers he can help me with the traps. That way we'll get more skins.' He raised the man's right arm and let it drop.

'I think we're in time.' The skin was mottled now. For a second the man's eyelids fluttered and opened.

'His eyes are dead as a carp,' said Pavel. 'Bring the tub.'

The trapper raised the stranger into a sitting position and thrust his arms into the melting snow.

'He'd be better to stay unconscious. When the blood begins to flow, the pain's enough to finish a man.'

Pavel needed all his strength to hold the writhing, twisting body. Sweat burst from the man's skin and rolled down the livid furrow of the scar; he arched his back, jerked his head from side to side, and his eyes grew wild with the pain of his waking limbs. But no sound escaped from his clenched teeth.

'This is a brave one,' said Pavel in admiration. 'Hold still there, friend, we're only trying to help you. Ah, so you feel your arms again. Now'—he turned to Uliana—'help me lift him.'

They lifted him and placed his feet in the tub. The stranger's eyes rolled upwards and this time, as his legs took fire, he uttered a harsh cry of agony.

They dried him with a rough cloth and laid him on a bearskin. With a grimace and a hiss of indrawn breath he turned on his side.

'Mother of God, just see this.' Uliana's eyes were wide as they rested on the man's back. With hot water and clean rags she loosened the bloody remains of his shirt from the long crusted weals, and her large hands were very gentle as they bathed the dirt and putrefaction from the torn flesh and washed his left wrist where the fetter had rubbed a raw circle.

'It might have been our son,' she kept repeating. 'It could have been Osip lying here.'

'I've seen a good few men after knouting but this—' He shook his head wonderingly. 'It'll take a lot to kill this man.'

They dressed him in an old shirt of their son's and laid him back on the bearskin.

The man's eyes were open now and he shook his head feebly, striving to focus on these strangers whose faces swam above him.

'How does it feel?' asked Pavel.

'He doesn't understand.'

'Pour some vodka down his throat then!'

The man choked on the raw spirit burning his cracked and blackened lips. After a while he tried to speak but the words came out in a croaking whisper and Pavel had to lean close. He shook his head.

'That's a funny sort of Russian. But I got a few words. 'Friends,' he said, mouthing his words very slowly, 'you're with friends. Understand?' The stranger seemed to for he nodded and something meant as a smile gleamed in his matted beard.

They fed him some soup, thick fatty stuff, and gave him more vodka until, partially restored, he tried to get up. He had wasted enough time; he was strong and must go back. Kasia would be waiting; she would be half crazy with worry—he must go back. But strong hands pushed him gently down.

'Easy, friend, you're not going anywhere.'

He struggled weakly, trying to explain, to make these good people understand how he must get back to Petersburg, now, this very instant. Tears of weakness and frustration filled his eyes. Using the Russian he had learnt during his year in St Petersburg, he implored them to help him on his way, but it was the Russian of the court, not the dialect of the northern Dvina, and the Tuntsevs understood little.

Then at last his croaking speech dropped to a whisper and he fell back on the rug with closed eyes.

'He'll sleep now,' Uliana said.

'I've know a hungry fox heavier than he is.' Pavel placed the man on the broad ledge above the stove, where he lay no longer struggling. The wind had gone and a most delicious warmth flooded his very bones; almost at once he slept.

For a while they sat watching this stranger who had come into their lives from the depths of the blizzard, now and then helping themselves to the vodka. His smile was nice, thought Uliana Tuntseva, and he had the hands of a noble, not rough heavy hands like their own.

'Tonight wife, we'll sleep in the furs.' The tip of Pavel's tongue was very red in his beard as it ran round his lips; his eyes strayed to his wife's heavy breasts and went suddenly hot. He got up from the table and seized her, biting her lips and her strong brown neck. Uliana returned his kisses, laughing softly, with one eye on the sleeping stranger.

'Gently, Pavel darling, gently. We don't want to wake His Excellency.' But, fumbling at her quilted jacket with impatient fingers, she went eagerly to the furs in the corner as he blew out the lamp.

With all the fury of a starving wolf the wind howled above their little darkened hut, driving the snow before it in a white fury.

*   *   *

For two days the stranger stirred and tossed above the stove in a high fever, muttering, shouting, clutching at Uliana's hands when she turned him to dress his festered back. Often she had to call her husband to hold him down.

'The heat of his skin's enough to flay your fingers.' Pavel scratched his head. 'Maybe we should bleed him.' He fingered the knife at his belt. But Uliana shook her head.

'D'you want to kill him?'

For two days the fugitive from the *prut* mumbled and cried out about things the peasants could not understand, in Polish, in French, sometimes in Italian or his strange, stilted Russian.

They could not know that he raved of betrayal and torture; of courts and kings and intrigue ranging from Paris to St Petersburg; of war and flashing sabres, of flame and death. When he shouted and muttered about the King's Secret and the Chevalier D'Eon and Queen Marie Lechynska of France, it was all so much gibberish to a fur trapper and his wife deep in the wilds of northern Russia. Little Figgy, Grand Duchess of Russia, and her childish husband Peter, who would succeed to the throne of All The Russias on the death of his aunt, the Empress Elizabeth . . . Louis de Valfons, soldier of France, and Jacques Beaufranchet dead from Prussian grape-shot on the field of Rossbach . . . the beautiful, wanton Amande de Valfons and the gentle Toinon, who gave him comfort and happiness in Paris . . . and always a woman called Kasia.

And this last at least Uliana understood.

'He must bear a heavy load of sorrow,' she commented, wiping the hot, dry brow with a rag dipped in snow-water.

'He won't be alone in that,' replied Pavel grumpily. He pulled on his big felt boots, loaded and primed his musket, and put on his long squirrel coat and cap of fox fur.

'I'll be back before dark.'

'I think he's better,' she said. 'His breathing is easier. Now he'll sleep.'

'Maybe we'll get some peace tonight then.' Pavel went out to search for his traps, banging the door behind him, his bad temper like an iron ball in his belly. They'd be stuck with the man for the winter now, and what would a noble know about anything except drinking and whoring and spending money? God had played a rotten trick sending such a fugitive here.

Pavel fastened on the clumsy snow-shoes and set off into the forest, slowly working off his ill humour in the rhythm of his long strides. He would teach him to work, by heaven he would; he, Pavel Tuntsev, would teach a noble to use his soft useless hands. The prospect cheered him; he said aloud, 'Oh yes, Your Honour, there's quite a surprise waiting for you.' Chuckling, he strode on through the white silent trees.

The wind had dropped away and in the hut it was quiet except for the man's steady breathing. The flush had faded from his skin and, looking at him, Uliana knew the crisis had passed. No longer did the names and unintelligible mutterings come tumbling in disorder from his lips. He slept quietly.

He must have travelled far, she thought, to speak in so many tongues. And who was Kasia? Did he call for someone already dead?

Uliana sighed and, taking up a knife, began to cut up an onion. What this man could tell us, what strange and wonderful adventures must be locked in his head, she thought. She sighed again.

At that moment the man stirred and opened his eyes.

'Where am I?' His voice was normal and pitched deep. The woman went and stood by him.

'With us you're quite safe,' she said. He looked at her thoughtfully from clear grey eyes no longer wild with fever. His face lit up in a quick smile, intensely alive yet at the same time sad.

'What is your name?' he asked in his slow, unfamiliar Russian. She told him.

'And mine,' he said, 'is Henryk Barinski.'

*　　*　　*

During the weeks that followed Henryk Barinski came to share their lives completely, hemmed in by the dark trees, trapped in the smelly little hut by the encircling snows. Slowly, under Uliana's care, he regained his health and strength; the open weals on his back healed into ugly ridged scars, and soon he was able to go out on shaky legs and breathe the bright, cold air. But his mind did not mend. For hours he would sit by the stove, wrapped in his own thoughts, or lie without a sound, gazing with wide-open eyes at the grimy logs above him. At such moments the Tuntsevs left him alone and went about their daily occupations quietly, for they were a kindly pair and did not want to intrude into his private world of suffering.

At nights he would lie awake in the blackness of the hut listening to Uliana muttering in her sleep, the winter wind prowling like a demon round the walls, and often the lonely misery of his loss and longing became so acute that he would bury his face in the furs and silently weep.

He rarely spoke, only nodding his thanks sometimes with that quick, sad smile which so stirred Uliana's heart. And then one day in early December, when he had been with them for nearly two months, he suddenly seemed to shake himself like a dog waking from a dream and said in his slow, curious Russian, 'I've been lying here like an old woman for too long and it's time I did something to help.'

He began to pace the earthern floor with rapid steps; he flexed his arms and picked up the axe from the corner.

'See, I can swing this as well as any man. Tell me what to do and I'll start now. Come on, now, there must be something.' His tone, though light, was imperious.

'Well,' began Pavel uncertainly. 'Perhaps Your Honour could —perhaps he might—' He glanced for help at his wife.

'Your Honour should not soil his hands,' she murmured, turning quickly to her cooking.

'Your Honour! Your Honour! Please, can't you call me by my name? You saved my life. You're my friends—let's have no more "Your Honours".' Pavel looked horror-struck.

Henryk took up a skin from the table, half stripped of flesh. 'Surely I could do this. Come on, Pavel, give me a knife and show me how it's done.' He flung himself on to the stool and, seizing the knife from Pavel's hand, began to scrape furiously at the skin.

'No!' Pavel burst out. 'No, not like that, Mother of God, you're cutting the skin. Here, I'll show you. Now, this is the way.'

Uliana smiled nervously to herself to hear them bickering for all the world like equals.

So, in payment for the food he ate and the warmth and security of their little home, Count Henryk Barinski, born of a noble Polish family, whose father owned more than five hundred souls, helped the fur-trapper with his traps, chopped birch-logs for the stove, cut ice from the river and learnt not only to scrape the

20

skins but to remove them from the carcases of foxes and ermine, and wolves.

But he found time to wander by himself, pushing deep into the forests or along the bank of the ice-bound river; he moved slowly, stopping often to listen, for as a boy he had learnt the ways of animals and birds and was happy to stand in the shadow unobserved to watch them going about their business. In this way he was able partially to forget, for a while at least, what it was that had brought him to this frozen place. But his thoughts always returned to St Petersburg and to Kasia Radienska. She was never far away; he heard her voice and laughter in the wind, and saw her as clearly as if she stood beside him, dressed in flowered blue brocade, her face ringed with sable fur, her blue eyes bright as the ice that covered the Neva.

Then he would groan aloud or curse savagely at Fate which had parted them so suddenly, so cruelly, and call her name and nothing would answer him except perhaps the distant howl of a wolf.

'Anyone can see he's a great noble,' remarked Uliana one day when the Tuntsevs were alone. 'Perhaps even a Prince.' Pavel merely gave his usual grunt.

'Yes,' repeated Uliana, half to herself, 'a Prince or at least a man born to lead.'

Pavel grunted again and remained silent. But later that day, as he lit his smelly little pipe after resetting a trap, he said slowly and carefully as though he had been planning it for weeks:

'The Dark People, Your Honour, that's us, you understand, the poor of Russia, the *mouzhiks*—'

Henryk nodded. Catherine had called them the Dark People.

'Well, they need a man to lead them. A man who understands them and can speak to them in their own language, and who has the brain and the learning of—' He could not think of how to go on but sat watching Henryk sharply through the blue smoke from the corners of his shrewd little eyes. 'A man who has felt the knout across his back.'

'And where would he lead them,' Henryk asked, 'this man you speak of?'

'To the gates of Moscow and St Petersburg,' said Pavel grimly, and would say no more but shut his mouth tighter than one of his own traps.

On another occasion Henryk stood looking down at a young

silver fox, teeth bared and splintered and dripping bloody froth from its terrible efforts to bite through the iron. Its eyes were filled with savage terror as it tore frantically at its shredded hind leg.

'Kill it.' Henryk spoke sharply, for he hated the sight of these poor mangled beasts. Pavel raised the short wooden club and brought it down with a loud crack on the fox's skull. The body leapt and jerked in the red snow and then lay still, the light fading at last from the tortured eyes.

'The peasants are like this poor devil here.' Pavel heaved at the peg in the frozen ground. 'They need someone to put 'em out of their misery—or to spring the trap they're in.'

On the slow way back to the hut, dragging the carcases on Pavel's home-made sledge, Henryk thought about the trapper's words. In the palaces, the embassies and the great houses of Petersburg and Moscow no one had the time or the inclination to discuss the Dark People or to wonder how they existed in their foetid wooden hovels. They were of no more interest than the countless trees or the mud which followed the melting of the snows in the spring.

Once he had heard Catherine say that any ruler of Russia who did anything at all to improve the lot of the serfs would bask in their loyalty and gratitude.

'For could they not one day, given a real leader, rise and sweep all this away?' And she had gestured with her fan round the magnificent blue and gold reception room lit by a thousand tall candles.

He and Pavel came out of the trees by the river-bank to the south; the sun was a silver ball low in the sky and ice crystals floated, glittering, in the pale light; the snow was like brittle, crackling salt beneath their snow-shoes and the hiss of the runners. A little breeze rattled the ice in the bare black branches of the birches, catching Henryk by the throat, for the sound brought a sharp memory of a day's hunting at Lipno when Kasia had worn a dark-green riding habit, and Figgy—in those days, Sophia von Anhalt-Zerbst, with her little pointed face and grown-up manners—had driven out in a sledge with her vivacious, errant mother, Princess Johanna, to watch the slaying of the boars. And Kasia's cousin Stanislas Poniatowski, a cultured, charming boy, had been dragged unwillingly from his French books, for hunting irked him (he was so short-sighted he never liked to ride at anything

faster than a trot) and he preferred to indulge his brain rather
than his body.

'There's a storm coming.' Pavel jerked his head at the yellowish
clouds massing to the north-east. The harsh rustle of the wind
was louder now and a fine mist of snow swirled above the ice.

As they reached the hut the first hard snow-flakes of the
blizzard were dancing on the rising wind.

*   *   *

That winter of 1758-59 was exceptionally severe; there were
many days when they had to dig themselves out of the hut to
fulfil their most pressing needs. Quickly Henryk came to understand and speak their rough dialect, for, in common with most
educated Polish gentlemen, he had both a natural ear for languages
and, what was more, a natural courtesy to those below him in
rank, absent from so many of his peers.

Yet he still did not speak much, nor often smile, but sat
wrapped in his thoughts, now and then rousing himself with an
effort to tell them something of his past life.

'Rome? Paris? What are they?' Pavel had once been down-river
to Archangel and his eyes still widened at the memory of a
spectacle which, to him, represented the whole wide world. But
Rome, Paris, these were more fabulous than the Arabian Nights
and Uliana sat wrapped in wonder as she listened to Henryk's
deep slow voice.

'It must be a—' she searched for a word to fit her sense of
awe—'a real miracle to see such places.' Her voice was wistful,
her eyes far away and full of God only knew what dreams,
inspired perhaps by unconscious visions of her Mongol ancestors
who had ridden with Batu Khan. But she? If she lived to be a
hundred she would never see anything beyond the river and the
tall dark trees that enclosed her little home.

And Pavel, puffing at his little pipe, would grunt and snort,
trying not to be impressed.

One day Henryk told them of his home in the Polish Ukraine,
over a thousand miles to the south, and of the Cossacks who

roamed the great southern steppes and with whom his people were constantly at war.

'I've heard of them devils,' said Pavel triumphantly. 'All this land and away to the east to where the Tatars live, it was all conquered by the Don Cossack, Yermak. Ah, yes, I may only be Pavel Tuntsev but there's still some things I know.'

They could never hear enough about St Petersburg and the huge white palaces of timber and stone rising along the Neva and of the great ships that came up the river from all over the world.

'Osip has talked about the ships—' began Uliana proudly.

'Have I not seen them with my own eyes in Archangel, like big white birds?' interrupted Pavel. 'Ships from France, or so Osip said, and the English island where Tsar Peter went to live many years ago.'

'Osip will be home when the ice breaks,' she said. Their son worked in a barge plying up-river from Archangel; he brought them provisions for the winter: lard and potatoes, lamp-oil, salt, vodka and hard black bread, and ship's biscuit that he begged or stole from the merchantmen. On his return journey he took the furs.

'Osip could take you to Archangel,' said Pavel, picking another thick pelt from the heap on the floor.

The two men sat at the table cleaning sable skins. Beyond the log walls the last of the blizzard raged through the trees, booming in the small, squat chimney, puffing white spurts of smoke from the stove. Uliana was preparing the evening meal, dropping gobbets of meat into the stew-pot.

For a while Henryk did not answer, working on in silence. If somehow he could get a passage to France or England—true they were at war, or they had been months before, but there would be ways and means; if you were determined enough there were always ways and means. . . . But until he reached Paris he had no money. Perhaps some captain, short-handed or sympathetic, would take him as deck-crew. Yet was there such a being as a sympathetic sea captain? The thoughts chased swiftly through his mind. If he could get to France, then from Paris he could somehow communicate with Kasia. But how, without implicating her? His knife worked at the skin by itself as once again Henryk's brain tried to grapple with the future.

Uliana turned from the stove and her eyes softened as they rested on the lean, swarthy face, the dark curls and wide mouth.

She realised with a little tug at her heart that she did not want him to leave. She had never met a man with such hidden fire, such restless smouldering energy, as this companion of princes and nobles; she had never seen such a set and serious face, the face of a man far older than his thirty years.

Feeling her eyes upon him, Henryk looked up with a smile.

It's strange, she thought, the scar does not spoil his looks; rather it makes his face fiercer, prouder, like a hawk or an eagle. At that moment, as if he had sensed her fanciful thoughts, Pavel put down his knife, began cleaning his pipe with a birch splinter and then asked Henryk deliberately, 'Was it in the wars you got that scar?'

'A Turkish scimitar,' replied Henryk shortly. Memory darkened his eyes and his fingers strayed to the scar as they did in moments of anger or preoccupation.

'I've heard tell of the Turks. A dangerous lot. It's said they eat new-born babies roasted on a spit. Could that be true, d'you think?'

Henryk did not answer. As clearly as if it was yesterday he saw the face of the Turk beneath the high white turban, a trickle of blood across his forehead, face twisted with the lust to kill, the crimson blade raised against the blackened walls of Volochisk and flames spurting from the windows—smoke and steel and a girl's voice crying his name as the scimitar swept down. . . .

Uliana cleared away the skins and put down the cooking-pot and the rough wooden platters. Pavel dipped his finger into the stew and brought out a lump of meat. They ate in silence. Then he sat back with a contented belch.

'Let's thank God the Turks don't come rampaging in these parts.' Grease shone in his beard as he licked his fingers clean; he would never use the pewter spoons Osip had brought from Archangel, cursing them for the inventions of foreigners and devils.

He took up his pipe and began to fill it.

'Aye, you'll have seen more in your life than we could ever dream of.' He was replete and wanting to talk. 'Tell us more about Her Majesty, the Empress. They say she's a fine woman and like her father, the Great Peter. Is this true?'

But Henryk was in no mood for conversation and, excusing himself, he put on his wolfskin coat and went out into the night.

The wind was gone; the sky had cleared and to the north the trees stood without stirring under their burden of snow against the flickering banners of the Northern Lights. He remembered another night three years ago when this same eerie beauty had spread across the skies of St Petersburg as he fought and killed his first man . . . the rasp of the blades as Apraxin, boorish but skilled, had pressed him hard in the shadows of the Peter and Paul fortress only to slip on the glazed snow and fall upon Henryk's lunging sword . . . the body buried beneath the ice of the Neva, the hurried flight from the city and the long and bitter journey across the snows of Europe . . . his return in disgrace to Paris where only D'Eon's considerable influence had saved him from the wrath of the Prince de Conti. Men who failed in the dangerous world of secret diplomacy could expect small sympathy, and now for the second time he had left St Petersburg, his task unfulfilled, and this time his failure was complete for he was a hunted criminal with a price on his head—torture and death waited in the dungeons of Elizabeth. To go back would spell disaster for them both. Kasia and himself—Henryk ground his teeth at the thought of her in such a place, her body exposed to the eyes of the torturers, naked beneath the hot cut of the lash.

What was she doing? Who was she laughing with as he stood there trapped by this awful loneliness? Had Alexei Orlov come home from the Prussian war to reclaim her? Henryk wanted to walk fast over the snowfields, to run until exhaustion dulled the visions that tormented his mind, but he could not move more than a few feet from the door for fresh banks of snow were piled six feet deep, shining in the greenish, golden glow.

He felt an overmastering hatred for the snow, treacherous, beautiful, impenetrable; he wanted to tear a way through with his bare hands, to the world that lay beyond this white prison, the world that somewhere would have a corner for Kasia and himself.

For Osip Tuntsev would be back when the ice broke in the spring and with him Henryk would go down the river to Archangel, and from there—Henryk shivered with the cold gripping his bones. How long before the waters of the river were free? Before there was warmth and new hope in this God-forsaken wilderness? Before he could escape?

As if to mock him a large white owl swooped low above him

on silent wings and away, above the brooding trees, away into the cold freedom of the night.

* * *

The spring came early that year and the snow vanished quickly, leaving the land sodden and steaming in the warmth of a sun that daily rose higher.

The snow slid with a soft *plumph* from bowed branches which now sprang up towards the sun, tipped with a brighter green; the trees were astir with a multitude of small birds whose chorus filled the bright dawns.

By mid-April the sun had prised the frozen crust from the earth, releasing the sweet scents of spring and only the breaking ice on the river served as a reminder of winter.

Henryk was cutting birch-logs in his shirt-sleeves at the edge of the marshes, enjoying the feel of the axe in his hands, the bite of the blade into the fragrant wood, the hum of the chips in the still afternoon. For his body was hard and fit and his restless energy increased within him like a swelling bud in the new warmth of the sun. But his face was still set in a sombre mask and his eyes rarely lit up with the smile that used to give such delight to all who knew him, more especially women.

After working hard for an hour he placed the logs in neat piles and sat down with a length of grass between his teeth. Then he lay back with his arms under his head, letting the sweat dry on his face in the sunshine. Above him the little fat birch-buds moved slightly in a soft breeze. There had been another small birch-tree standing on the ridge that lay along the boundary of the Barinski and Radienski lands, and there, on a day like this, with a gentle rain on their skins, he and Kasia had taken each other for the first time. That was the summer ten years ago when every afternoon she came riding on Kinga, the Arab mare, up the track through the trees, her black hair flowing in the wind, the dust on her tawny skin—and loved him beneath their little tree in a way no other woman had ever done. She had promised to wait for him. . . . 'Whatever happens, Rasulka'—he called her Rasulka,

27

'water-fairy', from the Polish folk-tale that tells of the sprites which, if seen by moonlight, are dangerous to men, luring them, dazzled by their beauty, to their deaths in the water—'whatever happens, will you wait?' 'Yes, Henryk, I'll wait.' And he said with infinite tenderness, 'You'll always be my woman, Kasia.' 'Say it again, my darling, say it.' Her head was thrown back, her lips parted in a smile of pure joy. He repeated the words and it was then the three Turkish horsemen came out of the trees and the nightmare began.

Now the nightmare was on him again. He shut his eyes. Had their love so offended God that He had twice torn them apart so cruelly?

'You will live many different lives but only one of these will bring you real happiness,' was what the gipsy woman had told him at Volochisk. There had been different lives; other women had enjoyed his body but it was to Kasia, with her gay courage and long blue eyes, that Henryk had given his heart.

Geese passed across the pale sky flying north and the wild music of their voices remained in the sky long after the birds had gone.

'They came from the sunrise, from beyond the great Mongol steppe,' Kasia always told him. 'They're Cossack birds because they're so truly free.'

From the direction of the hut he heard the sound of Uliana singing; she sang a lot with the coming of the sun. The sound grew louder and, turning his head, Henryk watched her go down to the river with a tub of clothes. He watched her strong back as she bent over her task, the thick white gleam of her legs; he heard the heavy wet slap of the clothes on the big stone above the rumble and rasp of the ice floes tumbling swiftly down-river, plunging and rearing from the grey snow-water, climbing one upon another like heifers in a field.

The sight of the woman and the grinding of the ice set off memories rarely absent from his mind. Staring at the small white clouds, so rounded and soft, he dreamt with open eyes. . . .

He was hurrying along the maze of corridors in the Winter Palace. He knew he was late and that Kasia would be anxious but the news he brought would surely hearten her. The sleepy sentries at the entrance to the Grand Ducal apartments let him past with friendly grins for they knew Henryk well.

Clocks all over the palace were striking eleven as he tapped twice on her door and Karzel's sullen little face peered out. Henryk disliked the dwarf; he hated his possessive manner towards Kasia, this stunted thing that called itself her major-domo and ordered her maids about in shrill, domineering tones and generally behaved as if no one else had the right to address his mistress. That he had originally belonged to Alexei Orlov made the business no better. 'Get rid of him, Kasia,' Henryk kept telling her. 'I don't trust him.' But she would not, saying he was efficient and useful and kept her informed of what went on behind many closed doors in the Palace. Henryk pushed past the dwarf without a word.

'You may go, Karzel, and thank you,' said Kasia quietly. She sat by the tiled stove, embroidery forgotten in her lap, her face glowing warm in the candlelight, her hair falling in glossy waves to the shoulders of a blue brocade dressing-gown. She smiled, not moving till the dwarf had removed himself with bad grace then, as the door closed, jumped up and ran to Henryk's outstretched arms.

'Darling, I thought you were never coming. What happened? Was it embassy business?' She spoke in French, for one never knew what ears were listening and to the world in general Henryk Barinski was the Frenchman de Bonville, *chargé d'affaires* at the Embassy of His Most Christian Majesty Louis XV—a Pole in the secret service of France.

Henryk held her at arm's length, drinking in her beauty. He never tired of looking at her face. Whether touched by laughter, anger, sorrow or love this was the face of the woman who, above all others, was his—truly and completely *his*. She gazed back at him, her head slightly on one side, a tender smile trembling at the corners of her wide mouth.

'Why do I love you so much?' she asked wonderingly. He shook his head, drawing her roughly to his body. He felt the sharp bite of the small crooked front tooth and his hands went to her breasts. She trembled violently, straining against him, then pushed him gently away, her eyes dark and teasing.

'First we'll have some wine, sweetheart. Tonight we'll need all our strength.' All day she had wanted him, with an even fiercer longing than usual if that were possible, counting the minutes until she would feel his hands on her. He watched her as she poured wine into the delicate crystal glasses.

She raised her glass. 'To us, my love.'

'To us,' he echoed. 'And to our future together.'

Her eyes clouded; she shook her head. 'No, Henryk, please. N-never tempt F-fate.' There was sudden fear in her expression. 'I know.' With him she rarely stammered, except when tired or in any way agitated; she had almost succeeded in conquering this disability brought on by the horror of the terrible night when the flames devoured her home and the bodies of her butchered parents.

But the experiences of that night and the years that followed in the hands of the Turks, then the Cossacks, had left their mark on Countess Kasia Radienska; they were sometimes to be seen, by those who looked carefully, in her eyes, in the firm set of her mouth, in her straight, calm gaze which had looked upon horror and death and could see no worse. She had suffered much in her twenty-eight years: fear and indignity; physical and mental pain; deep personal loss. And knowing such things never to be far away, she was afraid of too much happiness.

'But, my love, we must talk of the future.' He led her to the sofa and sat with his arm round her shoulders. She lay against him, listening with mounting excitement to what he had to tell her.

'. . . and so,' he finished with barely suppressed excitement, 'the ship, *our* ship, will sail for France as soon as the ice breaks.'

'O, Henryk. Oh, my dearest, I can hardly b-believe it. That we'll be away. Tears shone in her eyes. 'Just you and I.' For the moment she forgot her fear of Fate. 'Free and together.' She kissed the corner of his mouth. Free of a situation rapidly becoming unbearable for them both. Kasia shivered suddenly.

'What is it, love?' He drew her closer.

'It's—it's—oh, my God, if she were to find out.' Kasia knew well Catherine's anger, her ruthlessness, her feminine jealousy.

'She won't. Not if we're careful.'

'Perhaps we shouldn't see each other until the ship.' She clutched tightly at his arm. 'Yet, I don't know if I could bear that.' Henryk comforted her but the anxiety nagged his own mind.

If the Grand Duchess were ever to discover that it was not love but diplomatic intrigue which had brought him to St Petersburg and to her bed, and moreover that he was going from her arms to those of her most trusted friend—Henryk's mind froze at the prospect, not for himself, but for Kasia. Catherine was not Empress, her influence at the present was small, but nevertheless her vengeance would be swift and deadly. For that reason alone they must get away to safety.

'I can't go on seeing her,' he burst out. 'I won't do it any more.' His tone was that of the small boy who knows full well he is trapped and yet raises his voice in futile protest. 'How in hell can I go to bed—?' She put her finger to his lips, shaking her head.

'My dear, you must. You know you must. It's our only ch-chance.' Kasia's face was a mask. The thought of Henryk with Catherine made her sick with jealousy and revulsion but never once had she shown it, knowing well that the ironic charade must be played out to the bitter end.

'We won't think of her, not tonight. Will we, my darling?' She took the lobe of his ear between her lips, touching it with the sharp tip of her tongue. But he left her and went to the window; pulling back the curtain, he stood looking across the tumbled ice of the Neva. In the light of the full moon the floes were piled in grotesque confusion against the dark mass of the Island of the Strelka. Here and there white lumps twirled slowly in patches of open water.

'Another week and the river should be free,' he said, as Kasia joined him. The crash and groan of the ice never ceased.

'It's very beautiful—in a cruel way.' She remembered spring-time on the Don and suddenly, without warning, the death of her infant son as the blizzard raged across the steppes. Again she shivered, silently cursing the treacherous whim of memory.

'Come to bed, darling. Now.' Her voice was urgent.

Henryk glanced down at her upturned face; her eyes were black as the shadows in the ice, her expression radiant as the candlelight. He felt the firm softness of her flank against his side and slowly she took off the dressing-gown, his eyes never leaving her face.

As the long white shift fell in a soft, gleaming heap round her ankles, he saw the reflection of her body in the wall-mirror: slim and straight as a girl of seventeen; smooth, sloping shoulders and round, full breasts ready for him. Her skin glowed in the light of the hot little flames, her eyes glittered and the faint soft line of down was dark above her parted lips.

'You like to see me, don't you?'

'I've always liked to see you.'

She turned slowly round, watching him over her shoulders as he flung his clothes on the floor.

'You're the most beautiful thing I've ever seen,' he whispered.

31

'Tell me again.'

He repeated the words, beckoning to her, and she came into his arms. She drew his head down to her breasts, his hands to her thighs.

'I want you very badly,' she said and laughed aloud at the inadequacy of her words. 'If it were like this every night for a hundred years I would want you just as much.' His mouth came up to her throat and she flung her head back with a short gasp of joy.

That night they drove each other close to madness with their lips and hands and words. And, as accompaniment to her moaning cries, there was the grinding rumble of the ice, the heavy thump of snow sliding from the roof.

'Oh, my God. Oh, my God.' Kasia lay back panting. 'Oh, Henryk, that was marvellous, wonderful.' He brushed the wet hair from her face.

'The Turks are to be congratulated.' He grinned. 'They certainly taught you some lovely tricks.'

'I don't need anyone to teach me, not with you.'

They lay in sleepy, contented silence.

'Henryk?'

'Yes.'

'It was very complete, wasn't it? Was it the same for you?'

'Yes, darling. It's never anything else but complete.' Catherine knew how to love, sometimes in wild animal abandon, but compared to this—this was heart and mind and body working in wondrous unison.

'We do suit each other, don't we?'

'Go to sleep, Rasulka.'

The candle still burned, though very low, when they woke. They whispered together and laughed and moved against each other in the big curtained bed.

She took his hand and kissed the small scar running across the fingers; the mark of a bear's claws.

'I've loved this one for ten years.' She followed the line of the scar across his face with her lips, gently, tenderly.

'And this one for eight months.'

'And these?'

He brought her hand to the place where the Prussian bayonet had scored his thigh.

Pushing back the bed-clothes, she bent to kiss the long white mark on his skin.

'I'm lucky the thrust was poor,' he remarked.

She teased him with the tips of her fingers and, feeling the sharp nip of the crooked tooth, he turned on her roughly.

Kasia laughed deep in her throat. 'Slowly, Henryk, this time . . . slowly.'

He caressed and stroked, working her to a fine pitch, then lay motionless with his eyes closed, smiling to himself, as he waited for her to move.

There was passion and exquisite pain in the overwhelming tenderness of a love so very sure of itself. . . .

*   *   *

Memory was fed by the warmth of the sun and Henryk groaned in physical anguish as he lay on the bank of the Dvina. He opened his eyes.

Uliana stood above him, blocking out the sun, her wash-tub under her arm; she caught her breath at the look still smouldering in his eyes.

The hair was black on his bare, brown arms. He sat up. 'I'm sorry I've been so lazy, but the sun—' He saw her glance at his arms and her quick breathing. Any encouragement and she'd be down here in the grass beside him. He looked at her heavy figure still strong and supple, her hair hidden by the white kerchief, and got quickly to his feet.

Disappointment showed for an instant in the woman's eyes. She thought he looked absurdly young at that moment, slim and smiling. He stretched and yawned, reaching for the axe. More geese were calling to each other, flying low above the trees.

'They're going north,' he said, bringing the axe up in a glinting arc and down deep into the birch trunk. 'At last the winter's ended.'

Once he'd used those words to Kasia as he helped her into the saddle; she'd worn the red ribbon in her hair that day and promised to come to Warsaw with him—

33

Suddenly they heard a shout and Pavel came from the trees, his musket on his shoulder and a dead hare hanging from his belt.

'Aye,' Uliana agreed in a low, sad voice. 'The winter's ended, right enough.' And when the spring comes, she thought, he will go and life will sink back into a procession of empty days and nights. Oh, Pavel was a good enough husband, a good enough man, but—

She walked slowly towards the hut. 'This weather will soon bring Osip up the river.'

Pavel's glance took in the pile of cut logs. If he hadn't seen it with his own eyes he'd never have believed it. A noble, a great one, wielding an axe with all the strength and skill of a peasant. Shaking his head at the surprises of the world, he followed his wife and behind him the thud of the axe rang sharp and clear in the evening air.

Henryk worked on steadily till the shadows lengthened round him and owls began to call in the dusk. The axe rose and fell, rose and fell, as he drove his body towards the physical fatigue that would bring him the relief of sleep.

*   *   *

The furs were safely loaded into the big flat-bottomed barge and Osip Tuntsev glanced at the early sun already balanced on the treetops. 'We should go,' he said impatiently. He was a tall, gangling youth with the dark, secretive eyes of his mother and large, awkward hands.

Three days before he had come up river with his two companions, sailors by the looks of them, weather-stained men who slept off the trapper's vodka in the barge and seemed out of place on land.

But now Osip was in a fever to be away. 'Davidov will be here any day,' he kept repeating. 'This is the time he always comes and if he finds—' He never finished the sentence but muttered, at least twenty times a day, 'we'd best be getting him away.'

Henryk stood with the Tuntsevs at the water's edge, listening with half an ear to Pavel's instructions to Osip and himself. The sky was cloudless, the river free of ice, ruffled by a little breeze and no longer grey with melted snow. Water-fowl were calling in the marshes beyond the bright water, hidden by a thin dawn mist.

'. . . so it would be better for His Honour to remain hidden on board until you've found a ship. . . .'

Henryk turned to Uliana who stood silently with downcast eyes.

'I've been very happy,' he said quietly. She did not answer but he saw her skin flush darkly in the shadow of the white kerchief.

'. . . there will be government spies, Osip, and he is easily recognised. . . . Are you listening to me?'

'We must go,' said his son in answer. The two sailors sat on the side of the barge with closed eyes and nodding heads. It mattered little to them whether they stayed or went.

'Well—' began Pavel and stopped. Nor did Henryk know what to say. He had accepted the kindness of these people for over six months; enjoyed the rough hospitality they could ill afford and now he had nothing to give them, no way of showing the depth of his gratitude.

Uliana felt Henryk's lips on her cheek, the strength of his hands on her shoulders and kissed him awkwardly in return.

'Thank you both for saving my life,' he said simply, 'and for—' But he found he could not go on and, turning quickly away, he stepped on board the barge.

'God go with you,' Uliana called firmly.

His figure standing in the stern was blurred as the long pole pushed the barge out into the current. She heard the voice of her son calling farewells, the splash of water as the big sweep-oars began their slow rhythm.

'One day we shall see him again. I'm sure of it.' And the thought brought her some comfort.

'Nonsense, woman,' growled Pavel. But he, too, had the strange feeling that somehow the course of their lives was caught up with that of the Pole, Henryk Barinski.

They stood in silence as the barge dwindled rapidly on the broad expanse of the river. Uliana's hand caressed her cheek where his lips had touched and her eyes were far away.

Suddenly Pavel cupped his hands to his mouth and shouted with jocular gusto, 'Your Honour can always earn your living as a trapper or a woodcutter,' but his words vanished on the breeze long before they reached the distant boat.

Henryk watched his friends shading their eyes against the glare of the morning sun. Just before the barge rounded the wide bend of the river he raised his arm in farewell. Uliana waved once more and then they were gone and only a faint dark smudge of smoke hanging above the trees indicated the whereabouts of the little hut.

'Four days,' said Osip, leaning heavily on the long steering-oar. 'Four days till the smell of the sea.'

Henryk walked forward into the blunt bows. Ahead the Dvina flowed brown and shining between the dark green walls of the forest. They were running swiftly towards the sea, carried on the rush of the great river.

The oarsmen shipped their oars and struck up a merry song; duck rose in clouds from the reeds and scattered into the pale blue sky.

Henryk drew a deep breath and, as his lungs filled with the cool, sharp air, so his feeling of sadness gave way to an eager impatience to round the next bend, and the next, to glimpse what lay ahead.

And, all of a sudden, new hope sprang in his heart.

*   *   *

The big merchantman swung lazily to her anchor in the mouth of the Thames, waiting for the tide.

Henryk leant on the bulwarks, gazing at the three warships anchored off the flat shoreline; beyond the bright spit of land a tangle of masts and rigging rose against the dawn sky. Gulls wheeled and soared above the warships and boats moved across the shining sea between them. A light land breeze was cool on his face.

Kasia would love the sight of those ships; he imagined her excited comments and the flood of eager questions. This same dawn would shine on the Neva, on the myriad windows of the Winter Palace, on the room where she still lay asleep. And yet, as she always said, who could sleep in the strong luminous glow of the White Nights when the sun vanished for no more than an hour and they made love in perpetual sunlight?

But now, at this moment, was she waking luxuriously in her wide, curtained bed, stretching her long limbs? Was she turning to Orlov with little husky murmurs of love and desire?

Henryk moved restlessly, gripping the rail with white-boned strength, trying desperately to put these tormenting thoughts from his mind.

Three weeks before he had come aboard this English ship, at night, secretly, no questions asked. To the Captain he was a pair of hands to haul on a rope, nothing more.

Three weeks ago they had sailed from Archangel and now in a few hours they would move up-river to London. He would go ashore without money—the Captain, after all, saw no reason to pay an obvious fugitive; surely the passage to safety was enough? —without friends, in the rough shirt and breeches in which he stood. But his mind did not dwell on the difficulties ahead. He would beg, borrow or steal; something would surely turn up; with money in his pocket he would somehow get to France. But those warships, they were the only ships that went to France these days, to bring hunger and terror to the coasts. He had heard much about the war from the crew who spoke with fear and loathing of the Navy, for these were dangerous times when no man was safe from the long arm of the press-gangs. One of the warships he noticed especially, gleaming with new paint, her scarlet gun-ports open and brasswork twinkling in the sun. Men were working aloft in her rigging.

Behind him he heard the heavy thump of a wooden leg on the deck.

'Look pretty, don't they?' The cook emptied the wooden pail of galley refuse over the side, watched as the gulls swooped, screeching, and then sat himself down on a bollard.

'Third-raters,' he went on. 'One of 'em new by the looks of 'er.' He scratched himself reflectively.

'I was in the bloody Navy three years. Lost this at Finisterre.' He tapped the rough wooden stump. 'Topman in the old *Devonshire* under 'Awke. There was a sailor for you. Went after the bloody Monsieurs like a terrier, 'e did, *and* 'e looked after the lower deck—or tried to.' He fumbled inside his dirty striped shirt for his tobacco quid. 'Not many like old 'Awke.'

Henryk understood most of what the other was saying. During the voyage from Russia he had picked up a lot of English and, coupled with what he had learnt from an English friend in Rome, he now knew enough to carry on a reasonable conversation. By hard experience and the added spur of a rope's end across his back he had rapidly picked up the strange language of the sea, and he found moreover that, after the first two days of seasick agony, he enjoyed the feel of the ship beneath him and never tired of watching the play of the sea.

'We'll be docked inside of eight hours,' said the cook. 'What'll you do when you gets ashore, mate?' he asked curiously. He had come to like this fellow, Russian, Polack, whatever he was. Be sorry to see him go really. Helped him carry the buckets and the coal for the galley fire. Not a bad lad, for a foreigner.

'I don't know.'

In the silence that followed Henryk watched the sails of a small vessel moving beyond the spit of land; soon she would be in sight.

'I might be able to 'elp you.' The cook spat a brown squirt of tobacco into the scuppers. 'I knows a lad in Wapping, a real obliging wight 'e is, 'oo might—' He broke off to stare at the vessel which had appeared from behind the land and was standing out towards them. Henryk heard an oath.

'Gawd's teeth, that's a bloody pressing tender or my name's not Nathaniel Robb.'

Henryk saw the flash of a gun, sharp even in the sunlight, and heard the flat report, then something howled high above the bows. At the sound of it men came tumbling on deck with a rush of bare feet; there were shouts and bellowed orders.

'Up anchor! Sharply there.' The men put their shoulders desperately to the capstan bars. Water creamed at the bows of the schooner as she came up fast before the breeze.

'Get it up! Get it up!' The voice rang out, high-pitched with alarm. Slowly the anchor rose clear of the water.

'Make sail! Hands to the braces!' The Captain spun the wheel frantically.

The mainsail flapped for an instant then filled half-heartedly as the ship turned slowly from the wind. Henryk hauled with the rest at the lee-braces, infected by the same fear that drove the cursing men to work as if threatened by death itself.

The ship began to inch ahead and a ragged cheer rang out but it was quickly silenced as the gun fired again. This time spray pattered on them from a sudden waterspout close to the ship's side. A voice boomed through a speaking trumpet.

'Avast there! Heave to or I'll put the next shot into you.' The schooner was no more than a cable's length off the larboard side and they could see the gun's crew crouching over the deck-gun, a blue-coated figure beside them.

The Captain of the merchantman hesitated, glancing first at the schooner then at his own mainsail barely filling. With a shrug he brought her round. 'Mainsail aback!'

They drifted, barely moving. A boat, filled with men and an officer in the sternsheets, put off from the schooner, watched apathetically by the merchant seamen. They stood huddled like cattle mesmerised by the sight and smell of blood.

'You don't argue with the bloody Navy,' muttered a man near Henryk. 'Not without guns, you don't.' The sun glinted on pistol barrels and cutlasses.

The boarding party was led by a very young Lieutenant who seemed to know his business well.

'You will parade your men, if you please, Captain.'

'I have no trained seamen on board,' protested the Captain. 'This is a green crew, I tell you. How can I get my ship to London if you take all my men?' He alternately blustered and begged but the officer hardly listened.

'Where are you from?'

'Archangel.'

'You'll have had time to teach 'em a bit then.' The Lieutenant raised his voice. 'Look here,' he called out, 'England needs men—'

'And don't care much 'ow she gets 'em.' The cook spat over the side. He was safe; the Navy had no more use for a one-legged man.

The officer flushed angrily. 'Good pay and plentiful food for those who choose willingly to fight on the side of freedom and justice.'

He repeated the words he had used so often before on the decks of so many homecoming merchantmen. Nathaniel Robb made a rude sound; the crew of the merchantmen began to mutter and fidget.

'Great prospects for glory—and prize money—' He waxed more enthusiastic as he went on.

'Well? Any volunteers?' he concluded. Not a man moved as his angry eyes roamed along the line of sullen men.

'All right then.' Followed by two burly ratings, he inspected them slowly, choosing his men with a stabbing forefinger. As each unfortunate was marked so the two seamen grabbed and propelled him without ceremony to the side. A few struggled but mostly they went with the hopeless docility of sheep.

Henryk stood at the end of the line. The young officer looked him up and down and Henryk felt his anger rising at the haughty insolence in the other's cold eyes.

'You look a likely lad. Are you a seaman?'

Henryk did not answer.

'I'm speaking to you, fellow.'

In reply Henryk shouted loudly, 'Are we going to let ourselves be taken without a fight?'

'Silence!' roared the Lieutenant but stepped back from the look in Henryk's eyes. His men raised their pistols and cudgels menacingly. 'Take him!' The two men advanced on him.

Henryk hit one of the sailors full in the mouth, ducked a swinging cudgel and brought his knee up into the pit of the other's stomach. Cursing foully and spitting blood, his friend came at him.

'By Christ, you've asked for it, mate!'

Henryk made a dart for a belaying pin on the bulwark but before he could reach it a cudgel smashed across his head.

When he came to he was lying in the bottom of the boat, the blood sticky in his hair. He lay shutting his eyes against the glare of the sky with the sharp rush of water very close to his aching head.

On reaching the schooner, the eighteen of them were bunched in the bows and watched over by two seamen with muskets. The vessel turned to beat back into the breeze towards Sheerness. They rounded the land and made for the great cluster of ships. A little apart lay a dingy brown hulk, mastless and with rusted grilles across the gun-ports. The schooner came to anchor close to this unprepossessing vessel.

'The best receiving-ship in the Navy,' said one of the sailors.

' 'Ome sweet 'ome, me 'earties.' His mate guffawed.

'All the 'ospitality of 'is Majesty King George II,' he said with heavy humour. 'Gawd bless 'im.'

The pressed men gazed with frightened eyes at the hulk that

40

was to receive them, too dispirited and apprehensive to make a sound. Henryk, however, saw none of it. He sat with his head in his hands, staring at the deck between his knees.

He allowed himself to be herded with the others into the boat that carried them to the receiving-ship; in a semi-daze he climbed aboard and found a place away from the crowd which covered the deck. He sat there, not caring about anything except the fierce throbbing of his head.

He had no idea how long he remained like this, while a formless babel of sound swept over him as the two or three hundred men talked and argued, swore and shouted, and prayed. Every now and then the sound seemed to swell to a sudden peak of misery and terror. Red-coated Marines stood at intervals along the sides, leaning on their muskets, the long bayonets glinting coldly in the afternoon sun.

No one paid Henryk the least attention until a big man with bare, hairy arms and a frayed rope's end in his huge paw approached, shouting:

'You there with the scar across your face, off your arse and follow me.' Why do they bellow so? Henryk thought dully; why can't they speak normally?

He got slowly and shakily to his feet and, stepping over the many bodies sprawled on the deck, followed the big man down below into the gloom of a low cabin where two officers in uniform sat behind a table covered in papers.

The men were elegant and bewigged and the sharp, clean smell of vinegar rising from a little silver box on the green baize cloth vied with the musty dampness of the cabin. Another man stood before the table: a ragged, bearded fellow with reddish hair, thin hooked nose and angry restless eyes. The remains of a broadcloth suit and grimy shirt hung in stinking tatters on his thin frame, his shoes had gaping soles and rotting uppers. Henryk's nose wrinkled in disgust at the stench from the man's body. A Marine sentry stood by the door, only his eyes moving in a wooden face as they followed the course of a bluebottle buzzing in the hot cabin.

The men behind the table paid no heed to Henryk but continued to examine the bearded man.

'A Highlander, you say?'

'Yes.' The man held himself proudly for all his rags and filth.

'You were fortunate to escape the hangman,' observed one of the officers, a man with a thin, foxy look to him.

'Or the plantations,' added the other, fanning his pale sweaty face with a sheaf of papers.

'Were you one of the rabble who followed the Pretender?' The officer glanced with distaste at the man's long matted hair.

'I was.' He drew himself up.

'And now you will have the opportunity to serve your rightful King.' The examiner smirked, then nodded to the sentry. 'Take him below.'

The Marine flung open the door. The Highlander swept the officers with his fierce gaze and walked slowly from the cabin in his flapping shoes.

'Pah,' exclaimed the pale officer. 'I detest the Scotch.' He got up and stood by the barred port, helping himself noisily to snuff. 'They're so damnably pleased with themselves.' His companion poured wine from a pewter jug.

'It's thirteen years since the Rebellion,' he said, 'and yet they still come crawling from the gaols. It amazes me how lenient we were with the scum. We should have hanged the whole mangy pack.'

Both men appeared to have forgotten Henryk.

'Why am I here?' he demanded harshly.

They stared at him in utter amazement.

'Speak when we ask you a question,' said the foxy one softly. The bluebottle settled on his wig.

'You have no right to keep me,' Henryk burst out hotly.

'Right? *Right?* What does he mean?' They laughed without humour.

'Are you willing to join the King's service?' enquired the pale officer coldly.

'No.'

'And what reason can you give us?'

'This is not my country.'

'But you are here now.'

The silence was broken by a dull murmur of voices from somewhere below, the gentle slap of water and the frantic buzzing of the bluebottle caught in the wig.

'What are you? Where do you come from?'

'Poland.'

'You are a long way from home, then. Now listen, fellow,

42

there are many foreigners in our ships. Italians, Spaniards, Turks and blackamoors. Even Frenchmen are given the chance to earn money and glory in the service of England.'

'What should I do with glory?'

The officer emptied his glass and reached for the jug.

'Take my advice,' he said more kindly, 'and enter the service cheerfully. As a volunteer you will then have a bounty and be in a fair way for promotion. If you continue to refuse—' He leant forward, making a pyramid with his fingers. 'Just remember you are already aboard.'

'In fact I have no choice?'

'You're quite correct. You will be kept as a pressed man and treated accordingly.' He motioned languidly with his hand and the sentry again opened the door, calling out, 'A pressed man to go below.'

'Is this the way England fights for her precious freedom and justice?' Henryk asked bitterly and went from the cabin.

'So you're going to be a sailorman,' said the big man as he led Henryk below. 'Look 'ere, I'll give you some advice. It ain't a flaming bit of good to fight the Navy. You'll only get the cat across yer back—or worse.' They crossed an empty gun-deck to a hatchway. 'This 'ere used to be the cockpit where many a good lad's 'ad 'is limbs sawn orf and many another's breathed 'is last. Now, get down and pray to Gawd you gets a decent captain.'

Henryk descended the ladder into a foetid gloom lit by two small tallow dips and the grating in the deck above. About forty men lay on the deck or sat with their backs against the curved sweating sides. Half a dozen men were grouped round one of the candles, noisily throwing dice; others lay motionless and silent on the deck; in one corner a rasping voice uttered a stream of blasphemies, in another a youthful cry called again and again on God for help. When Henryk's eyes grew accustomed to the flickering gloom he made out the figure of the bearded Scotsman and went to stand beside him. On his other side a fat middle-aged man with tears running down his quivering cheeks kept repeating, 'They would never believe it. Never.'

'So they've got you too,' said the Scotsman, glancing up at Henryk.

'What will they do to us?' quavered the fat man, pulling at his white neck-cloth. 'My dear sirs, what will they do?'

43

'Do? Put us in one of their stinking ships till we rot or get ourselves blown to pieces or tossed overboard, dead of the putrid
fever. That's what they'll do.' The Scotsman spoke in a kind of
snarl.

'Oh my God, my God, if they saw me now. They'd never
believe it.' The fat man moaned, rocking backwards and forwards,
his wig askew.

'Here, sit down,' the Scotsman said to Henryk, indicating the
deck beside him. 'If you can stand my filthy stink.' A brief smile
glimmered in his beard. His eyes were sunken under a broad
forehead deeply scored with black lines and the hands which
plucked at his crawling beard or scratched the reddened, spotted
skin visible through the rents in his clothing, were hooked and
bony as a vulture's claws. The timbers moved slightly at Henryk's
back as the hulk shifted gently on the tide. He felt the Highlander's
eyes fixed on him, dark and sombre in the hollow face. Then the
smile showed again.

'The last time we met,' said the Scotsman in excellent French,
with courtly politeness, 'was in Paris—oh, it must have been four
years ago. In the *salle d'armes*. I never forget a scar.' His laugh
was short, harsh, rasping as a broken file. Henryk gazed at him
in amazement.

'Let me jog your memory, friend. One day, after I had been
fencing with the Chevalier D'Eon, you praised his skill with the
blade. You said—'

Henryk interrupted. ' "His wrists may be those of a woman but
they belong to the finest swordsman in Europe." Or something
like that.' The scene was clear in his mind. . . . A hot afternoon
at the *salle d'armes* . . . friendly bout with Jacques Beaufranchet,
then drinking wine as they watched the small, slender Chevalier
give a lesson to one of the Scotsmen, a thin red-haired man in his
middle twenties, lithe and fast but no match for the Frenchman
. . a group of Jacobites standing aloof in their usual corner of
the gallery where Amande flirted outrageously with richly dressed
young men . . . the day that the Prince de Conti had come with
the Duc de Richelieu to watch . . . the look in Amande's eyes
and the revealing quality of her laughter as she caught the attention of the most renowned libertine of France, the noble goat who
must have been born with a woman in his arms.

That was the day he himself had been introduced to Conti and
because of that meeting he was here now. If Conti had not

44

chosen him to go to Petersburg . . . if Amande had not persuaded him to go that first time to the *salle d'armes* . . . if he had not ridden across the river from Lipno that day ten years ago and found Kasia sleeping by the birch tree. . . . If. If. Retire to bed for your life or to a monastery, plant yourself in the earth as a cabbage and you would have no destiny. But you would, he thought with a flash of bitter humour. In bed the roof would fall on you; in a cabbage patch someone would pick and eat you. You can no more escape your destiny than you can escape death. He remembered the Jacobites. Proud, penniless, touchy as gunpowder and still brooding, eight years after leaving Scotland, on their misfortunes; nostalgic for the mountains and heather; full of memories—turning a little sour—of the magnetic young man who had set them on the long road to Culloden. And this one—he glanced at the wasted scarecrow beside him—had kept himself even more aloof than the rest, the haughty look of the mountain dweller to him, a hint of the eagle in his gaze.

'By God, you remember.' The Scotsman held out his hand. Henryk felt the grip of a skeleton.

'My name is Cameron. Ewen Cameron.'

PART TWO

LIEUTENANT WILLIAM STODART stood on the quarterdeck of His Majesty's ship *Huntress*, looking about him with keen eyes. For a while he watched the men at work on their various tasks, listening with pleasure to the contented murmur of talk. They sounded reasonably happy and a happy ship was, in his opinion, a good ship. And, as First Lieutenant, it was his job, his sole reason for existence, to turn out a good ship.

'Amazing,' he said to the Midshipman of the watch, who stood solemnly waiting for what the moment might bring. 'Look at 'em.' Stodart nodded at a party reeving ropes through the blocks newly arrived from the dockyard. 'You'd think to hear 'em, they were born to the sea.'

Midshipman Lloyd did not venture an opinion.

'Yet, three months ago they'd never so much as smelt a ship.' There was pride in Stodart's voice, pride in the change he had made in these men, turning them from a rag-bag collection of humanity into trained seamen worthy to sail the finest seventy-four in the Navy.

Gaol-birds, decayed artists, debtors; bankrupt merchants, rapists; brawny ploughmen, elegant fops; beggars and dismissed footmen. He took what came and welded them—some with rough kindness and encouragement, some with oaths and threats—into a crew that would not fail the ship, or each other, when the moment came. He looked at them working in the sunshine. Treat 'em as well as conditions allowed and they'd fight better than any men on earth.

To his disappointment the moment was overlong in coming. A new ship, an excellent captain, willing men—and nothing. Other ships reaped the glory, saw the action, raked in the prize money, but *Huntress* had so far not fired a gun in anger, unless you counted that sorry business with the privateer in the Basque Road some months before.

But the crew then had been green, the ship sluggishly handled. Stodart frowned at the memory of the Frenchmen's jeering cries, the miserable shooting made by the lower-deck guns, Captain Primrose's cold anger.

The Lieutenant glanced at the gleaming decks, the neat coils of tarred rope, the white heap of a sail being sewn on the forecastle; from the towering white masts to the dull gleam of the quarter-deck 9-pounders. Now if they met a Frenchman the affair would end very differently, whatever his size.

'We should be ready for sea by Tuesday,' he said. Then, raising his voice, he shouted, 'If I catch you spitting on the deck again, Fitch, I'll have you at the masthead for a week.'

The seaman called Fitch looked up with a startled expression on his sharp face, then grinned sheepishly. Stodart prided himself on knowing, out of a complement of six hundred, the names of three-quarters of his crew, not including the latest batch of pressed men down there under Yorston, Captain of the Afterguard, who were trying to learn the mysteries of splicing. The officer took his watch from his fob. Gore should be back soon with the final scrapings. Thirty men needed and he'd be lucky if he got ten. He heard Fitch make one of his jokes and the laughter of his mates. An unmitigated scoundrel, he thought, but one he had hopes for.

He turned back to Lloyd. 'In *Culloden* he'd have got a dozen lashes.' The Midshipman followed his superior's gaze to where the flagship lay at anchor astern.

'She needs a lick of paint,' added Stodart smugly.

'So does *Edgar*, sir,' squeaked the boy.

When Lloyd had reported aboard *Huntress* for the first time on his fourteenth birthday six months before, in his white knee-breeches and small uniform coat with broad white cuffs, he had almost burst with pride and joy at her appearance. Built at Chatham in 1758: one of Pitt's new ships which were taking to the seas in place of the leaking, rotten, undermanned vessels sent out in Newcastle's time, ships which on occasions literally fell to pieces in heavy weather. One hundred and sixty-five feet long, forty-six feet in beam—he knew her dimensions by heart. Fifteen hundred and fifty tons and drawing twenty feet unladen, she carried twenty-eight 32-pounders on her lower gun-deck, thirty 18-pounders on her upper gun-deck and fourteen 9-pounders on the quarterdeck. Black, with gun-ports picked out in yellow and a

47

broad red band running along the side; bright blue stern galleries ablaze with gold; red caps to the tall white masts, black yards and shrouds and her guns polished like fire-irons. He never ceased to marvel at the beauty of this ship and at his good fortune to be posted to her.

But his real delight was the figurehead: the great gilded lion, common to all the third-raters, crowned and thrust forward defiantly into wind and sea.

'Where will it be this time, sir?' he enquired.

'God knows. Another spell with the Western Squadron beating up and down off Brest. Or stuck in the Basque Road, like as not.' Many of the ships blockading France's west coast were over six months foul and long due for relief.

'Not the West Indies?' said Lloyd wistfully. 'Or the Mediterranean?' He'd heard a lot about the Med. from Midshipman Tregotha.

'No. It'll be Ushant for us, m'lad, mark my words. Most of the winter keeping the Monsieurs safe and snug in their harbours while we play at corks on the edge of the Atlantic. Ah well, that's the Navy for you.'

Still, they should get a couple of months good weather for training the new men and keeping the old ones up to the mark. Mr Hay would want to exercise his gunners and the Master-at-Arms to practise the men in handling small-arms.

Stodart's mind leapt ahead to the problems of keeping the crew trained without making them stale. Two hours aloft . . . gun drill . . . boarding drill . . . fire drill . . . No, perhaps three hours aloft. No use having expert gunners if you couldn't put the ship where you wanted her. He'd have to draw up a scheme of further training for the Captain's approval. . . . There were the quarter bills to be altered when he saw how many men Gore had managed to scrape up from the receiving hulk. . . . It was too hot for problems. A mug of beer was more like it. Stodart removed his three-cornered hat and mopped his wide forehead.

'Longboat in sight, sir.'

'Sharper, Mr Lloyd. None of your drawling, if you please.'

Midshipman Lloyd flushed, drew a deep breath and snapped out the words as he had been taught at the Naval Academy. No useless words to muddle the men. Say what you mean, gentlemen, and no more.

'That's better.'

Stodart ran up the ladder on to the poop and watched over the rail, counting the heads, as the boat passed round the stern. He swore. Only eight. They would sail short of two dozen men. Not many perhaps, but when you took into account sickness and the daily accidents at sea among the landsmen—he swore again, hearing already the Captain's cutting reproof, and went down to the waist.

'Well, Mr Gore, what have we this time?' He spoke cheerfully, not allowing his annoyance to show, glancing without much interest at the eight pressed men shuffling sullenly into some sort of line.

'A Scotchman and a Pole,' said the Third Lieutenant. 'And some sort of a merchant. The fat one.' The Hon. Richard Gore might have been discussing the latest batch of cattle. Stodart looked them over in silence, then he stepped back a pace and addressed them.

'There are a hundred and fifty ships of the line,' he said, repeating his customary speech of welcome. 'And this one is the best. Do your duty well and you'll have little to complain of. Keep your wits about you—your lives and those of your mates depend on every man obeying orders quickly and without question.' There's only one of the rascals listening, he thought, meeting Henryk's steady gaze. He's like Walenski, my father's agent at Lipno, Henryk was thinking, the same saturnine look, the same long jaw. Everything about him was long: the blue frock coat, patched and stained, ill-fitting on his narrow shoulders, the dingy white waistcoat and wrinkled stockings. A tall, lean, untidy man with a strong, incisive voice. 'Right, Mr Gore, read 'em in, if you please.'

The Third Lieutenant read the Articles of War in his slow, precise way.

'... every person in the Fleet who, through cowardice, negligence or dissatisfaction, shall, in time of action, withdraw, or keep back, or not come into the fight ... every such person ... shall suffer death.'

Death. Again and again the word. For doing this, death; for not doing that, death. The men fidgeted and shuffled their feet, staring at the bleached deck or up at the gulls soaring above the yards or across at the green line of the shore, so close and yet lost to them forever, or so it seemed at the moment. Henryk fixed his eyes on Gore's freckled face. This one was neat and well

49

turned out, slim as a girl in his new blue coat; not a crease or a stain. Behind him stood a huge bear of a man with enormous arms folded across a barrel chest bursting his striped shirt. His thick, greying hair was drawn back into a long, greasy queue tied with a black ribbon; his canvas trousers were rolled up his hairy, muscular calves. From one hand hung a thin cane tipped with rope and his expression, cast in weatherbeaten rock, never altered.

'... and for this the punishment shall be death or such less penalty.'

Bunch, the merchant, was shivering violently with his mouth wide open and terrified little eyes darting in pale, sweating fat, the Scotsman muttered angrily beneath his breath; the remainder listened in dazed silence.

The Third Lieutenant finished reading.

'Is that understood then?' he asked.

The men nodded apathetically; no one spoke except for Bunch.

'You can't mean me,' he began in a high, shaky voice. 'Not me—I shouldn't be here—I—'

'Scrub 'em down, Bos'n,' interrupted Stodart coldly. 'Get the stink of the gaols off 'em.'

'Aye, aye, sir.'

The big man stepped forward. He stood before them on straddled legs, growing like some great tree from the deck.

'My name's Jem Pike.' His voice was a rumbling growl. 'And I'm the Bos'n of this ship.' He spoke with the broad vowels of a countryman. 'And you'll listen to what I say. Understand?' There was no mistaking the men's attention. 'If I don't make something of you, then there ain't no snakes in Virginia.' He fingered the small silver whistle hanging from a chain round his neck. 'This 'ere's the Bos'n's call. When you 'ear it you come running, understand?' The sun flashed on the little gold rings in his ears. 'Whether you're soused, sick or dead you come on deck to this call.'

He jerked his head at the quarterdeck. 'Those are your officers and you 'eard what Mr Stodart 'ad to say. You obeys them but—' he paused—'but it's me you'll come to love.' He grinned, exposing a few brown teeth. 'And this—' he struck the side of his leg with the cane—'is a switcher.' It swished viciously in the air. Bunch uttered a low moan. 'Behave yourselves and you'll 'ave no cause to feel it. Give me or any of my Mates any lip and you'll be bloody dancing, understand?' His hard blue eyes looked them over, coming to rest on Henryk. 'It don't matter 'oo you are nor where you comes from. You're in the Navy now and just don't you forget it.' He leant forward. 'You the Pole?'

'Yes.'

'Understand what I say, do you?'

'Yes.'

'I've 'ad plenty of furriners in this ship. Some of 'em couldn't 'ardly understand the difference between the anchor and the bloody mizzen but they understood *me* all right.' He bounced lightly on the soles of his bare feet. 'And which of you's the Scotchman?' The man in rags nodded. 'The last 'ighlander we 'ad fell out of the topmast trees and smashed 'imself to jelly, and the ship 'ardly moving.' He shook his head sadly. 'Now, me 'earties, we'll start by scraping some of the muck off you.'

He took them forward to the deck-pumps where he made them strip naked and stand under the gushing sea-water. Two grinning seamen worked the pumps; others gathered round to watch while the eight men scrubbed themselves and each other with lumps of holystone. There was much coarse amusement at Bunch's flabby white body and trembling paunch and rough encouragement for the Scotsman as his filthy, crawling hair was shorn to the skull.

Henryk gasped from the shock of the cold water. But, when he stood back to dry, the warmth of the sun on his body was pleasant. His head still ached from the blow received—was it only that morning? Was it really him standing stark naked, watched by a crowd of gaping, grinning monkeys? He felt the warmth of the sun on his body and stooped for his clothes.

'Not yet, lad. The Surgeon wants a look at you.' Jem Pike herded them into line again, laying his switcher lightly across Bunch's quivering behind. A roar of laughter greeted the fat man's frightened yelp. 'Like a lump 'o white lard in the pan,' Pike pronounced. 'Nothing for a woman to 'ang on to there, eh lads?'

Bunch tried vainly to cover himself, bending almost double in an access of modesty.

'Lay it on again,' suggested a voice helpfully. The Surgeon came stamping across the deck on his short bandy legs, a bad-tempered expression on his red face. Ebenezer Boosey had been disturbed from his backgammon with the Chaplain, the Reverend Dunsterville, and somebody would pay. The usual weedy lot, he thought sourly, regarding the half-starved bodies and filthy skins; thieves,

51

debtors, back-street scum. He jabbed his thumb into Bunch's stomach. Nothing starved about this one.

'Stand up, man. You've nothing to hide.'

'I'm not fit,' wailed the unfortunate man. 'My dear, kind sir, really I am not fit. My heart—if only you knew—'

'A couple of trips to the masthead and back and you'll be fit enough.' Boosey snorted. He inspected the Scotsman in contemptuous silence then asked, 'Newgate?'

'Among other places, yes.'

Cameron's whole body was horribly marked and spotted with the bites of the prison vermin; his skin had the greyish tinge of one who had been starved of sun and air for long months.

'As a rebel you'll know a bit about war,' remarked Stodart from where he stood, hands behind his back.

The Scotsman swept him with angry eyes but did not answer.

'You'll speak up with respect when an officer addresses you and say "sir",' growled the Boatswain, bending his cane into a bow. 'I've 'ad your sort before, my fine Highland gentleman, and I knows very well how to deal with them—as you'll soon find.'

Boosey stood looking Henryk up and down with his rheumy little eyes. 'Turn round.' He inspected the scarred body with interest. 'It wasn't a naval lash that made those marks.'

'No,' Henryk agreed.

'And this one?' Boosey pointed at the puckered, purple line on Henryk's thigh.

'A bayonet.'

The Surgeon's eyes went to the star-shaped scar on the lower ribs. 'And this?'

'A horse's hoof.'

Stodart had advanced closer to see for himself. 'A fighting-man, eh? We get too few of those,' he said. 'Soldier?'

'Yes.'

'You'll know about guns then?'

'From the wrong end, yes, a little.'

Anger rumbled in the Boatswain's throat. 'A bloody wit, is it.'

'Two gunners in this lot,' said Stodart to Gore pointing at the Highlander. 'Right, get dressed, lads. Except the Scotchman. Throw his rags over the side.' He turned to shout at a little man hurrying along the deck followed by three seamen carrying a

52

huge chest and a table and a pasty-faced clerk staggering under the weight of an enormous ledger.

'Come on, Purser. Would you have this good man here catch his death of cold?' asked Stodart.

'Set up the table. No, over here, fool. Yes, yes, quickly does it. And the slop-chest there. Hurry, man. Pen, ink.' Wheezing and mopping himself, Mr Francis Columbine sat himself at his table, the clerk beside him. 'Step up here. You first.'

Henryk waited before the table while Mr Columbine arranged coins into little piles with his fat fingers.

'Volunteer?'

'No. I was taken against my will from—'

'All right, all right. Not your life story . . . Name. Age. Religion.'

The quill scratched busily in the ledger as the clerk wrote in the few details of Henryk as a human being the Navy thought fit to record. 'B-a-r-i-n-s-k-i.' Boosey snorted. 'Thirty-one years. Roman Catholic.' He snorted again. 'Smoke?'

'No.'

'You're entitled to one pound and fifteen shillings,' said the Purser. 'Two months advance. Want any clothes? Help yourself, lad, help yourself.'

Henryk rummaged in the pile.

'One pea-jacket,' said the Purser, 'nine shillings and sixpence. One shirt, three shillings and twopence. One pair of Kersey breeches, four shillings and sixpence. One pair striped linen trousers. . . .' The clerk wrote it all down in his neat sloping hand. 'Fifteen shillings and fourpence for you, lad. Don't spend it all on loose living.' The Purser chuckled hoarsely. 'Next.'

Henryk stood back and watched the others. A musty smell rose from the pile of clothes in his arms. The Scotsman stepped forward naked to the table.

'Pah,' exclaimed the Purser and wrinkled his strawberry nose in mock disgust. 'Have you no shame?'

When it came to Bunch's turn he elected to keep his shiny broadcloth suit.

'Can you write?' asked Columbine.

'Me, sir. Can I write? Why, of course—'

The Purser interrupted the excited flow. 'I need another clerk.' He glanced at Stodart. 'Will that be convenient to you, sir?'

Stodart nodded. 'He hasn't the build for a topman, nor the eyes of a gunner. Take him, Mr Columbine, with my blessing.'

'Oh, good sweet sirs—' began the rapturous Bunch, clasping his hands. 'God will bless you and—'

'God will lay 'old of your breeches and throw you down the 'atch unless you shuts up,' growled Jem Pike.

The First Lieutenant turned away to hide a smile.

The Boatswain cupped his hands to his mouth and bellowed, '*Yorston!*' A broad-shouldered man in a red shirt and patched brown trousers appeared at a trot. 'This lot's yours. Take 'em below.'

The Captain of the Afterguard swung his rope's-end 'starter' lazily. All his movements were deceptively slow.

'Come on, you pig-brained bunch of idlers.'

He spoke very deliberately, seeming to choose every word with great care; his low forehead was wrinkled in a permanent puzzled frown as though he found life altogether too difficult. His brown eyes were set a fraction too close.

Wearily the pressed men followed their master as he led them below to their new home.

* * *

'*Whe-e-e-ugh!* All hands to wash decks, aho-o-oy!'

Henryk lay with the cry ringing vaguely in his ears, drugged with sleep.

'D'you hear the news there below?' the voice roared.

He sat up in his hammock, struck his head on the deck-beams, and fell back cursing. On his right, so close that he could have touched his face, the Scotsman still slept with his mouth open; on his left Bunch's hammock sagged deeply towards the deck. Here and there men were rolling sleepily from their hammocks, yawning and spitting. The early-morning sunshine through the gun-ports lightened the frowsty gloom of the lower deck, patterned by the nets which hung across the ports to prevent men slipping out in the darkness and swimming for the shore to freedom.

'Rouse up every man and mother's son of you. D'you hear, you idlers?' Three boatswain's mates moved swiftly along the neat lines of sleeping shapes, punching the curves in the canvas. Men spilled out, began feverishly to lash up their hammocks.

'Out! Out!' A knife flashed in the dusty sunlight as one of the mates cut down a laggard head first. The deck rang to the heavy thump, a yell of pain and shock.

Henryk shook the Scotsman violently. 'Wake up. Come on, for God's sake!'

'All hands on deck. Rouse out, you limbs of Satan, the sun's burning yer bloody eyes out!'

With his hammock slung over his shoulder Henryk scrambled clumsily up the ladders to the main deck.

'Into the nets. Come on there. Sharply now.' They piled the canvas bundles in the nettings along the bulwarks.

There was a chill in the air and the hands stood on the poop scratching and shivering after the musty fug of their hammocks. Gulls were perched in rows on the upper yards, turning their white breasts to a sun just clear of the sea; a thin bar of mist lay along the shoreline. For those in a position to enjoy it there was a lot of beauty in the windless morning.

'Here, you with the scar, take it.' A man thrust a large flat piece of holystone at Henryk. 'The bible, this is. And this—' he himself held a smaller bit—'is the prayer book. Closest to the Church you'll get with the Chaplain we've got.'

'On your knees,' shouted Yorston. 'And I want this deck whiter than a harlot's arse.'

They got down in a line and scrubbed and scraped and sluiced the smooth white planking. After twenty minutes Henryk's knees were red-hot agony; he sat up on his haunches. At once the rope's end curled across his shoulders.

'I'll tell you when to stop.' Yorston spoke softly and with no particular animosity. 'And if you looks at me like that again, me fine fellow, I'll have you before the First Lieutenant. Or maybe—' he added reflectively—'I'll knock some of them white teeth down your throat.'

They finished the poop before Yorston let them rest. Henryk sat against the rail leaning his head back to catch the sun between the great gilded stern lanterns.

'I'll get that bastard one o' these days,' growled Fitch. He was a powerfully built man with a sharp evil face and shifty brown eyes which could not meet a steady look.

'Easy, Fitchie. You don't know when you're well off. You've

never been in a rotten ship. Well, listen here, you two new men—' Matthew Swaine, the leading hand of their mess, a grizzled, stooping man with one eye and wearing a red flannel shirt, addressed his words to Henryk and the sullen Scotsman who sat with his eyes shut. 'I went to sea when I was a lad of ten, that's nigh on forty years ago, m'dears. I carried powder for the bleedin' guns in the little *Seahorse* when you were pinching apples and chasing cats.'

Henryk had a sudden vivid memory of Cornu, the little drummer boy, beating out the *pas de charge* at Rossbach.

'Tell us about when you went round the Horn with Anson.' Isaac Mendel winked slyly at his companions.

'The old *Centurion*. Ah, me lads, there was a ship—' But Swaine was not to be drawn further on that. 'I tell you,' he went on in his deep Cornish voice, 'I tell you, I've had to serve in some proper rotten scows under captains and officers who should by rights have been public hangmen. I've felt the cat across me back Jesus knows how many times. Court-martialled once and two hundred lashes, for hitting bo's'n.'

Henryk remembered the knout and gazed in amazement at this man who had survived two hundred strokes.

'Of course, I didn't get 'em all in one day. Oh no, down to the sick-bay and vinegar on me back, then next day the 'ands drawn up to witness punishment again.' His one eye regarded them. 'But that won't happen in this ship, m'dears, not with the captain we've got. 'E'll put you to the mast'ead, by Christ 'e will, or below with the holders to clean out the rats or stop yer grog maybe, but 'e won't use the cat—not unless you really makes 'im.'

'Fancy uniforms don't make a man,' muttered Fitch. 'Why don't 'e let us 'ave our women at sea like some captains do?'

'That's his way,' said Swaine. 'Thinks they cause trouble. I heard him say that to Stodart one time. A ship's a ship, Mr Stodart, not a bawdy 'ouse. That's what 'e said.'

'They're often just poor harbour drabs,' put in Mendel. He spoke in a quiet, well-mannered way. 'They'll face all the dangers of the sea and the rotten food to be the sweetheart of some lucky wight. They'll mend his shirts and hold his hand in the black hell of the cockpit. All they seem to ask is to be with him to the end. My God, I've seen some brave ones.'

'It don't matter if they're brave or not,' said Fitch. 'If they've got what I need in the right place and know 'ow to use it, that's all I want of them. God's teeth, this Captain of ours,' he went on, ' 'e don't know a woman from a bleeding cow, that's my opinion.' When Fitch spoke, every other word was an oath.

'His job's to look after the ship,' said Swaine. 'Not to mess about with women at sea.'

'And fight her,' added Mendel.

'Fight 'er! It's us 'oo fights this ship. You and me, mate.' Fitch lowered his voice. 'Not the officers, God curse 'em. It's us poor sods 'as our bleeding bollocks blown off.' He stared across the placid water to where the mist was dispersing in the mounting heat of the day. 'Women,' he said with terrible longing. 'Lying there between the bleeding sheets, naked as the day they was born.' He clenched his fists convulsively. 'Oh, my Gawd,' he groaned. 'Crying out for Joseph Fitch's—' He sketched a graphic and obscene picture with his grimy hands.

'An edifying picture,' murmured the Scotsman without opening his eyes.

Fitch swung round glaring angrily from under the dark black line of his eyebrows. He small mouth curled. 'Listen to the precious gentleman.' His hard, contemptuous gaze swept the speaker from head to toe. 'No. 8 mess. The *gentlemen's* mess.' Fitch spat out the words.

'It was naturally not of our choosing,' Henryk said mildly.

'Your sort should be in the wardroom—' began Fitch but Swaine interrupted peaceably, 'Now, m'dears, it's too early in the morning for fighting.'

Yorston's call ordered them down to the quarterdeck and on to their knees again. They worked in silence broken by the harsh sound of the scrapers, the sluice of water. As Henryk rubbed the planking with the holystone he tried to abstract his mind from the pain in his knees, the stab of the old wound in his side. He thought of the men he had been put among. No. 8 mess, larboard side, lower gun deck. . . . The Scotsman who had known him in Paris; Joseph Fitch, the foul-mouthed Cockney, sentenced to the gaols for petty thieving; Isaac Mendel, the dark-eyed Jew from London—a man of some education; Elmquist, pressed from a Swedish vessel off the Nore, a vast Viking of a fellow with a shock of fair hair and hands that could bend an iron bar; poor frightened Joshua Bunch, merchant from Brighton, a strange mixture of cringing fear and pompous bombast, Dick Gammon, a red-faced country lad who gazed round him with round, fascinated eyes and mumbled shyly when addressed. And Mat Swaine, the oldest seaman in the ship, quarter gunner in command of the two 32-pounders that squatted, grim and expectant, below the swinging hammocks of No. 8 mess, and the two opposite numbers of the starboard side—one-time prisoner of the French, whom he had fought throughout forty years of open war and uneasy peace. Swaine, whose faded black patch hid the ugly cavity where a deck splinter had mashed his eye to jelly; a giant of a man, as big in stature as the Orlovs, a man who should have been a boatswain if only he could have controlled his hasty temper.... 'Listen here, m'dears,' he was fond of saying, 'if I'd had a mind for it, I could be walking the quarterdeck of me own first-rater.' Then he would laugh so that tears ran from his one twinkling eye....

The sun was hot on Henryk's back; he worked on, finding that the circular sweep of the holystone had already become automatic. A jumble of impressions from his first night below crowded his mind.... The mess table slung from hooks, one of forty similar ones stretched along the sides ... wooden mugs and platters, a few rough spoons, dirty fingers shovelling the lob-scows, a salty stew of meat, crumbled ship's biscuit, and onions—'after three months at sea there'll only be the biscuits and the worms'—rough wine mixed with sour water, beer, cheese hard as wood —'makes good buttons does this stuff'....

The complaints of the bullocks and pigs penned in the manger above them on the upper deck—the midshipmen singing in the gunroom beyond the after bulkhead ... Mat Swaine telling the new men about the organisation of the ship, having to shout against the raucous roar of sound, deafening beneath the low deck: quarter bills. Watch bills ... 'Starboard watch in the afterguard you'll be, that's the landsmen, idlers we calls 'em. When all 'ands are mustered on deck you, being an afterguard man, will muster aft, back end of the ship to you.... When they calls you you'll jump to it. Don't matter if you're the watch below, snoozing in your 'ammick or under a gun, you gets up on deck, fully dressed, 'arf naked, it don't matter, m'dears, not if it's blowing a t'gallant gale....' Swaine patted the round black curve of the gun beside him. 'You'll be gunners, you two. What's your name again? Aye, well Brinski, you'll be on No. 8 gun, this one 'ere, and you—' he squinted at the Scotsman—'we'll 'ave

58

you too, Cameron.' He emptied his mug of beer, smacking his lips.

'Good stuff this is. Not like the rotten muck we takes aboard at Plymouth. The rats won't look at Plymouth beer, bless their little 'earts.' He belched and unfastened his belt. 'We're all gunners in this mess but you, Bunch. But that don't mean we don't 'ave no other duties. When there's no Frenchie to lay alongside of you'll be painting, scraping, cleaning, carrying barrels of salt-tack. They'll 'ave you chipping rust, 'ogging ship, sweating at the pumps or bending your bloody backs at the oars of the long boat. Or you'll be practising with these.' He patted the gun lovingly. 'They'll be running you out, running you in, won't they, my beauty?—swabbing you out and feeding you with powder and iron to send a few more Monseers to meet their Maker—if they 'ave one, the slimy toads. Aye, there'll be times when Bull Frobisher—e's the officer in charge of this section o' guns—will make your guts ache with 'atred of these long black devils.' Swaine looked round the little mess table. 'But that's what you're 'ere for, to fight this rascal till you've got no bloody legs to stand on. Midships, larboard side. That's your place in action. This gun, see, and you sticks by 'er till you're dead, see. You'll 'ave your name posted on the quarter bill above this gun and it won't be taken off till you goes over the side. And those 'oo can't read will ask those few 'oo can to tell 'em where to go when the drums beat to quarters.'

He had told them a lot more, puffing at his short clay pipe: about the ship herself, the Captain, the officers, the iniquities of the clerks and pen-pushers, who cheated the seamen of their rights and their pay.... Later, in his hammock, Henryk could hear the deep voice still rolling on till finally it ceased and the lower deck was given over to the snores and gruntings, the unintelligible mutterings of sleeping men. For hours he had lain awake, too tired and tense for sleep, sickened and breathless from the smell. No air came through the ports to sweeten the mixture of unwashed bodies, tobacco smoke, stale food, tarred rope, the putrid stench of the bilges, sweat, rum and rancid butter. In the dim light of a few candle lanterns the red sides and the deck-head close above his face, the rats moving between the dark shapes of the guns, the gleam of the cutlasses in the racks, the shot piled in the garlands—all combined to build in his mind a picture of some flickering red hell.... On each side of him the pressure of two hammocks, twenty inches to a man, moved against his own whenever Cameron or Bunch stirred in his sleep. No privacy, his every action exposed to public curiosity ... Nowhere in this packed sweat-hole could man escape the eyes of his mates; not for one moment could he ever be alone again.

'My God,' he had asked himself in a wave of self-pity, 'oh my God, what have I done to deserve this?' And the only answer was the sigh of the water along the side as *Huntress* moved gently to her anchor. ...

Eight bells were struck, disturbing his unsavoury recollections, the sharp clear note of the bell carrying across the flat water.

'Hands to breakfast!'

The others trooped below but Henryk remained leaning on the bulwark, gazing at the shore, unwilling to leave the sweet, clean air for the stifling fug of the lower deck. Three lighters came round the land from Sheerness, barely moving in the tiny breeze, and with much bustle and noise the watch on deck began to rig the derricks in preparation for taking on stores.

*　　*　　*

A barrel of salt meat spun slowly at the end of the rope as it was raised from the deck of the victualling lighter. 'Easy now. Lower away.'

For the last two hours the blocks had squealed, the lightermen had cursed and the Officer of the Deck, the Second Lieutenant, Charles Wood ('Mr You-sir'), had leant over the side, shouting furiously, 'You, sir, down there. Go easy with that damned tub of yours.' The lighter bumped the side and the stores came slowly aboard, hauled up by a hot and sweating party from the afterguard under Yorston's watchful eye, most of them stripped to the waist in the warm sunshine.

Mr Columbine stood near by with Bunch respectfully behind him, ticking off the items as the former called out the stores which would feed them for the next three months.

'... twelve tons of biscuit ... twenty casks salted pork ... eighteen firkins butter ... Mind how you go, you clumsy cow.' Columbine's double chins wobbled and his face gleamed in the midday heat.

'Fat swine,' muttered Fitch. 'I'd like to see him dancing at the yard-arm.'

'He'd need an anchor cable to hold him up,' said Mendel quietly. The men within earshot laughed.

'Keep some of it for us, Bunch,' they called, for the day was fine, and they were well rested. Oatmeal. Cheese. Sides of good fresh beef; peas, potatoes for the officers; butts of Chatham beer, ankers of rum and barrels oozing water. The first lighter drew away followed by a stream of abuse from the Second Lieutenant answered in full measure by the lightermen who cared little for naval discipline.

Henryk and Cameron worked together, rolling the heavy barrels to the lip of the after hold.

'Half an hour on yer backsides,' said Yorston, grudgingly, when the last of the barrels had vanished into the depths of the ship. He hated to see men idle.

They drank a pannikin of water each from the water-butt on deck then squatted wearily on their haunches. Mat Swaine got out his pipe.

Henryk sat with Cameron slightly apart. For a while they did not speak, then the Highlander said, 'God, Paris seems a long way.' He inspected his hands, raw and blistered from the friction of the rope, and shook his head in slow disbelief, letting out a heavy sigh. 'And yet, after the Thames hulk, this is a heaven on earth. Everything in this rotten life's comparative.'

'How did you come to be here from Paris already?' Henryk's English though good, now and again contained small errors.

'To put it shortly I lost my temper and stabbed an English sergeant in Inverness one night, and for that they gave me the chance to go in chains to the Barbados plantations or join His Hanoverian Majesty's Navy. But it all really began fifteen years ago when Prince Charles Edward landed in Scotland.'

Henryk listened quietly as his companion talked in his soft, slightly lilting voice, of his life before and after Culloden, speaking in short, clipped phrases, while the deck moved soothingly to the slow, shining swell and a man's deep voice was raised in song on the forecastle.

Ewen Cameron, two years older than Henryk, was a man twisted with bitterness and dark secret thoughts of vengeance—born a close cousin of Lochiel, the Chief of Clan Cameron—gentle Lochiel—'a king in his own lands'—and with yearnings since earliest youth to be a soldier. He spoke of the year of triumph when England trembled at the prospect of the dreaded Highland charge. When he came to the retreat from Derby Cameron's voice trembled slightly with anger. 'Why in God's name we did not go on . . . many of us begged, implored. London lay open before us and the Hanoverian was packing his baggage. But His Royal Highness was badly advised and those damned English sympathisers who'd talked so loud before he arrived did nothing but watch and wait like the Lowland Scots with their sentimental pretences and ready smiles.'

Henryk knew little of the Prince who had brought ruin to his followers, had condemned men like Cameron to lie on the stones in the holds of the prison ships, sucking air through the chinks of the timbers, suffering the lash, hunger, the scaffold. In the coffee-houses of Rome he had heard the rumours surrounding Prince Charles's future: marriage to a Radziwill, to a Princess of Massa, to a Miss Walkenshaw; his frequent affairs, his despairing addiction to the bottle; how he revisited London in disguise and renounced his Catholic faith; half a dozen plans to return to Scotland which came to nothing. On one occasion he had even seen him leave a coach and stumble, swaying in the lantern light into the Muti Palace to join his sad, melancholy father and his brother, the resplendent young Cardinal, Henry Duke of York.

The gossips had spread stories of a man degenerating: his sensitive courage blunted to brutality. Selfish and mean, all traces of his courtly manners gone—a boasting swaggerer drowned in drunken dreams of the past, of what might have been.

Henryk did not understand some of what Cameron said, for the latter talked as if the Pole had been there with him, had run beside him over the heather during that last desperate charge of hungry weary men, into the sleet and the fire of the merciless guns. But Henryk could visualise the scene only too well, remembering the thunder of Seydlitz's horsemen, the breaking of the Regiment de Mailly by the little village of Rossback.

Cameron told him of months of wandering, slinking from cave to cave, island to island, with the redcoats and the Highland levies breathing down their necks. 'We became animals in our cunning . . . we did not have to hear the tramp of their boots, for the smell of the brutes came to us on the wind.'

Cameron had lain in the woods of Borrodale above Loch nan

Uamh as the English sloops came in to attack the French frigates, and watched as the ships pounded each other. The screams of the wounded were borne loud across the calm waters of the loch, echoing hideously from the hills. 'I remember thinking at the time, God help the poor fellows caught in such an inferno. And now—' He patted the gun-truck of the 9-pounder beside him and, smiling, fell silent, slowly scratching his shaven head.

From the Highlander's vivid description Henryk could clearly see the sails white against the loch, hear the gunfire reverberating among the mountains. Suddenly Swaine's voice cut across his thoughts.

'When Anson took us round the 'Orn in the old *Centurion*—'

'Aye, Mattie lad, tell us about the seas at Cape 'Orn. Big as churches was they?' Fitch's mocking tones.

'Heh, you, sir,' shouted the Second Lieutenant from above them. 'You, sir, with the bucket, what in hell's name are you doing?'

The man, newly pressed, paused with the bucket poised above the side. 'I—I was going to empty it, sir,' he stuttered nervously.

'Not that side. The wind, you brainless clod. Watch the wind, can't you. I'll not have the decks a mess of galley sweepings.' Muffled laughter swept the deck as the unfortunate man scuttled across to the other side and emptied his bucket into the sea.

The Second Lieutenant resumed his self-important strutting of the quarterdeck, his glass stuck stiffly under his arm. The Captain was expected aboard within the hour—it would have been a disaster. He shuddered, hearing the quiet reprimand in his mind. 'Mr Wood, I suggest you keep your eyes about you in future. This is a ship of war, Mr Wood, not a Medway lugger.'

Who would be an officer, thought Wood, and be stifling in this heavy blue uniform, with an overtight waistcoat and pinching shoes? He paused. Look at those two now—with envy he watched Henryk and Cameron lounging on the deck—damned gentlemen of leisure, no responsibilities except to carry out simple orders, wearing what they liked—as officers had been allowed to until that damned silly Admiralty order ten years before.

'He looks hot,' remarked Henryk, returning the officer's stare.

'But he has his own cabin where he can lie and fan himself,' said Cameron.

'Oh, I know, there are indeed to an officer's life certain small compensations,' said Henryk drily.

'Lighter coming alongside,' yelled a voice from the gangway. 'Very well then, get off them, you lazy rascals,' shouted Wood. This time they hauled up the Captain's stores while his steward, Sweetapple, jumped about in a paroxysm of anxiety as the precious barrels, crates and boxes swung aboard. 'Mind how you go. Oh, mind it, I say.' He nearly wept as a shower of small pears cascaded from a split sack, going on his knees to retrieve the squashed, bruised fruit. Cases of wine followed: brandy and claret for the Captain's table; then crates of squawking chickens and fresh, brown eggs.

Joseph Fitch kept up a ceaseless monotone of blasphemy under his breath but Swaine ticked him off roundly.

'Less o' that, Fitch. We've fresh vegetables and meat and a cow to give milk to the sick-bay. And that's all Stodart, that is.'

'Hoist away! That's it, lads.' Yorston was in one of his good moods. A wine-cask swung slowly to the top of its ascent. 'Lower. Handsomely does it. Easy.' The cask had slipped and hung dangerously from the tackle. 'Look out! She's going!'

The cask fell from ten feet on to the deck and split in half a dozen places so that the wine spurted across the white planking and ran red in the scuppers.

'Get it overboard!' yelled Wood. 'Over the side!' They heaved the broken cask over the side and by the time they had finished their bodies were splashed purple from neck to ankle. 'And those men, there, get them out of the scuppers! I'll have no drunken sots, d'you hear?'

Fitch and some others were on their faces in the scuppers, sucking noisily at the trickling wine. Yorston laid about him, raising angry weals with his starter. The men got to their feet with wine running down their chins, merriment in their eyes.

'God blast it,' Wood screamed, 'get that mess cleaned up!'

Men ran for buckets, swabs, holystone. In the water the cask floated in a spreading crimson stain and not a cable's length away the Captain's gig approached the ship, a blaze of blue and gold in the stern.

'What's he going to say? What's he going to say? Oh, my Lord, it'll be Sweetapple for the lower deck.' The unfortunate steward hung over the side flapping his soft white hands.

The Second Lieutenant was giving his orders in a voice of self-contained fury, very conscious of how his voice would carry to the gig. The whole ship, except for the party of Marines clumping to their posts at the entry port, seemed to be concentrated on the wine-stained deck.

One party, entirely on their own initiative, had laid hold of the derrick rope and were busy hauling up a large crate of chickens.

'You left-handed lubbers. You slovenly pack of farmers' boys. You bloody useless bunch of tinkers.' Yorston cursed them in his rasping voice with a single-minded fluency occasioned by the knowledge that the fault had been in some way his own.

'I'll have your hide, Yorston, God damn me, but I'll have it in strips if you don't get that mess cleaned up this instant.' Wood's face was dangerously suffused.

Henryk felt closer to laughter than he had been in all the months since his golden summer with Kasia.

The men ran to and fro, purposely getting in each other's way, tripping over ropes, colliding with each other and spilling their buckets, so that Mr You-sir was reduced to a bursting frenzy of rage and Mr Midshipman Lloyd had to stuff his mouth with a grubby handkerchief to stifle his unseemly mirth and gaze with shaking shoulders to where the boat drew close to the gangway. In a muffled squeak he announced the fact.

'Stand up, you men. Stand still down there,' bellowed Wood. 'You, sir, stop dancing about there. Stand still, I say.'

The Marines presented arms with a crash of huge boots and a cloud of pipeclay; the shrilling of the Boatswain's call rose and fell and the four sideboys held themselves stiffly to attention with set faces as Captain Thomas Primrose stepped on board his ship.

He acknowledged the salutes by raising his braided three-cornered hat and replacing it firmly on his thick brown hair. His sharp eyes, as blue as his coat, took in the scene in one sharp sweeping glance; his mouth tightened slightly but he said nothing as he picked his way over the ropes and spars, a short, stocky figure in full-dress uniform.

By the group of seamen he stopped, staring up at the chickens which were twirling slowly in their crate and squawking in terrified surprise. 'Let 'em down. They—er—don't appear to like it up there.' A few of the men grinned and that pleased him. Stodart was doing a good job with the crew.

He looked down at the remains of the dull red stains partially scrubbed from the deck and at the horror-struck face of that well-meaning fool, Sweetapple. Frightened of being returned to duty, thought Primrose, suppressing an urge to smile. Why, the man looked as worried as those hens. Then his eye was caught by a seaman whose swarthy good looks were cut in half by a shocking scar, a man who met his glance squarely. One of the newly pressed men. He must speak to them, he supposed, not relishing the prospect for he could never think of anything to say.

'I'll see the latest batch,' he said quietly.

'Over here, the men who came aboard yesterday.' Yorston bustled them into line.

The Captain stood facing them in silence, his hand on his sword-hilt, then he cleared his throat.

'Tell me your names.'

They did so in turn.

'You—er—don't like being here,' he went on, fixing his gaze on the scarred man with the outlandish name. An intelligent look to him. A possible fellow for petty officer one day. 'But I—this ship —needs men, good men and—well, you are here now and must make the best of it.' He paused, looking up at the cloudless sky. They were due to sail tomorrow and he hoped for a steadier wind. He cleared his throat again.

'You will have had the Articles of War read out to you. Now, lads, remember them and do your duty as your officers tell you—'

Henryk did not listen to the dry, rather hoarse tones, but his eyes took in the details of this man who had the power of life and death over every man jack of them, whose every word was a law to itself and who could never be disobeyed. A man in his middle thirties, a few years older than Henryk, twenty years younger than Swaine, in excellent health, with a complexion made ruddy by wind and sun. He was magnificent in blue and white, heavy with gold braid. His linen and the facings of his coat were snowy and the sun was reflected fiercely from his buckled shoes. There was a sheen of heat on his face. Henryk, remembering the elaborate discomfort of his French officer's uniform in the heat of the Saxon summer, knew exactly what it must be like to stand in the eye of the sun.

'...do your best and—er—you'll not find me ungrateful.' Primrose brushed a drip of perspiration from his large, beaky nose. 'This—I think—is a good ship with a good crew so I hope you men will—er—I hope you will settle to your work.' His whole body was awash, his fine lawn shirt sticking to his back;

he had no more to say but, as always, found great difficulty in knowing how to terminate the proceedings. . . . 'Right, well—' Abruptly he turned on his heel and strode away.

They watched him go up the ladder to his quarterdeck, say a word to the red-faced Wood and vanish to his quarters below the poop, to what was known as the coach or roundhouse—sitting-room, dining-room, two sleeping cabins, clerk's office and a pantry where Sweetapple reigned supreme. The Boatswain's voice broke the silence.

'You 'eard what the Captain said. Let's not forget, shall we? But remember, it's me you've got to love. And I'm not as kind-'earted as 'e is. Now get 'em back to it, Yorston.'

As the sun sank beyond England's green countryside they toiled to unload the lighters which came in endless procession. At dusk the tired men trooped below to fresh beef, peas and biscuit in the mighty din and stench of the mess-deck.

'He don't speak with—' Dick Gammon struggled to find the right word.

'Authority,' said Mendel, cutting hard at the tough meat.

The Captain's little speech had been far from impressive, yet his look and his walk belied the hesitancy of his words.

'Don't you go thinking he's a softy,' put in Swaine. 'Why, I've seen 'im take this ship through a storm in the Bay that should by rights 'ave lifted the masts from 'er and no more damage than a split jib boom.' He drained his beer and wiped his mouth with the back of his hand.

'We sails tomorrow,' said Fitch. 'Then you'll get to know Primmy.'

'He looks an honest man,' said Henryk.

Exhausted by the day's work he soon slept, lulled by the creak of the hull, which was never silent, even on the calmest of nights, and by the sound of the little breeze in the rigging, running down the shrouds and magnified by the chains so that every corner of the ship was filled with a strange, vibrant hum. And in his dreams Kasia came to him so vividly that when he awoke some time in the night the whole of him was alive with the feel of her body and desperately he tried to close his ears to the disgusting sounds of men snoring and spitting, groaning, whispering unclean things and laughing as they sought some relief in each other.

*   *   *

At the turn of the tide next morning they sailed, in company with the *Edgar* and *Culloden*, to join the Western Squadron. Captain Primrose walked his quarterdeck in the sunshine, feigning a total lack of interest in the noisy, bustling preparations for sea, leaving it all in the capable hands of his First Lieutenant, but missing nothing: the topmen manning the yards, ready to shake out the sails; the Marine band, six drummers and three fifers, waiting to play on the poop-deck; the men standing by the braces; the boats in-board on the chocks.

He glanced at the smoke from the galley chimney curling in the rigging and at the gulls hanging in the air on motionless wings. A fair breeze on the larboard bow. A band was playing in *Edgar; Culloden's* anchor was almost apeak. *Huntress* was a fraction late. As he opened his mouth to speak, Stodart said, 'Ready to weigh, sir.'

Henryk, waiting by the lee braces a few paces from the officers, heard the Captain's quiet order.

'Very well, Mr Stodart. Carry on, if you please.'

Stodart raised his speaking trumpet.

'Are you ready there forrard?'

'All ready, sir.' The Boatswain's call shrilled. 'Heave round the capstan.'

Primrose's eyes were everywhere. He raised his face to the little breeze.

'Let fall, sheet home,' he ordered. 'Hoist away.'

Stodart repeated the order through the trumpet. The three sails fell together in a cloud of white canvas, billowed for a moment, then, as the sheets tautened, filled.

'Lee braces!'

The yards came round, the sails swelled and the ship heeled slightly and began to move through the water. The Boatswain and his Mates rushed up and down the decks, bawling at the inexperienced landsmen. 'Clap on there, you drunken sons of whores. Together, Yorston, get them together . . . God's teeth, you ignorant bastards, don't you know a rope when you see one?'

Henryk, from his time in the merchantman, had some idea of what was going on and knew how to put his weight on a rope, but Cameron and the other pressed men, with their hands already torn, wasted their strength in useless effort, obeying the flood of orders with sullen desperation.

'Belay there!'

Thankfully they secured the braces and rested for a moment. Below the great gilded stern lanterns the Marine band burst into a rousing march, the fifes squealing in rivalry with the ropes in the new blocks and the thin song of the wind in the rigging; the roll and thunder of the drums beat out a stirring rhythm and the faces of the bandsmen grew redder than their bright scarlet coats.

Half a mile to larboard *Culloden* and *Edgar* shook out their topgallants.

'Set all sails to the royals, Mr Stodart.'

Henryk watched the topmen swarm along the yards a hundred feet above him and his stomach turned at the thought of going up the mast.

The mountain of sail cut off the sun from the deck and the ship heeled more sharply so that the men had to lean in order to keep their balance. Already the taller men were walking with the stoop caused by the lowness of the deckheads below, so that now they moved with a curious twisted look to them.

Stodart glanced about him with satisfaction. The sails were filling handsomely; the snaking lengths of rope were being coiled; the decks shone, and the hiss of the water along the sides, which could be heard now that damned band had packed up, warmed his heart. He turned smartly to face the Captain.

'All-a-taut, sir.'

Primrose's face showed nothing.

'Very good, Mr Stodart. But I'll expect it done quicker next time. Too much bumbling, Mr Stodart, far too much bumbling.'

'Yes, sir,' said Stodart, crestfallen.

*   *   *

The three ships of the line swept down the Channel under full sail, bearing south-west for Ushant and sailing free with the wind on their starboard beam.

'A real soldier's wind, this,' said Isaac Mendel, joining Henryk by the side. 'A horse dragoon could handle her today.'

His arrival irritated Henryk who was in that mood of gentle

melancholy which scorns the conversation of others. He nodded shortly in answer, continuing to gaze down at the sea rushing below.

'Beautiful, aren't they?' Mendel looked across to where *Culloden* and *Edgar* held station some half-mile to starboard, hugging the wind, the sea creaming at their bows. New sails caught the afternoon sun full on their swelling curves and shone with the same white lustre as the fleecy little clouds. Blue ensigns stood out proudly from the mizzen peaks and a broad pennant fled before the wind at *Culloden's* main. 'Aye, they're beauties all right,' affirmed Mendel, 'till you know what goes on inside them. Still, to many a poor fellow they're better than the home he left behind.'

Henryk took his gaze from the ships and looked at Mendel curiously. He had met few Jews, only the money-lenders in Krakow from whom his father and his fellow nobles had sometimes borrowed money: fawning, cringing creatures usually too frightened to demand repayment. At Konarski's, that liberal establishment, he had been taught how the Jews had fled from the swords of the Crusaders, bringing with them to Poland a host of arts and skills and financial wizardry, and of how certain Polish kings had granted them charters guaranteeing religious freedom—though, God knows, that had not lasted long. Others, on the other hand, had brought him up to regard a Jew as a blood-sucking, avaricious animal, though unfortunately often a necessary one.

Now, for the first time, he had met one on equal terms, and he liked what he saw. Mendel was pale-skinned, with the same curly black hair as Henryk; quiet-spoken and intelligent. His dark eyes were watchful as those of a cat, watchful and a little suspicious, searching beyond the kind word or smile for the hint of patronage or contempt he had so often found.

'Look at me, now,' he went on. 'One of eight brothers and sisters and never anything but thin soup to eat, rags to wear. Whatever else it does, the Navy gives you decent clothes and you know where the next meal's coming from—though, by God, it may be stinking rotten when it comes. But you, now, you're not like the rest of us. One can see that. You've known power and position: that shows in the way you look about you.' At that moment the ship's bell was struck. 'Seven bells in the afternoon watch!' came the cry.

70

'Ushant'll be in sight,' said Mendel. 'We'll be turning south.'

Sure enough, as though he had heard the words, Captain Primrose came on deck, sniffed the air, glanced across at the *Culloden*, then to larboard where the dark line of Brittany lay along the sea.

'Sail broad, Mr Gore. South south-west.'

'Aye, aye, sir. Lee braces! South south-west, helmsman.' The man spun the wheel and the ship fell away before the wind on her beam.

'Sou' sou'-west it is, sir.'

'Very good,' said Primrose and vanished again, back into his cabin.

Huntress began to move in a different fashion; no longer did she lift and plunge in the short white-capped Channel seas but rolled nastily as the first outriders of the Atlantic took her by the keel.

'This'll catch the news lads,' said Mendel. 'They'll be emptying their stomachs all over the decks, poor devils.'

The gun-tackles squeaked in protest as the 9-pounder beside them strained to break away down the sloping deck, the wheels turning slightly as the ship heeled the other way.

'The big ones below make a noise like mating cats,' said Mendel. 'Here, come on, I'll show you Ushant.' They crossed the deck to the lee side. 'There she is, the black bitch.'

Shading his eyes against the bright glare, Henryk made out a small flat island surrounded by black rocks protruding from the milky surf.

'Take a good look,' said Mendel. 'Christ knows, you'll see her often enough. Today she looks harmless but wait till we're beating off here in half a gale. Heh, watch out, you filthy swab, get it over the side, can't you?'

A green-faced sailor vomited helplessly at their feet, then staggered to the side where he clung on, moaning and glassy-eyed. All over the deck men were giving up their oatmeal and peas and salt beef while the petty officers drove them with frantic oaths to the rail.

'Hell's blood,' shouted Gore. 'Into the sea. Into the bloody sea.'

The sudden boom of a single gun called his attention to the flagship. Within a moment Primrose was beside him, his glass to his eye. He could make out the crew mustering on deck, the Marines drawn up, the cluster of officers on the quarterdeck.

'Call up the hands, if you please, Mr Gore.' He shut his glass with a snap.

'All hands on deck!'

They fell in facing *Culloden*, those already too weak from seasickness being supported by their comrades. Cameron stood beside Henryk, proudly and angrily spurning assistance, his face ghastly. All along the ranks men bowed forward, groaning and gasping in agony as they retched and vomited.

The petty officers cursed the sufferers. 'Stand still! Stand up, God blast you.' Here and there a man sank down among his comrades' feet, no longer caring what happened to him if only the awful sensation would pass.

From the flagship came the faint roll of drums as the body of a man rose slowly to the yard arm. Henryk watched the toy figure jerking and kicking at the end of the rope; the drums continued to sound until the limbs were still and the body swung to and fro with the movement of the ship. Then the gun fired again and a man went out along the yard and cut down the corpse. It fell into the green sea with a bright splash. The head showed briefly, a tiny black dot on the crest of a long, smooth wave, then it was gone.

'If a man goes against the laws of the Navy,' called out Primrose, 'that is the penalty he must pay. Fall out the hands, if you please, Mr Stodart.'

For a moment Henryk remained watching the two ships. An unknown man strangling above the sunlit sea. At the moment of his death he had played his part in keeping these beautiful ships at sea. Possibly a larger part than all the admirals and captains put together. He went below.

The scene was revolting. Dozens of seasick men lay on the slippery, heaving deck, too far gone in their misery to sling their hammocks let alone climb into them. Cameron had fallen forward across the mess table, his head on his arms, and every lurch of the ship forced another groan from his tortured body.

Only four of No. 8 mess could face the sea-pie—a greasy mixture of meat and biscuit. Their faces were deeply shadowed by the light of the candle-lanterns, for the ports were closed against the slapping seas and the mess table was some distance from the hatchway.

'No use trying to clear up decks,' said Swaine. 'Not yet, least.'

'Why did they have to hang him?' asked young Gammon. He

was not eating, but sat hunched, his upper lip beaded with sweat, swallowing hard now and then.

'Refused to obey an order, like as not,' said Swaine. 'Or raised 'is 'and to an officer.' He pushed his wooden platter away and sat back with a loud belch. 'You're not a bad cook, Mendel.'

'That's where you end up, if you don't jump to it.' Fitch speared a piece of floating fat on the end of his knife and waved it across Gammon's nose. The boy went green; his eyes started and he gulped convulsively.

' 'E's better orf than you are. Rather be under the sea with 'im, wouldn't you?' Fitch laughed unpleasantly.

'Leave him alone,' said Elmquist in his slow deliberate voice. 'Leave him alone or I break your damned head.' He put his arm round the boy's shoulders.

'Just try it.' Fitch leapt to his feet, his knife raised, the point at the Swede's throat.

'It's no use fighting, m'dears.' Swaine spoke firmly. 'We're likely to be at sea for a long time and 'tis best to keep your angers for the Frenchies.'

In the close confines of the lower deck tempers were dangerous, often at flash point; fights and brawls—black eyes or split lips—were frequent but, unless a man was stabbed or badly cut about, little notice was taken.

'You and your pretty boy,' snarled Fitch, glaring at Elmquist. Leaving the table with an oath, he swaggered across to join his cronies on the starboard side, with whom he was in the habit of throwing dice for their non-existent pay.

'I do not like him,' said the Swede flatly. 'Some day I think I put him overboard.' He turned to Gammon. 'Get up on deck, Dick. Best to breathe fresh air when you feel like this.' They watched the lad staggering to the ladder, clutching at the great bulk of the mainmast as he went.

'I've seen some who never get over the sickness.' Mendel, who was duty cook, gathered up the platters. 'Poor swabs. Look at them, they'd rather be dead or rotting on the plantations.'

'I did not know a captain could sentence a man to hang.' Henryk had heard no word of sympathy for the dead man.

Cameron lifted his livid face. 'What d'you expect in a ship with that name?' he ground out bitterly between clenched teeth.

'An 'anging's a court-martial job,' said Swaine. 'And they usually does it in 'arbour or leastways at anchor. Then they leave the

73

poor wight swinging there for two days or more. But I seen it done this way once before in the West Indies.' He grabbed his mug as it slid across the tilting table slopping beer. The candle flames bent sharply, then straightened. 'The Atlantic, bless its loving 'eart.' Swaine grinned.

'By rights,' put in Mendel, 'a captain can sentence a man to twelve lashes, and no more. But once out of sight of the Admiralty most of them gives more than that—'

'Aye, and how they enjoy doing it, the bastards,' said Elmquist.

'They'll keep his name on the muster book,' remarked Mendel, scraping the platters into a scummy bucket. 'He'll be floating to France swollen like a wine-skin, but someone'll go on drawing his pay and eating his rations.'

'Aye, they'll be keeping him alive for a while longer.'

Henryk slung his own hammock, then Cameron's, and helped him in.

'Thank you,' whispered the Scotsman. 'Oh my God, make it stop. I—' With his head over the canvas he retched violently but nothing came.

The creaking of the timbers all round them was very loud and never ceased, and with every breath they drew, the stench grew more horrible. Henryk's head was splitting; he knew he must have air.

The last of the sunset moved like living flame across the slow Atlantic swell and on the horizon, silhouetted against the red furnace, Henryk made out the sails and upperworks of fifteen warships. A sailor paused in his task of coiling a rope.

'The Western Squadron,' he said laconically. 'Hawke's over there. If anyone can bring us to action with the Monseers it's him. If it's glory or a berth in the cockpit you're after, mate, then by God, you've come to the right place.'

As the sun vanished below the sea, so the colour fled from the water and the sky grew darker and more immense. Eight bells were struck; the watch changed, and Henryk sat dozing with his back to the longboat, waiting for any orders that might come. His thoughts were miles away from the rolling, creaking ship, the dark sails dipping and sweeping across the soft starlit sky. He was thinking not of the present nor of the future, for present and future were as black as the shrouds vanishing into the night above him, but they had taken refuge in the past. . . .

He was strolling through the golden, scented gardens of Peterhof beside a different, quieter sea and at his side walked Kasia, the woman he loved above all else. The rustle of her flowered dress was soothing as the whisper of the tide on the pebbles beside Monplaisir, Peter the Great's little summer palace. Her soft, husky voice was saying sweet seductive things to him, her eyes were huge in the dusk. She leant close and kissed him; the touch of her lips was warm. He placed his hand on the soft swell of her breasts

'Life is rather wonderful, my darling,' she whispered. Somewhere beyond the trees, the flowers and the fountains they heard the tinkling laughter of Catherine's other ladies.

He took her in his arms. 'Come, sweetheart. Now.'

She shook her head as he kissed her hair, her neck, her closed eyes. 'No—Catherine—there are watching eyes everywhere.'

But he had overcome her fears and taken her to their favourite little grove, a secret place tucked away among the lime trees, within sight of the sea. There he made love to her till she buried her face in the grass to stifle her wild cries of love and joy.

That night they had promised each other the earth.

'We'll go to Paris, my dearest.'

'Yes, together.'

'This life cannot go on.'

'No, no, my love, it cannot. We must escape.'

'Catherine will never forgive me.'

'She'll forget.'

He lay on his side, kissing her satin shoulders, drawing his fingers lightly down the length of her body, feeling her yearn for him and raise herself against him.

'I'll make enquiries, find out about another ship. This time we *shall* succeed.'

'Money, we'll need money.'

'Yes. I've got a few jewels.'

Presents to her from Orlov, Bubin. A moment of jealous anger overcome by her love. What did it matter where they came from if the baubles would purchase their freedom?

So they had planned to try again to escape from Petersburg, determined to risk everything, and then, when all was arranged and a ship for France awaited the midnight tide, Fate stepped in for the second time, causing the Empress to send for Catherine late that night. Kasia went with her, leaving Henryk to wait in a black fever of suspicion and impatience.

With a clatter the coach had arrived at the quayside. Together

75

the lovers had watched hopelessly as the stern galleries of their ship vanished in the mist, and Henryk, turning away in a fury of disappointment, caught the flash of triumph in Karzel's eyes and knew for certain the dwarf had somehow had a hand in this, their second failure. . . . Now he felt the ridged skin of his back hard against the boat. If I get to Russia, if I ever see him again, if it's the last thing I ever do, I shall kill him.

'I want the ship put about, Mr Wood.' The Captain's order broke into Henryk's memories, jerking him back into the present.

'Hands to the braces for going about!'

Henryk got wearily to his feet.

*　　*　　*

Admiral Hawke and the ships of the blockading Western Squadron kept ceaseless watch off the coast of France, never out of sight of land, sailing slowly up and down in the light August winds between Ushant and the Pointe du Raz. The weather was fine, day after day of cloudless skies and kindly seas, and at night the clear breezes blew cool through the lower decks.

Food was still plentiful and good; the beer showed no signs of turning sour. The men were fit and hard and burnt black by the continuous sunshine; even Bunch allowed himself a little discreet sunbathing on the forecastle. There was as yet little sickness in the ship.

From time to time the ships did fleet exercises, sometimes manoeuvring to a rash of bad-tempered signals from the flagship and the angry booming of the signal gun, sometimes forming line ahead with a smooth precision that won praise even from Hawke, the perfectionist.

Captain Primrose kept his men busy. Every day they trained and practised: at handling the ship in every sort of situation his ingenuity could devise, at firing the big guns till their minds and bodies rebelled against the continual toil—running them out, running them in; levering with the handspikes, hauling, heaving at those devilish lumps of iron which, like women, seemed to know well how to thwart and annoy: lowering and manning the boats—till, in his own words, 'every man among them could do a dozen different jobs blindfolded'.

Henryk was a gunner and also found himself painting, burnishing, keeping look-out, taking the wheel, running below to man the relieving tackles when the wheel had been carried away by imaginary shot. For, though their main purpose in life was to man the guns, if necessary until they died, Primrose was determined that the gun-crews should be able to perform the other duties of the ship. He even sent them aloft, knowing how quickly sickness could deplete his trained topmen.

'But,' he was always telling his officers, 'I will have good gunners. As I see it, gentlemen, to sail this ship well is vital, to lay her alongside the enemy in the shortest space of time is equally so but—' and here he would always strike his fist against the palm of his hand—'but to destroy that enemy with our fire is the most important of all. So I must and will have expert gunners.'

To achieve this state of perfection Mr Hay, the gunner, kept his gun-crews together as far as possible; they came to know each other by sleeping side by side, eating in the same messes. Their names, for those who could read, were posted above the guns they served, on the quarter bills in Stodart's spidery writing.

Henryk exercised with the boats' crews, running and vaulting on deck, pulling at the heavy oars of the quarter-boat till the muscles in his shoulders took fire. He practised with musket and boarding-pike and, remembering his boyhood training with the Polish cavalry sabre, showed his mates how to wield a cutlass in many ways not taught by the Master-at-Arms.

The watch sat one morning in the sunshine flooding between the sails, chattering happily as children. Mat Swaine was carving buttons from a hunk of cheese. He was always carving something: knife handles, tiny erotic female figures—very popular, these, with the men, who would lie in their hammocks fondling the little statues rubbed smooth and shiny by the touch of calloused fingers.

It would soon be midday and the First Lieutenant would issue the grog on the spar-deck as was the custom in fine weather—a pint of fiery rum to a quart of water to three men. And, as some did not drink it, there was always spare for those who did.

At moments like these a sailorman's life was not too bad. They were as close to contentment as they could be without women to squeeze and paw, and if they couldn't have them, there was always food to think about.

'Boat's crew away!' The cry echoed along the deck.

They watched the longboat being lowered with the smug enjoyment of those off duty who see others working in the heat, but without undue interest, for there was much coming and going between the ships, much entertaining by the captains. Then they saw the empty casks being lowered into the boat and groaned.

'Gun-drill,' said Fitch and spat over the side. It was too hot for heaving at the handspikes, running the guns in and out. Yet, on the other hand, there'd be extra rum for the gun-crew that smashed a cask to splinters.

They stood by their guns, waiting. There was a lot of waiting in their lives. Henryk blew on the slow-match—a bunch of tow dipped in spirits of wine and gunpowder—and wrapped it round the linstock. He looked out through the gun-port. About nine hundred yards away a minute dot floated in the water, appearing and disappearing on the easy swell. 'Pay attention to me, lads.' They knew Frobisher's lectures by heart. He was a big, blustering man with the neck and voice of a bull and small, keen eyes on the look-out for slovenliness.

'It takes six weeks to make a passable gunner,' muttered Fitch, leaning on the handspike. 'But I'm damned well going to do it in five. Go on, say it.'

Frobisher stalked along the line of guns. 'Get that powder barrel out of the way. The other side of the gun, you mangy fool, the *other* side.'

They heard the shouted commands from the deck above and with a crash an 18-pounder fired. Looking along the barrel of No. 8, Henryk saw the little white plume rise from the water a long way short.

After half an hour of fruitless shooting by the 18-pounders Mr Midshipman Lloyd, at his battle-station by the hatch, yelled in his cracking voice, 'Mr Frobished, sir. The Captain's compliments and will you please commence—and he hopes you'll make better shooting.'

'No. 1 gun! Take your aim! Fire when your gun bears!' The crash of the gun was deafening in the confined space. Smoke rolled over the gun-deck and drifted along the ship's side. The ball landed to the right of the cask.

'No. 2 gun!' Down the line the guns fired in turn and, though the shooting was better than that of the 18-pounders, the cask still floated intact.

'No. 8 gun ready!' called Henryk, crouching with the linstock, peering along the barrel.

'Stand steady!' Swaine shouted, his eyes on Frobisher. 'Take your aim!'

Henryk saw the black dot on a distant swell, then it had gone. 'Left,' he ordered. The handspikes levered the gun to the left. 'A little more.' The wheels ground on the deck. 'Steady as she is. Steady.'

He waited as the ship rolled lazily and he could see only water, then as the line of the horizon swung into view he put the slow-match to the vent. The powder fizzed briefly then the charge exploded, the gun-truck leapt back to the limit of the breechings, black gritty smoke blew from the vent staining Henryk's face. A pause, then a cheer from the gun-crews as the target was blotted out by a curtain of spray. 'Stop your vents!'

'A fine shot, No. 8.' Frobisher beamed his delight. They were showing Wood and his 18-pounder crews how guns should be handled, by God they were.

'Good, Brinski.' Swaine clapped Henryk on the back. 'You'll make a gunner yet.' Henryk smiled. All the afternoon, till every corner of the ship was thick with smoke and the bell sounded the end of the watch, they banged away at the casks, and above them in the sunshine Primrose watched the silver splashes and was pleased by what he saw.

'Bring the ship close,' he said. 'We'll try two broadsides, Mr Stodart. I want half a dozen casks in the water.'

'Aye, aye, sir.'

The decks vibrated to the rumble of twenty-eight gun-trucks on the two-gun-decks. Mr Hay, old 'Blue-Lights', grizzled and tough as weathered oak, hurried about the ship in a fever of anxiety. This was the first time the Captain had ordered a full broadside and God only knew what might not go wrong.

'Breechings,' he kept bellowing as he stumped along the lines of blackened sweating men. 'Watch those breechings! And I want it together. Not anyhow like cattle farting in a field, but together.'

Primrose stood watching at the rail as the ship ran up towards the casks. Judging the moment when the guns would bear and allowing for the time his order would take to reach the gun-crews, he gave the order to fire.

'Fire!' The midshipmen yelled the word excitedly down the hatchways. Primrose's grip tightened on the rail.

Every gun on the starboard side went off. The ship leapt in the water, the deck shivered violently beneath the Captain's polished shoes. All round the casks the water was torn to boiling foam; smoke filled with black fragments billowed up and stung his eyes.

Amazingly, two casks still survived in the white, eddying water. In the far distance little spurts of spray appeared as the shot ricocheted, bounding slowly towards the shimmering coast of France.

'They're going in the right direction,' remarked Stodart happily.

'Ragged,' snapped Primrose. 'Too damned ragged. Let's see what the larboard battery can do.'

They came about and ran down on the two remaining casks, moving faster with the wind on the quarter.

Henryk held the linstock ready. His head sang from the monstrous din of the broadside.

'Fire!' Down came the linstocks; a sheet of flame enveloped the ship's side; Henryk's head expanded and even though his mouth was open, the blast of sound struck his ear-drums with sharp agony.

'Stop your vents!'

The smoke was thicker than a Channel fog and from somewhere in it came the sound of a man's high demented scream.

As the smoke thinned Henryk saw that No. 12 gun had broken its tackles and slammed back against the mainmast. Squashed between two tons of iron and the massive trunk of the mast the upper half of a man's body writhed and wriggled like a trapped worm.

'The surgeon! Get the surgeon!' The cry was taken up and Midshipman Tregotha flew below for Mr Boosey.

'Christ's teeth, it isn't a surgeon he needs,' said Cameron. He and Henryk joined the men frantically heaving to shift the gun. The man's mouth gaped in a continuous scream as he clawed at the iron that had mashed his lower half to pulp.

The gun came clear; the man was lowered genetly into the terrible remains of his legs, his screams growing weaker till they finally ceased and only a faint bubbling sound issued from his bloodless mouth.

'Gangway for the Captain. Make way there.'

They drew aside and Primrose reached the dying seaman as the Surgeon came hurrying up.

'Well, Mr Boosey?'

'There's nothing I can do, sir.' Boosey got to his feet wiping his hands on a cloth. 'The man is dead.'

'God rest his soul,' said the Captain and stood in silence for a moment looking down at the drained torso and sunken grey face, the blood gathering thickly round his own shoes.

A strangled gasp came from behind him where Midshipman Lloyd stood with starting eyes, staring at the raw, quivering flesh and splintered red bone.

'Oh, my God!' His hand went to his mouth; he lurched away, pushing through the silent men, his handkerchief to his mouth.

'Have him moved,' the Captain ordered quietly. Then, raising his voice, he spoke to the men gathered round him. 'Now, all of you listen to me.' His voice was harsh, his eyes bleak, there was no trace of awkwardness or hesitancy. 'I don't know who was responsible for this.' Frobisher looked down at his stained shoes, a flush spreading over his neck. 'And I don't intend to enquire further, for I shall assume the death of this poor fellow to be punishment enough. But—' he paused as the body was lifted and carried away—'but I will have this understood: every man of you on this gun-deck is responsible that such a thing never occurs again. Upon the ability of *all* of you to do your duty efficiently depends not only the lives of your mates but the very existence of the ship herself. And I will not have the safety of this ship threatened by the carelessness of one individual—whoever he may be.'

The men looked away from the anger in his eyes.

'Mr Frobisher, you will come with me, if you please.'

They stared after the officers in silence.

'Right. Get back to the job. Come on, there. Sharply now. Have you never seen a dead man before?' The quarter gunners took charge of their crews. The guns were sponged out, the vents cleaned, the shot piled neatly in the garlands; everything put back in its place.

'Get this mess cleaned up.' The boatswain's mate gave his orders sharply.

'You there, with the scar. And you.'

Henryk and Mendel washed down the scored mast, followed the trail of blood to the ladder, mopping away the drying stains.

'It's not wine this time,' said Mendel. And that was all they said.

The dead man was put over the side in sight of the full ship's company, with the surf on St Matthew's Point as distant background to his burial. He had been a newly pressed man, a family man wrapped in his memories and worries, a man who kept to himself and made no friends, and as the water closed over the canvas bundle there were few who could even remember his face.

'His effects to be sold before the mast,' announced the Purser. 'Within the hour.' With commendable—and unusual honesty— Mr Columbine told Bunch to score out the man's name in the muster book. His few pathetic possessions were auctioned amid much merriment, for death lurked too close to be treated with anything but a pretence of coarse and cynical nonchalance.

But, if it did nothing else, the death of this single lonely man showed them what manner of treacherous animals were these long black guns.

The watches changed; the sun dipped into the Atlantic, the look-outs gazed ahead into a molten blaze of light and Mr Frobisher, his mind full of the biting words with which Primrose had lashed him and the other officers, took the deck.

Life went on as usual with the loud sigh of the evening wind in the rigging, the creaking of the timbers, the surge of the water along the sides.

As daylight faded the breeze fell away completely as they let go the best bower and came to anchor on the darkening swell a few miles to the south of Ushant.

*   *   *

The Reverend Samuel Dunsterville, robes stirring in the warm August breeze, stood at the quarterdeck rail and delivered a rousing sermon from among the three dozen he had brought aboard.

'. . . and so my friends,' he concluded, raising his arms to the pale blue sky as if seeking confirmation, 'we know that God is with us. Knowing that, each among us can go forward cheerfully about his duties and face whatever dangers—'

82

Henryk was not listening. He was more interested in the scene round him. The sun, blinking among light clouds, glittered on the officers' gold braid and on the brass-bound wheel. The Captain stood behind the Chaplain, resplendent in full dress, an expression of seeming attentiveness on his healthy, shining face.

Beside him the First Lieutenant bent and smoothed the wrinkles from his dazzling new stockings. Straightening up, he let his professional gaze wander about the ship: over the lines of men drawn up below, clean and tidy in their Sunday best, up at the neatness of the furled sails—surely the envy of the Fleet?—forwards to where the ship tugged gently at the bower cable.

Beyond the men facing him, Henryk saw the sea breaking round the Black Rocks and beyond, so clear he felt he could reach out and touch it, a little white church steeple rose from the green line of France.

'. . . with the Lord at our right hand we shall prevail against our foes,' cried the Chaplain in his most ringing voice, gesturing dramatically at the French coast.

Even at this moment, thought Henryk with quiet amusement, some earnest French *curé* is exhorting his flock in much the same terms, against the ships anchored so contemptuously off their coast.

'And now let us sing the hymn.'

Black Bob drew the bow across his fiddle. Captain Primrose's voice rose into the rigging, untuned and cracking.

The men gave of their best, singing lustily and with surprising feeling, rendering loud praise to the God who had condemned them to the Navy and the sea. Henryk shut his eyes. Only a year ago he had gone with Kasia to worship in the Kazan Cathedral. . . . The brilliant vestments of the chanting priests; the blaze of precious stones; the heat of ten thousand candles; the thunderous sound of singing echoing round the great painted dome. Priests, their arms raised like golden wings before the altar or moving in the smoky, golden glow among the nobles and the peasants, and beside him Kasia with shining eyes and voice uplifted to a God who had allowed them to be together. . . . A lump came to his throat and he blinked. Different singing, the plain black cassock of this English priest, a makeshift altar, the cloth rippling in the sea wind, the smell of the sea, the plaintive mewing of the gulls. . . .

In the *salons* of Paris Henryk had heard the very existence of

God questioned, mocked. After the sack of Volochisk he endured torments of doubt, railed bitterly against a God who could tear her away from him and let her die. Then they were reunited, and his faith gathered fresh strength. And now . . . Henryk shifted restlessly, shaking his head slightly. Ten ships of the line lay at anchor here. Six thousand men, he thought, raising their voices to an Almighty who, as many among them must believe, would help them when the time came and nothing stood between their bodies and the howling storm of iron but this strange blind thing called faith.

The last of the hymn rolled across the water; the Reverend Dunsterville pronounced the Blessing and disappeared rapidly to the Captain's cabin where he was in the habit of joining Primrose and his officers in a Sunday glass of claret.

The silence accompanying his departure was filled with the slap and chuckle of the water along the sides; the squeak of a dry block; a loud banging of pots from the galley and the mournful lowing of Stodart's cow from the manger.

The officers turned to face their men. Gore had a few sharp words to say concerning the state of his men's turn-out. 'I'll not have you coming to church as if you were going to quarters expecting to meet the whole French fleet.' Then he let them go to their Sunday leisure.

'I expect every man to be clean and properly dressed,' mimicked Fitch in Gore's slow drawl. 'We don't all have gold lace and tight breeches across our arses,' he went on, raising a laugh with his imitation. 'But that's no excuse for appearing like a bunch of Tyburn rogues, ho no.'

'The Holy Crow was in a hurry to get finished,' said Swaine.

'Holy Parrot, more like,' put in Fitch. 'Arsk 'im wot 'arf of it meant and 'e wouldn't 'ave a notion.'

The Chaplain was not popular, being thought too much of an officer's man.

'Men of God, I've found, are often of a bloody disposition,' said Mendel, 'calling down death and damnation on the Monsieurs, but their behaviour when the shot's flying is often very womanish, even as helpers in the cockpit.'

They sat or sprawled round the forward hatch drinking their rum and water, sipping the 'pale death' appreciatively, talking idly among themselves or lying back with eyes closed, the sun hot on their eyelids while Matthew Swaine gave them a tune on his German flute. Unless the wind rose or the signal gun banged in the *Royal George* or the French appeared from Brest, the afternoon was their own to spend as they wished.

Near where Henryk sat with Cameron on the hatch one of the sailmaker's mates was sewing the ragged edges of a large blue ensign. The Scotsman watched the little flash of the needle for a while then, reaching into his jacket pocket, he took out a piece of dirty crumpled silk.

'It's amazing what men will do for a coloured symbol,' he said in French, turning the remnants of the white cockade over in his hand.

' 'Ere, the Monseers are at it again,' said Fitch pausing in his task of paring his toenails with his knife. ' 'ark at the 'eathen lingo.'

But it was too warm and they were all too contented with the midday grog inside them for more than a few lazy comments.

'Let's have a jig, Mat.'

'Aye, clear a space there.'

Two young seamen got to their feet and the notes of the flute were gay and catchy and away went the sailors in the lively steps of the dance amid cheers and hand-clapping, up and down the deck in a heel-and-toe.

Cameron regarded the dancing sailors sombrely, then read out the faded words still legible on the material: '. . . or nobly serve our country'. He sighed. 'I've carried this scrap of silk since Culloden. Thirteen years, during which I've served nothing and nobody. And now—' he made a small gesture of disgust at the ensign—'I've got to bow to that.'

'I once wore the uniform of France,' said Henryk, 'and now—' He repeated Cameron's gesture. He swirled the grog in his mug. He had drunk from gold goblets in the Winter Palace and the finest crystal glasses in Warsaw, Rome and Paris, but none of the rare wines had warmed him as did this thick dark brew.

'When I was young I used to dream of taking my sword to Europe,' said Cameron.

'There've always been many Scots in Poland—merchants, soldiers of fortune. We'd have welcomed another,' replied Henryk.

'But then Prince Charles came to Loch Moidart and—' Cameron fell silent, his eyes dark with memory.

A shouted order drifted across the water from another ship;

the gulls, perched in a row on the top-gallant yards, bickered and preened in the sun.

Joshua Bunch came hurring along the deck on his way to the heads, clutching his ample stomach, a contorted expression on his face. Ribald cries followed his desperate progress.

That morning, pleading sickness, the merchant had refused to leave his hammock. A short-tempered boatswain's mate tipped him from his hammock and took him before the First Lieutenant.

'Stand up, man,' ordered Stodart, trying not to smile.

Bunch moaned and clutched his belly. 'It's the fire of hell,' he gasped. 'Oh, my dear sir, my vitals are burning up.' His little eyes rolled wildly.

Stodart, feeling in need of entertainment, took him before the Captain, who gave Bunch the choice of half a dozen lashes with a split and tarred rope's end or a course of physic. Groaning but grateful, Bunch chose the latter.

In the sick-bay the Surgeon diagnosed a surfeit of ship's biscuit, and the grinning assistant, the 'lob-lolly' boy, administered a clyster of soapy water followed by senna pods in lard.

'That's the fifth go . . . no, the sixth. . . . He'll be back.' Wagers were laid; the men held their ribs, laughing till the tears ran down their sunburnt faces. Henryk smiled almost against his will. Bunch in his dire need was serving a more useful purpose than in his capacity of Purser's Clerk, today he was providing amusement to men with precious little in the way of entertainment. They faced hardships, danger, mutilation, death, with a readiness which amazed him, and yet when they had something to laugh at they seized the moment, with the whole-hearted joy of children. Kasia had described the Cossacks as resembling children: rowdy, courageous, murderous children. But they at least were free.

'Would you do it again?' Henryk asked. 'If the Prince went back to Scotland would you follow him?'

'Yes!'

'Even though it were to end in the same way?'

Cameron nodded and broke into a lilting Jacobite song, in English, very low.

> 'Fill, fill a bumper high!
> Drain, drain your glasses dry
> Out upon him, fie oh fie
> That winna do't again.'

Cameron emptied his mug, wiped his mouth with the back of his long, thin hand, showing the palm engrained black with tar. 'I see his failings,' he went on. 'I know what the black bottle has done. But I'd still follow him.'

Henryk felt a quick twinge of envy for his friend who still clung to his dream, who still, however forlornly, gazed into the future. He had come to like the Scotsman. Not only for the similarity of their upbringing and backgrounds; for the fact that they could converse together on subjects other than the habits of the officers, food and women; that they shared the common memories of Paris and a comfortable life, and that they were both exiles. He liked him for his intelligence, for the occasional flashes of dry humour which broke through the bitter mask; he recognised the same spirit of romantic idealism that thrives on lost causes and hopeless battles. In some ways Cameron reminded him a little of Louis de Valfons, even to the streak of fanaticism that revealed itself now and then when he spoke of the Stuart cause.

'Tell me,' demanded Henryk after a pause. 'If you do not mind my asking, are you married?'

'No.' Cameron's mouth tightened. 'I might have been once.' He paused and then added curtly, 'She preferred the Hanoverians.'

Henryk felt pity for his friend. He himself had at least been granted a few perfect months with the woman he loved.

'And you?' asked Cameron.

Henryk shook his head. 'There's someone—' he began but stopped. Though at that moment he had a sudden blinding urge to talk about Kasia, to pour out his longings and his memories to this man who had become his friend, he did not go on, for once the dam had burst he felt he would never stop and besides, if he was never to see her again, she was too precious a memory to be shared with anyone.

A great gust of laughter among the men greeted some coarse witticism.

Mr Midshipman Prendergast's childish voice rang out at the gangway, calling for the Captain's gig to lay alongside and be sharp about it. With his long, pitted face and popping eyes the Junior Midshipman reminded Henryk of a miniature Grand Duke Peter.

'How old would you say he is?'

87

'Fourteen ... fifteen? I don't know,' answered Cameron without much interest.

The boy stood importantly at the gangway, minute in his little blue coat beside the sentry, with his hands folded behind his back.

'He's like a very small admiral,' remarked Henryk, 'surveying his fleet.' Cameron grunted. Henryk scratched inside his shirt. Soon he would go and wash at the deck-pump, before the watch changed.

'When I was his age,' said Cameron, 'I was running free in the hills of Lochaber above Achnacarry; I was brought up there through the kindness of my cousin after the death of my parents, stalking the wild deer and catching trout in the burns, free as a savage. Then in '46 the English came to Achnacarry.' He plucked at the hatch-cover. 'It's a terrible thing to watch your home burn,' he said with empty sadness.

A picture formed in Henryk's mind. Flames spurting from melting windows, rushing up white walls, bursting through a green roof ... blazing rafters crumbling ... Kasia crying out his name ... the clash of steel and a scimitar bright with blood. His hand went to the scar on his face.

'Yes,' he agreed very softly. 'It is.'

The glittering figure of the Captain appeared. He crossed the deck and the men made way for him hastily.

'A fine day, lads,' he said stiffly.

'Aye, it is that, sir,' they chorused.

He met the returning Bunch, contented now, hurrying back to his hammock in the purser's store.

'Ah—er—Bunch. I trust the medicine has proved—er—efficacious.' Bunch stood confused, twisting his pudgy hands.

'Yes, sir. Aye, aye, sir.'

'That's it, Bunch. Carry on then.' The Captain strode on and laughter followed him to the boat. Prendergast raised his huge hat; the sentry crashed his musket into the present; Jem Pike piped Primrose over the side; on the boat the Captain's coxwain raised his stentorian voice:

'Give way!'

Six oar-blades bit into the water and the gig shot away from the side. As the boat climbed a long, curving swell, Primrose looked over his shoulder at his ship. The lion rose and fell slowly against a blue sky; the white masts and black shrouds—most effective, he thought with a little thrill of pride. He settled back in the stern sheets well content.

'He'll come back full to bursting with roast beef and Madeira,' said Cameron sourly.

'Yes,' agreed Henryk, lying back in the sun. 'But at least we have no responsibilities.'

* * *

They continued to ride at anchor off St Matthew's Point, doing little but enjoying the sunshine and smarten a ship already a scrubbed and gleaming picture.

Then on the afternoon of the 27th Primrose came back from a visit to the flagship and shortly after his return the hands went to quarters. Frobisher ran down the ladder to the gun-deck. 'Quarter charges! No shot.'

They stood by their guns. Flags were hoisted at every vantage point in the Fleet, the great ensigns barely stirring in the windless afternoon. The bands took station on a dozen poop-decks.

'What's going on, sir?'

'A salute, Swaine. We're to fire a salute.'

'What for, sir? Can you tell us that?'

'A great victory at Minden, Swaine. With the help of our gallant lads the Prussians have well and truly beaten the Frogs.'

'Them Proossians have all the luck, sir. Why can't we—'

'Stand by,' roared Frobisher.

The ship leapt in the water as every gun went off and the Fleet was enveloped in smoke as the great sound rolled across the water and rattled the windows in Brest itself; all along the coast the startled inhabitants came tumbling from their cottages thinking a bombardment had begun.

There was an extra tot of rum for the hands that evening..

'Gawd bless Prince Ferdinand of bloody Brunswick, 'ooever 'e may be,' toasted the irrepressible Fitch.

A few days later they watched enviously from the rigging as three sail of the line went in close to engage the forts in Camaret Bay. The big shore batteries sent the water spouting high round the

British ships; a ball came skipping over the surface, passing two cables' lengths astern of *Huntress* and Captain Primrose paced his quarterdeck in a black fury of frustration.

Well away from the forts the population lined the shore, drinking their wine and gnawing their chicken bones, enjoying the spectacle in the sunshine. Two shots blew dust from the forts, bringing cheers from the watching sailors; a ball passed through the main course of the *Edgar*, raising counter-cheers from the French on the beaches and cliffs. A thoroughly picnic atmosphere reigned.

After an hour's fruitless duel the ships withdrew out of range to derisive whistles and catcalls from *Huntress*'s crew, every man of whom was firmly of the opinion that if only they had been allowed to take their turn the forts would have been battered into submission with little trouble.

But *Huntress* saw no action as the fine weather slowly began to break and the wispy mare's-tail clouds reached farther across the sky from the west. The song of the rigging altered, was pitched higher, and white-capped seas came at the ship in endless procession. Windswept rain hissed on the deck and lashed the cursing topmen as they struggled with the soaking canvas.

Hawke took his ships to the safety of the open sea. They clawed their way to windward from the iron-bound coast; they beat slowly and uncomfortably westwards under topsails, drenched by rain and stinging spray. And every man in the *Huntress*, from the Captain to the youngest snotty-faced boy, knew that the bearable days were over and that they now had to face the bleak prospect of the autumn gales—and then would come the winter. As Henryk put it, 'The holiday is over and now we must be earning our grog.'

Matthew Swaine, who knew more than any of them what a winter at sea could do to a ship and her crew, gazed throughfully at the Pole.

'There'll be times, m'dears, when you'll wish you'd never left your mothers' wombs.' His eye twinkled through the pipe smoke.

PART THREE

FOR the last few months the threat of invasion had hung over England. In an effort to relieve the mounting pressure on France's colonial empire Marshal Belleisle planned a twin-pronged attack on the British Isles. One army of twenty thousand men under the Duc d'Aiguille, conveyed by the combined Atlantic and Mediterranean Squadrons, was to land on the west coast of Scotland and march on Edinburgh. To assist this ambitious project a second army of similar strength under Chevert would sail from Ostend to effect a landing in Essex. As an extra diversion the notorious privateer, Thurot, was to make for Northern Ireland with eight hundred men in five frigates.

And, in the great port of Brest, M. le Comte de Conflans, Vice-amiral des Mers du Levant and Marshal of France, lay with a powerful fleet, waiting for the weather to worsen and drive the blockading squadron from its station, thus allowing him to slip out and sail south to pick up the troop transports gathered a hundred miles to the south in Quiberon Bay.

But they knew very little of these threats, the men who stood between their country and possible disaster, being too occupied with their own privations and discomforts, for the gales came tearing from the Atlantic and the ships lay-to under storm canvas, struggling to keep station in the mounting seas.

Though Hawke took his ships farther to the west whenever the wind drove the ships uncomfortably close to the surf, they were rarely out of sight of France; the black threat of Ushant loomed large in the mind of every captain and officer of the watch clinging to the quarterdeck rail throughout the long, black nights, often hearing the deep thunder of the surf above the shriek of the gale.

Below, the men lived in semi-darkness lit by the little flickering lanterns, for every chink, every crack round the gun-ports, closed now for three weeks, was stuffed with oakum. Water oozed and spurted and sloshed up and down the gun-decks as the *Huntress* performed her endless, creaking dance, and the lower decks were foul with mildew and stale damp air.

The men were never dry. Stumbling below down the heaving ladders, they chewed the cold salt pork and biscuit in a stupor of exhaustion while their sodden clothes dried on their bodies. At one point they existed for five days on cold food, tainted by sea-water, for the galley fires were drowned as soon as lit.

The men crawled into soaking hammocks, and fell into drugged and steaming sleep, impervious to the heavy bumping against their mates, the frenzied squeak and creak of timber round them and of straining gun-tackles, the groan and clatter of the pumps, the batter of the seas so close beyond the streaming sides. Impervious even to the hoarse shouts of the Boatswain's Mates, the dread cries of 'All hands to shorten sail!'

'All hands on deck! Come on, rouse out, rouse out!'

Twice, three, four times in a single night they were ordered up into a howling darkness out of which came high, curling seas to sweep the deck thigh-deep from stem to stern so that the men clung stunned and gasping to the lifelines. And above the roar of the wind and sea came the orders; the ceaseless, relentless orders which would perhaps keep them from the hungry seas.

Men were flung about by the crazy motion, bruised and bleeding, kept going by the rum inside them. In a week they lost ten men, two by flying blocks, six swept overboard without a sound, and two topmen torn from the upper yards as they fought to control the tattered remnants of a split topsail.

For hours on end the sleepless Captain never left the quarter-deck, stocky and sturdy in his tarpaulin coat, the rain dripping from his hat into bloodshot eyes and down his stubbled jaw. And seeing him there, holding on to the rail, now and then shouting to the three men on the wheel, brought the men some small comfort.

Other ships were sent into the blessed relief of Plymouth to refit and plug the leaks, but *Huntress*, being a new ship and but lately cleaned, remained on station.

'You should thank the Lord you're in a sound ship,' said Swaine, stuffing his mouth with cold pork.

His one eye though red-rimmed still twinkled; he never seemed perturbed nor unduly tired, for like Cameron he possessed the happy knack of being able to sleep anywhere and under any conditions. With his head on the mess table he would sleep; with an arm hooked round a lifeline or a shroud he would doze on his feet.

'Jesus, what's it like in some of they other ships.' He jerked his head towards the side. A big sea struck the ports and tiny jets of water spurted over the mess table. 'I've been in ships that took in water like a rotten sponge. Opening at the seams every time they went through a big sea.' He opened and closed his big hands.

'If this is a dry ship, then it must have been like living in a swamp,' said Henryk, wrinkling his nose at the stink of the bilges, the thick damp odour of mould. His eyes prickled with fatigue; water trickled down his back; his limbs ached painfully.

Swaine banged a biscuit against the table and watched the weevil fall out. Slowly he squashed it with the side of his fist. Henryk threw down his own biscuit with a grimace of disgust.

'Douse the glim if you're too dainty to look at 'em,' said Fitch scornfully. 'Crunch 'em up in the dark. Ah, Christ above, 'ere she goes again.'

They clung to the chains of the mess-table trying to steady the sliding cascade of platters, knives and mugs as the ship came back slowly from the vicious roll, shaking herself free of the sea which had threatened to press her under.

'Don't you be worrying your head about 'er going down, lad.' Swaine had seen the panic spark in Henryk's eyes. 'If she goes, she goes and there ain't no one but God can do nothing about it.'

Henryk did not answer but chewed slowly at the tough salty meat, his eyes fixed on the wet red wall standing between him and the death he feared more than any other.

*　　*　　*

For a brief spell towards the end of September the gales eased, the seas went down and, strengthened slightly by regular hot food, the crew cleaned up the ship and dried out their belongings in the sun. They shaved and cut each other's hair and skylarked on the warm deck, the misery of the past weeks quickly forgotten.

The days were calm and hazy with a good heat in the sun that eased their aching bones and dried the steaming sails; the ship herself seemed to be resting after her struggles, sliding easily up and down the swells.

The Third Lieutenant was officer of the deck. He still had two hours to go. 'Meet her,' he growled at the helmsman, irritable in his boredom.

'Aye, aye, sir.'

The ship came back on the wind. Gore yawned and Midshipman Lloyd strode up and down on his little legs, looking very serious and manly. They passed and repassed each other without speaking, along the lee side of the deck as befitted junior officers. Gore smiled to himself. Dreaming of being a captain, he supposed. Sometimes he dreamt such things himself.

'Four bells in the fore-noon watch!' came the cry.

Gore leant on the rail watching a party practising with cutlasses under the Master-at-Arms. That Pole, Barinski—gun-captain on No. 8, wasn't he? He'd noticed his shooting the other day—certainly knew how to handle a cutlass. After a while they were dismissed and, struck by a sudden thought, Gore called out:

'You, Barinski. Just a moment, please.'

Henryk came up the ladder, lithe and dark as a cat. He touched his forehead with his knuckles and stood carelessly looking at the officer with watchful interest. There was a trace of arrogance in his bearing, the way he held his head slightly to one side, the look in his steady grey eyes, which might have irritated a man of less intelligence than Gore. But the officer merely smiled.

'You speak French, don't you?'

'Yes.'

Midshipman Lloyd bristled at the casual tone. Impudent foreigner. Not even the word 'sir'. His youthful intolerance boiled within him.

'I should like to learn the language. I can read a little but that's all. Would you be prepared to speak with me sometimes?' Strange, he thought, I'm addressing this man as an equal and it seems quite natural.

'Certainly, sir.'

'I'll try some phrases,' said Gore. 'Perhaps you could correct me.'

'Of course.'

'Do you enjoy life in the Royal Navy?' said Gore, slowly in French.

'No,' Henryk answered with a quick smile. 'No, I do not.'

'What would you be doing if you were not here?'

Henryk corrected the inaccurate French then thought for a moment. 'I should be eating delicious food at a table which did not rock and sleeping between sheets in a bed which did not swing.'

Gore laughed at what he understood. They got on well with the lesson, and the helmsman listened amazed to the French gibberish and Midshipman Lloyd ceased his pacing and stood at the starboard rail within earshot, pretending a consuming interest in the shining sails of the squadron.

'When we've finally put an end to the Frenchies I should like to visit that Paris of theirs!' Gore said in English at the end of half an hour of stumbling French. 'Especially Versailles. They say it can hold upwards of five thousand people.'

'Seven thousand,' corrected Henryk. 'It's like a rabbit warren.'

'You've been there then?'

'Yes.' Henryk smiled faintly. He remembered how men and women had schemed and plotted, sold and humbled themselves to get a few square feet of attic space and be able to say, 'I am living at Versailles.'

Gore reminded him a little of Poniatowski. He had a sudden flash of memory . . . a coach arriving at Versailles, rumbling over the cobbles of the great forecourt and into the Cour de Marbre. Walking with Poniatowski along endless gilded corridors past the Swiss Guards, motionless and stony as statues . . . supercilious looks at his sober clothes from men gorgeously attired, glittering peacocks . . . admiring glances from the women . . . his shoes slipping on the polished parquet of the Hall of Mirrors and three thousand candles glowing hotly in the glittering glass . . . the doors of the Queen's apartments thrown open . . . *'Messieurs le Comte de Poniatowski et le Comte de Barinski'* . . . a plain, pleasant-faced woman looking up with sad eyes from the card-table, a plump, heavily beringed hand held out limply.

'You are most welcome, *Monsieur.*' Maria Lechynska returned to her game of *canapé.* . . .

'Tell me,' asked Gore curiously. 'What were you doing at Versailles?'

Midshipman Lloyd strained his ear so as not to miss the answer.

'I was Gentleman-in-Waiting to Her Majesty the Queen of France,' said Henryk quietly, enjoying the expression on the officer's face. Gore's mouth had fallen open.

'Good God,' was all he said. He stared up at the sky between the sails.

So the man's a liar as well, thought Midshipman Lloyd severely.

Gore whistled softly between his teeth, quite stumped for what to say next, and, as if in answer to the sound, the ship heeled suddenly to a stronger gust of wind with a thrill squeal of blocks.

'The wind's backing westerly. It's going to blow hard again,' said the Third Lieutenant unnecessarily.

Captain Primrose came on deck. Gore and Lloyd stiffened to attention, raising their hats.

'That'll do, Barinski. And thank you,' said Gore. Henryk knuckled his forehead and went down the ladder. As he reached the deck he heard the Captain's voice.

'I'll have the t'gallants taken in, if you please, Mr Gore. More dirty weather, I'm afraid.'

Henryk felt the wind strong on his face and the first thin spray from a wave bursting at the bows drifted along the deck.

*   *   *

In the following days Gore had no further chance to practise his French, for once again they met the big Atlantic seas head on. The ship shuddered to the ceaseless plunge and slam of the blunt stem into the rolling walls of water, and solid sheets of spray enveloped her to the topmast trees.

But *Huntress* was sound; her fastenings held tight and she rode the seas quite freely, not in the water-logged and sluggish fashion of the older ships.

Whenever possible Captain Primrose had the lower ports triced up so as to give his depleted gun-crews practice in handling their guns in heavy weather. Knee-deep in swirling water, the gunners learnt how to keep the slow-matches alight; how to load and aim and fire when the gun-muzzles were now pointing to the angry grey sky, now dipping into rushing white water.

'Wait for the roll, damn you!' Old Blue Lights shouting at them; Frobisher bellowing. 'Fire on the roll! Judge it, you stupid swabs. A shot above the masthead's no damned use. Nor into the belly of a wave.'

Primrose kept them at it. Better to keep them busy, he reasoned, however tired, than allow them to idle, wallowing in their sufferings. He never once allowed his pity for them to show. If a man could stand on his feet then he was driven on deck.

'Now's the time, gentlemen,' Primrose insisted, 'when all our efforts to make *Huntress* a well-run ship, contented ship, can go for naught.'

His officers sat round his big table, gripping the edge to steady themselves against the crazy movement of the cabin much magnified here in the very stern. He turned to the Surgeon. 'How many sick today, Mr Boosey?'

'Another six of the scurvy, sir. Three of the fever. Making a total of—' he checked his sick-list—'sixty.'

'Of these, how many fit for duty?'

Boosey shrugged. 'Strictly speaking, none, sir. But if the ship was sinking I dare say most of 'em could crawl on deck.'

Primrose frowned and tapped his tilting desk. Already eight bodies had gone over the side into the roaring sea along with the casks of rotting meat and cheese. Only yesterday the last remaining barrels of pork were opened and found to contain nothing but pigs' heads and feet, greenish and thick with bristles, the iron rings still in the swollen snouts.

'God knows how long it'll be before we go in to clean,' he said. 'Or before the victuallers can get out to us.'

All fresh food was finished; the butter was rancid and was being used for greasing the iron-work and the blocks. What cheese remained could climb the ladders on its own and, what was worse, the ale was tainted with sea water, leaving only a few casks of Guernsey wine to mix with the foul green water.

And yet, worried though he was, Primrose well knew his ship was no worse off than the rest of the squadron. If the French were to come out, he thought grimly, they would meet ships undermanned by tired, hungry men who had fought the seas for weeks on end while they themselves were well rested in port. But he'd still back his sullen, soaking crew against the largest three-decker in the French Navy. As seamen, as fighters, the men of the Royal Navy had no equals; that he knew for absolute certainty. He must remember to tell Sweetapple, a much thinner, bonier Sweetapple, to take wine to the worst cases in the sick-bay, with his compliments. Lord knows, he could do little enough for the men who were dying for a country that gave so little thought or care to their well-being.

'Anything else, gentlemen?'

The officers rose from the daily conference, steadying themselves as the stern lifted high and dropped with horrible speed into a trough, then made their way from the spacious cabin.

*   *   *

Fog lay heavy on the sea, pressing closely round the ship, clutching at the rigging with thick white fingers, swirling so thickly that the topmasts were invisible from the decks and the look-outs called from another disembodied world above the dense grey carpet.

The officers on deck drew their cloaks across their mouths, the watch cursed the raw clamminess which closed round their throats and crept below down the hatchways and along the lower decks so that the lanterns burnt in little hazy circles of weak light.

At measured intervals one of the quarterdeck guns barked its warning, to be answered by flat, muffled reports from other hidden ships. Now and then a voice shouted or a ship's bell clanged, and the sea moved silently and darkly in the fog until it met a ship, when the water ran along the side with a curiously subdued sound.

Henryk lay in his hammock with his knees drawn up; now and then, as the row of hammocks swung in unison, his knee-caps brushed the beam above him. Provided he remained absolutely still, he managed to retain the illusion of clammy warmth put into his body by the rum—two rations, for Mendel had no more use for grog. Tomorrow they would slide him overboard from a grating, dead and black, his jerking limbs and body free at last from the burning hell of the spotted fever. All round in the dim red haze of the gun-deck the night was hideous with the mutterings and ravings of men in the grip of fever, men swollen and discoloured in the last stages of scurvy. The airless place was thick with the horrible stench of the sores that disfigured their bodies.

The shadowy figure of the Surgeon moved along the lines of hammocks but there was little he could do; a little elixir of vitriol for the scurvy; Doctor James's Fever Powders for the fevers, though the devil only knew it was hard enough in this light to distinguish between the two. Croaking voices begged for the fresh fruit he could not give them. His assistants carried a butt between them, stopping here and there to give a small ladle of foul water to some moaning sufferer.

Henryk put his hands to his ears to shut out the sounds. His head throbbed, his gums ached, his teeth felt loose; he could smell his own mouth, foul as swamp air; his tongue felt too large and his week-old beard seemed to be crawling over his face. Never dry, water wherever you looked but none for shaving; four pints a day cut to one and a half, and that green and solid with matter. A wicked irony for those who longed for anything green. His mind was filled with visions: of cold silvery water gushing from the hillside among the oak trees at Lipno, where they used to dismount to slake their thirst during the hunt; a knife cutting through the cool pink flesh of a melon; pears and peaches melting in his mouth; the sweet juice of an orange bright on Kasia's chin as she looked at him with smiling eyes by the water's edge at Peterhof—was it only ten months ago? . . . Now a voice was shrieking for mercy: 'Oh, my God, help me. Help me. I'm burning. Oh, help me!' The cry was cut off by a thick, strangled rattle.

To Henryk it was as if that last despairing cry would continue to sound forever, trapped beneath the deck beams as he himself was trapped. No future, no past, nothing for him ever again except the wet, the numb clutch of exhaustion and sickness, the devilish creaking of the timbers; the clatter of the pumps, the dirge of the wind in the rigging, the hopeful squeaking of the hold rats lured to the gun-decks by the stink of death and decay. Officers and men stubbled and bearded, red-eyed and filthy-tempered; the cruel summons of the Boatswain's call . . . naked frozen feet stumbling up the ladders—those who could still walk— into yet another black, blustering night—and another. They had forgotten the feel of the sun; the tan had faded from their faces, leaving skins as grey beneath the beards as the scudding clouds, the weeping skies, the autumn fogs which enclosed them.

Henryk jerked his head from side to side in a sudden fury of disbelief. Was it only a year since he had lain with Kasia and felt her breasts tighten against his skin? Was it for this stinking hell-hole that he had cheated death in the Siberian snows?

Lying in the black depths, sick in body and at heart, Henryk fought for his very sanity, praying to his God for the strength to go on, to get out of the hammock when the call came again, which it would for he felt the movement of the ship change as the returning wind took her on the beam and the thrum of the chains began again. If I give in now, he knew with absolute certainty, I'll never leave this hammock. They'll sew me up and tip me into the sea.

Once, years ago, Kasia had seen him slumped against a blackened wall, his face a mask of blood, and had taken him for dead, but he returned to her. This time he would not come back; he would fall with a splash into the water—the last minute disturbance he would make in this mad world—and she would never know. She would marry Orlov or take up her life with Lev Bubin again—or perhaps in a convent she'd forget her stormy, tragic past and come to find the peace that only he had been able to give her. The thoughts flashed through his mind like eels in a dark, murky pond, twisting and turning upon themselves, darting this way and that.

The thud of the gun had ceased.

'Fog's lifting,' he heard a voice say somewhere near him. 'Wind's getting up.'

A sea struck the side; the hammock-lines vibrated.

'You there.' Ebenezer Boosey held his lantern above Henryk's face. 'What's meant to be wrong with you?' Boosey was not a naturally callous man but under those conditions his trade was of necessity a rough and ready one. With the equipment and facilities available it could hardly be otherwise.

'Nothing,' said Henryk, without opening his eyes.

'Good,' grunted Boosey. 'That makes a change.' To his assistants he said, 'One more dead. See that he's brought up tomorrow.' The Surgeon shoved his way among the hammocks of the sick. The dead would lie in their hammocks, swinging against the living as they stiffened. Even in death, thought Henryk, they could not escape the packed bodily contact he had come to detest with a loathing which was almost horror: jostling on the ladders, pressed close at the mess-tables, in sleep, waiting in the shelter of the bulwarks for orders. Never a moment's escape from this pack of coarse, loud-mouthed humanity, many of them as brutish in their habits as animals.

For one moment, just one moment by himself, on a horse or lying in the shade of apple trees in dry summer grass on ground which did not move ... to hear, instead of the ceaseless surge of the sea, the thud of hooves on the open steppe, smell the dust of summer in his nostrils instead of the horrible odours round him—for any of these things he would have given many years of his life.

'All hands on deck!' The shout was loud and healthy above the moaning of the sick.

'Come on, rouse out there below, you lazy bunch of shirkers! Hands on deck to shorten sail!'

Men barely able to stand rose shivering from the hammocks and stumbled on deck, too numb with sickness and misery even to groan or complain.

'All hands on deck! Every man jack of yer 'oo can stand!'

Henryk's legs were weak and he had some difficulty in getting up the swaying ladders to the open deck. It was raining again and the night was black as sin. A figure loomed before him, bulky in wet-weather clothes.

'Right,' it shouted above the rising wind, 'mizzen topsail. Reef 'er. Well, get on with it then.'

Yorston thrust his face close to Henryk's. The latter glanced up into the dark where the white trunk of the mast vanished in the black rain. His stomach turned over. Oh, my God, not up there. He heard more than felt the swipe of Yorston's starter across his heavy jacket. He put his hands to the ratlines.

As he went up, desperately overcoming the weakness in his limbs, shaking his head to clear the rain from his face, the fever from his brain, the wind took hold of him and he clung with his arms round the shroud. Up, up, eyes tight shut, hauling himself slowly to the mizzen top; hanging out above the black abyss as he negotiated the futtock shrouds, his panting mouth filling with rain.

For a moment he clung dizzily to the mast as it swung through a long arc. He was falling backwards, then rushing up, hovering before the plunge down with the mast crushing his chest. The vague shape of the yard led out above him, too narrow for a cat;

he couldn't do it. A steep roll sent the mast hurtling on its downward plunge; he realised the cry torn away on the wind came from his own throat. The fever was driven out by naked fear. He heard a shout from the yard where shadowy shapes were bent over, struggling with the sail. But still he could not move.

Then a thought entered his mind and fought with the fear. If Kasia wanted me to do this—if this act would save her. . . . Once, in a mood of supreme self-confidence induced by love, he had told her: 'With you beside me, my darling, there's nothing I couldn't achieve.' He had not visualised, as he lay in her arms, a moment when he would sway a hundred feet above a sea which leapt at him with white ravening jaws, when a wind threatened to pluck his body from its hold and fling it into the waiting night.

Slowly he went on up the shrouds. In the grip of the despairing determination that conquers fear he hauled himself out along the yard, his feet slipping on the wet foot-ropes. Lying forwards across the bucking spar, he clawed with the topmen at the stiff wet canvas. In the wind the sail struggled wickedly and blood oozed from under his torn nails as his groping fingers felt the reef-points hanging like rats' tails.

The yard dipped with appalling speed to the white blur of the sea. He licked salt spray from his lips; water ran down his spine, ice-cold on the sweat.

They were hurled through the sky at speeds which left him gasping, his stomach far behind. Slowly, and with stubborn effort, they hauled up the sail, secured the points while the ship dipped her yards to the sea, trying to fling them off.

'That's the bastard secure,' yelled a voice in Henryk's ear. 'Let's get below out o' this.'

On the way down Henryk could not delay, with the horny feet of the man above crushing his fingers. He swung himself off the shrouds on to the deck, stood for a second gazing up in disbelief, then his legs gave way and he collapsed insensible on the planking.

'Get 'im below,' ordered Yorston. Leaning down, he bellowed at Henryk, 'You did all right, lad.'

But Henryk did not hear.

*   *   *

'Strike the t'gallants yards, please, Mr Stodart.'

With great difficulty the heavy spars were lowered to the heaving deck and lashed down and the masts stabbed at the dirty grey clouds like trees stripped of their upper branches.

'Double lashings on anything that moves.'

'Aye, aye, sir.'

The Captain and his First Lieutenant leant forward against the wind that was whipping their coats about them. Fifteen sail of the line lay-to under storm canvas some ten miles to windward of Ushant. November had come in on the skirts of a full westerly gale. For close on a week it had blown, increasing at intervals to savage black squalls which tore at the ships and ripped the tops from the waves in drifting veils of spray.

Primrose, bearded now, like his men, in his heavy weather uniform of tarpaulin coat, canvas trousers and short sea-boots, never seemed to take his tired eyes from the sea, the straining sails and the mast moving in the decks.

The faint reports of two guns—the distress signal—came to him on the wind.

'*Royal Anne*, sir. Looks to be in trouble.'

They watched her as she turned across the seas, a topsail flying loose and tattered, rolled almost under, righted herself and bore away to the north-east, to England.

What's the use of firing guns? thought Stodart. No one can do a damned thing in this sort of weather, except try to stay afloat. His thoughts were as bleak as the dark clouds driving low above the mastheads.

Huntress rose high on the broken back of the next sea, lurched forward into the trough with a crash which jarred her horribly.

'My God, sir. They can't keep us out here in this. We'll have to put into shelter.'

'The Admiral knows what he's about, Mr Stodart.' Primrose trusted Hawke, a seaman for nearly forty years.

'Yes, sir.'

Primrose's trust was justified for within the hour they turned away and were rolling and bucking across a quartering sea, homewards for the shelter of England.

But Henryk knew none of this. He lay half-conscious, drying the damp blankets with the heat of his fever; his delirious ravings mingled with those of the sick men round him, drowned by the crash and groan of the struggling ship.

Faces swam above his own in the dim red light: Cameron, Gammon, Swaine—but he did not know them. A little gruel was forced between his dry, crusted lips and kept him alive; he hardly noticed the foul taste of the water they gave him.

For three days he fought the fever, determined in the tiny conscious corner of his mind not to die without a struggle. He had the absurd notion that if the ship could fight for her life then so could he. Helped by his iron constitution, built up in his youth, tough and wiry and hardened by the months with the Tuntsevs and at sea, Henryk went on living.

'By rights he should be over the side,' said Elmquist, shaking his fair, shaggy head in wonder.

'He's one of those born to die in battle,' said Cameron, raising his friend's head. 'Here, take a little of this. It's filthy, but it's food.'

Henryk groaned and flung an arm across his face. He had been riding with Kasia at his side along the ridge where they had first loved each other and where the Turks had appeared from the trees. The sun glittered on the snowfields and the frosted birch trees ... the sound of the hooves on the frozen snow was harsh and crisp ... her eyes shone bluer than the velvet of her riding habit ... everything was cold, sparkling, clean. ...

For the first time he tasted the thin gruel trickling down his throat. His eyes felt hot and swollen but at last they could focus properly. He tried to raise himself but was too weak.

'Lie still,' said Cameron, gently as a woman.

'How long have I been—?' He realised with horrified digust that his hammock was foul.

'Easy,' Cameron's hand was comforting on his shoulder. 'We'll have you out of there.'

'The sea's gone down,' said Henryk. His voice was very feeble.

'We're at anchor in Torbay. For the moment at least we're out of it.'

'They say we put into Plymouth soon,' said Elmquist. 'Then beer—and women.' He smacked his lips.

'Vitaller in sight.' Swaine joined them, rain dripping from his beard. 'Fresh food, m'dears. The galley fire's burning like a furnace and we'll get out gear dried out.' His spirit was infectious; even the sick poked their heads up and grinned with their bleeding gums. Excited talk broke out and laughter which had not been heard for days.

'All hands on deck for loading stores.'

Henryk lay listening to the faint thuds above as the stores came aboard, an occasional grinding bump as the swell rolled a lighter against the side.

And on deck the Captain watched approvingly as the men worked with a will to unload the food which would give them the new strength to go back out there.

'Just in time I fancy, Mr Frobisher.'

'Yes, sir,' roared Frobisher from a few feet away. The Fourth Lieutenant always spoke as if addressing a gang of mutineers three hundred yards distant.

'I'll have the band play,' said Primrose quietly.

'Aye, aye, sir.'

To the accompaniment of a rousing march the stores came swinging inboard; the ensign snapped bravely in a light shore breeze and another lighter came butting through the easy swell, laden to the gunwales with fresh beef, bread, vegetables, cheese, butter; not to mention lemons and apples for the scurvy cases, bought by Primrose with his own money.

Some of the men raised a ragged song. The past was behind them, the present was good, and the future—not one among them thought of the future, or at least not beyond the immediate vision of Plymouth, sleep and women.

*   *   *

Primrose allowed the ship to rest. He allowed the men to eat their fill of the fresh provisions, to drink an extra tot of rum and to sleep undisturbed for a full twelve hours. For anchor watch he took the idlers, men who had not been continually called on deck: men like Bunch, clerks, storekeepers; the pallid, ghost-like holders who blinked in the light of day and coughed in the cold air.

When the men had slept and eaten again he set them to clean up the mess of the lower decks and to dry out their clothes and bedding at the heat of the roaring galley fire. The ship was fumigated from main deck to keel with loggerheads—hot irons dipped in tar—the fungus washed from the beams with vinegar. The gun-decks smelt sweeter for a day or so, the noisome air cleaned by heated pannikins of sulphur and tobacco.

The Captain toured the ship with the surgeon and the carpenter, inspecting every inch from the f'c'sle head to the darkest bilges; he stopped to talk in his awkward fashion to the men working cheerfully at their tasks, to encourage the sick with a few words of sympathy.

'How is it, Barinski?'

The Pole was very thin, the scar stood out vividly against the yellowish skin. He turned from tidying his hammock.

'Better, sir, thank you.' His eyes were enormous in his wasted face.

'Good, good.' Primrose hesitated. 'Well, see that you take advantage of the—er—lemons and things.'

'Yes, sir.' Henryk's eyes softened with quiet amusement. He could almost feel the strength returning, flowing through his body. His limbs and teeth ceased to ache and his gums hardened to the bitter tang of the lemon juice; the fever had cooled, leaving him clear-headed.

With the prospect of Plymouth above the horizon they worked with a will to clean up the ship; even Jem Pike was in a benevolent mood and was heard to crack jokes. Only the few poor wretches dying in their hammocks were unaffected by the infectious good spirits in the ship, as they were unaffected by the appearance of a cutter bobbing over the swell towards the ship. An officer stood in the stern-sheets, one hand cupped at his mouth.

As the cutter passed below the counter and down the side he shouted up to the men lining the bulwarks, 'The French are out! Conflans and a big fleet, heading south from Brest.'

The boat took the news to the next ship in the line, leaving a ripple of excitement spreading through *Huntress*. Men poured on deck, questions on their lips.

'What is it? What's the news?'

'The Monseers are out!'

'By God, they are, are they?'

Plymouth was forgotten. At last there would be an end to what had become a senseless misery. They cheered as the *Royal George* passed down the line, the Union flag at the main. A brilliant figure stood impassively on the quarterdeck, now and then raising a hand to its hat.

'There's 'Awke!'

'Aye, that's 'im.'

The salutes boomed out: seventeen guns each from twenty sail of the line and three frigates: the crash of close on four hundred guns rolled along the line echoing from Berry Head. And still the men cheered and waved, quite carried away by the prospects of meeting the French in action at last.

Henryk watched the scene with amazement. 'It seems they really *want* to fight.' He shook his head in disbelief.

'They'll get their bellyful soon enough.' Cameron looked at them scornfully.

'All hands make sail! Prepare for going to sea!'

In the late afternoon the Fleet made sail to the south-west with the thunder and rattle of the drums audible to the many spectators gathered along the shore in the cold sunshine, waving God-speed to the ships.

And a courier galloped out of Brixham with the news that Hawke had sailed, riding hard for London, a rising westerly wind helping him on his road.

*　　*　　*

Dawn on 20 November 1759 was grey and lowering and filled with driving rain. The Fleet lay on the starboard tack, plunging southwards under reefed topsails with the cruel lee shore of Brittany lurking far too close for comfort along the broken, tumbled horizon.

For a day and a night the British ships had driven through the gathering storm, searching vainly for the French, and every captain knew the fate of England was hidden somewhere behind the scudding clouds and long white streamers flying like battle pennants from the wavetops. The captains cast anxious glances at the straining canvas and bending masts, and wondered how long their ships could endure such punishment. But not one of them shortened sail.

Captain Primrose hung on to the mizzen-stays, assessing every detail of the ship's behaviour. He knew what she could take, what her limit was likely to be. But today, he thought grimly,

if we sight the French, then she'll be called on to exceed this
limit. We all will. He had to lean steeply to hold his balance. He
looked at the watch huddled in the meagre shelter of the hammock
nettings, drenched by the endless procession of waves that struck
the ship. Poor devils, what was *their* limit? The blunt bows
punched hard into a big white-veined sea with a great explosion
of spray and fell away sharply.

'Hold her, lads! Bring her back!' he shouted at the men on
the wheel.

The cry from the masthead was very faint. Primrose gestured to
the look-out to come down.

'Well, what is it, Morrison?'

'Frigate, sir. Think it's *Maidstone*.' The man was panting slightly.
'But couldn't properly see 'er.' He wiped the rain and salt from
his eyes. 'Flying 'er t'gallants loose, sir.'

'Thank you, Morrison. You've got sharp eyes.' Primrose
watched the man climb back to his perch. Topgallants loose, signal
for 'enemy in sight'. 'Beat to quarters, if you please, Mr Stodart.
Clear for action.' On a lee shore, in this sea—Primrose shuddered
mentally.

'Shall I have the galley fire doused?'

'Not yet,' said Primrose. 'I want the men to get a hot meal. God
knows when the next chance'll be. It looks like being a lively day.'

'It does that, sir.' Stodart sounded happier than he had done
for the last three months.

The urgent message of the drums sounded above the deep roar
of the wind as the Marines beat out the call to quarters, struggling
to keep their balance on the tilting decks, rain blackening their
red coats.

Henryk rose from where he had been trying to snatch some
sleep wedged against the gun-truck of No. 8.

The gun-captains checked their crews, ran an expert eye over
the equipment: rammer, sponge, handspikes, the shot piled ready.

Henryk made sure the slow-match was burning and that the
vent was dry and plugged with tow. The boys came hurrying
from the magazine with the cartridges and loose powder.

Water slopped from the fire-buckets; sand was spread on the
wet deck to help the grip of the bare feet.

Throughout the ship the carpenter and his mates unshipped the
bulkheads and laid them flat. Far below in the cockpit Mr Boosey
put away his backgammon board and laid out the rough tools of

his trade on the midshipmen's sea-chests: a saw, some dubious-looking needles, a fiendish selection of probes, cauterising pitch and two butcher's knives bought from a Jew's kitchen in Deptford.

The Reverend Samuel Dunsterville moved about the ship, giving comfort and encouragement in his most lugubrious voice and getting in the way on the ladders. 'Be of good heart, men. The Lord is with us this day.'

'How do 'e know that?' muttered Dick Gammon, stumbling under the weight of two 32-pound shot clutched to his stomach.

'He's in constant touch with the Almighty.' Cameron leant on the long rammer.

Since the death of Mendel the crew of number eight had been reorganised.

'Breechings, lads. And the tackles. Watch the tackles.' Swaine went between his four straining guns.

'Cameron. Powder. Wads. Rammer,' called out Henryk.

'Here.'

'Croaker... sponge.' Croaker was a f'c'sle man newly transferred to this deck. A slow, sad-faced individual but capable at least of sponging out a gun.

' 'Ere.'

'Gammon. Shot.'

'Here.'

Henryk called the names of his crew then saw to a dozen things, glad to have his mind taken from the thought of the seas pounding the side only a few feet away. Some of the guns were moving dangerously as the deck heeled and canted; the men worked with handspikes, banged in wedges, tightened the heavy ropes holding the hulks of iron.

They waited by their guns behind the closed ports, watching the water spurt through the cracks in the oakum whenever their side of the ship dipped more deeply.

If they opened the ports... Henryk moved uneasily, the sand gritty beneath his feet. He'd heard stories of ships going in a few moments, dragged down by the sea flooding the lower decks, and he shivered, not only from the chill of his wet clothes; the canvas trousers clung to his thighs, yet the sweat had broken out on his body. At least let him die above decks under the open sky. A sudden thought twisted his lips in an ironic smile. Afraid of heights; terrified of drowning, and he a common seaman. Fate had a peculiar sense of humour.

'Watch that gun, No. 6. She's shifting.'

Frobisher moved ponderously along his line of guns. On the starboard side Gore looked as slim and slight as a girl in comparison with the burly Fourth Lieutenant.

Henryk fixed his eyes on the battle lantern above the gun. The flame flattened this way, that way, trembling violently as a big sea picked up the ship and flung her aside with a jarring crash.

'Christ damn her for a stupid bitch!' snarled Fitch, rubbing his bruised shin.

They waited.

'Shouldn't be long now, lads.... I'll have good shooting today.... Remember your drill...' But after a while Frobisher got tired of this and went to stand by the mainmast with Gore.

Henryk remembered how he himself had walked among the Regiment de Mailly as they waited to go forward against the Prussians, with much the same inane encouragement.

Except for the glimmer of light down the hatchway it could have been night on the gun-deck. The men hung on to the guns in silence, seeing nothing but the wet trickling sides, the scared, set faces of their mates, knowing nothing except that they were soaked, hungry, and, in most cases, afraid.

Torbay was long behind; so was the time for cheering. The cries of the sick men in delirium, tossing in their hammocks by the hatchway, added to the apprehension gripping the men.

The shrill voice of Midshipman Lloyd shouted down the hatchway for Mr Frobisher.

'Listen to me, you men.' Frobisher relayed the message. 'Twenty-one sail of the line on the larboard beam. No more than two miles away.'

'And they're Frenchies!' The boy's voice cracked alarmingly in his excitement. A buzz of talk swept the gun-deck.

The Midshipman's excitement spread among the men. Here at last, perhaps, after these months of discomfort, disease and boredom, was the chance to vent their pent-up anger and frustration on an enemy ship; regain the wild satisfaction of seeing limbs and splinters fly and masts crashing to the decks.

'They're turning away! They're running for it, God blast 'em for a pack of cowardly Frogs!' The oath sounded strange in the boy's high, squeaky voice. 'We're going to larboard.'

They could feel by the altered movements of the ship that the seas were coming at her from astern. She no longer rolled and lay over but dipped and reared, alternately hanging stationary and rushing forward at dizzy speeds on the following waves. A few men whose stomachs had never fully got used to the tricks of the sea were sickened by the new motion and green and retching, bent over the guns.

'General chase!' yelled Lloyd. 'Signal from *Royal George* for general chase. By God, we're going after 'em!'

The topmen clawed their way aloft to shake out the reefs in the tearing wind, battered by a sudden hailstorm.

'More sail.' The boy's tone was disbelieving. 'We're setting more sail.'

'Jesus, they'll take the sticks right out of her.' Cameron's eyes were wide.

'We're passing *Swiftsure*,' yelled Lloyd. 'We're showing her a clean pair of heels. Oh, come on, Tregotha, what's happening up there?'

But Midshipman Tregotha, stationed on the upper gun-deck, could see nothing either, and had to wait for Midshipman Prendergast to relay news from the main-deck hatchway.

'The French rear's in plain view, hull-up. . . . *Torbay*, *Magnanime* and *Dorsetshire* are ahead of us, but we're catching 'em. . . .'

On deck Primrose stood by the rail, watching the sails taut as carved wood, the bending masts. Glancing ahead, he saw the lion bury itself completely in a dark trough, rise from the water, shake itself like a living animal and dip once again. He leant out over the rail, looking astern at the mountainous seas chasing his ship, rising high above the stern lanterns. He swung round on the men at the wheel, envying them, dry and sheltered under the poop deck, as he felt the ship begin to yaw.

'Keep her steady!'

Her blunt bows were a help in running before these seas; for with this heavy press of canvas there was always the danger of being driven under.

Ahead, just visible in the gathering murk, he could make out the plunging shape of *Dorsetshire*.

'Great heavens, sir, they're going into the bay,' reported the Master, Mr Cromer.

'Then we'll just have to follow,' replied Primrose, regaining his balance.

'But the shoals, sir, the rocks. The French'll have pilots. And a ship at this speed—we'll never get through.' His face was white; the fear showed in his eyes.

'If the Admiral wants us in hell, Mr Cromer, then we shall be there.' He pulled out his watch. 'Half an hour to noon. Hell's teeth, it could be dusk.' The clouds, black with menace, were driving low above the masts.

Then, just as the light was fading into near darkness, the clouds lifted and parted. A watery sun lit on the dark shape of Belle Isle away to larboard and picked up the twinkling sails of the French ships no more than a mile ahead, very white against the black bank of cloud above the coast.

Primrose heard the faint report of a gun, then another, as the leading British ship opened fire.

'*Torbay* or *Magnanime*,' said Stodart. He looked round to where the rest of the British fleet was pounding after them. 'Hullo, what's this?' He steadied his glass against a shroud. 'Red flag at flagship's foretop masthead, sir.' He closed his glass with a sharp snap.

'Very good.' All ships to engage closely, thought Primrose. Well, at least they were not going to try any fleet manoevures. From now on it was every ship for herself; every captain on his own. No tidy forming line, just get in close and engage as you hurtled by at twelve knots. And the real enemies today were not the French but the hidden rocks waiting to rip the bottom from a ship in long, splintering wounds. The ships vanished beyond fresh sheets of rain.

'I'll have the upper-deck guns loaded and run out, if you please, Mr Stodart. The lower deck stand by, ports closed, ready for action.'

Primrose heard the orders passing below; saw the crews of the quarterdeck 9-pounders spring into action. Along the bulwarks the Marines were priming their muskets, trying to shelter the pans from the rain.

Huntress had drawn level with *Dorsetshire* and was hard on the heels of *Magnanime* and *Torbay*. Primrose gauged the distance. Perhaps a quarter of a mile and the rear of the French line no more than that beyond.

Praying to God for luck and a passage through the shoals, Captain Primrose took his ship into Quiberon Bay.

Below, the men on No. 8 heard the rumble of gun-trucks above them as the 18-pounders were run out.

'Be ready for action!' yelled Lloyd.

The water swirling round their feet, lapping the piled shot, was bitterly cold. In his mind Henryk saw the solid red wall burst open and the foaming rush of the sea. To calm his nerves he checked the touch-hole was dry and swung the linstock in the air so that the slow-match glowed bright as a burning ember. He glanced at Ewen Cameron. The Highlander's face was set, his long fingers picked at a breeching-rope; Fitch was chewing his quid, squirting brown gobs of tobacco juice from the corner of his mouth; young Gammon's eyes were never still, going from the gun to the Fourth Lieutenant, to the massive figure of Matthew Swaine, as if seeking comfort from those emblems of authority. The Cornishman squatted on his heels impervious to the water, his face impassive, his one eye watchful. He's like a good horseman, Henryk thought; he's part of the deck; he and his kind are the greatness of these ships.

'Trice up the ports!'

They hauled on the thin ropes and the ports burst from their beds of oakum and came slowly up.

Henryk peered along the barrel and saw a square of streaky grey water rising to blot out the torn grey sky.

'Stand to your guns!'

He felt Swaine's hand on his shoulder.

'Don't 'ee go letting her off too soon, not too late neither, see?' Henryk nodded, calmed by the touch of the big hard hand.

'No. 8 gun ready!' Henryk raised his arm as he had done so often in training. A fierce lurch sent them staggering.

'Run out your guns!'

The gun ran forward easily on the downward roll and at once the muzzle was buried deep in a slope of water, came up dripping.

'Hell's damnation, we'll never keep the powder dry.' Cameron held a paper cartridge close to his chest.

The glimmer of the lanterns had paled but the gun-deck was still dark, for the waves cut off the light from the sky—at times the ship could have been racing below the surface. If they were to turn across the seas they were finished; every man on the lower deck knew that. So did their Captain.

He at least had the doubtful pleasure of seeing the French ships as they twisted among the reefs and shoals, with the surf breaking on the Cardinal Rocks beyond.

The British fleet was sweeping into the bay under every stitch of canvas it could carry, the great battle ensigns whipping forward in the gale, every ship enveloped in her own white cloud of spray.

'Look, sir! Larboard bow!' Stodart's cry was urgent.

The rain lifted. And there, suddenly from out of nowhere, a bare three cables' length ahead, appeared a two-decker, the white flag of the Bourbons clearly visible at her mizzen-peak. As the British ship came out of the rain squall a puff of smoke blew away from the Frenchman's stern. Primrose heard the flat thud of the gun but no sound of the shot.

'They're quick on it,' said Stodart admiringly. *Huntress* was closing the enemy ship at frightening speed.

'Point to starboard,' ordered Primrose, standing close to the wheel. 'Hold her.' She couldn't take much more; already he could feel the nasty slew of the stern. Any more and the lower deck would flood. 'Hold her,' Primrose repeated.

He'd run down to windward of her and try a broadside as they went by. There was another spurt of smoke and this time a loud crack as a hole appeared in the stretche_ foretopsail. Better shooting than he'd expected from men who'd been rotting in port for months on end.

'Hands to the braces! Meet her, damn you,' the Captain snarled at the helmsmen.

The men strained at the lee braces, the yards kicking violently in the wind, jerking the ropes through their hands, flaying their palms.

'Orders for the larboard guns, Mr Stodart. I want a broadside on my order, then guns to fire when they bear. I'll stay by her as long as I can.'

'Aye, aye, sir.'

'And close the lower starboard ports.'

Four ships were following in his wake, well back, led by *Royal George*. Plenty of sea-room and he'd need every inch of it. Damn this wind. You couldn't hear yourself think with the noise of the rigging.

'Bow guns. Open fire,' he shouted. The order was relayed forward. The long 9-pounders banged out almost together. He saw a little white splash plucked from the top of a wave a few yards to starboard of the Frenchman's stern, to be answered at once by a flash of flame and this time he thought he heard the faint howl of the shot.

The two ships were very close now; he could see figures lining the taffrail. The bow-chasers fired again, point-blank range for guns which could throw a ball over two miles. A shower of glass and splinters flew up from the enemy's stern galleries and one of the figures vanished utterly. He heard faint cheers from the fo'c's'le. Another ten minutes and they'd be level with her.

A shot hit the mainmast fair and square; splinters whirred and he saw a Marine fall clutching his thigh. With a loud twang a forestay parted. Primrose's mouth tightened. They knew their job, those French gunners. A curtain of rain came down between the ships; when it lifted there was not half a cable's length between them. He could see the French officers grouped on her quarterdeck, the little spurts of musket smoke along her bulwarks. A ball smacked into a deck-ring and went whining above him.

He gauged the closing gap and judged the time it would take for his orders to reach the gun-deck.

'Ready for broadside, Mr Stodart.'

Stodart yelled the word. Midshipman Prendergast leant down the hatchway. 'Larboard battery, stand ready!' Frobisher's voice rose above the storm. On both the gun-decks the gun-captains crouched, linstocks poised; the men stood back, out of the way of the guns. Suddenly the little square of grey light was filled by a ship's side with gaping ports, hungry black muzzles. A sea rose between them, the ship vanished. Water slopped over the gun, tugged at Henryk's ankles; he held his hand tight over the touch-hole.

The ship's side reappeared, towering to the sky; if he reached out he could surely shake hands with the enemy gunners.

'Stand steady. Steady.' They rose on a wave level with the Frenchman's rail, then dropped.

'Fire!'

Twenty-eight guns leapt back in a roar of flame. Smoke rolled over the gun-crews; they could see nothing, but felt the ship tremble as the enemy shot struck home.

'Stop your vents!'

'Powder—ram—load and ram! Ready!' Spitting the gritty powder-smoke from his mouth, Henryk gave his orders automatically.

'Fire when your guns bear!' Frobisher's orders were faint through the thunder of the 18-pounders above.

Henryk sighted. The Frenchman's bows were visible; they were drawing ahead.

'Left!' Fitch and Elmquist heaved at the handspikes.

'More! Put your backs into it! Come on, *left!* Stand clear.' Henryk waited till the gun dipped, hovered, rose again, then put the match to the powder. With wild joy he saw the strike of his shot just below the bulwarks. His eyes watered, smarted horribly; his face was black. The smoke thinned. He saw his third shot knock a lump from the figurehead, then the jib-boom vanished slowly from his view and they were past. They reloaded and waited as the water crept higher up their ankles and Gammon had to reach below the surface for the shot.

Now and then Henryk caught a glimpse of sails and masts swaying across the sky. They engaged a ship half hidden in spray and a ball came through the port of No. 12 right through the chest of the handspike man. His smashed body floated in red water, sliding about, humping against the feet of his mates until they slung it in an empty hammock.

'We'll have to close ports,' shouted Gore.

'What?' Frobisher's ears were singing.

The Third Lieutenant put his mouth close to Frobisher's ear.

Frobisher nodded, watching as another sea surged round the gun-trucks.

'Mr Lloyd!'

'Mr Frobisher's compliments, sir,' said Stodart very correctly a moment later, 'and permission to close the lower-deck gun-ports.'

'Very well, Mr Stodart.'

As Primrose spoke, a shot from somewhere in the flying spindrift smashed into the bulwarks close by the quarterdeck 9-pounder; he heard the savage whine of the splinters, felt a sharp blow on his hip; glancing down, he saw the bent hilt of his dress-sword. But his brain was filled with the screams of the gun-crew. A man—Christie, wasn't it? How could you tell when half his face had gone?—staggered across the deck, hands to the crimson mess, blood spraying between his fingers. Two men with ghastly wounds writhed in the scuppers; the other three were mercifully dead. But the gun was intact. And from now on only the upper-deck guns would be of any use.

'Get 'em below.' Marines carried away the screaming remains of what a moment before had been strong, well-built men.

Shot were whispering high above; plumes of spray whipped from the tumbled water. A big three-decker loomed to starboard with ragged flame stabbing from her side. The heavy shot tore the air round *Huntress*, riddling her upper sails, bringing down a foremast yard, smashing the jib-boom and severing the main shrouds in two places.

From below came the answering crash of *Huntress's* guns, her last broadside before the ports closed and the men coughed and choked in the thick acrid smoke trapped below decks.

'Get that mess cleared! Cut it away!'

The topsail flapped wildly in the wind, crumpled half on deck, half trailing over the side; the broken stump of the jib-boom hung in the water. Her way was cut down dangerously and Primrose felt her wallowing. On his larboard beam the Cardinal Rocks rose hideously like black teeth from the seething water.

The hands swarmed over the damage, hacking with axes, striving to bundle the sail under control.

'Tell Mr Frobisher to send up a good crew for the quarterdeck 9-pounder,' ordered Primrose.

'Wind's veering north-westerly, sir,' Cromer called out anxiously.

Primrose felt it on his left cheek, still as strong. 'Bring her up.'

The men strained at the wheel, hardly able to shift the spokes.

'Man the relieving tables! Lee braces!'

The yards came round. But still the mass of sail and cordage hung over the side, dragging *Huntress* off the wind. From the corner of his eye Primrose caught sight of the new crew running up the ladder and across the bloodstained deck.

At least four British ships had overhauled *Huntress*, including the *Royal George*, which went past with the leaping golden horses of her figurehead plunging through the spray, and the red signal for Close Action whipping defiantly from the foremast.

'I'll wager she's going after Conflans,' shouted Stodart excitedly. 'A guinea piece she's looking for *Soleil Royal*.'

On her quarterdeck stood the figure of Hawke. As he passed *Huntress* he raised his hat and waved it in the air.

Beside the 9-pounder Henryk found himself waving in answer and shouting with the rest. He heard the Captain's voice.

'I'll want that gun handled well.' Primrose's white stockings were spattered red. 'Load with cartridge.'

It took them a minute or so to get into the way of the 9-pounder: there was some clumsiness. But Henryk and Cameron had fired the lighter guns and knew them to be more accurate.

'Run her out!'

Henryk averted his eyes from the ragged hole gouged in the

bulwarks and looked across the leaping, tumbled sea. There were ships in every direction, a mass of tossing masts and swollen sails; here and there a blue ensign showed up vividly among the white flags. No horizon was visible, only the wicked line of surf breaking on the rocks away to starboard beyond the smoke of two ships engaged in close action.

Lightning flickered across the black sky to the south-west and sleety rain beat cold against their backs as they stood by the gun, waiting for orders, for a target. Shot landed short, sending up a dozen white fountains. 'God knows where that came from,' shouted Cameron.

The shriek of the wind in the rigging was augmented by the angry hum of shot, British and French; the storm was full of flying iron. Then the damaged rigging and sail went over the side and at once the ship moved more freely, lighter in the water.

'Lay her close to the wind, Mr Cromer.' She began to move faster, heading for a cluster of ships milling on the starboard bow. 'Fire at any Frenchman within range.'

'Aye, aye, sir.' Henryk smiled at the Captain. The simple orders were always the best.

They came up with a two-decker. Henryk tried to sight on the enemy quarterdeck but the muzzle curved wildly in the air. On a downward plunge he fired, lost his shot in the Frenchman's broadside. The sea erupted in a blinding white wall as the water was flung high; they felt the heavy crash as a few balls hit below. Bundled hammocks flew in the air from the nettings.

'. . . wad. Ram. Stand clear.' The powder sputtered in the touch-hole. A shower of wood exploded from the base of the French mainmast. Henryk saw figures go down; red pieces rose among the rigging.

'A fine shot,' shouted Stodart.

'. . . sponge. Cartridge—wad—shot . . .'

A three-decker towered, huge with menace fifty yards away. The 9-pounder struck her, and struck her again. *Huntress* heeled from the recoil of the 18-pounders below. Great furrows were ploughed across the Frenchman's crowded decks. Henryk saw her lower ports go up, felt his stomach tighten, heard the muskets pop, the hiss and rattle of the balls in the shrouds, smacking against wood, metal, bone, heard sharp yells of pain, vicious oaths, shouts of rage.

'Great God, look!'

A curling sea came rolling at the big ship. The lower ports vanished. For an instant she seemed to stand stock-still as if wondering what to do next, then with a terrible slow finality she listed and fell over on her side flat on the sea, masts towards *Huntress*.

Henryk saw men and guns tumbling in a flailing, jumbled mass down the vertical deck; others jumping from the upper bulwarks. Some clung to the yards a few feet above the raging sea. All their mouths were open but the sounds of their fear and despair were barely audible to the fascinated watchers in *Huntress*.

She took two more seas, breaking against the steep deck, then she was gone, leaving arms and legs thrusting to the sky, heads appearing, faces contorted as men were pulped between a mass of grinding spars.

We can't leave them, Henryk thought vaguely. What an awful way to die—we can't leave them. But Primrose gazed stolidly ahead, desperately closing his mind to the frantic cries dying in the wind. Close on a thousand men, gone, just like that. God, how he loathed the sea at times. But the red flag still flew in the wind and the French had to be destroyed. He turned his attention to putting his ship where she could do the most harm to his enemies.

From that moment, for Captain and gunners, topmen and helmsmen, everything became wild and beyond reason. Ships came and went with bewildering speed and the rain-squalls were dark with smoke. . . .

A dismasted ship drifting out of control close across their bows . . . a French ship anchored with her wheel shot away and colours struck . . . more men struggling in the water by the blackened ruin of their ship; the scene stark in the blinding flare of the lightning: white faces, arms imploring, an officer lying hatless across an upturned boat, the dead flung up on the rearing waves; the formless hubbub of human voices crying for help, faint on the wind. . . . The roar of the guns dwarfed by the roll and crash of thunder overhead and hail bouncing from the slippery decks.

Twisting, turning among wreckage; the heavy growl of the surf closer . . . the sky inky, slashed with crimson across the sunset behind them.

Primrose hoarse from shouting quick, urgent orders, for normal speech was useless now. Henryk streaked wet and black with powder, eyes smarting from the smoke and the brilliant flash of the gun. The huge roar of *Royal George*'s broadside as she sank *Superbe* . . . sheets of orange flame tearing vivid holes in the dark murk, lighting up the sides of ships themselves almost invisible.

'Hard over!' Just in time Primrose saw the glimmer of sails. Then the sound of surf breaking too close, dead ahead. 'Must be the Isle of Dumet,' he yelled at Stodart. 'We've done with the French,' he added. 'Now we've just the sea.'

He turned and shouted to Henryk. 'There'll be no more shooting tonight. Well done. Gun-crews to stand down, Mr Stodart.' Thunder drowned his words and he had to repeat them, blinking his eyes against the lightning. Far astern, two ships still blasted each other, ringed with flame.

Henryk shook his head to clear the numbness in his ears, wiped the black water from his face, letting some of it run into his parched mouth, spitting out the powder taste. The rest of the crew had sunk down beside the gun, utterly spent. A fresh squall of hail beat at them from the north-west, white and wintry in the lightning.

Quiberon Bay was full of ships yet *Huntress* might have been alone in the storm. All the captains sought what safety they could in the wild, roaring darkness, using God's candlepower to light their way. No orders, no signals, no contact with any other vessel; nothing but the bellow of the storm in the rigging, the pale glimmer of waves high above the bulwarks. Now, as Primrose said, it was just the sea.

All we can do, he though hazily through his exhaustion, is to anchor and pray for the dawn.

*   *   *

Lanterns moved about the ship, puny as fireflies in the black night, as the weary men went about the job of securing the worst of the damage. Squalls of rain and spray washed the blood from the decks, streaked the powder stains on soaking skin. Thunder rolled to and fro across the bay; the lightning lit up the ships pitching at straining cables, played round the bare masts. The pumps kept up their clanking tune without a pause and the

120

carpenters struggled to patch the shotholes at the waterline.

Captain Primrose went among the men, hauling himself along the lifelines, encouraging and cheering, or stood on the poop-deck, listening for the heavy booming of the surf on Castelli Point, waiting for them somewhere beyond the darkness, feeling his ship jerk and strain at the two bowers.

Then, too wide awake and strung up for sleep, he went below, through the snoring fug of the lower decks, stooping between the lines of hammocks, addressing a word here and there to the Marine sentries on the hatchways, down to the smoky red light of the cockpit.

The faces of the wounded were livid in the eerie glow, black-shadowed and gleaming. Now and then a man groaned or drew in his breath with a hiss, moving convulsively on the soiled sails bundled under him.

The surgeon sat with his body sprawled forward over the sea-chest table, his head on his arms, dead asleep, snoring like a hog beside an open bottle.

Primrose's mouth twitched at the foul stench of the place.

A man rose to his feet from beside a still form. Primrose saw the scar black across his face. 'Barinski?'

'Yes, sir.'

'Were you hit?'

'No.' He nodded his head at the shape on the deck. 'It's Gammon, sir.'

Primrose remembered the splinter sticking from the boy's chest. He stood looking down. Gammon's eyes were open; there was blood at the corners of his mouth. Linen was bound loosely round the middle of his body, soaking red; his hands were clenched.

'How—' The Captain stopped. Why ask? The answer lay at his feet. He went down on one knee beside the boy. It would be better if he died quickly. 'You did well, Gammon. I saw how you went about your duty.'

'I—' Gammon's lips drew back, baring his teeth in a ghastly imitation of a smile, his features twisted with the unbearable agony but he made no sound. Then—

'Brinski,' he ground out.

'Yes.' Henryk stooped on his other side.

'You—didn't have—no—cause—to complain—?'

The words were slow and gasping. His eyes were half mad with pain.

121

'Of course not.' Henryk took the boy's hand. It lay in his, help-less and with no trace of strength.

A man without his right hand cried out for water and the surgeon's mate held a pannikin to his lips. Mr Boosey's snores rose to a crescendo then ceased. He stirred, raised his head, mut-tered something and fell asleep again. Rats squeaked in the shad-ows.

Henryk wiped the sweat from Gammon's face, remembering Beaufranchet dying in the drenching Saxon night. If he had had a pistol in his hand at this moment he would have killed the boy, as Louis de Valfons had killed his dearest friend by the little vil-lage of Rossbach.

'He's going,' whispered Primrose.

Gammon's breathing had grown uneven; he was twisting his head from side to side. His eyes stared huge in a shrunken face, and Henryk could already see the skull peering through. The boy raised his head with the last of his strength.

'I didn't want to fight no one.' His slow countryman's voice was clear but very bewildered. 'Why couldn't they 'ave left me alone to follow the plough?' He sank back; his eyelids fluttered and closed. 'That's all I wanted.'

A rush of blood choked the words. They thought he had gone but he rallied and asked, so faintly that Henryk had to put his ear to the straining mouth, 'Now I've got this, will they let me go? You're a gentleman and knows about such things, will—they —let me—go—' the pauses lengthened—'go—back—to—the—farm?' His life went out from him on the last words; his eyes opened and stayed open, staring sightless at the lantern on the beam above his dead body.

For a moment Primrose did not move then, without a word, he rose, glanced slowly round at the other men, touched his hat almost shyly as if in some form of unspoken tribute and went slowly up the ladder.

Henryk squatted on his heels. Without thinking he waved his hand at the rats which crept forward to sniff at the dead feet, their eyes blazing like hot embers in the light. He looked at the wax face, very peaceful now, the lines of pain smoothed away by the awesome mystery of death. What a waste, he thought bitterly, for he had liked the boy. What a damnable waste. And what good had he done his country? He had seen that a gun was served with shot for its hungry mouth; he had obeyed orders uncomplainingly and had never fully understood why he was there. 'He's one that won't be catching cockroaches no more,' said the surgeon's mate.

Henryk gave the man a hard look.

Boosey's snores reverberated from the table. His mate swayed gently, then sat down in a heap, his head falling on his chest, beside an unconscious man whose breath bubbled in pink foam on his lips.

After a while Henryk went slowly up to the lower deck, his mind troubled, and lay down in half an inch of water with his back against a gun-truck. In his stomach were a ship's biscuit, a lump of cold pork and a tot of unwatered rum already grown cold.

They had been at action stations and served their guns for nine hours. They knew nothing except what had passed in the smoke immediately before their eyes and gun-muzzles. Victory? Defeat? The words meant nothing to men whose hammocks had been blown to shreds, who did not know if the ship would last the night, who only wanted sleep and warmth.

And the night was very long. Dawn, when at last it came on an easterly wind, was greyer than the stubble on Swaine's face; grey and wet, but the wind had eased and they made light sail for the open sea.

An uncertain sun broke through, shining on the sails in the bay, as they moved slowly. The signal gun thudded again and again from *Royal George*, as Hawke strove to marshal his scattered fleet. The French ships had vanished as though spirited from the sea.

'They'll have got into the Vilaine,' surmised Stodart. 'Before the wind changed.'

Primrose grunted. 'Or down the coast to Rochefort.'

'Perhaps.'

The Captain looked to starboard and saw three ships with flapping sails come round as one into the wind, saw the splash of their anchors.

'We'll anchor, Mr Stodart.'

Huntress rode there, more comfortable this time within sight of *Essex* and *Resolution*, broken on the Four Shoals. Beyond them, damp smoke rose from the smouldering hulk of a French two-decker.

There was the sound of distant gun-fire from the mouth of the Vilaine river but no one felt envy for their comrades still engaged.

'I'd rather stand on Drummossie Moor and wait the order to charge,' said Cameron, 'than go through something like that again.' He touched the jagged edge of a long tear in the deck with his toe.

'Call that a fight?' Fitch spat scornfully. 'Wait till we closes with a Frenchie, then you'll get a proper taste of powder.'

'At any rate,' said Henryk with a smile. 'We have something to look forward to.'

He felt the stirring of a new confidence, he knew he had acquitted himself well, had handled the gun with skill and had not shown his fear; he knew himself a match for any man in the ship.

They waited in line for hot sea-water from the galley. With gasps and oaths others turned swiftly in the jets of the pumps. A sound of banging came from the bows where a new jib-boom was being rigged; men were splicing the severed rigging, sorting and counting hammocks, swabbing out the scuppers.

Below in the reeking cockpit, Ebenezer Boosey still struggled with his saw and probes. And the six dead were sewn expertly into their canvas shrouds.

Order had returned to the ship.

The clouds were clearing, showing strips of blue sky, and the sea was going down. With luck there would be a hot meal and sleep. Meanwhile, on the capstan, Black Bob was scraping out a tune and old Primmy was up there in his usual place, red-faced and freshly shaved, wearing new white stockings.

Already the horror and fear of the past hours were fading from the men's minds, which was as well for England, for possibly if they remembered too well they would not have fought another battle so willingly in her name.

*　　*　　*

'Lads,' began Captain Primrose. 'Lads—' He cleared his throat noisily. God damn it, he must not keep them hanging about for much longer. Already an inspection and the Articles of War—the hands were moving restlessly in the bitter little wind. There'd be snow before night—he smelt it in the clouds piled to the north-east.

'Come on, for Christ's sake,' muttered Fitch, burying his hands in the sleeves of his heavy jacket. 'Spit it out and let's get below to the grog.'

'Lads,' repeated Primrose for the third time, 'it's a month since the—er—glorious—' the word sounded false to his ears but it was what they expected—'the glorious victory of Quiberon Bay.'

Well, whatever else the sailors called it, the day had been a victory for England. The fleet of M. de Conflans scattered and broken; his flagship abandoned on the rocks; seven sail of the line burnt or sunk, one captured; five others helpless in the Vilaine. Bodies were thrown ashore for days by the careless sea, many of them Bretons from the district, cast up on the sands where they had played as children, and the crowds who had lined the cliffs of Croisic to watch the exciting spectacle had returned shocked to their homes. Soon all France had known the true extent of the disaster. As for Hawke, he had lost one officer and thirty-nine seamen killed, two hundred wounded.

'The power of the French at sea would appear to be broken.' That was true, for the moment. 'But—er—as we know, they are brave men with many good ships—er, still afloat, and who can tell when they will not try again. So it is the duty of everyone among us to see that Mister Conflans remains where he is until —er—until the weeds grow thick on his bottom.'

A few men tittered politely at the stilted joke.

Henryk, listening curiously to the harsh, flat voice quite devoid of expression or life, knew exactly what Primrose was feeling. He himself had been the same with the men—Frenchmen— under him. In action it was a simple enough matter to inspire and to lead, but in cold blood to find the right words, the words to stir their interest, to make them laugh or forget, that he had always found an agonising task.

This man, fidgeting with the bent hilt of his sword, plucking at the buttons of his dress-coat, had handled his ship through Quiberon Bay with cool professional skill. His split-second judgement had never for one instant failed and every man in *Huntress* knew that. But if only he'd stop and let them get out of this damned wind.

'If they put to sea again, then of course we shall destroy them.' For a moment his tone was firmer, more confident. 'Our job now is to keep ourselves ready for—' He paused, glancing for inspiration at his First Lieutenant, but Stodart gazed ahead as if he found the shape of the mainmast of exceptional interest. 'Ready for anything,' Primrose tailed off lamely.

The first snow-flakes drifted through the rigging, striking softly against the faces upturned to the quarterdeck.

'Tomorrow is Christmas Day.' He could not bring himself to talk a lot of nonsense about wishing they were all snug in the bosoms of their families. 'If the weather's kind—and the French—' He was encouraged by a few smiles, noticed just below him the scarred gun-captain who had laid the 9-pounder with such rare skill. He must have a word with the Pole one day. Gore said he was an intelligent, well-educated fellow with a lively imagination and some cock-and-bull tale of having been at the French court. They'd be getting Louis himself next—as a topman.

'Tomorrow, the day will be your own.' He thought he heard a slight hiss of disapproval from Stodart; he could tell that Jem Pike was growling angrily to himself. Let them, he thought with a hint of mischief. This was his ship. If he said the men were to lie in their hammocks for a week then lie they damned well would. He felt the snow on his face, the wind icy round his calves.

'Fall out the hands, Mr Stodart.'

They left the decks to the look-outs for the glass was steady, the wind gentle, bringing occasional snow-showers sweeping slowly across the ship, whitening the rigging, softening the outlines of the yards and the upper-deck guns.

The Second Lieutenant stamped his frozen feet, thinking with longing of the warm good cheer of the wardroom awaiting the end of his watch. Midshipman Tregotha swung his arms vigorously. 'This is my first Christmas at sea, sir.'

'Mr You-sir' did not answer. He waited until Ushant reappeared from behind a dark, drifting shower. 'It won't be your last,' he said grumpily. His shoe pinched a chilblain, fat as a short red sausage, on his little toe. Three more hours of this and every French sailor safely tucked up at home. The remainder of the blockading squadron was strung out along the western horizon. 'No, by God, it won't be your last. This Christmas, and the next —and the next—and—you'll have grown a long white beard before you see a log fire crackling or taste roast goose again.' They'd have finished all the claret before he got below, he thought irritably. 'This flaming war'll go on forever, and tomorrow the hands'll all be foxed. Take a week to get the ship cleaned up again. Heh, you-sir, up there, keep your eyes open. You're not paid to sit in the cross-trees and snooze.' He glared at Tregotha. 'Great God, I don't know what the Navy's coming to these days. Call themselves seamen. Why, they couldn't even push a bloody plough straight.'

A hundred feet above him Henryk narrowed his eyes against a fresh swirl of snow and went back to his interrupted memories. He watched a snowflake melt away on the back of his hand ... Christmas Eve at Lipno: breaking the wafer among the family —his father, scarlet in the face from honey-mead; his brother, Adam, serious and solemn as befitted the eldest son; cousins and uncles, and the servants at the other end of the long low room, the sturdy peasant girls giggling and nudging each other in their embroidered finery, flashing sideways glances. Out to the stables, singing and laughing, to share the crumbs with the horses ... beetroot soup, fish, cakes of honey and poppy-seed and the empty place set for the stranger who might arrive out of the white, frozen night ... his seventeenth Christmas ending awash with corn-brandy in the barn, warm and excited in the hay with Wanda, the stout daughter of the cook ... she'd had a sore on her leg and her body had smelt of smoke and earth, but he still remembered the strength in her square hands and the bite of her splendid teeth, the first time he suffered the savage joy of a woman's teeth. ... She would be married now and her children running among the hens in the big courtyard, playing among the sunflowers as he and Adam had done ....

The bell sounded below; six bells in the forenoon watch. ... Sleigh-bells clear as tinkling glass in the frosty stillness of the morning, the hiss of the runners on crusted snow, sparkling spray flying from under the horses' hooves ... riding to the hunt, the wolves running, the boar crashing through dead thickets, the brazen sound of the horns echoing among the silent trees ... his father sitting on his great black horse, even redder in the face from the gallop, watching with ill-concealed pride as the fourteen-year-old Henryk leapt down and advanced on the boar, spear held low ... The snarling hounds fell back, red foam on their teeth ... the stricken beast, doomed fury in its little eyes ... the flurry of snow as it came for him.

Kasia's childish cry of fear ... Longing to run, the boy had stood his ground ... blood melting the snow ... his father's grunting praise ... Henryk looked up at the godlike figure, magnificent in dark red caftan, soft hunting-boots, fur-edged pelisse thrown back over his shoulders, jewelled hunting-knife in the broad golden sash, a jewel pinning the plume to his hat of leopard fur. Not for him the new-fangled wigs and breeches and fancy waistcoats of the Western world; nor the Saxon Kings imposed on Poland ... Count Barinski was a true patriot—had not his father ridden with the Winged Hussars and received the green standard of Mahomet from the beaten Turks outside Vienna?

With his ruddy complexion and wide blue Polish eyes he was a barbaric version of Primrose. A big, roaring man with the long drooping moustache of a Tatar and huge capacity for mead and vodka and dark Polish beer. Unlike most of his fellow nobles he would not touch champagne and wines, not even the Hungarian *tokay* that was becoming so popular. He rode to Krakow, to the Diet in Warsaw, in all weathers, on horseback, disdaining the use of a carriage.

'The nobles *are* Poland,' he was fond of saying, 'and should behave as Poles, not foreigners.' And away he'd gallop, straight and proud in the saddle, with his dogs barking at his heels, to hunt some animal across the rolling Ukrainian hills.

Henryk blew on his fingers. Snow on a spar of wood high above the Atlantic ... snow falling with a soft *plumph* from the sloping roof of Lipno ... the blue autumn haze lying above the trees and in the little valleys ... the open steppe shimmering in the heat of midsummer ... the tall grass swaying and rippling in the wind; or brown and dead, flattened by the blizzards. Was it for this he had cheated the blizzard—and death—in Siberia? To sit vacantly, mindlessly, halfway up a mast, watching snow-flakes vanish in the water? Kasia would appreciate the humour of it. He allowed his mind to go to her, his thoughts a mixture of empty longing, sadness, despair and worry; only desire was missing in that cold, bleak spot.

'Masthead! D'you see anything?' 'Mr You-sir' was showing off his authority.

'No, sir,' Henryk shouted down. Stupid oaf. What the hell did he think could be seen in the depths of a snow-storm? He tried to recapture his memories.

But his thoughts were broken. The officer's voice had dragged him back to the present, to the cold wrinkled swell moving vaguely below him, the bitter sigh of the wind in the rigging, and the wet touch of the snow on his skin.

*   *   *

Christmas Day was windless, clear and cold; the sea was kind.

The Reverend Dunsterville had held his short service; the crew had thundered out the Christmas hymn, and had then been dismissed to occupy themselves as they wanted: to sleep or drink the day away.

Primrose sat in his easy chair, his waistcoat unbuttoned, his feet up on a footstool. They'd earned a respite. Back on blockade straight out of Quiberon Bay and never a hint of going into port, and the worst of the winter still to come. By God, they had. From the big day-cabin he heard the clatter and clink as Sweetapple prepared the table for dinner. He listened apprehensively to the distant noises. Hell above, it sounded like a fairground. Could it get out of control? Jem Pike and his Mates were watch-keeping with the petty officers, the ship lay at anchor; a certain proportion of the men were teetotal. In a sudden crisis they could raise enough sober hands to man the ship. Besides, the comforting bulk of *Warspite* and *Hero* lay between *Huntress* and the French coast. Moreover, Catholics would never come out today; they'd never violate the unofficial Christmas truce, that was certain. And he knew he could depend on Stodart.

An outburst of singing, cheering, catcalling broke out. He heard the thud of bare feet, a splash below his cabin window. Not yet noon and they're falling overboard already. He stirred uneasily. Perhaps this licence was unwise, madness even. But it would be the same throughout the Fleet. He comforted himself with the thought. Yet it would not be taken as an excuse. And, even if he had wanted to do such a thing, he could hardly put the blame on Hawke. Visions of a court martial rose before him.

'. . . Are we to believe, Captain Primrose, that you, as the Captain of His Majesty's ship *Huntress*, allowed the hands to drink to excess?'

'Yes, sir.'

'... Christmas Day or not, Captain ... a ship of war, Captain, not a dockside tavern ... Endangering your ship in time of war ... Dismissed the service, Captain Primrose. With ignominy ...' On the bench, ridiculed and disgraced.

Primrose swung his legs off the footstool and stood up calling for his steward. 'My compliments to the First Lieutenant and I should like to see him in my cabin.'

As the door opened the loud sounds of merriment increased sharply.

'Ah, there you are, Stodart. How—er—how goes everything?'

There was no answering smile from the First Lieutenant who stood very erect, his hat under his arm, a look of pursed disapproval on his face. 'The hands are getting in a disgraceful condition, sir,' he said coldly. 'The ship'll be a pig-sty by nightfall.'

'Very likely.' Primrose was not going to be browbeaten in his own cabin. 'They'll just have to make everything shipshape again, won't they?'

Stodart's mouth tightened. In his heart he knew the Captain was right but, God damn it, who would have the task of getting her back to normal?

'Yes, sir.'

'They sound happy.'

'Happy!' The word burst out. 'I should say they're happy. D'you know what they've done, sir?'

'No,' enquired Primrose innocently. 'What have they done?'

'They've painted Mary, sir. In green and yellow stripes.'

'God bless my soul.' Primrose burst into one of his rare laughs. 'Green and yellow ... well, good Lord—she can't have liked that, can she?'

Stodart was too indignant to answer. Mary, his beloved cow, who had survived the autumn gales, heroine of Quiberon Bay, patient provider of milk, made a spectacle of by a crowd of drunken sots.

'Who is the officer of the deck?'

'Mr Frobisher, sir.'

'Good,' said Primrose, still chuckling. 'Well, at least they're not likely to paint him with stripes. Green and yellow—I wonder who thought of that.'

'Fitch, sir. Leastways he was laying on the paint. And he's already been on the poop-deck declaring at the top of his voice that he was Admiral Hawke and wished the ship to make instant sail for London Bridge.'

Primrose got up and went to the window. A dripping figure was hauling himself from the sea up a rope, spitting water and a garbled song from his mouth.

'A blind eye today, Stodart, a blind eye. Unless of course there's anything promising violence, or damage to the ship. Tomorrow, I promise you, you can make them jump as sharply as you will. A detachment of Marines is being kept sober, I hope?'

'Yes, sir.'

'And the sentries of the magazines are reliable men?'

'Yes.'

'Good. We don't want to be blown to our Maker on this day of good cheer, do we?'

Full of jokes today, aren't we? thought Stodart sourly.

'No, sir,' he said woodenly.

'I shall be having the honour of entertaining yourself and the other officers at dinner this afternoon. And now you'll want to get back to the wardroom, I'm sure.'

Stodart went without another word. Primrose wanted to ask him more; wanted to go out on the quarterdeck and watch them enjoy themselves; wanted to drink deeply himself, to sing and roister without a care and, for one day at least, throw off the weight of his uniform and with it the responsibilities, the leaden burden of command; wanted to show them that he was a human animal like themselves and not a gold-braided god.

Whatever the men might think of him, he thought suddenly, he suffered the same desires and torments as they themselves. None of them knew, not even Stodart, that he had once been married when he was Second Lieutenant of the *Monarch*. He rarely allowed himself to think of Louise, nor of the son he lost with her all those years ago. He had buried his grief deep within him and had returned to the sea a dedicated professional with little ashore to distract him. True he had an elder sister living in Shropshire with her dull husband and three spoilt brats, but he tried not to visit her more often than the faint stirrings of family conscience dictated, preferring to spend his leaves within sight of the sea he had come both to love and to hate. He shuddered at the thought of the lower decks: the promiscuity, the unholy temptation of bodies packed like herrings in a barrel, the lure of flesh —male flesh, any flesh. He wanted to rinse his mouth with sea water and spit out his foul imaginings which he knew well to be fact. . . .

He heard Sweetapple's return, a raucous voice yelling some-where: 'Signal to flagship, Mr Swaine, a hundred ankers of rum for *Huntress*!'

'They've painted Mr Stodart's cow, Sweetapple.'

'Yes, sir. An unholy liberty, if you asks me.' The steward held an unopened bottle of claret in each hand. Give me those, Primrose longed to say. And two more. Leave me with them on my cot. Leave me to sleep for ever. But instead he said. 'What other pranks have they been up to?'

'The rigging's full to the cross-trees with men 'unting for monkeys and white mice.' Sweetapple sniffed scornfully as he busied himself at the table, bringing up the sheen of the polished wood with a soft cloth.

'Today they'll probably find 'em,' said Primrose.

Until the coming of dusk and long after, the ship resounded to bawdy singing and merry-making.

They ate—those capable—as well as Mr Columbine could pro-vide: the last of the fresh beef—long past its prime, but who cared on such a day?—peas, beans, butter, cheese and two quarts of good Portsmouth beer per man. But, despite his efforts, the cook was tried for his life by a party of fo'c's'le men on the charge of poisoning the crew, found guilty and had to be rescued from his stove, with most of his hair singed off, by a sergeant of Marines. Bunch set up his table in the waist and issued tobacco; later he was seen clinging to the mizzen-shrouds, swearing he could see sixty-five sail of the line bearing down on them, and shouting for the guns to be run out. Beside him Mr Midshipman Lloyd hung over the side, listening with drunken concentration for the dogfish to bark.

A sailmaker known to the ship as Hallelujah Jones sat in the captain's gig, quoting at the top of his voice from the Bible, until dragged out by two boatswain's mates and held gurgling beneath the pump.

The longboat, manned by grinning abstainers, pulled slowly round the ship rescuing the drunks as they fell from the ship like smoke-dazed insects.

Parties of men, mugs in hand, went whooping round the ship playing a mad follow-my-leader among the rigging; others danced on the fo'c's'le to Black Bob's fiddle; some sat on the bitts or the spars, slowly glazing till they toppled over and lay where they fell, snoring and mumbling.

The worst cases were pulled from where they lay, giggling or insensible in the scuppers by the petty officers, a line was fastened under their arms and they were lowered over the side to trail in the icy water until the drink was shocked from their brains and they spluttered and cried for help.

Many men never left the lower decks; many drank themselves into a stupor in their hammocks; many lay all day like snoring logs under the mess-tables.

Of No. 8 mess only Henryk, Cameron and Swaine remained capable of speech. Fitch was insensible, lashed in his hammock; the Swede had not been seen since the morning.

'Where were you last Christmas?' Cameron's voice was slurred.

'Last Christmas? Where was I?' Henryk's eyes were spinning. Cameron's face went blurred at the edges, seemed to be falling apart, lurched back into focus. 'I was with good friends, yes, very good friends. I'll tell you about them, one day I'll tell you about them.' He reached unsteadily for his mug and rum slopped down his chin and on to his shirt. Strange, the stuff hardly tasted any more. It burnt but had no taste. He shook his head. 'God, I'm drunk.'

'I was in Newgate,' said Cameron. 'Christmas is a happy time in Newgate. Oh, yes. Remind me to tell you—' His voice trailed off into a thick groan; his eyes rolled in his head as it fell forward on to the table.

'You're not like the seamen when I first joined,' said Swaine impassively. He had drunk enormously yet showed nothing except an added deliberation in his slow speech. 'A little rum and—' he glanced about him—'a broadside could have hit the ship.' From the gun-room came a confused din of boyish singing, the sound of breaking glass. 'They'll be captains on their own quarterdecks one day. But us, Barinski, you and I, we'll still be down 'ere, fighting the ships for 'em.' He looked at Henryk thoughtfully. 'I dunno about you. You're not one of us—yet you does all right none the less.'

Henryk swayed gently in his seat. 'My God, will we ever get out of here?' His sudden cry was sober and despairing.

'No, lad. Not till the war ends or we goes over the side on a grating.'

'We all go over the side sometime, somewhere. On a grating.' Henryk spoke with drunken solemnity, wagging his finger at Swaine. 'I don't want to slide into the sea. I want—I want—a

133

charge. Yes, that's what I want, a charge. Full gallop on a good horse and a musket-ball between the eyes—poof, like that, not know what hit me. That's war, my friend, trumpets, and hooves kicking up the dust, not this—' He gestured fiercely with his arm, knocking over his mug. The dregs dripped steadily from the table-edge on to the face of the man sleeping below.

How clearly he was seeing things, his mind razor-sharp. There was no doubt the rum he had drunk heightened his awareness to a rapier point. Wine, champagne, vodka, raw Naval rum, what did it matter? They made him lord of all he surveyed, an equal to all men, be they Conti, Voltaire, Primrose—Swaine even. He laid his head on his arms and drifted into unconsciousness.

Swaine lit his pipe and sat for a long while wrapped in thought, then he went slowly on deck, picking his way over the prone bodies.

The sky was clear and cold, the stars sparkling ice-chips. From the direction of *Warspite* or *Hero* came the sounds of a song float-ing across the gleam of the water. A man shouted something from the fo'c's'le, then the ship was silent.

Above him Swaine could see the dark figure of the officer of the watch; the bell was struck; the sea swept softly along the sides. He ran his hand down the curve of the main mast, took hold of a rope, felt it moving in his hand to the slow creaking of the ship. His ship. This was his life, the only one he knew.

Tears filled his eye and he let them roll down his face unheeded. Standing by the mast, hearing the sweet sounds of a gentle sea, Matthew Swaine wept quietly—and could have told no one why.

*   *   *

Boxing Day was a day of reckoning. Sore heads, red eyes, mouths like the inside of a lime-kiln; snarling bad temper from the officers and boatswain's mates as they drove the men to their work.

Half a dozen times within an hour Stodart got his own back on the crew; half a dozen times the topmen groaned as the order, 'Prepare to go about!' split their aching heads. And below the gunners sweated the alcohol from their bodies, running out the guns, running them in; closing the ports, tricing them up.

On the quarterdeck Henryk laid his gun on the distant shape of *Warspite* dancing hazily in a cloud of black spots. Muskets were going off in Henryk's skull; he had to put out his hand for support. Nausea welled in his stomach.

The wardroom steward emptied three pailfuls of broken glass over the side grinning spitefully as he banged the buckets noisily against the bulwarks, watching the sufferers as they clutched their foreheads at the metallic din.

'Run her out!' Henryk's voice was hoarse and thick. The gentle squeak of the rigging pierced his brain like the screech of guinea-fowl. He could hear Jem Pike bawling somewhere. 'Come on, there, rouse yerselves. Sharper yet!'

Once again the ship came slowly round, hung in irons while Stodart cursed and shouted, then slowly heeled on her new course. Once again he wearily laid the barrel on the dancing black spot of Ushant.

'No. 1 gun, ready.' He raised his arm, let it drop. 'Fire!' He put the empty linstock shakily to the imaginary powder in the touch-hole.

'A fine shot, Barinski,' observed Primrose, attempting to join in the spirit of the occasion. No one laughed. Crestfallen, he moved away. It was not often he tried a joke in public.

'I'd like to lie down and die,' muttered Cameron.

'You'll die when I damned well tell you,' snapped Stodart. 'And not before. Now then, Barinski, let's do it again and faster this time. A pack of old women could do it better. Just because we had a brush with the Monseers at Quiberon—' A brush! Henryk found the strength to smile.

And far above them Fitch clung at the masthead where the First Lieutenant had sent him on some excuse or other. 'Oh, my Gawd,' he repeated over and over again. 'Oh, my Gawd.' Now and then he was sick, to the loud fury of those unfortunate enough to be below.

Mary the cow was avenged.

For the next months *Huntress* endured the weather and privations of the winter. They sat in the Basque Road watching the seven sail of the line trapped in Rochefort. But the enemy masts remained as bare as December trees, and the only sails they saw, as winter gave way unwillingly to a bright blustery spring, were British.

Fever took its usual toll; dully they tapped the weevils from their biscuits, were sickened by maggots moving on their tongues, the foul odour of crawling cheese; as before, past, present and future merged in a grey waste of wet misery in which they trained —and trained—until they could have fought their guns or taken in a reef in the pitch blackness of Hell itself.

As always the real enemy, the relentless enemy which never let up until the coming of summer, was the sea.

Then one day towards the end of May, Bunch came hurrying along the lower deck, self-important with the news.

'Plymouth, lads. We're going into Plymouth within the week. You may be sure I'm right for I got it straight from Sweetapple himself.'

'I'll believe it when we're past the Eddystone,' said Fitch.

'And what will you do, Mr Cameron, when you first step ashore?' Henryk asked gravely.

'I shall take myself to the best tailor in the town and order a suit of the richest watered silk. And you, Mr Barinski?'

Henryk scratched in his dirty beard, pretended to think deeply. 'A shave, I think. A bath. An excellent meal with carefully chosen wine. A full night's sleep between scented sheets and then—ah, then—who knows?'

Fitch regarded them with his angry little eyes. ''Ark at the gentlemen now. Ashore you says. As if we walked the quarter-deck. You'll not get a run ashore me fine pair. No one gets ashore, not from King George's Navy. Primmy may love us but 'e don't trust us, no more than any other captain. They'll 'ang the nettings across the ports, and there'll be none of your swimming for the shore, I tell you that.'

'The run men don't have a chance,' said Swaine. 'Should you make it to land, they'll pick you up, m'dears, sure as I left me eye in the West Indies. Pick you up and bring you back to lose two years' pay and a thousand lashes.'

For a moment they sat in silence, Henryk trying to visualise a thousand lashes.

'But at least we may expect feminine company,' he said at last with a smile.

Fitch snorted. 'If you mean do we gets the bleedin' women aboard, aye, they'll come swarming up the side, petticoats flying, squealing for Joseph Fitch.'

Henryk had come, if not to like, at least to tolerate the foul-mouthed Fitch. He was an ill-tempered swab, but, for all his grumbling and blasphemies, he was a useful member of the gun-crew who did his duty with the best.

'You'll have to wait, Fitch, m'lad, till the ship's ready for sea,' Swaine pointed out. 'And if we have to go into dock that won't be for a week or more.' Groans greeted this warning. 'Break our bloody backs clearing the ship, guns, cordage—into the hulk— then scrape 'er clean. Brimstone and tallow till every bit o' weed is off 'er. Work first. Then play. That's our Primmy.'

'All hands on deck! All hands to make sail! Rouse out! Rouse out!' The call came down the hatchways.

Elmquist swore loudly. 'Are they never leaving us alone?'

But this time they ran to their jobs willingly enough, for the wind was fair for Plymouth and the water curled and sparkled at *Huntress*'s bow as she bore up for England with all sails set to the royals.

*   *   *

'There she is, the beauty.' The tall finger of the Eddystone lighthouse, newly built the previous year, pointed into an almost cloudless sky. 'Another hour and we'll be past Penleep Point.' Swaine's tone was cheerful.

Spirits were high, the whole ship, from the Captain to the youngest boy, eager for his first glimpse of Plymouth, was infected by a mood of keen anticipation; even 'Mr You-sir' was seen to smile. Ushant at last lay below the shimmering horizon; France was hidden far beyond the heat-haze.

The ship lay over comfortably to a light westerly breeze, the sails full-rounded and the song of the wind in the rigging was light and gay.

Astern, at the end of the foaming wake, *Monmouth* followed under full press of canvas and once again Henryk was struck by the sheer beauty of a big square-rigged ship under sail.

'I served in *Monmouth*,' said Fitch. 'I was in 'er when we met *Foudroyant* in 'fifty-eight. Christ above, that was a fight. Close on five 'ours port to port we 'ammered away in the moonlight, and pissing on the guns to cool 'em. Eighty-four guns she carried to us with sixty-four, and Captain Gardiner with 'is arm 'anging by a string after the first exchange. But 'e wouldn't give in, not even when a ball took 'im through the 'ead. 'E lay there on the quarterdeck under 'is cloak and told 'is Number One to lay 'er closer. Closer!' Fitch watched a fulmar planing on stiff wings along the length of the ship. 'Closer! Jesus, we could see the powder fizzing in their touch'oles.'

Looking at the gilded figurehead and the proud tiers of bleached canvas, Henryk found it hard to believe she could ever have been a smoking, blackened wreck. He listened as Fitch told them of the single-ship action famed throughout the Navy; he looked at their own white decks, the perfect coils of rope, the Second Lieutenant's snowy stockings. Then he remembered the men in the waters of Quiberon Bay; the 9-pounder crew scattered in pieces; the thunder of Seydlitz's horsemen in another battle. There's a lot of beauty in war, he thought, but how very swiftly it changes to red horror, especially in the sunshine.

' ... I'd always 'eard that cannon shot couldn't be seen, but by Gawd that day I saw a few of the little black devils ... one of 'em dashed a mate of mine into a dozen bits. I collected 'em and the flesh creeped to my 'and as if not wanting to let go ... We blasted the sticks right out of 'er. But the Frogs were a game bunch, they wouldn't strike, not even with smoke pouring out of 'er like a leaky galley fire and 'er decks a bleeding slaughter-yard.' He fell silent. The taut braces squeaked softly; the sound of the ship thrusting through the water was soothing.

'The Lord keep us from such a fight,' said a man quietly.

'Amen to that,' Bunch echoed fervently as he joined them. A Bunch much leaner now but still plumper than anyone else in the ship, with his ledger tucked under the arm of his faded black coat.

'What have you planned for us in that book of yours, Bunch?' asked Cameron lightly.

'Ah, my good sirs, Mr Columbine and I have made out the lists of fresh victuals. Your mouths will water, I assure you. Twelve pigs and four bullocks among other rare delicacies. Oh, I tell you, we shall not let you starve.'

'Pigs! Bullocks!' Fitch bit off a piece of tobacco.

'What about women, you fat merchant? 'Ave you no women on your lists? Or 'as Fitch, the 'ero of *Monmouth*, got to make do with a bleeding pig?'

In great good humour they chattered away, the coarse jokes

flying round the deck as Rame Head came up closer on the larboard bow.

They dropped anchor in the Roads and lay there all night, and the lights of Plymouth were bright and tantalising in the thin June darkness.

Next morning the two ships were joined by eight sail of the line and two weather-stained frigates. There was a great to-ing and fro-ing of gigs, a great shrilling of bosun's calls and stamp of Marine boots as the captains paid courtesy visits to each other.

'Waste of bloody time,' grumbled the crews. 'Let's get in first before this other bunch of idlers.'

They need not have worried, for *Huntress* went in on the early morning tide, past Drake Island as the sun came up, dispersing the mist from the roofs of the town, and into the mouth of the Hamoaze where she anchored close inshore off the building yards.

For the first time in almost a year the timbers were silent, the thrumming of the chains had ceased; the ship, utterly still at her anchor, was at rest.

*   *   *

The hands lined the side gazing at the dockyards lying beyond a cable's length of scummy water. Henryk leant on the rail, feasting his eyes on houses and people and, most of all, the green tops of trees rising beyond the shining wet roofs.

Already the steady beat of the shipwrights' hammers and the long rasp of saws filled the morning air as men swarmed over the rough hulls of two third-raters in the frames.

A gentle land-breeze brought the smell of tar, paint and wood-shavings from the piles of timber and cordage, the rows of un-cut logs waiting to be turned into yet more vessels to sweep England's enemies from the seas.

The cook emptied his scrap-pails over the side and a cloud of gulls dived screaming.

'It's so close, you could almost jump ashore,' said Henryk softly.

'You'd find it a long way with musket-balls churning up the water like those birds.' Cameron watched them fight over the offal 'I had to swim just about that distance once with twenty red-

coats practising their marksmanship on "the Highland animal".
It was the longest journey of my life.'

'This would be nothing to a good swimmer.'

But Cameron shook his head. 'No,' he said. 'I've had my fill of
running.'

Below them, under the shrill direction of Midshipman Lloyd,
men were hanging the nettings over the open ports, joking and
laughing with the women lining the quay. Here and there a man
recognised his wife or sweetheart and shouted a warm greeting.

'At least they've got something to come back to,' said Cameron.

'Take a closer look at some of them,' remarked a seaman standing near, 'and you'll want to dive straight into the Bay.'

*　　*　　*

The Clerk of the Cheque, a little man in a hat too large for him
and a brown velveteen coat, came aboard to go through the muster
rolls; the Captain went ashore; the patient gulls lined the yards
in the sunshine, the patient women sat waiting on coils of rope
and rows of new gun-trucks. Nothing seemed to happen until late
in the afternoon watch when Primrose returned, even redder in
the face, and the ship sprang to feverish life as the crew prepared,
angry and frustrated, to go into dock.

Five days of hard toil and *Huntress* was cleaned, refitted, re-
victualled and back at her berth off the building yards.

'Today the women's coming aboard.' The news spread through
the ship and the men's faces brightened; there was more activity
round the wash-pumps, clean shirts were dragged out, the long
razors wielded with extra care and skill; they played and joked
like schoolchildren on an outing.

They lined the hammock nettings and stared at the women on
the quay, many of whom did not appear to have moved since the
week before, and this time the remarks shouted across the water
were filled with anticipation and the promise of what was to
come.

But the women did not come aboard that day either.

*　　*　　*

The longboat slowly approached the ship, the oars flashing rhythmically above the sunlit water. On deck could be heard the dull thud of the drum as the drummer in the stern of the boat beat out the Rogue's March. At half-minute intervals the ships' bells clanged dolefully. Astern of the boat followed ten boats filled with Marines sitting rigidly to attention. At the foot of the ladder Jem Pike stood with sleeves rolled up, slowly pulling the knotted cords of the cat through his hand.

'Hands to witness punishment!'

They lined the bulwarks and watched in silence as the fleet of boats came closer across the smiling sea.

'Those hands who cannot see, into the shrouds with you.' Primrose's voice was curt. He loathed the macabre ceremony to come.

'Fleet flogging,' hissed Swaine from the corner of his mouth. 'Poor bastard.'

'Keep silence!' ordered Gore sharply.

Eight sail of the line and four frigates lay in the Roads. Twelve lashes alongside each ship. The striped and bleeding thing bound face down across the thwarts, an iron bar in its torn mouth, had already received one hundred and forty-four lashes.

The boat came alongside the ladder.

'His Majesty's ship *Huntress*,' roared out Pike.

Primrose came to the top of the ladder. For a moment he looked down with pity and revulsion at what lay in the spattered boat. Then, clearing his throat loudly, he began to read the charge.

Henryk stared at the boat in horrified fascination. The open back shone wetly in the June sun, the white curve of the back-bone visible in three places. The white breeches and pipe clayed equipment of the drummer were as scarlet as his coat.

' ... in that he, Zachary Spurrier—' Primrose's voice was tone-less—'did attempt to desert from His Majesty's ship *Temeraire* on the twenty-second day of May, in the year of Our Lord, seventeen hundred and sixty ...'

Henryk tore his gaze from the twitching legs and a hand that slowly opened and closed, and fixed his eyes on a small round cloud low above a green, wooded, English hill. But in his mind he did not see the peaceful beauty of summer trees, he saw the leaping shadows in a dungeon lit by torches of naked flame; the vile instruments contained in that devilish place: the rack, the wheel, the branding irons and pincers heating in the glowing coals, the roasting spit. He saw the flat bearded face of the executioner, expressionless, small-eyed and deadly. Beyond the powerful body, naked to the waist, the sharp gloating face of Lev Bubin; Shuvalov's cold, bored look. Henryk heard his soft insistent question. 'Monsieur, for the last time, why were you sent to Petersburg?'

His own voice answering, echoing from the dark vaulted stone, 'I've already told you. I was on the staff of the French Embassy. You know that. You've no right to bring me here. You—'

'*Right*, Monsieur?' Softer still. 'Who sent you? Why are you, a Pole, in French service? What secrets were you paid to learn in Her Imperial Highness's bed? Give me the answers to these questions, Monsieur, and you will be allowed to return to France unharmed.'

. . . A woman appeared on a track near a little house driving two cows before her; rooks rose circling above the trees.

'A dozen lashes, Bos'n. Do your duty.'

'Sir,' called up the surgeon in the boat. 'Sir, this man is unconscious.'

Three times the tortured wretch had been revived with rum, then the iron was thrust back between his chipped and broken teeth and the punishment went on.

Jem Pike glanced up enquiringly.

'Carry out the punishment.' Primrose snapped out the words, hating every one of them.

'Aye, aye, sir.'

Henryk winced at the whistle and thud of the lashes tearing live flesh from the quivering body, feeling the scars on his own back crawl from the memory of the knout. A voice called out the number.

'Punishment completed, sir.'

'Very well, Bos'n. Thank you.'

Primrose turned and strode quickly away, not looking down. For an instant the din of the hammers ceased and in the sudden silence Henryk heard the distant cawing of the rooks. The Boatswain bent and drew the slimy red lashes through the water, swished them through the air then ran up the ladder to the deck.

The boat pushed off; the drum took up its melancholy beat as the funeral procession drew away from the ship and headed up-river to the remaining four ships, the Marines staring woodenly to the front, the tattered body of Zachary Spurrier dripping into the bottom boards.

'Hands fall out!' ordered Stodart when the thump of the drum had faded into the renewed clatter of the shipyards.

Most of the men remained on deck, a few gazing morbidly down at the empty water, at the foot of the ladder; the chatter was subdued; many of the glances directed at the quarterdeck were sullen and bitter.

'Tweren't his fault,' said Swaine. ' 'Tis the law of the Navy, m'dears. 'Tis not the captains who write the Articles of War.'

'Damn them all to Hell,' growled Fitch.

'If it weren't for that—' Cameron nodded at the distant boats. 'How many ships would ever get to sea?'

'They'll take him ashore tonight,' said Croaker in his mournful voice. 'And bury him in the mud without a prayer for his soul.'

'I knew a man 'oo lived after three 'undred lashes. An 'undred and fifty on the Monday an 'undred and fifty on the Tuesday. A topman in *Swiftsure*,' put in Fitch, rolling the tobacco plug from one side of his mouth to the other. 'Got foxed as a pickled 'erring and cried mutiny from the fo'c's'le. A real tough wight I tell yer, why 'e were back aloft within the week. Allo, what's this?'

Two lighters had put off and were making for the ship, casting long evening shadows. Midshipman Lloyd's voice was heard shouting, 'It's the women, Mr Gore.'

'By Gawd, 'e's right.' Fitch spat the tobacco over the side, rubbed his hands, flexed his muscles.

Across the water came the sound of feminine laughter rising to a screeching pitch as the lighters drew close. Henryk watched the last boatload of Marines vanish round Devil's Point and looked down at the women packed in the lighters. Hot, flushed faces, bold eyes, hair straggling from beneath dingy mob caps; brawny arms folded across massive bosoms, pock-marked skins, rotten teeth.

The remarks flung up at the waiting sailors were ribald and obscene; the language as foul as anything heard in the ship.

'By God, are they to be let loose among us?' Henryk asked in amazement.

'Give them weapons and they'd be a match for the best.' Cameron's lips curled.

'The women are waiting, Mr Gore.' Stodart's sharp voice rose above the shindy. 'Look 'em over, Mr Gore, look 'em over.'

143

Blushing slightly, the Third Lieutenant ordered the women up the ladder.

'One at a time now.'

A confused shindy greeted his words.

'Let us on board, sonny,' cried a huge, shapeless woman with a large red handkerchief knotted round her throat. 'We've waited for it long enough. Haven't we girls?' A roar of assent and laughter greeted this sally. Gore's flush deepened.

'One at a time, damn you.'

Stodart hid a smile behind the broad cuff of his sleeve.

'Wives and sweethearts first.'

As each woman reached the deck, moist and puffing from the climb, her husband or lover from the previous visit to Plymouth pushed through the throng round the gangway to claim her. Amid shouts of rude encouragement and advice each couple vanished below.

Henryk sat on a gun and watched the scene, stirred despite himself by the sight of female flesh, the grubby gleam of a naked calf as a woman raised her skirts extra high. He felt a sudden hot envy for the men who swaggered below, their arms encircling women's waists or shoulders, their lips already searching.

He turned away from Cameron to hide the look he felt smouldering in his eyes, reflected in the eyes of every man on deck, and went to the side. As he watched, the sun slipped below Tor Point and the water darkened. The shipyards were silent except for the work which continued on the skeleton ribs of a frigate taking shape by the light of flaring resin torches.

He stood without moving, watching the night come down. The drum sounded the setting of the night watch; a master's mate took the deck, the sentries their posts along the bulwarks, for the shore lay no more than a cable's length away. Nothing for even an indifferent swimmer like himself.

The light of the torches shone on the water in tracks of rippled flame; between them stretched lanes of blackness. If he swam underwater ... Glancing at the nearest sentry and the glint of the bayonet, he raised himself slowly on to the bulwarks. The nettings hung down right to the water. A man could slide down those and into the sea without a sound.

Shrill cries of pain and delight rose from the open gun-ports, mingled with the drunken laughter floating across the water from *Monmouth*.

Henryk had a sudden memory of Zachary Spurrier; the thud of the whistling lash on torn flesh ... And yet over there, in the darkness beyond the torchlight, lay freedom, so close he could feel it in his hands. He had no money, a pair of canvas trousers and a seaman's shirt, but he would feel the solid earth beneath his feet and smell the sweet scents of grass and trees. He would see—

Hearing the clump of boots, he lowered himself quickly to the deck.

'A fine night, matey,' observed the sentry in a friendly way.

'It is.' Henryk cursed him in his heart.

'What keeps you up 'ere with the women aboard and extra grog a-flowin'?' The sentry sounded curious.

'The gun-deck's like a furnace. I needed the air.'

The Marine grunted, then, lowering his voice, said, 'I knows wot ye're 'ere for but don't 'ee do it, mate. 'Tain't worth it. They'll get you, they allus do.'

Henryk heard Primrose's harsh voice: '... in that he, Henryk Barinski, did attempt to desert from His Majesty's ship *Huntress*' ... Choking on an iron gag; his last conscious view of life the bottom-boards of a boat, discoloured with his own blood. But, by God, the risk was worth it.

The sentry's face was dark in the shadow of the wide hat. 'Course, if I sees anything I'll 'ave to shoot. But I'm no use with a musket. Can't 'it a bullock cart at twenty paces.' He chuckled quietly and went on in a normal voice, 'If I was you, mate, I'd get below before all the women's played out.'

He marched ponderously away and halted with his back to Henryk, gazing towards the sounds of revelry from *Monmouth*.

The deck was deserted, the figures on the quarterdeck too far away. There'd never be a better moment than this.

As Henryk swung his leg over the bulwarks he heard the rush of bare feet, a muttered oath, the hiss of words: 'Get him!' then something came down very hard on the back of his head and a bright flash exploded inside his skull.

Silently Cameron and Swaine carried him below.

'Too much grog, sir,' they assured an inquisitive Midshipman Lloyd, who was hovering near the lower-deck ladder, excited by the animal sounds rising from the gun-deck. 'Taking him to his hammock, sir. Night air finished him.'

Midshipman Lloyd peered down through the hatchway, watching them as they pushed their way through, stepping over the recumbent forms. Never in his fourteen years had he seen anything like that which now met his popping eyes.

Most of the deck seemed to be moving with the prone bodies of half-naked men and women. Couples full to the eyes with rum mated freely, noisily and without shame; some on the mess-tables, some underneath. A woman was bent back over a gun by a large, panting sailor, her mouth open in a moaning cry of joy, watched by Hallelujah Jones in a foaming frenzy of rum and religion; a couple spilled from a swaying, bulging hammock crashing to the deck, continuing their business entirely oblivious to those who stumbled over them.

The noises beat against the boy's ear-drums; the grog-fumes rose with the lantern heat and the tobacco smoke in stifling waves.

A huge woman, stark naked except for a torn mob-cap on her greasy curls, staggered from man to man, rum trickling down her chin, bawling out that she was ready for anyone on the gun-deck who called himself a man. Catching sight of the boy on the ladder, she spread out her arms towards him.

'Come here, sonny. Come down here to Kate and let her—'
But the boy had fled, more terrified than he had been facing the guns of Quiberon Bay.

After two days and two nights, during which Henryk lay semi-conscious, pale, and breathing so thickly that Cameron had feared his blow was fatal, the ship, much to Primrose's relief, was ordered unexpectedly to sea.

'A gun-deck's a gun-deck, Mr Stodart, and not a blasted brothel.'
But Primrose knew, as he watched the crew go about their duties, many of them wan and hollow-eyed, that these last forty-eight hours of licence had been all too short. God knew, they deserved their women, their brief brush with humanity, for longer than that.

They sailed shortly after dawn with the Boatswain's loud abuse audible above the wailing and lamentation of the women making for the shore in the lighters.

With Rame Head on the starboard beam they set sail to the topgallants, feeling the westerly wind cool on their heated skins.

Henryk stood at the braces, eyes smouldering with sullen resentment.

'Did you want to end up like that poor devil with your backbone stripped?'

146

He did not answer Cameron's question. Yet he knew his friends had acted to save him. He knew in his heart they were right; that he would not have got far, would have groaned away his life face down across a thwart. He knew now he would remain in the ship till released by the end of the war—or by death and, accepting this knowledge with all the philosophical courage of his race, felt a sudden lightening of the spirit. It was unlikely there'd be another chance. Well, so be it. If God wanted him to eke out his years in this way there was small point in weeping and complaining.

'Two days of it,' cried Fitch. 'Till the old marlin-spike were fair black and blue. But what does Gentleman Brinski do? Gets isself 'it over the 'ead with a belaying pin by some drab 'oo didn't want 'is attentions and ends up lying like a dead pig in 'is 'ammick missing all the bloody fun. Oh, that were rich, that were.' Fitch laughed till the tears poured down his face. He was in fine fettle, sated at last. 'You missed it, eh,' he gasped between fresh paroxysms. 'But maybe they weren't grand enough for 'Is 'Ighness.'

'Ah, stow it, Fitch,' growled Swaine.

Fitch chuckled away to himself.

'Ease off the sheets and lee braces there to leeward. Round in the weather braces, you afterguard! Come on, Yorston, get 'em moving there!' shouted Primrose.

'Primmy's 'ad the 'ell of a time of it with some randy bitch,' muttered Fitch. 'Ark at 'im.'

'Less o' that, Fitch, or you'll feel this starter across yer arse,' said Yorston.

'How's her head, Quartermaster?'

'West by sou'west, sir.'

'Steady so. Ste—de—ey!'

The deck tilted slightly. The bubbling of the water along her sides and the rising sigh of the wind in the rigging merged into the familiar song of the open sea as *Huntress* sailed to war again.

PART FOUR

H.M.S. *Huntress* moved slowly before a light breeze, a few miles to the east of Madeira. Most of the hands off watch lay about in the waist, shaded from the September sun by makeshift awnings. It was too hot for much talking and the men got up frequently to wander lazily to the water-butt or to watch the efforts of a few energetic souls to catch fish from the chains.

The water was tepid but fresh; the men were surfeited with the oranges, mangoes and pomegranates of Madeira. For the first few days off Funchal they had torn ravenously at the fruit, their faces wet with juice, stuffing the sweet grapes into their mouths in handfuls, not caring that they had to rush continually for the heads, full and yet not satisfied.

The griping pains in their bellies did not matter, nothing mattered except the glorious fact of tasting fruit fresh from the trees and vines after six months without so much as a wizened apple. Fingering the smooth round grapes, stroking the rough curves of oranges, lemons, limes, had been a sensual delight.

'Think of they lucky swabs in Havana,' said Fitch, breaking a long, lazy silence. 'All the prize money, all the women.' He stuffed a date into his mouth.

'The West Indies station is putrid with fever.' Matthew Swaine did not open his eye. 'It ain't no rest cure to serve out there.'

The words of a song floated from the forecastle:
'Sally Brown's a bright mullater
she drinks rum and chews tobaccer—'

'Think of them, all panting for us over there.' Fitch pointed towards the mountains of Madeira shimmering in the midday heat-haze.

He lay pleasuring himself with lecherous memories of the women who had come out in the bumboats to *Huntress* as she lay with the rest of the squadron in the Roads off Funchal. Black-eyed, flashing grins in dark, olive faces; the smell of 'em enough to send a man wild. 'I'll wager Primmy got 'is breeches down for one o' them half-breed bitches.' He sat eyeing the fishermen tugging gently at their lines. Shirts were drying in the warm wind.

Merry noises rose from forward where a few enthusiasts were hanging from the cathead hoping to trap flying-fish in a home-made net.

'All the glory in Havana—and the gold. Twelve Spanish sail of the line taken at anchor, or so I've heard. Suffering Jesus but that's the war for us, lads.' Fitch shifted his quid to the other cheek. 'And what do we get? It's more'n a year since Belle Isle and what've we done, I asks yer?'

'Old Primmy gets 'isself made Commodore,' said Swaine. The broad pennant moved uncertainly in the dying wind above them. Commodore Thomas Primrose, thirty-nine years old, in command of a detached squadron patrolling between Madeira and Morocco on the watch for Spanish treasure ships bound for Cadiz from Brazil and the Rio de la Plata. 'And Brinski 'ere gets made a quarter gunner with six shillings a week all to 'isself. Oh, they're all right, these two. But us common sailor lads, what do we get, eh? The fevers and the belly-rot and never a whiff of the Frenchies, nor the bloody Dagoes neither.'

Since January of that year they had been at war with Spain but had not sighted so much as a Spanish topsail.

'If you asks me,' Swaine went on, 'we ain't never going to see any action in this ship. We'll all be 'ere in another twenty years' time, white beards down to our damned—'

Loud shouts of excitement drowned his words as a man hauled up a large green fish. Black Bob's fiddle took up a tune and near them Hallelujah Jones's lips moved soundlessly as he read to himself from his worn Bible.

Bunch sat with his back to the mainmast quietly scratching away in his ledger, now and then pausing to dip his quill in the inkwell on the deck beside him. A fat drop of sweat gathered on his chin and fell with a splash on the page. But he did not even click his tongue; it was too hot and peaceful for annoyance.

Henryk leant with his back to the bulwark, looking down at these men he had lived with now for three long years. Three years in which he had felt the earth beneath his feet only once, and then only for a week.

He glanced across the sea towards the distant Desertas poking above the horizon, remembering his wild rapture at the feel of the warm sand round his feet, the wonder of touching a tree, a leaf; of holding a deep red flower in his hand; of drinking from a running stream and rolling, shouting and laughing under the sparkling white coolness of a mountain waterfall. All round him his shipmates had gone mad as they romped in the sands or scrambled among the rocks, shouting with childish wonder and delight as they caught the brilliant flash of birds in the thick, luxuriant foliage or tore up handfuls of dewy grass, tossing it in the air so that it fell on them in cool green showers.

He had thought he loved the very earth of Poland but never had he experienced such a moment of sheer joy as when he stepped from the longboat on to the beach of Ilheo Chao.

Since the expedition under Keppel which resulted in the capture of Belle Isle in the spring and summer of '61, another autumn had passed, then another bleak winter off Finisterre, broken by cleaning ship in Lisbon. In the spring of 1762 *Huntress* sailed south of the Mediterranean for a three months' vigil off the Spanish coast: to and fro with unvarying monotony between Malaga and Cape Palos, where *Monmouth* and *Foudroyant* had fought their epic action.

But no ship came out to challenge *Huntress* and No. 8 mess was wearied to death by Fitch's constant references to the battle of long ago.

They fired their long guns at a Spanish lugger, hitting her once before she escaped into Almeria. Venturing too close on her heels, they lost the wind and were fired upon by large guns to the east of the town and got out under tow, the boats' crews drenched by water from the heavy shot, the gunners answering with futile broadsides which fell at least a hundred yards short.

They were tantalised by the smell of the land and the sight of dust rising from the wheels of carts, the smoke rising from the little cottages.

Then in July the frigate *Wild Goose* had brought despatches promoting Captain Primrose and placing him in command of three sail of the line and one frigate, and they had sailed to join the little squadron in the Horse Latitudes where the light airs played as fickle as a wanton woman.

With *Wild Goose* in close company, the remaining ships in line astern, they beat slowly across the fitful breezes to the north of Madeira, to within sight of the Atlas Mountains, then back on their tracks, blocking the gateway to Spain. They took on stores from the three victuallers and went into Ilheo Chao—Willy Chow, as the men called it—put ashore, for careening and slept under the stars for a week on a warm sand bed that did not move.

After leaving Willy Chow they cruised to the southeast of Madeira; they fished and swam in the green sea; when they were not working aloft or exercising the guns they lay in the hammock nettings and watched the porpoises and flying-fish and dreamt of women.

Fitch, as always, was talking of women, but now Henryk found himself listening. He saw the familiar look in other men's eyes as they hung on the lewd words, hot and secretive; they moved where they sat or lay and their tongues ran round their lips. He found his own palms were wet, his body stirring at the pictures of women forming in his mind, and he turned away in self-disgust. Not Kasia, not Catherine, nor Amande, just women. He put his hand on the curve of the gun; with an oath he snatched it away from the hot kiss of the metal.

The sea shone cleanly and sparkled at *Wild Goose*'s stem as she kept station three cables' length to starboard under shortened sail, schooling her pace to that of the two-deckers. Gazing at the frigate's swelling sails, he thought at once of a woman's white breasts and found his hands were clenched.

'Aye, Fitchie, go on, tell us what you'd do to her then.'

'I'd put 'er down and then I'd put this marlin-spike o' mine—'

'Ah, stop it, I say, stop it!'

Hallelujah Jones, his eyes wild, had leapt to his feet. Flicking the pages of his Bible, he began to read, shouting the words in a high, cracked voice, so that all over the deck men stopped what they were doing and listened with their mouths open.

'Thy two breasts are like two young roes that are twins—' low groans came from his listeners— 'which feed upon the lilies.' The sailmaker was beside himself with excitement. The fore-top lookout neglected his sweeping search of the seas and gazed down in amazement.

In his cabin Primrose stirred on his cot, woken from a doze. He lay for a moment in his shirt and breeches, listening to the familiar slap of the water under the stern, the steady sigh of the wind round the cabin windows. A sticky, warm wind coming from Africa, bringing no relief. Blast it, but he'd be glad when they could go north again—even the Bay in January was preferable to this oven.

He scratched irritably at the itching rash round his waist, loathing the heat. No wonder the horses died in ships becalmed in these latitudes.

But the men seemed to enjoy it, though to him the lower decks seemed an inferno, even with the ventilators blowing every hour, God knows how they could endure the stink down there.

Faintly he heard a voice shouting something, and, listening more intently, Primrose made out some of the words.

'Shall we not lie with the whores and strumpets of Babylon and send them mad with our bodies?'

Primrose moved uneasily, then, getting up, he went into his day-cabin. He helped himself to a glass of luke-warm madeira and stuck his head out of a stern window. The wind had practically gone. Astern he saw the topsails of his other two ships flapping feebly like fishes gasping for oxygen. The wisps of cloud reached out ahead of a dark mass gathering low to the north east.

On the quarterdeck the Second Lieutenant watched the clouds and did not like what he saw. The glass was dropping too fast. He wondered whether to call Primrose.

'An unclean abomination in the guise of white and—'

The sails rattled like small arms fire.

'Turn up the hands, Bos'n. Mr Lloyd, my compliments to the Captain and I don't like the look of the weather. You, sir, down there, stop that blasted caterwauling. Get out on the jib-boom and read the first chapter of Genesis to clean the filth from your tongue. Smartly there, or I'll have the hide off you.' Mr Wood roared out his varied orders almost on one long breath.

The hands were piped, running to the braces as Jones made his way out on to the jib-boom, in no way abashed, and settled himself to read in a ringing voice about the beginning of the world.

' ... And God said, let us make man in our own image ...'
In the sultry, windless silence his words carried clearly to all parts of the deck.

Primrose, emerging on deck, enquired very loudly indeed:
'What the devil's that man doing, Mr Wood?'
'It's Jones, sir. He—'
'Bad weather coming, Mr Wood, and a madman on the—'
'Thus the heavens and the earth were finished and all the host

of them. *Hallelujah*. And praise be to God.'

A sudden gust of wind rushed across the sea, darkening the water and filling the flaccid sails with a thuderous crack.

'Have the goodness to take in the main course, Mr Wood, and remove that religious maniac from the jib-boom.' Primrose was too experienced a seaman not to know what was coming. And yet with no wind to take them from the path of the storm what on earth could he do?

'Sheet home!' The Second Lieutenant passed on the order in a bellow, eager to make amends.

Henryk, hauling on the thin rope, thought with a smile, that only the English could manage their affairs in this strange manner. Perhaps that was the secret of their greatness.

'I'll have the ship secured for heavy weather, Mr Stodart.'

The glass continued to plummet and by sunset the sky astern had turned to glowing copper; the sun went down in a furnace blaze among long bars of cloud burnt ragged at the edges. The wind which had threatened dropped away completely and left the squadron rolling slackly on a long oily swell from the north-east, totally unable to escape the path of the storm.

Throughout the night the wind stayed away but the watches worked to secure the ship by the light of lanterns swaying in the rigging. Henryk saw to the securing of his four quarterdeck guns till they did not move an inch to the roll.

'There's trouble coming,' said Croaker dismally, lifting his face to the dark night. 'You can smell it.'

Henryk watched the reflection of a lantern gleam on a high curve of water, felt the ship lift beneath him and then fall away into deeper darkness. A few heavy raindrops spattered on the deck.

Dawn was red and angry. But that was all they saw of the sun, for the overcast thickened till the sky was dark and more deeply tinged with that eerie, copper glow. And the air was utterly still as though the world around them held its breath.

By God, thought Stodart wonderingly. The damned glass can't get any lower, surely. He glanced at the sails firmly secured; the t'gallant yards safely struck, the main topsail and jib hanging slack, waiting for the wind. Lifelines rigged, double lashings on everything that could shift, guns double-breeched and storm-cleated; a sea anchor of spare spars lashed and ready forrard. He'd been through a storm with Primrose once before, a near hurricane off the Azores when the ship was newly commissioned; he knew the Captain would not run before a gale if he could help it, he'd turn at the first opportunity and face the devil. At least when the storm comes the ship will be ready, he thought, with the inward satisfaction of a man who knows he has done all in his power to meet impending danger.

He listened to the Captain's voice:

' ... according to the Act of Parliament passed in the second year of the reign of His Present Majesty, King George the Third, the said Articles of War were read in the presence of the officers and seamen belonging to His Majesty's ship *Huntress*, on board the said ship on this the first day of October, 1762.'

The Captain stopped reading, cleared his throat and, as he turned away, felt the first touch of the wind, no more than a faint stirring of the air, on his cheek.

'Fall out the hands, Mr Stodart.' In a lower voice he added, 'Here it comes.'

The wind came gently at first as if exploring the sky in front of it, ruffling the swell with light fingers, whispering in the rigging.

Wild Goose was the only ship plainly visible, riding the swell with an easy grace, stripped to her maincourse and fore-staysail. The two-deckers astern were partially hidden in the overcast; the four ships were cut off from the world, alone and with nothing to help them but the skill of their Captains and the strength of their timbers.

The first of the storm struck *Huntress* in a vicious squall of drenching rain, followed by a wind which came at them savagely like an animal bent on destroying this puny obstacle in its path, scything the tops from the mounting seas, roaring like a thousand banshees in the taut rigging.

For half a day the ship fled before the gale at ten knots under storm-canvas while the crew hung on below decks, listening to the seas crashing on the battened hatches and the feverish clatter of the straining pumps.

On deck the Captain, dressed in tarpaulins and canvas trousers, barefooted like his men, clung to the mizzen halliards beside his First Lieutenant, shouting encouragement to the men lashed to the wheel—the most reliable quartermaster in the ship and three of the strongest seamen, and they could barely hold her.

In the grey chaos of scudding clouds and lashing rain long streamers of spume flew from the crests of huge seas rearing high above the stern, so that the air was thick with stinging spray smacking against the bent backs of the men on deck.

Breathless from the force of the wind and the choking spray Primrose leant close and shouted in Stodart's ear, 'We'll have to shorten sail. She'll be driven under.'

Above them the bulging topsail was forcing her forward into the bottomless troughs too fast, with too great an impact; she was burying her bows too deep.

'Aye, aye, sir.'

'Flying jib—all she'll carry. Get the hands on deck. By heavens,' he added, 'it's worse than Quiberon.' But no one heard.

In the bedlam of the lower deck the voices of the boatswain's mates were lost in the grinding of the timbers, the shrill squeal of the gun breechings, the loud protests of the rudder cables, the deafening vibrations of the chains and the thunder of the seas. The mates had to move along, whipping the reluctant men on deck.

As Henryk's head cleared the hatchway it was buried in a heavy surge of water cascading down the ladder. He shook himself, gasping, grabbing for a lifeline, hauling himself upright. Slowly he made his way out and up to the quarterdeck, dragging himself along the line against the mighty pressure of the wind; now and then his legs were plucked from under him by a sea sweeping the deck thigh-deep.

His guns, he found, were secure. Hooking his arm round a shroud, he watched with horrified fascination as the topmen fought desperately to take in the sail, clinging for their lives to the bucking yard.

The evening was already very dark, lit faintly to the west and by the great white seas.

'Get below.' Faintly he heard Stodart's order, but did not move. Nothing would make him return to that packed red coffin.

'Permission to stay at my guns, sir?' His request was torn from his lips by a wild gust but the officer heard and nodded.

All over the ship men who preferred to die in the open remained on deck, clinging to whatever hand-holds they could find.

Night came and still she ran before the storm, lurching, twisting, now hurled high into the screaming blackness, now deep into the very bowels of the tormented sea. Still the wind increased, flinging itself at them out of the darkness.

Sometime during the first watch the cutter carried away,

going over the side like a sliver of wood on the crest of a mountainous sea, taking with it three men knocked from the lifeline, then, as if to atone for such behaviour, the wind rushed away into the blackness ahead.

They were in the very eye of the storm. When the wind returned it should be from the west; they would be heading into the wind.

'Mr Stodart!' Primrose's voice was audible in the comparative silence. 'Have the sea anchor put over the side. Smartly does it.'

Cursed on by Frobisher, a party under Jem Pike somehow manhandled the unwieldy mass over the side on a derrick. Every other minute they were forced to cling on, dazed and half drowned by yet another sea bursting over the bulwarks. The pause would be all too short; the wind, when it returned, would be stronger, much stronger.

They heard it coming from the pitch black sky ahead; with a roar as it swooped over the broken sea, flattening the wave-tops and filling the air with grey curtains of driving spume. The ship shuddered violently. Forced back by the wind she was brought up head to sea by the weight of the makeshift anchor. Her bows met the relentless procession of steep-fronted waves and reared to meet them.

Inky mountains of water rolled past, their hissing peaks level with the lower yards. Upwards she rose till she seemed to be standing on her stern, hovered, then dived forward down the far slope, stabbing back defiantly at her enemy with her bowsprit.

Sometimes she fell away and twisted horribly, rolling her yards down till solid water ran along the top of the bulwarks as though along a tightrope; sometimes the whole Atlantic came sweeping at them from darkness to break over her bows and rush waist deep along the whole length of the ship, leaving men bruised and gasping, spitting out the sea.

With the altered direction of the wind the seas, steeper now, rushed at her from unexpected angles, so that, until the slow coming of dawn, *Huntress* was pounded and hammered till the men who manned her were begging God for a respite from the wild lurching, plunging, rolling.

'He must have heard,' said Primrose with a tired smile as the sunrise broke through the storm clouds, the wind moderated, striking in gusts now, and no longer with the same steady shriek in the rigging.

For the first time since he came on deck some twelve hours before Henryk was able partially to relax his grip. He felt dazed and battered, blinded, utterly exhausted.

The sky flew past in tatters; here and there blue showed through great rents in the scudding clouds.

Huntress was as tired as her crew; she rose more sluggishly to the seas, buried her stern more heavily; the faint clatter of the pumps was more ragged.

'She's by the head, sir.' Gazard, haggard and filthy from his tour of the holds and bilges, made his report to the Captain.

'Very good, Gazard. Keep her afloat for another hour and we should be clear of—' Primrose stopped, eyes widening as they stared ahead into the dawn sky. 'My God!' He whispered the words, then shouted, 'Hold on!'

What was rolling at them was not a wave; it was a mountain of water, forced up from the very depths.

Henryk watched open-mouthed, held motionless in sheer awe. He saw the bows dip into the valley as the towering wall rose high above them to blot out the sunrise, to blot out all life itself.

As the ship began her struggle to surmount that monstrous upheaval he flung himself down, his arms round the breech of the gun; he closed his eyes and clung on with all his strength.

Huntress climbed very steeply up, up towards the clouds. Somewhere a voice was calling on God to save them. She went back on her stern like a rearing horse, but the sea anchor held and dragged her bows through the curling twenty-foot crest of the wave. For an instant she teetered on the top, then plunged downwards with sickening speed, crashing her bows deep into the trough, flooding the forecastle, jarring the very bones of every man in the ship.

But the shipwrights of Chatham had done a good job; her oak timbers were truly laid, and though the fastenings protested in a wild chorus they did not give. The masts shivered in their steps and, here and there, a deck-seam opened under the appalling strain, but she came up shaking herself like a dog, into the sunrise. Bright silver light fanned down through the thinning clouds ahead, striking pale gleams from the tumbled waters.

Henryk got to his feet. His eyes were bloodshot and smarting from the driving spray; he had to clench his chattering teeth;

gingerly he felt the bruises on his aching body. Gazing numbly at the sun he had never expected to see again, he heard vaguely Primrose's calm voice saying, 'There's work to be done, Mr Stodart. Turn up the hands, if you please.'

The Captain emptied water from his hat. He gave the shivering men on the quarterdeck a tired smile.

'A mug of grog would be welcome, eh, lads?'

They nodded silently, still dazed by the night they had spent.

'Rum, Mr Stodart, without the water.'

'Aye, aye, sir.'

'And an extra tot for the man who spots the rest of the squadron.'

But though they went up the swaying shrouds, warmed by the raw rum, staring across the wastes of sea, now slackening to a heavy swell over which the ship soared and swooped, they saw nothing except a minute storm-petrel beating into the last of the wind.

The topmen loosed the courses and topsails to dry; they struck the main yard for inspection, then rigged the top-gallant yards in a gentle north-east breeze, the fringes of the trade winds. As swiftly as it had dropped, the glass rose again, bringing blue skies and life-giving warmth to the ship.

The pumps worked to empty the ship; Gazard inspected every inch. Then hammocks and bedding were brought up to dry and wet clothing flapped in the rigging.

Primrose took sights with prickling eyes and pored over his charts in company with Mr Cromer, striving to fix the position, to guess—for that was all he could do—the whereabouts of his other ships. If they'd run before the storm they could be a hundred miles to the south-west of him. But at least they'd got their orders; in the event of dispersal rendezvous to the west of the Canaries. He came on to the quarterdeck, immaculate in proper uniform again.

'Two points to larboard, helmsman. Course east by south-east.'

'East by sou'-east it is, sir.'

The man spun the wheel.

'Set all sail to the royals, Mr Stodart.' They would head to the south-east on the north-east trades, then turn northwards and make a sweep towards the distant Azores, then east again to get on to the Spanish trade route for, with or without the squadron, his orders were to watch for the convoys; then eastwards to wait off the Canaries. Though what he could achieve with one ship of the line ... He stifled his gloomy thoughts and commenced to walk the deck, glancing now and then at the men drying out the guns, up at the sails, revelling in the ordered bustle of the decks. Reassured, he went to his cabin for the first moment's rest he had taken in the last twenty-eight hours.

*   *   *

For two days now the wind had lain two points abaft the beam and so steady there was no need to do more than glance with relief at the well-filled sails as the ship rose and fell across a polished green swell. Extra look-outs manned every vantage point but sighted no sails.

'They'll 've been blown over the Line,' Swaine opined. 'Or else foundered with all 'ands.'

Primrose clambered to the maintop and swept the rim of the sea with his glass. For a while he remained there, the wind cool on his neck, watching the silver glint of the flying-fish bouncing and ricocheting over the swell; the faithful petrel running in their wake on skittering legs and outstretched wings, hopping over lanes of bronze weed drifting south-west across their path.

Then a minute patch of white gleamed for an instant, thrusting above the western horizon, sinking back out of sight. He held the sails in his glass as they rose one by one from the Atlantic.

He waited, curious to see which man would report the sighting first.

'Sail-ho!' the foretop look-out called excitedly to the deck.

'Report position then,' snapped 'Mr You-sir'.

'One point off starboard bow, sir. Six miles. A ship of the line, sir. I can see her rig.'

Primrose made his way to the deck.

'Frigate, Mr Wood,' he corrected quietly. 'I think it's *Wild Goose*.'

'You, sir, in the fore-top,' bawled the Second Lieutenant. 'Don't you know the difference between a seventy-four and a frigate? Great God, sir, I think your eyes—'

Wild Goose rejoined them shortly before dusk, looking as jaunty as ever and amazingly beautiful against the glow of sunset. She took station two cables' length on the starboard beam and both crews lined the bulwarks listening to the frigate captain shouting his news through a speaking trumpet.

'. . . ran before the storm . . . damned lucky not to founder . . lost sight of *Hurricane* and *Termagant* . . .'

'Good to have you back,' shouted Primrose. The crews waved and cheered and ceased to feel quite so on their own.

For the morning watch Henryk went on look-out in the bows. The night was clear and brilliant with stars; a few glowing wisps of cloud hung round a three-quarter moon. He made his way towards the forecastle, stepping over the motionless forms, for the lower deck was an oven and many of the hands chose to sleep in the open.

'Nothing to report, mate. *Wild Goose* over there—' he jerked his thumb at the shadowy vessel gliding level with them across the track of the moon.

The man departed.

Henryk leant over the rail. The sea curled away from the bows in rolls of pale sparkling flame and the phosphorus twinkled along the side. The wind was steady and warm and carried a sea-weed smell; the rigging sang with a contented, peaceful note. He watched the glittering sea and the masts swaying across the stars and looked ahead into the shining darkness, wondering briefly what lay there, waiting beyond the starlit curtain. A block squealed, a man called out in his sleep; a drowsy murmur of talk rose from a group of the watch sitting on the longboat among the clear-cut shadows of the sails.

At that moment Henryk felt a sudden sense of great well-being and, in some strange way, security. His body was fit and brown; his hands and feet hard as the deck and ropes below them; every muscle tuned to a peak by the physical exercise. Since Funchal they had eaten well and sucked the sunshine into their bodies with the flesh and juice of unlimited fruit and vegetables.

Round him were men he had come to admire and even, in a few cases, to like. They might be illiterate, foul-mouthed, ignorant of anything beyond this ship that was their home, their life, and yet when the shot and the splinters were flying you knew they would fight till they died. After all, he thought drily, what else could they do? A soldier could at least turn tail and run but here, in this wooden prison, where was there to run? Hearing a quiet step behind him Henryk straightened up from the rail.

'A fine night, Barinski. But too hot for sleep.'

Primrose was without his coat but his sword-belt hung across his white shirt; the buckles of his shoes caught the moonlight. He stood in silence, gazing towards the frigate, one raised hand gripping the forestay.

'A pretty sight,' he said. 'A very pretty sight.' Henryk remembered Mendel's words as he had gazed across at *Culloden* and *Edgar*—how many years ago?

'Yes,' he agreed.

'Somewhere out there,' went on Primrose, nodding at the moonlit sea, 'enemy ships are heading for Spain.'

Extraordinary how easy he found it to talk to this man; his own conversation did not have the usual contrived, almost false, ring in his own ears.

'Under the same bright moon,' said Henryk quietly.

Primrose looked at Henryk. The line of the scar cut his face in two; his teeth gleamed in the dark shadows of his beard. What must it be like for a man of intelligence, a sensitive man and a foreigner, to endure the rigours and privations of the lower deck?

'This is not your war,' he said abruptly.

'No,' answered Henryk. 'It is not.'

'Yet the Third Lieutenant tells me you fought for the French.'

Henryk nodded.

'As an officer?'

'Yes.'

It did not seem strange to Primrose that the Pole, in the privacy of the darkness with only the sea and the wind to hear them, should address him as an equal. But had Stodart heard Barinski's tone he would certainly have suffered a seizure. The thought afforded Primrose quiet amusement.

'Last time I went to war,' Henryk said musingly, 'I wore the uniform of France. Now I go barefoot and am expected to blow anything French to small fragments. To me that is quite ironic. Yet it does not matter so much. The shot sound the same whichever flag you follow. You fire first, you fire fast, and you do not allow yourself to think too much of what you are doing. In that way you become a good soldier—or sailor—and perhaps you stay alive. If Fate wants me to live my life at war, well then' Henryk shrugged, 'I suppose I must make the best of it and fight to the best of my ability.' He stopped and looked up at the moon. 'With my head, Captain, but not my heart. There is only one country I'd fight for with my heart and that is Poland.'

Primrose heard the fire and sadness in his voice. 'I have always had a great curiosity to visit your country,' he said. 'And Russia too. The Navy has sent me to many strange corners of the world but I've never been closer to Europe than the shores of Quiberon Bay.'

'Perhaps, after this war is ended?'

'No, Barinski. My life is here. Until old age or a round shot gets me, my life is here.' He patted the rail, looking along the dark deck of his ship. 'You have been to Russia?' he asked wistfully.

'Yes.'

'To Moscow?'

Henryk nodded again.

Primrose sighed. Here he was, Commodore in command of a squadron—even though the greater part of it was missing, he thought wrily—lord of all he surveyed, and yet it was this man, a lowly quarter gunner for all his background, who had seen the golden domes of Muscovy.

For Primrose had read books by travellers who had visited the land of the Tsars; his imagination had been fired by their tales of strange and savage peoples: Tatars and Cossacks and such, and barbaric wonders quite beyond the province of a dull sea-dog like himself. Not only was he an avid reader but, to the best of his ability, a keen student of history, of events beyond the narrow confines of his ship. He liked to feel that *Huntress* was playing some part in these events, however unimportant; that one day her name might feature in the accounts of this war.

He questioned Henryk keenly about life in Russia, listening with rapt interest as Henryk told him of St Petersburg and the magnificent palaces lying along the Gulf of Finland. 'Do they wear Western dress? ... Is it true that Peter the Great was seven foot tall? ... Does the snow really cover the houses right to the eaves? ... The nobles now, can they read and write ...?'

Henryk answered everything to the best of his ability.

'Tell me,' Primrose continued after a little silence. 'Those scars on your back. How—'

'They wanted information I could not give.'

'Could not—or *would* not?' The Captain smiled. This would be a difficult man to break. If three years of the Navy—

'I think if they'd gone further with me I would have told them everything they asked.' He'd have told them his purpose in Russia, he'd have brought Kasia herself to the dungeons of the Secret Chancellery—anything to escape the unendurable torture of the knout. He knew that, had always known it, and the knowledge made him sick with disgust.

'When the war is over, will you go back?' asked Primrose in an effort to ease the pain he saw on the other's face. 'To Poland, that is.'

For a long moment Henryk did not answer. 'I don't know,' he said at last, his eyes fixed on the jib-boom gently rising and falling. 'I don't know.'

The years of unquestioning service, of dumbly carrying out his duty, of rarely having to think for himself, had impaired his power of decision; they had toughened his body and weakened his mind. He had become a machine, a fighting machine, expert at his job but with few thoughts of any future beyond the next meal, the next dawn.

'Let's get this war over first. Then perhaps—' Perhaps what? 'Perhaps I'll remain at sea and become an admiral.' He laughed softly. 'The first Polish admiral ever to walk a quarterdeck.'

Primrose regarded him quizzically, but did not speak. Both men stood immersed in their own thoughts.

'You're a good gunner,' said Primrose suddenly. 'The Navy has cause to thank men like you.'

And you too, Henryk thought. England could never repay the debt she owed to men like Commodore Primrose.

'Where did you learn your English?' the latter asked.

'In Rome.'

'You were there long?'

'Three years.'

Three years of trying to forget the horror of Volochisk; trying to forget the steel that opened his face, the girl he had loved and lost: three wasted years of drifting, drinking, whoring—until Amande de Stainville lured him to Paris with her big white body and hungry mouth, to the great house of her uncle, the Duc de Choiseul, where, after six short and hectic months, he found that lust was no substitute for love.

The Captain yawned and stretched, glancing at the first streaks of dawn pink across the eastern darkness. 'It'll soon be daylight. Another hot day by the feel of it. Well, I've enjoyed our chat.

Some other day you must tell me more of your travels.'

'With much pleasure,' said Henryk and meant it.

'Well, good-night, Barinski,' Primrose said abruptly, and walked away.

'Good-night, sir.'

He watched the white figure vanish in the darkness.

'Deck below!' The cry from the foretop was urgent. 'Sail-ho! To the sou'-east. Three sail of the line, sir, and more topsails coming up fast from the sunrise.'

Henryk sprang into the rigging. Along the horizon, he made out rows of little white patches; the upper sails of at least ten ships.

For the moment at least his own problems were resolved.

* * *

By ten o'clock the enemy convoy was hull-up, beating slowly across the light wind which had veered easterly and slackened appreciably on a course that would take the leading ships close to windward of *Huntress* and *Wild Goose*.

As yet Primrose had not given the orders to go to quarters but the men had moved instinctively to be near their action stations, and the crews of Henryk's four 9-pounders were lounging in the sunshine near their guns.

'Christ above,' swore Fitch. 'Look at all that bloody prize money going past our noses.'

Fifteen merchantmen crammed with the riches of Peru, escorted by four sail of the line and two frigates. Leading to leeward of the left hand line of ships, a big three-decker flying the red and gold of Spain.

'By God, what a sight,' exclaimed Cameron. The ships were carrying every stitch of canvas they could hold; the water sparkled at the blunt bows as they drove stolidly northwards for Spain, seeming to disregard the two British ships tacking slowly towards them into the teeth of the flaccid little wind.

'About ship,' ordered Primrose for the tenth time. The helmsman put the wheel over.

'Helm's a'lee, sir,' he sang out.

'Fore-sheet, jib and staysail-sheets let go!' Stodart roared angrily in a filthy temper. Fitch had echoed the thoughts of every man in *Huntress*: all that gold so near, enough to make rich men of them all, and yet with the wind against them and treacherous —the sails flapped thunderously as the ship came round—and without *Hurricane* and *Termagant*, it might just as well be safely in the vaults of Cadiz.

'Off tacks and sheets! Come on, wake up there! Get 'em moving smarter, Bos'n, or I'll know the reason why.'

The ship lay head to wind, momentarily in irons. 'Mainsail haul!' The hands hauled on the lee-braces. 'Walk away with 'em lads!' She heeled slowly on her new course that might, if the wind held, bring her within range of the three-decker.

'Beat to quarters, Mr Stodart.'

'Aye, *aye*, sir.'

The brave challenge of the drum carried across the water towards the Spaniard now no more than four miles away. In her path lay *Wild Goose*, in trouble with her fore topmast, sprung during the storm and not adequately repaired.

'Get her out of there. For God's sake, man.'

Henryk was close enough to hear the Captain's muttered words; he saw Primrose's fingers tapping on the bulwark and did not envy him his position.

Since dawn Primrose's brain had grappled with the situation. He knew he must close and cause what damage he could to the convoy before himself being overwhelmed. Make the merchantmen scatter, delay them, perhaps even sink a couple. With *Wild Goose* —but the frigate was semi-crippled, without a shot being fired. Anxiously he watched the men swarming in the fore rigging, working desperately to free the hanging topmast with its mass of sail and cordage, then his eyes shifted to the Spanish ship. With her huge spread of canvas she was moving faster than *Huntress*; she'd reach the frigate first. He swung round.

'Secure for action. Load the guns.'

With the swift orderly chaos of disciplined men the ship was prepared for action as she inched closer to *Wild Goose*, creeping into the wind.

'Ship secured for action, sir. Guns loaded and run out.'

'Very good, Mr Stodart.'

Primrose never took his eyes off the disabled frigate. Another

165

quarter of an hour and they'd be close enough to help her. Raising his voice he called out, 'I'll want straight shooting today, you gunners.'

'You'll get it, sir,' said Henryk in answer.

Six hundred men stood at their battle stations; the sail trimmers waited aloft on the yards; the Marines had run clumping to line the bulwarks and up into the rigging with muskets primed. The screens before the magazine were drenched with water; the decks were thickly sanded, the shot piled ready and the gun layers swung their linstocks. In the Captain's cabin Sweetapple cursed indignantly at the gun-crews manning the twin 12-pounders as he stowed away Primrose's precious books and glass in a packing-case.

Far below, Mr Boosey placed the rum bottle on the sea-chests among his tools and waited.

The whole ship waited as the sun rose higher in a bright blue sky.

If I was in command of the convoy, thought Primrose, and with the wind as it is, I would keep them together and shepherd them northwards, detaching two ships of the line to contain the threat of *Huntress* and *Wild Goose*.

In the distance, beyond the Spaniard on the same course, his glass picked up a two-decker, French by the looks of her; the other two must lie to windward of the convoy. Vainly he searched the sea astern for a sight of his own missing ships. With them he could have smashed this convoy, ripped it apart.

The sharp report of a gun brought him to the weather rail in time to see the spray falling back from a near miss on *Wild Goose*'s quarter. Smoke puffed from the frigate's deck as she answered with her 6-pounder pop guns; holes appeared in the Spaniard's sails; splinters flew from her fore-peak but she did not alter course.

Huntress's bow guns were masked by *Wild Goose* and could not fire. In a fury of frustration, Stodart cursed the seamen at the braces, but it was not their fault the ship moved so slowly for the wind had grown more fickle, now and then dying away completely. The crew watched horrified and helpless as the towering ninety-gun ship bore down slowly, massively, relentlessly, on the hapless frigate.

At a bare cable's length, with the frigate's small shot thudding home, the Spaniard put his helm up and came into the wind.

Henryk just had time to take in her beauty—brown and scarlet streaks between the gaping gun-ports; great gilded poop lanterns, raking black masts and her rigging brilliant with banners, a fierce glitter of steel along her rail—and then all was hidden in a pall of dirty white smoke ripped with flame as she gave *Wild Goose* her full broadside.

In a splitting roar of flame and whirling debris the little ship simply disappeared, flung in fragments to the sky, blown from the face of the sea by her exploding magazines. Black smoke hung above the water as the shattered remains of the frigate and her crew fell back into the boiling sea.

Wild Goose no longer existed, destroyed with an ease as contemptuous as it was thorough, leaving the crew of *Huntress* stunned by the suddenness of her end. They watched in bitter silence as the Spanish ship resumed her course, her rigging alive with cheering, waving men.

'Any gun that bears, fire,' shouted Primrose hoarsely. If they could not save her they could at least try, from this moment, to avenge the frigate which had sailed in close company with them for the last five months. The bow guns opened fire but the range was too great and the balls pitched harmlessly into the sea well short of the Spanish ship.

For *Huntress* now the wind died completely and they lay utterly becalmed watching helplessly as the convoy crept slowly past well out of range. In a torment of self-recrimination Primrose had the hands dismissed from quarters, except three men standing by each gun.

'Lay a course to intercept her, Mr Stodart.' He pointed towards the French ship of the line coming up very slowly to starboard. Without another word he went to his cabin, his face set in a taut mask.

''E couldn't 'ave done nothing else,' said Fitch with surprising sympathy. 'None of us couldn't, not with this damned wind.'

Henryk found his gaze drawn, against his will, to the mess of planking and blackened canvas, broken spars, barrels and other objects that marked *Wild Goose*'s grave. Beyond it, the merchantmen, close-hauled, catching a kinder breeze, sailed serenely past. Now and then *Huntress*'s sails felt a breath of this same wind and she heeled slightly on her new course which would bring them some time that day within range of the French two-decker. He sat himself down with his back to the gun-truck and closed his eyes.

'Before Culloden,' said Cameron, squatting beside him, 'I remember I had no sleep for two days.'

'Before Rossbach,' said Henryk with a smile, 'I ate and slept like a hog. It doesn't make any difference once the guns are shouting—they keep you awake well enough.'

He lifted his face to the sunshine and tried not to dwell too deeply on what was approaching over the shining sea.

*   *   *

Slowly, in silence, *Huntress* drifted down the track of the moon towards the enemy ship, her sails set so as to drive her sideways down the wind.

Since late afternoon of the previous day the two ships had manoeuvred to obtain the weather gauge.

The Frenchman, the *Richelieu*, an eighty-gun ship, was handled well; her Captain and crew knew their jobs, but *Huntress* had the edge and, sailed superbly by Primrose, had hauled to windward as the moon rose at two o'clock.

'Here's one that's not going to shirk a fight,' Primrose remarked to Stodart. 'She's been left to deal with us.' The moonlight shone coldly on the gold lace and snowy breeches of the Captain's full-dress uniform, on the extra polish given to his shoes by a shaking but willing Sweetapple. His hand rested on the bent hilt of his sword as he watched intently the dark shape of the *Richelieu* growing larger and more distinct. She bulked huge and menacing in the night.

Both ships were silent. Usually the French seamen gave loud and excited vent to their feelings for some considerable time before action, but now they manned their ship in menacing silence.

On *Huntress's* quarterdeck gunners held the glowing linstocks hidden below the bulwark, crouching beside their guns, eyes fixed in helpless fascination on the black squares of the enemy gun-ports.

'I'll have the battle ensign run up,' ordered Primrose.

The great blue flag broke at the main, standing out towards the French ship.

'Steady, lads. Stand steady. If any man fires before the order I'll have him on a grating.' Primrose's clear warning could be heard travelling through the silent ship, passed below by the midshipmen.

'Jesus,' muttered Fitch. 'I'd take fifty lashes, only let 'im give the order to fire.'

Not more than two cable lengths separated the ships; in the Frenchman a drum rattled briefly. When the French drums had beaten out the *pas de charge* at Rossbach, Henryk remembered grimly, the soldiers of France had fought like demons. Now he moved between his two starboard guns, encouraging quietly, looking along the barrels, correcting—'Left, Elmquist ... Bring her up a bit, Fitch. D'you want to soak us all with the shot?' His mouth was very dry, his palms sticky, he imagined they must all hear the urgent thump of his heart.

Now and then Primrose gave out a quiet order that altered the trim of the sails, kept her beam-on to the *Richelieu*.

Closer. Closer. Relentlessly the gap closed. Henryk could not keep still; his head moved continuously, glancing at Primrose, at his guns, back to the looming shape from which, any second now, would come a storm of death. He swallowed repeatedly to keep down the sickness in his stomach. He heard an order in French telling men to stand ready to fire, and found he was shivering violently though the night was warm and most of the men were naked to the waist.

The little song of the wind in the rigging was low and sweet; between the ships the sea was ruffled silver and surged with a wonderfully peaceful note. Henryk, screwing his eyes tight shut and clenching his hands till the nails bit into his palms, prayed silently for life.

'Steady. St-e-ady.' The captain's voice was calm.

Less than a cable between them now. Primrose gripped the bulwark; the sweat trickled down his body; he also prayed that he should keep his nerve and not give the order too soon—or too late. He raised the speaking trumpet, moistened his dry lips. No, not yet.

The faces of the French showed as pale dots; dark figures clustered in the tops. Close on eighty guns faced each other: eighty muzzles, poking black and silent from the ports, waiting to fling a hurricane of iron.

'Helm up a little,' he ordered sharply. She was falling away, pointing her bows too much at the French ship. When the moment came, and by God it was near, every gun must bear.

'Steady as she goes.'

'Steady it is, sir.' The Quartermaster's voice was as imperturbable as if he were taking her into Torbay. *Huntress* is a lovely ship, Primrose thought with a sudden twinge of sadness, she's too lovely to be destroyed. He shook his head quickly.

'Ready, gunners?' he asked over his shoulder.

'Ready, sir.' Henryk's answer was calm.

'God be with you then,' said Primrose under his breath; 'God be with us all.' He longed to call out to them, good luck to you all, but this was no moment for histrionics.

'Mr Stodart. Pass the order below. Stand by to fire.'

'Aye, aye, sir.'

At every gun the crew stood clear, the gun-layer blew on the raised linstock, the men were frozen in the dim light of the battle-lanterns, and on the open decks in the cold wash of the moon.

'Now,' breathed Cameron. 'Claymore—*now*.' He broke into a little Gaelic song, fierce and mournful as a gull's cry. Henryk crossed himself, instinctively crouching slightly below the protection of the bulwark. If I get through this, he thought bleakly, then all I'll ask of God is a life of peace miles from the sea and the sound of guns.

Primrose forced himself to stand erect, though every nerve in his body cried out for him to fall on the deck and crawl away to safety. He put his lips to the speaking trumpet. The range below a hundred yards. He took a deep breath. Give it to the count of five. Slowly. Slowly.

'Three—four—' He heard a sharp command from across the water and shouted with the full strength of his lungs, '*FIRE!*'

The night was shattered by the blast of flame and the roar of *Huntress*'s broadside; the ship heeled against the wind as nearly forty guns leapt back in the tackles. Smoke enveloped her and through it came the shrieks of the men wounded by that first murderous discharge.

'Good work boys! Fire at will. Fire at will—' The Captain's words were drowned by the *Richelieu*'s answering broadside, aimed high for the rigging as was the French custom.

Blinded by the sheets of flame, Henryk threw up his hand across his eyes. The air all round him trembled to the passage of the shot; shrouds, stays, braces parted, curling like whips in the smoke. The deck jumped to the impact of the balls below and a blizzard of splinters scythed among a group of Marines, tumbling men from the yards.

Henryk's guns had already fired again.

'That's m'beauty,' Fitch was shouting. 'That's m'darling.'

'Powder—ram—load and ram!'

Back leapt the gun as the flame ripped the smoke through which *Richelieu* was hardly visible; in went the sponge with a hiss to clean out the hot barrel.

The smoke was pierced and lit by the flash of guns, the little stabs of flame from the muskets and the balls whispering, spattering on the masts, whining into the air, lost in the gigantic noise.

The ships lay at seventy yards, blindly pounding each other; no careful aim was possible for, with every gun that fired, the smoke thickened into a reeking fog.

Henryk's fear had gone, blown away by the crazed din of battle. His only thought was to keep his guns in action. Croaker, in the act of loading No. 1, fell forward over the gun, a dirty purple hole in his forehead.

'Get him clear! Get this gun firing!' With Cameron, Henryk pulled the dead man clear.

'It's hot work.' Cameron's eyes glittered in his blackened face. He laughed wildly. Henryk laid and fired the gun himself, aiming at a patch of deck visible for an instant. He saw figures flying in the air from his shot. Spray pattered on him from a ball striking short.

'Mr Tregotha!' Primrose had to use his trumpet to make himself heard above the crash of the guns. 'Get below. Mr Frobisher —I want two broadsides—'

'Aye, aye, sir.' As the boy turned to obey his head vanished from his body. For a second the trunk remained upright on its feet, then crashed to the deck.

Primrose gulped horribly and wiped frantically at his face; from the corner of his eye he saw the Quartermaster go down, part of the wheel vanish.

'Mr Stodart. A man on the wheel!' Though God knows why. There were no orders he could give him, except to stay there until he too was killed. 'Barinski! *Barinski!*'

Henryk shook his head to clear it.

'Get below and tell Mr Frobisher—'

Primrose repeated his order so close that Henryk felt the Captain's mouth against his ear. He shoved past Midshipman Lloyd at the hatchway; the boy's eyes stared at him blindly, his mouth hung open, he was shaking his head like a dog emerging from the water.

The heat of the lower deck was appalling; figures were just visible in the swirling smoke; here and there the dim red glimmer of a lantern played on dismounted guns and bodies sprawling half buried in debris. Beneath his feet the deck shuddered and trembled to the heavy thud of shot striking the sides. Tears blinded him from the raw sting of the powder. He saw Swaine bring down the linstock; the explosion of the gun was obliterated in the monstrous din. Swaine grinned at him, shouted something, but he might just as well have been a mute.

Black torsos streaming with sweat, teeth gleaming in snarls of rage, fear, frantic effort ... the powder monkeys staggered through the smoke bringing more powder, more shot for the ravenous guns, clambering over the dead and wounded with their loads.

Henryk, searching for Frobisher in the dark, choking fog, came upon Bunch. The merchant of Brighton, his flabby white body thick with powder grime, was lugging a bucket of shot, yelling in a high voice, 'Give it to 'em! Oh, my God, give it to 'em!'

Henryk put his face close to Bunch's.

'Frobisher? Where's Frobisher?'

Bunch pointed to the shadowy main mast.

The Fourth Lieutenant lay against the base of the mast. His normally ruddy face was ghastly in the lantern light; a splinter a foot long had pierced his stomach. But he was still gasping out orders, unheard, more and more weakly.

'Fire—when—guns—bear. Steady, lads, steady ...'

Gore appeared from the smoke, rubbing his eyes. His hat had gone, his soaking hair was over his face; he was bleeding from a furrow on his scalp.

'Broadsides, sir. Captain's orders. Two broadsides.'

Gore shook his head.

'No use—never hear—will try.'

As Henryk left the dying Frobisher and felt his way back to the open deck he heard a few guns going off together, but the broadside was a ragged, feeble affair. On the quarterdeck Cameron and Fitch were fighting the gun alone; Elmquist lay in the scuppers with a shattered leg. The other two men were sprawled headless near the mizzen mast.

Henryk took three men from the idle larboard guns, sending another to the magazine.

'More powder! Hurry, damn you! Hurry!'

The ships were much closer now. Only about thirty yards of water lay between them, already black with wreckage, bodies and *Huntress's* foretopmast hanging over the side. By now all speech was useless. Stunned and half blind they fought on, yard to yard, muzzle to muzzle, so that when opposing guns fired together the ships were linked by a solid sheet of flame.

The decks were slippery, the sand thick with blood. Below, in the hell of the gun-decks, the men were yelling and cursing insanely as the world round them dissolved in flaming horror. Henryk found himself praying wildly for even a moment's pause— please God, let it stop, just for a second. His mind reeled; he felt himself going mad. But he laid the gun at some men gesticulating in the shrouds; yet again it leapt in the tackles and the figures flew apart.

Though the French fought magnificently the years of Primrose's training began to tell, and slowly the *Richelieu's* fire slackened, but her guns still crashed out; stubbornly other men took the place of her gun-crews and fought on blindly. Her Captain fell, three of her officers were swept away in one discharge, yet she would not give in.

The smoke clouds lightened; somewhere the dawn must be coming up. Primrose gazed with a sort of fearful admiration at the blackened, blistered ship, at the tattered white flag still defiant at the mizzen peak. He winced violently, unable any more to control his nerves, at the close hawl of a shot. It was time to finish the business.

'Load with grape!' His hoarse order was passed on by voices. 'Fire at will. Boarders stand by!'

The guns were loaded with eight pounds of broken iron. Each gun that fired spread a tearing storm of death across the *Richelieu's* decks; a blizzard of flying metal entered her gun-ports, smashing down the dazed gunners, ripping her timbers. From that moment the noise abated, and the animal sound of men's voices could be heard again.

Henryk and Cameron seized weapons from the racks and crouched with the rest of the boarders below the bulwarks.

'Lay her alongside, Mr Cromer.' But Mr Cromer was dead with a musket ball in the heart and Primrose took the wheel himself, putting the helm hard down.

Stodart was heard.

'Boarders!' He drew his sword and leapt on the side, clinging to the shrouds. 'Into them, m'lads. Give them the cold steel!'

As the ships came together with a grinding crash the boarders sprang into the shrouds.

Cameron was shouting the war cry of his clan, swinging a boarding axe—'Ye sons of dogs, come here on flesh to feed!'—his eyes red with battle-lust.

Henryk found himself poised to jump the gap, his cutlass ready to cut and hack. A few Frenchmen faced them; he caught the gleam of steel. This was war, when you saw your enemy, felt your hands at his throat. He was calling out in Polish to the men round him, to follow him—Then, suddenly, voices yelling, crying:

'She's struck! Oh, sweet Jesus, she's struck!'

As the rising sun pierced the smoke-pall hanging over the ships, so the flag of France came slowly down. The guns gradually stopped firing. It was over.

The smoke thinned, seeping from the blackened, blistering ships as they drifted gently apart, quiet now except for the screams of the wounded floating hideously across the placid green sea.

'Christ,' said Fitch weakly. 'Suffering Christ, that was worse than *Monmouth*.' He spat on the bloody deck and sat down with his head on his knees.

His words came to Henryk as if from miles away.

*   *   *

The whole ship was filled with the racking sounds of men coughing the powder from their lungs. Along the length of the gun-decks men collapsed by their guns, stretched out face down in the sticky red sand, utterly finished; here and there a man stumbled vacantly among the wreckage.

The morning sun entered through the gun-ports and the shot-

174

holes, the last of the smoke moving lazily in the sunbeams which played warmly on the devastation: on the overturned guns, smashed mess-tables, the welter of broken buckets, ramrods, spilt powder; on the dead and on the maimed.

On the gouged and splintered quarterdeck the sun shone very brightly, blackening the streams of blood and warming the waxen faces of the dying.

Henryk was slumped on the breech of No. 1 with Cameron lying on his back beside him, his chest heaving as if he had run a gruelling race. From head to foot Henryk was slimy with thick black sweat, and trembling as if in the grip of a high fever; his eyes were stinging fiercely and his head ached cruelly; he kept opening and shutting his mouth to clear his ears. He was very conscious of his physical reactions but his brain was hazy and confused; in a sort of dazed way he gradually realised he was still alive and feeling the sun on his face.

A few feet away Croaker gazed back at him with his fixed white stare; Elmquist, half conscious, was groaning softly. Flames were crackling somewhere and the stink of burning drifted across from the *Richelieu*.

'Well done, you gunners. Well done.'

Primrose's voice was a rasping croak. His eyes took in Croaker and the rest of the dead.

Henryk got uncertainly to his feet, trying to smile.

'May I say the same to you, sir.'

'Thank you. Thank you,' the Captain mumbled absently. His dress uniform was torn in a dozen places; his stockings and breeches were splashed; his fresh white linen was almost completely black. His left arm hung limply at his side, blood dripping between the fingers.

Slowly dragging his steps, he went to the rail and stood like a man in a dream, trying to take in the death and destruction dealt to his beautiful ship. Then, with tears running unashamedly down his face, he raised his hat in silent salute to his men and went down among them, picking his way over the torn hammocks and broken spars to the remains of his gig, pausing to pull out a long white splinter sticking up like a spear; to put his hand on the shaking shoulder of Midshipman Lloyd who sat on an overturned gun weeping noisily—he was only just seventeen years old.

Now and then he went on one knee in the sand beside a dying

man, trying to find the right words. He moved about his battered ship, croaking encouragement to the exhausted men who, in many cases, gaped at him uncomprehendingly, stone deaf from the blast of the guns.

In the sunshine Henryk pulled himself together and stirred Cameron with his foot. 'Come on, Ewen, we'll get the Swede to the Surgeon.' It was the first time Henryk had ever used his first name.

They carried the groaning Elmquist below. The ladders leading to the 'tween decks were choked with wounded, and amid a wild chorus of pain they waited their turn by the lower-deck hatchway, gazing dully at the shambles.

Henryk remembered once longing for a war, for a chance to draw his sword as a man of courage, of honour. Well, by heavens, he'd got his war—and what honour was there in this butcher's yard?

'Bring 'em down!' The cry rose from the bedlam of the cockpit where forty-eight wounded lay packed close as herrings in a barrel in the dim light of lanterns and tallow dips.

'Put him here!' Surgeon Boosey, spattered from forehead to ankle, his bare arms bright with a red sheen, wiped the pink sweat from his eyes.

Henryk lowered Elmquist's shoulders on to the stained and crumpled sail covering the sea-chests, deafened by the medley of groaning, shrieking, praying.

Boosey poured rum into the Swede's open mouth, tipped the bottle to his own, then, nodding to his Mate who thrust the slimy length of wood between the man's teeth, he took up his saw.

'Hold him, you two!'

Henryk, sickened by the awful rasp of metal on bone, held down the writhing shoulders, fixing his attention on a boy who crouched scaring the huge hold-rats from the wounded, trying desperately not to hear the high strangled screams of unbearable agony.

'*Hold* him, damn you! How can I work if you let him wriggle?'

The sizzle and stink of cauterising pitch, a convulsive twisting jerk, lips rolled back, a long moaning sigh and Elmquist mercifully lost consciousness.

'Put him over there.'

They laid him between a man with no jaw and one newly dead, and made for the ladder.

Once in the open Henryk took great shuddering breaths of the clean morning air. The *Richelieu* still smoked lazily. A heavy jumble of spars, topmasts and sails trailed over the side; the gilded cherubim on her stern galleries had been blown to pieces; the figurehead of the great Cardinal was smashed to ragged shreds. There was no sign of movement.

He felt the sun on his shoulders and watched with a kind of awe a few fat clouds moving across the blue sky, let his eyes roam slowly, lovingly over the shimmering green sea. Lowering his head, Henryk gave thanks to God for letting him live.

'Get hold of 'em, Bos'n.' Stodart's voice rang out harshly. 'There's work to be done. There's a ship to be put to rights.'

Jem Pike's voice echoed through the ship.

'Off your backsides, m'lads. Rouse up there. Smartly does it now.'

But his voice held a kinder note and he did not use his switcher.

*   *   *

'You'll take her back to England, Mr Gore.'

'Aye, aye, sir.'

The Third Lieutenant stood waiting for Primrose's further instructions while a worried Sweetapple bound up the flesh wound and put the arm into a rough sling. Gore's head was done up in a dirty bandage; his hat was very correctly beneath his arm.

'That's it, sir. Soon be right as rain.'

'Thank you, Sweetapple, you've made a good job. And now my shoes if you please.' His steward searched in the ruins of the cabin, struck by two 24-pound shot.

Primrose had removed his stained clothes and was clean again; in a moment he would return on deck and see to the tidying up of the ship.

'Yes, Mr Gore. Those are your orders. You'll have thirty seamen plus twenty Marines, two midshipmen, Prendergast and Lloyd, two—'

'Prendergast's in the cockpit, sir, without his right arm.'

'Oh—' Thirteen years of age and without his right arm. Damn, thought Primrose savagely. Damn this war. Damn it to hell.

177

'Two bos'n's mates and Yorston,' he went on quietly. 'All I can spare, but you shouldn't find the Frenchmen any trouble, not after—ah, there you are, Stodart.' The First Lieutenant's shoes crunched on the broken glass. 'Help yourself to a glass of claret. It's about the only bottle left unscathed,' Primrose added ruefully.

Every window had gone; the packing-case was matchwood; the sides were scorched and great lengths of veneer were ripped from his dining table.

'A cold voyage home, I fear. With little to read.' He stooped to pick up a mangled book. 'Poor Swift. No critic ever treated him so roughly.' Then he raised his glass. 'To *Huntress*, gentlemen— and to all those who fought her.' His eyes clouded. He did not dare ask the whole awful total of her losses.

It was Stodart who spoke first.

'I've made an assessment of damage and casualties received.'

'Very well, Stodart. I'll hear it if you please.'

He listened quietly to Stodart's mounting catalogue, staring into his glass. The ship rang with the sound of hammers and axes as the wreckage was cleared and the carpenters banged home the shot-plugs.

' . . . Gazard reports her making a little water in the after hold, sir, but nothing the pumps cannot control. Fifty shot-holes in the hull between wind and water; fourteen guns dismounted and two a total loss. Mr Hay reports ninety barrels of powder consumed—'

'Yes, yes, but what about the men?' Primrose could control his anxiety no longer.

'Two officers, two midshipmen and seventy-five hands killed or missing,' said Stodart woodenly. 'Frobisher, sir, and Wood. Midshipman Prendergast died on the table.' Stretched on a sea-chest full of his own small possessions, thought Primrose irrelevantly. He stood with his right hand shading his eyes.

'One officer—er—two officers—' Stodart corrected himself hastily, glancing at the sling. Primrose made a slight gesture of impatience.

'—and sixty-two hands wounded, including the Chaplain, sir, who has lost an eye. By all accounts for a man of God he behaved with great courage, carrying shot to the guns and exhorting the men in the very thickest of the fight.' Stodart sipped his claret. 'A total of one hundred and forty-two dead and wounded.'

'More dead than wounded,' said Primrose without expression. 'That doesn't often happen. Did you say Wood as well?'

'Yes, sir. He died before they got him below. And a mercy it was too.'

Primrose looked out of the broken windows for a long moment then swung round briskly.

'I am sending this prize home under Gore. He speaks French well enough after all his lessons.' He paused. 'By the way, gentlemen, what would your reactions be if I suggested promoting Barinski to Master's Mate?' The officers glanced at each other.

'Come, Mr Gore, you know the man. Have you no views on the subject?'

'Yes, sir, I have. I think he could do it.'

'I agree,' said Stodart with none of his usual argumentativeness.

'And what about the Scotchman?'

Stodart shook his head vehemently.

'Why? He's good material. An educated man.'

'He's a Highlander, sir. Temperamental, moody. A rebel. Still disaffected. Not the right type. Promote him and you'll promote trouble.'

'Very well, Stodart, I'll bow to your judgement in this matter. For the while. Please have the goodness to send for the Pole.'

Henryk was summoned from the grisly task of collecting the dead. Wiping his hands on his trousers, he followed the Marine messenger aft to the Captain's cabin.

'Come in, Barinski, come in.'

Henryk faced the three officers, very conscious of his filthy appearance, and then glanced round the wrecked cabin. Cannonballs, he thought grimly, were impartial things.

'I've decided to promote you,' said Primrose without preamble. 'I have observed your conduct closely, especially in the course of this last action and—'

'Excuse me, sir, but I'd rather not.'

He saw the look on Stodart's face, the tightening of Primrose's mouth.

'Rather not?' burst out the First Lieutenant indignantly.

'I'm a foreigner, sir,' said Henryk quietly and firmly. 'The men would not take kindly to my being put over them.'

'Pray allow me to be the judge of that,' replied Primrose coldly.

'Yes, sir. But I do not want to leave my friends on the lower deck,' he added calmly.

Primrose stared at him in silence, anger sparking in his tired eyes. Henryk met his gaze evenly. For a full half-minute no one spoke.

Two officers dead; the master dead and now he'd be losing Gore. That left him with Stodart, one master's mate and two midshipmen to run the ship. Stodart's shoulders were broad—well, my God, they'd need to be. With a slight shrug, the Captain said, 'I won't force you.' He was himself utterly drained by the last hours. 'But think it over. Later I'll speak to you again.'

'I much appreciate the honour you've done me, sir,' said Henryk very politely.

There was silence broken by the Boatswain's raucous encouragement as he supervised the clearing of the decks. Primrose spoke. 'I shall need you to come with me to the Frenchman, Barinski. My French—but for the moment—you may go now.' The officers watched him leave the cabin, treading carefully among the glass.

'Evidently a proud and stubborn man, gentlemen.'

'He is that, sir,' agreed Gore.

Stodart muttered something under his breath.

For a while Henryk stood at the rail, wrapped in his thoughts. What madness had made him give that answer when another one would have freed him from the gun-deck and, at least, given him slightly better food to eat?

To avoid responsibility? Because he didn't want to be in the position of having to give orders to men who had fought beside him and who were his mates? Though he was excellent at obeying orders, had he perhaps forgotten how to give them? Yet in action, command had come quite easily to him even after three years of knuckling his forehead to gold braid.

He shrugged with a little twisted smile. Whatever the reason at least he had made the decision himself.

As Primrose stood with Gore, Henryk and the surgeon's mate on the *Richelieu*'s torn deck a young French officer came limping up, sketching a vague salute. His frightened eyes and faintly twitching mouth showed what it must have been like to endure the terror of *Huntress*'s broadsides. He began speaking rapidly. Primrose cut him off curtly.

'What does he say, Barinski?'

'He says that two of the officers are wounded and need immediate attention.'

'Oh, he does, does he?' Primrose's tone was savage. He had

been below and the sight had sickened him. God knows, his own ship was in a bad enough state, but this—

Richelieu's hull was ragged with shot-holes, two of her top-masts lay across the waist, guns were flung back pointing to the sky; one hundred and ninety dead, including her Captain, lay hideously scattered about the decks; the living—not one of whom was not spattered and streaked with rusted blood—sat or lay about gazing apathetically at their conquerors. Looking round the decks and listening to the demented bedlam of screams and howls trapped below, rising in formless agony from the hatchways, Henryk was not proud of his gunnery.

'There's scores of poor dogs lying below whose wounds is still open,' put in the Surgeon's Mate.

'The officers—please. Those *canaille* later.' Henryk translated.

'In a British man-o'-war,' said Gore in his slow French, 'all the injured are equal. The officers wait their turn even if it's only a common seaman under the knife.'

'Savages,' spat the French officer, his eyes sparking with anger. 'What savages!'

'Was it not your own King who said, "I am at war with England, but not with humanity?"' asked Henryk quietly.

'All right then,' snapped Primrose. 'Enough of this palavering. There's the devil of a lot to be done, Mr Gore, before this ship's ready to make sail.'

Gore gazed round him, wondering rather hopelessly where to start; he too was suffering badly from reaction and wanted only to lie down or get drunk or both.

'Yes, sir.'

'First, get the dead overboard.' The sickly sweet smell of death rose with the mounting heat of the sun, clinging to the very shrouds.

'The Frenchies won't like that, sir. They take their dead home with 'em for Christian burial. I don't—'

'I'm well aware of their habits,' snapped Primrose. 'But I'll advise you to heave 'em over the side. You've eighteen hundred miles between you and Drake Island; you've a ship taking water faster than a thirsty cow and God's own hell to clear up below. You can't have your holds packed with rotting bodies. Over the side, Mr Gore, over the side.'

'Aye, aye, sir,' said Gore, grateful to Primrose for taking the decision from his shoulders.

On the way back to *Huntress* Primrose sat hunched in the stern-sheets of the quarterboat with his eyes closed. Just before they reached the ladder he looked up, met Henryk's eye and said in a low bitter voice, 'By God, it's a bloody business we're in.'

His eyes were deeply troubled.

*   *   *

Seventy-eight canvas shapes lay in neat rows along the deck; two of them covered by Union flags. Henryk wondered which hammock contained what was left of Matthew Swaine who had served in England's ships for almost all of his life and ended it smashed in a dozen bits by case-shot. Unhonoured, unmourned except for a short while by those who remembered his rough kindness, he would go with the others; the brave, the cowards, the true seamen, the pressed men, the officers, sliding down the grating.

The Reverend Dunsterville, ashen-faced, suffering terribly from his wound, ground out a few short phrases, holding to the rail for support. The Captain and his officers removed their hats.

' ... and so we commit these, the bodies of our brave, departed comrades to the deep.' Dunsterville's voice faded weakly. Staggering slightly and pressing the bandage to the red darkness of his empty eye-socket, he left the deck.

'Commence,' ordered Primrose sharply.

The Marines raised their muskets to the sky; the disciplined crash of six volleys rang out as Frobisher and Wood went down the grating from under the flags.

A single drummer struck the dead-beat as the long procession went into the sea. A white splash, a canvas shape for a moment erect from the water and then each was gone, dragged into the depths by the weight of a shot at the feet.

The last of their bodies went over; the water smoothed over the hole it had made; the drum was silent.

As *Huntress* rose to the swell, the breeze hummed an uneven little song in her damaged rigging and the sound of Primrose's preparatory throat-clearing was loud.

'They've gone, lads, and may God rest their souls.' He raised his voice. 'And now, if any of us want to see the Lizard again, there's more work to be done.'

He replaced his hat, made as if to go, then turned back to face his crew. They were filthy still, for a shot had smashed the galley stove and there would be no hot water, nor hot food either for many hours. The black sweat of battle clung to their bodies; they stank of powder and the blood of their comrades.

'England will be grateful when she hears of this day's work,' he said. Then, feeling that possibly his words had been altogether too fanciful, he growled out a brusque, 'Carry on, Mr Stodart,' and retired hurriedly towards the round house, followed by a few feeble cheers.

'That'll do,' roared Stodart. 'Get back to your work. I want this deck shipshape by sunset.'

'There goes a great man,' said Cameron as they bent to the task of sorting out the damaged hammocks.

Henryk glanced at his friend in some surprise.

'He may be an Englishman but by God he's a good one.' Cameron bent stiffly to pull a long sliver of wood from the planking and toss it over the side.

'Aye,' agreed Fitch. 'They'll make an admiral of 'im one day or there ain't no bloomin' justice nowhere.'

He swore at a tangle of hammock netting and shredded canvas.

Before he came to *Huntress* Henryk had never given much thought to England or the English. In Paris he had listened to impassioned denunciations of their hypocrisy, double-dealing, complacency and well-disguised lust for world dominance. In Rome he had met Englishmen and Scotsmen and for the first time marvelled that so small an island could contain two such different peoples. At Konarski's he had learnt of the Englishmen's great love of freedom secured for them by their barrier of sea and by these ships in which freedom was unknown.

But now he knew them better for what at heart they were: stubborn men, slow to real anger but when roused then truly murderous. Less excitable than the peasants of Poland but born with the same inherited breed of dogged courage mixed with a strange brand of fighting madness.

Yes, he knew more of the English now.

'England may be grateful but I'll be mighty glad when I sees the colour of her money.' Fitch inspected a blackened object closely, turning it over in his hand before tossing it over the side.

They worked on steadily, slowly restoring order to their ship as the sun fell lower in the sky and the breeze fell away, leaving the two crippled ships rising and falling over the long, lazy swell.

'The Jew,' said Fitch. 'Young Gammon, poor old Mat, all gone, every one of 'em. And look at Brinski and me, not a scratch on us.' He chuckled. 'No bloody round shot'll ever get Joseph Fitch, Christ no, 'e were born for the gallows.'

Eight bells were struck. Jem Pike's voice echoed along the deck. 'Starboard watch to the deck pumps! Get some o' that stink off yer hides! Come on, move yerselves there!'

Henryk waited his turn, standing by a jagged hole in the bulwarks, hearing the laughter of men as they twisted and turned under the pump, revelling in the play of water on bodies that still lived and felt. A few hours before, they had cursed and bellowed with fear and the lust to kill, destroy, and now their gaiety drowned the faint screams that still rose from the bowels of the ship.

As the sun sank into the sea beyond the *Richelieu*, so the battered hulk stood out blacker, her damaged rigging like a broken spider's web against the dying glow.

For the fourth time God had let him live. Volochisk, Rossbach, Quiberon Bay and now this. In the last hours he had felt the wind of fifty shot and yet his skin was unbroken.

A corpse, unshrouded, floated past the ship face-up, just visible, rising to the smooth crest of the swell, down a long dark slope, and it looked as if the man slept.

Why was that man bobbing in the water, staring at the sunset with sightless eyes, while he had himself felt the dying warmth of that sun on his face?

Why was one man spared, he asked himself in weary wonder, and the next smashed into oblivion? Was it chance where the shot went, where a man was standing or did God, Fate—? He shook off these profitless thoughts. He'd be better employed below, clearing up the mess, than asking himself riddles. Besides, as Kasia used to tease him when he got too introspective, 'the bread would never be baked if we all sat round asking ourselves and each other questions that have no answer'. 'Be patient, my darling. Wait till you get to Heaven; some know-all up there's sure to have an answer.'

Henryk fingered the torn wood of the shot-hole remembering

her with all the old longing. 'Oh, Kasia,' he whispered. 'Oh, my love.'

The feel of the splintered wood on his fingertips, the whispering breeze on his prickling skin; the breath filling his lungs, even the hunger-ache in his belly, the laughing relief round him, the gentle surge of the sea: he experienced these simple things so vividly, so fiercely that he could only just restrain himself from crying out, 'I am alive. Look at me, all of you, I'm alive—*alive*.'

Suddenly he found himself smiling. Then the smile turned to laughter and, throwing back his head, Henryk laughed as he had not done since he and Kasia had shared the wonder of life together.

*   *   *

On a cold blue day in the New Year three sail-of-the-line headed up the Solent, close-hauled to a brisk northerly breeze, punching aside the choppy little seas in thick dollops of spray.

'I never thought I'd ever be glad to see England.' Cameron blew on his fingers.

'Even Siberia would be welcome after four years of mould and ship's biscuit,' said Henryk.

They were waiting on watch, wrapped in their pea-jackets against the biting February wind, crouching in the shelter of the hammock nettings, the sunshine and warmth of the last six months no more than an improbable dream.

After *Richelieu*, patched and jury-rigged, had started on her long slow journey home, *Huntress* had made for the Canaries where, a week later, she had been rejoined by *Hurricane* and *Termagant* in a joyful reunion. For six weeks the little squadron quartered the ocean, their hunting ground the triangle of sea bounded by Madeira, the Canaries and the Coast of Morocco, but saw nothing except flying fish and dolphins. Then in mid-January a frigate came over the horizon with news of recall to home waters, and now, within the next two hours, they would let go their anchors and come to rest.

The ship was buzzing with rumours: they were to revictual and, after a week of rum and women, to join an expedition to the wondrous islands of the South Pacific. That had come to the lower deck via Bunch and was by far the most popular of the possibilities, except, of course, the miracle that they might be paid off—but few dared even to think of that. They were returning to the Mediterranean—Fitch had overheard the Captain's secretary talking to Mr Columbine. That in all probability they would simply refit and rejoin the Western Squadron off Brest was never mentioned aloud.

'Cutter on the larboard bow, sir.'

Henryk raised himself and peered over the nettings.

From ahead, beyond the Isle of Wight, came the heavy thud of gunfire. Men were on their feet, staring into the wind. The little craft danced towards them over the hurrying white horses.

'What's happening? ... What's ado? ... Are the Frenchies out in the Channel?'

Primrose emerged on to the quarterdeck, joining Stodart and Mr Midshipman Lloyd.

'What's the news, Mr Stodart?'

In answer a voice from the cutter came faintly to them on the wind. Through his glass Primrose made out an officer standing in the bows, a trumpet to his lips.

Midshipman Lloyd's eyes lit up; he commenced his usual excited little dance on the deck.

'Stand still, can't you?' said Stodart. But the boy was too excited.

'It's peace—' he suddenly cried. 'He's saying peace has been declared—'

By now the officer's words were clear to every man on deck and as the cutter came by very close, he waved his hat as he shouted up 'Nivenais and Bedford signed yesterday. The war's over.' He was past, on his way to *Hurricane* with the glorious news.

'The war's over! The war's over!' Up and down the deck the men shook each other's hands, threw their arms round each other's necks; some laughed, some wept; they clambered into the shrouds, on to the guns, into the nettings, cheering, waving.

'Hoist the battle ensign,' said Primrose.

The men's huzza-ing grew louder, wilder, as the stained ensign,

186

holed and ripped, broke from the peak. The watch below came tumbling on deck to share the unbelievable news. But the Captain stood apart. After seven years, suddenly there was no war. At that moment the future for him was uncertain and bleak.

Henryk and Cameron looked at each other in silence, unable to find words.

'I'll have the quarterdeck guns loaded with quarter charges and run out,' ordered Primrose above the happy din. 'Mr Stodart, remind this rabble that we are still at sea, if you please.'

Jem Pike and his Mates moved about the crowded deck restoring order but the men took the blows and curses with a grinning good humour.

'Load with cartridge! Ram home your wad ... Run out your guns!'

For the last time Henryk gave his orders very completely, very correctly.

'No. 1 gun, ready!' Cameron's hand was raised.

'No. 4 gun ready!' yelled Fitch.

Henryk held up his hand to show his four guns were ready.

'Stand steady!' called Stodart when No. 14 had reported.

The linstocks glowed in the wind.

'Fire!' shouted Primrose for the last time.

Huntress shivered as the 9-pounders roared out; the echoes were flung back from the two shores and gulls fled downwind with shrill frightened cries.

'Stop your vents! Sponge out!'

'Secure your guns,' ordered Henryk after they had fired six charges.

'An extra tot of rum for all hands, Mr Stodart,' Primrose called out.

'Aye, aye, sir.'

Henryk sat beside Cameron on a gun, holding his mug between his hands. On the starboard side of the deck Primrose stood by the rail with his back to them, facing England, his hands clasped beneath his coat-tails.

'I know how he must feel,' said Henryk with deep sympathy. 'He loves this ship. And now suddenly he'll find himself without work.'

'He won't be unemployed for long,' said Cameron. 'The world's too small for two great empires. You'll see; France and England will soon be at each other's throats again.'

'But for you and me this could mean freedom.' It was a word Henryk had not dared to allow in his mind for four long years. 'What will you do when we're paid off? *If* we're paid off,' he corrected himself with a smile.

'I? Do? God only knows. I don't know how welcome I'll be in England, though possibly,' he added drily, 'my service for the Hanoverian may count as payment for the crime of having fought for the Stuarts.' His gaze was fixed on the Captain's broad back and for a while he did not speak, then, suddenly turning to Henryk with his eyes alight, he asked impulsively, 'Will you come to Scotland with me?' Not waiting for an answer, he went on, excited as a boy, 'I'll show you the mountains of Lochaber. We can fish as I used to do and go after a stag or two and—'

He broke off crestfallen as Henryk shook his head. 'I'm sorry, Ewen. One day perhaps. But first I am going to Paris.' As he said the words a great weight lifted from his mind.

'Oh . . .' Cameron tried to hide his disappointment. 'If you should change your mind—'

More cheering broke out among the ships and Primrose moved restlessly, shaking his head slightly as though in irritation or disbelief.

'By God,' exclaimed Cameron, striking the gun with his fist, 'I might come to Paris too. His Royal Highness is in France— yes, I'll come, but first I must see Scotland again.' He talked on but Henryk was busy with his own thoughts as he began to consider the decision so suddenly made.

'Tell me,' asked his friend softly, 'that someone you once mentioned, is she in Paris?'

'If only she was, how simple things would be,' Henryk said, and at that moment the future, a second ago so bright, clouded darkly again and seemed once more without hope.

*　　*　　*

Commodore Primrose stood in his usual place at the quarter-deck rail. Within a few hours *Huntress* would be empty and silent. He would spend one more night aboard his ship, then until the renewal of the war he would fret ashore on half pay, useless as a fish out of water, unless by some chance Their Lordships decided to keep his ship in commission and allowed him to retain command.

But he expected she'd join a hundred other ships of the line to idle in ordinary, watched over by a few so-called seamen who knew nothing of her history: of how she had sailed with the van into Quiberon Bay; and had fought an eighty-gun ship to a standstill. They'd treat her simply as a hulk of timber, he thought with a hot surge of anger; they'd allow the cobwebs to grow and the dust to settle and her name to die.

His gaze wandered over the crew mustered below him for the last time. And these were the men who had done it; who had made *Huntress* into the finest seventy-four of the Navy. He sighed.

'They're waiting, sir.' Stodart's sharp whisper cut into his thoughts.

'Ah, yes—ah, thank you.' He took a deep breath.

'Lads,' he began, and stuck. Damn and blast it, what *does* one say at a moment like this? He tried again. 'We've been together now for a long time. Yes, a long time. Some of it was good, some of it was—ah—rotten—' A ripple of laughter rose from the crowded waist. He took courage from the sound.

'I want to thank you for what you've done and to wish you God speed wherever you may go.' He paused. And thank you, thought Henryk warmly, for teaching me the true meanings of kindness and courage, for showing me truly how to lead. The men were very quiet, very attentive, and every face was raised towards the Captain. Just below he caught sight of the Pole's scarred face, the red hair of the Scotchman, the sharp, impertinent face of that rogue Fitch.

'Should *Huntress* sail again and should I be in command then —ah—every man of you will be very welcome back aboard—and that includes you, Fitch.'

That brought a great roar of laughter.

'That's a kindness, sir,' called out Fitch equably.

'Well then, I think that's all I—er—have to say.' Primrose stood clasping and unclasping the rail uncertainly.

A slight commotion was taking place below as Henryk pushed his way to an open space. Raising his voice, he shouted, 'I speak for the ship's company when I say to you, thank you for what you have always tried to do for us. We shall not forget you, sir.'

'No,' echoed a dozen voices. 'We'll always remember old Primmy.'

Primrose stared through a mist at his hands, unable to do more than nod his appreciation.

'A cheer for old Primmy—' yelled an anonymous voice. And not all Jem Pike's invective could stop the thunderous wave of cheering that swept the deck and echoed from the warehouses, startling the gulls from the bollards and bringing sour looks to the cold, pinched faces of the loafers on the quay.

Primrose waved his hand in answer, then, with a last choked 'Carry on, Mr Stodart', went blindly to his cabin.

* * *

The Commssioner, a portly, fussy man, came aboard and paid off the ship's company with a tedious, long-winded reading out of rules and regulations, interrupted by the frequently noisy taking of snuff and the loud fidgeting of impatient men.

They filed past Mr Columbine's table collecting their certificates of money—months of arrears plus the share of prize due to each man for the capture of the *Richelieu.*

'Tower Hill, lads,' he kept repeating. 'Cash 'em on Tower Hill.'

The four original members of No. 8 mess stood together in the line: Henryk, Cameron, Fitch and Elmquist, still clumsy on the wooden leg carved for him by Gazard from a broken spar.

'This all I get?' asked Fitch, waving his certificate indignantly in the air. 'A man wot fought at Quiberon and—'

'Get on, there, move on! Out of the way, Fitchie lad.'

'You're lucky they didn't 'ave you dancing at the yard-arm.'

'See you back when the war starts again.'

'Not me, mate, I'd rather live like an 'og in the woods than serve another spell in the Navy.'

They chattered and shouted, happy as crickets in clover.

'You're a rich man, Brinski,' said Bunch, glancing up from his ledger. 'You'll be able to buy yourself a velvet suit—'

'—and go back to that strange country of yours, eh?' Stodart put in from where he stood by the table.

Henryk smiled at him. 'Should you ever find yourself in Poland, you must of course come and visit me,' he said courteously.

Stodart stared with his mouth open, then burst out laughing. 'Well, God damn me, I will.'

'Will you be asking the Bos'n as well?' enquired a voice. 'Aye, and Yorston too?'

Below, Henryk packed his few possessions in his ditty-bag. The gun-deck was almost deserted, most of the men having already poured ashore in a jostling, shouting throng. Fitch had gone; Elmquist and he had not even said farewell. The mess-tables hung motionless, the guns, secured behind closed ports, stood in black silent rows in the lantern light. Timbers creaked very faintly and he heard the soft sigh of the water along the side as *Huntress* moved to the tide.

The deck was silent but the flickering red shadows were alive with ghosts. The ghosts of men who had gone from the ship; Mat Swaine's slow deep voice; Frobisher's blustering shout. Old Blue Lights—'Breechings, watch the breechings.' Henryk heard in his mind the rumble of the gun-trucks, the pounding of the seas, the ceaseless deep-throated hum of the wind in the chains.

He looked down at Mat's initials carved on the table, at the mast where Frobisher had died, at the cutlasses in the racks and the shot waiting. The voices of the ghosts were very loud in his head. With these men he had shared dangers, hardship, rotten food; with them he had fought the sea and fought the guns; had cursed and wept and laughed, and learnt that there is more to life than oneself.

'Come on, for God's sake, d'you want us pressed into another ship?' Cameron's voice jerked him from the past.

On the quayside Henryk looked up at the scarred, blistered sides, the red mouths of the gun-ports, the naked yards lined with gulls.

'This is the second time we've seen her from the outside in four years.'

'It's the only way I want to see her,' said Cameron shortly. He shouldered his ditty-bag and made for the entrance to a narrow street.

Primrose came on to the quarterdeck. He stood utterly motionless, hunched forward in his cloak, looking about his deserted, silent ship. But what he saw, what his thoughts were, no one could tell.

Henryk raised his hand in salute and farewell. For a moment the two men looked at each other but Primrose did not move except to turn his eyes to the empty topmasts.

Henryk took up his bag.

One of the loafers approached him.

'Spare a copper for a poor man, mate,' whined the man. His breath was sickening with stale gin.

'Get out of my way,' said Henryk with quiet savageness.

'Ah, you blasted sailors. You're all alike. Think you're Jesus Christ and all 'is bloody disciples.'

Henryk glanced back past him. Primrose still stood alone on his quarterdeck, not moving, as if a very part of the ship herself.

Then he was round the corner and the ship and her Captain had gone.

* * *

The wind was fair for France and the Channel packet, under full sail, swooped over a sparkling sea.

Henryk stood in the bows, strangely constricted in his broadcloth suit, neckcloth and the heavy shoes which slid on the heaving deck and had not the grip of horny bare feet. His clothes he had bought out of his accumulated pay and his share of the prize money. In the heavy belt round his waist was enough money to enable him to find cheap apartments and live in modest comfort until he visited the Paris bank and discovered whether after all these years his father's allowance was still being sent from Krakow.

He was shaved and neat, the grease washed from his hair by a London barber; his stomach filled with good food, good wine. He stood in silence watching the coast of France come up ahead, deep in his own thoughts.

It was two days since he had watched Ewen Cameron leave for Scotland. His friend had been light-hearted, laughing at the prospect of seeing his beloved mountains again.

'But I'll come to Paris, never fear.'

'You know where to find news of me then, at Madame Geoffrin's, 372 Rue St Honoré. She'll know where I am.'

Whips had cracked, horns had blown, and the coach was away, rattling and swaying over the rough road that led past Tyburn to the north. Ewen waving and shouting. 'God-speed, Henryk,' until dust hid the coach.

Sadly Henryk had watched it vanish. They had been together for exactly three years, seven months and twenty-one days; they'd worked it out over mugs of ale in a Cheapside tavern. That was a long time in which to share the hardships, privations and dangers which bind men together.

But now the future lay ahead. He must try and put away *Huntress* from his mind, though God knows there were things he would never forget until his death. Just as a man with two broken legs learns to walk again, so he must learn afresh the ways of normal civilised life.

'My God, sir. Is that not a glad sight?' The loud voice brought him from his reflections.

To starboard a British man of war, a seventy-four, patched and worn, was passing on the opposite course. In a flurry of loud orders the packet dipped her topsails in salute. The white ensign at the warship's peak fluttered down in brief acknowledgement.

'By Heavens,' burst out his fellow passenger, a tall young dandy in a suit of yellow velvet and a brown fantail hat, 'It makes the heart of an Englishman beat faster when he sees a ship like that.' He raised his glass and regarded Henryk superciliously, his eyes travelling up and down his simple clothes as if unable to believe what they saw. 'Well, my dear sir, is that not a fact?'

'Oh yes,' said Henryk politely. 'It is indeed.'

'Would we have come through this last war victorious without the brave sailor-lads and their ships?'

'Probably not,' said Henryk coldly.

'You appear to be unmoved by the sight of that magnificent vessel.' The other waved a pale hand towards the gleaming stern galleries beyond the white wake. 'England's glory rests upon the might of her Navy and—'

'The fact is,' interrupted Henryk, putting on his most foreign accent, 'I have not the good fortune to be an Englishman. You must please excuse me, sir, but I know nothing of the sea. In fact it makes me so frightened and I find the motion of this boat not too pleasant.' He put his handkerchief to his mouth in simulated distress.

The stranger stared at him with a barely concealed contempt, then with a muttered 'I'll bid you good-day, then' turned on his heel and went to join a group of passengers who were praising the two-decker loudly.

For a moment Henryk watched the sun striking on the towering sails, the scarlet gun-ports, the sea foaming along her faded side. With what was half a sigh, half a silent laugh, he turned his face towards the coast of France, towards the future.

PART FIVE

THE blustering March wind rushed through the streets of Paris, roaring among the chimney pots, filling the darkness with rain. But in the room where Henryk waited before a fire of sweet-smelling juniper logs, it was warm and snug, even though now and then the heavy crimson curtains stirred uneasily as a squall of lashing rain struck the windows, and the candle-flames bent to the draught. At least, he thought with a little smile, the room doesn't lift and plunge below me. Poor devils at sea in this; there'd be water down the hatches tonight all right.

He glanced round the room. Accustomed for so long to the Spartan squalor of the gun-decks he found the opulence of his present surroundings almost unbelievable: tapestried armchairs stood beside Boulle bureaux of tortoiseshell and brass; griffons played across the rich carpet among the shapely legs of marquetry tables and cabinets; tulipwood and kingwood gleamed in the soft light of naked flame. On the silken limegreen walls hung pictures by Fragonard, Van Loo, Chardin; a seascape by Vernet—if only the sea was always like that, he thought wryly—two miniatures by La Tour.

Beautiful things ... but arranged with no sense of taste or style; too crowded, too heavy for the size of the room, touching on vulgarity. A hotchpotch of lacquer, brocade, marble and porcelain—and more gilt than Primrose's dress uniform.

A footman appeared. 'Madame de Valfons presents her compliments and will be down immediately.' He put the tray on a table by the fire. 'Should Monsieur require a glass of wine he is please to help himself.' The man retired without a sound.

Henryk filled a glass and stood sipping reflectively. He looked at the gilded, white marble clock. Eight o'clock and still in bed. Indisposed the man had said. Henryk remembered these 'indispositions' of Amande's; they were already growing more frequent

195

even before she had left him to marry Louis—days when she could not bear to face the light and lay groaning, with splitting head, behind closed curtains until the blessed evening came and she emerged once again, looking magnificent, to the cards, the dancing and the wine-bottle.

Above the mantelpiece was the picture of a naked woman lying on her front among velvet cushions and cunningly arranged draperies, her face half-turned, with the hint of a mischievous smile, towards the viewer. The glowing curves of her body were warm in the candlelight and reminded him of the summer sunset reflecting from the rounded swell of a wave. Though the face was not specifically that of Amande, Henryk recognised her body. So she'd achieved her ambition and that virile old goat, Boucher, had added her to his collection of willing, naked ladies who, or so all Paris had always averred, lay before him to be painted and pawed.

In the old days, Henryk, nervous of the painter's reputation and still retaining a naïve faith in Amande's character and habits, had always forbidden her to visit his studio. 'Puritan' was one of the least offensive epithets she had flung at him. 'You don't own me ... I shall see whom I please. ...' A week later she had announced her intention of marrying Louis de Valfons. And Henryk's main reaction had been one of deep and heartfelt sympathy for his friend.

He heard her come into the room but did not move, wondering what her first words would be.

'It's nine years since you stood before that fire,' she said in a matter-of-fact voice.

'Only six. After Rossbach, remember?'

'Was it? Yes, I expect you're right. You were usually right.' She poured herself a glass of wine. 'God, it used to annoy me, the number of times you were right.' She drank half the glass and put it on the mantelpiece, then held out her hands to him.

'Too many years,' she said.

He took her hands and felt them tighten slightly on his fingers.

'Aren't you going to kiss me, darling?'

Henryk kissed her on the cheek, smelling the smoke in her hair, the familiar scent of her skin.

'Should I not call you darling?' Her voice held the teasing note he had once found so irresistible. 'Perhaps we should start afresh as two strangers. Yes, that might be more fun.' She regarded him thoughtfully, inclining her head, first to this side then the other. 'You're thinner, Henryk. Thin, brown, hard. You must have been to the Indies or somewhere. It suits you.'

'Thank you.'

She's changed too, he thought, from the girl he had first met in Rome. Still the same thick fair hair, the same superb shoulders and bosom swelling from her green and silver dress, the same big red mouth—but her body had thickened; there were dark shadows smudged beneath the large brown eyes that seemed a little faded somehow; her skin had lost its former splendid lustre. Though he knew her age to be only thirty-two, her face and figure were those of a woman ten years older. But still a magnificent creature, more opulent even than her surroundings, soft, white, sensual; her every movement, her every glance an invitation to the delights of love.

'So you still don't wear a wig,' she said lightly, quite at ease. His dark hair was clubbed back in a short queue, touched here and there with grey; neat, simple like his plain brown coat and breeches. 'D'you remember how we used to fight over that?'

'What didn't we fight over?'

'I know. Yet we had our good times too.'

Henryk saw the wine trembling in her glass as she raised it to her lips. The wind boomed in the chimney and then was gone, leaving silence before the next squall.

'Where's Louis?' he asked abruptly.

'Somewhere.' Amande shrugged. 'With his regiment, I expect.' The subject did not appear to hold much interest for her. 'I've had no news of him for months.' She gazed into the flames for a moment. 'We no longer see much of each other these days.'

'I see.'

'He has his army life—that's his *real* life.'

'And you?'

'You know me, darling. You know I couldn't live away from Paris.'

'He must be doing well as a soldier—all this.' Henryk gestured round the room.

'Oh yes, Louis does very well—as a soldier.' She sat down and the shimmering folds of her wide skirt spilled over the arms of the chair. Henryk remembered Louis at Rossbach, powder-stained, his white uniform mottled with blood, a broken sword in his hand, trying desperately to rally the men of the Regiment de

Mailly dazed and broken by the Prussian cavalry; a true, professional soldier, one day destined perhaps to become a Marshal of France. But she would never see this picture of her husband. Henryk wondered if she had yet found the man she could love more than she loved herself, whether she ever would. His head ached and he felt suddenly depressed. Since the fight with the *Richelieu* he had been troubled by headaches, sometimes quite blinding in their intensity; and the journey from Calais had been long and tedious. The heat of the room had become uncomfortable; he felt hemmed-in; trapped by the sheer, overpowering richness of his surroundings, by the look he saw sparking in her eyes as she glanced up at him; the look he remembered so well: avid, hungry, begging.

All his old dislike of her welled up inside him even as her eyes, the shameless swell of her breasts, the tip of her pointed tongue moving along her full lower lip, stirred his body. He wanted to strike her, hurt her, punish her savagely in a way they both enjoyed, for her treatment of Louis.

He knew quite well why he had come here. The excuse in his mind had been the urge to see Louis again but the truth was in the hot stirring of his body; the urgent, desperate longing for a woman and, after these years of abstinence, a woman like Amande without shame or inhibition, who did not care how she behaved with a man once she had him in her bed.

He could have gone to Toinon and she would have loved him as she had before but with restraint, tenderness and some understanding, and that he did not want—not yet at least. Later perhaps he would go to Toinon for the enjoyment of her wit and intelligence. But now, at this moment, he wanted a woman's body, not her mind. Yes, he realised with a bitter spasm of self-disgust, it was lust that had brought him to Amande de Valfons.

'You'll stay and sup with me,' she said without query in her voice.

'Why not?'

'For old times' sake.'

'Of course.'

At the table she was gay, talkative; her eyes brightened, the colour came back to her cheeks; as the silent footman filled and refilled her glass she began to laugh too much and too loudly. No, he thought without undue sympathy, the years have not been kind to this woman who, but for the grace of God, might have been his wife.

'And now,' she said after a short pause in her prattle, 'I've talked too long about myself. Tell me what you've been doing all these years. Where have you been hiding yourself, my pet?'

'Me? Oh, I've been travelling; seeing a bit more of the big world. Enjoying myself in a leisurely sort of way.'

'How fascinating, darling. You must tell me all about it. Where you've been, all the exciting things you've done, all the women who've fallen in love with you.' She laughed with her head thrown back. There was gravy shining on her chin. 'But first I must tell you the latest tidbit—all Paris is talking about it. They say the King has formed a new attachment, a Mlle Romains—another one of absolutely no family, a lawyer's daughter or something ... Well, he's bought her a delicious little house at Passy—oh goodness no, not the Parc au Cerfs for her.' Amande picked up a drumstick and gnawed at the flesh, slowly turning the bone between her teeth.

Henryk pushed away his plate; he found he could eat no more; rich food still upset his stomach. His glance wandered over the gleaming table: silver plates, delicate Venetian goblets, finger-bowls of chased silver; hot-house flowers floating in a great golden basin. Everything shining with a soft, rich sheen; precious metal, polished wood, velvet curtains, the pearls in her hair, round white arms, the wetness of her lips.

'Of course Pompadour's very put out ...' Amande dabbled her fingers in the water. Henryk remembered scraping the scummy wooden platters into the pail; the abominable Fitch cramming meat and biscuit into his mouth with his hands; the stink of rotten cheese.

'It's not supposed to be generally known, but she's dying— they say it can't be long now—oh, darling, you really must try this—it's a wonderful new water-ice from Italy.' The cold of it burned his tongue and hurt his eyes. The wine was working on his brain. He felt very sleepy. Now and then he put in some remark or asked a question but it did not matter, she was happy with her endless tittle-tattle. He listened with half an ear as she chattered on, now and then recognising a name from the past.

' ... Monsieur le Duc is more than ever like an old scarecrow —drenched in scent as always.' Her tongue had grown even sharper with the years and when she spoke of the Duc de Richelieu her eyes went hard and spiteful. She had not spoken like this when she had first set her cap at the most notorious womaniser in the whole of France, possibly the whole of Europe.

'But now he's losing his famous powers.' Wine spilled from her glass and trickled down into the deep cleft of her breasts where it lay like blood. 'The *dompteur de femmes!*' Her voice held a sneer. 'Tamer of wild animals! Now look at him. A senile old man who can only have a woman if he pays for her.'

Henryk wondered how long it had been before Richelieu had tired of her. Perhaps she had seen herself as a second Duchesse de Chateauroux or Mlle de Charolais or even, in her wildest dreams, as the woman who would reign supreme during his declining years. But Monsieur le Duc had grown bored as any man would grow bored once his body had lost interest in hers. Poor Louis, he thought, these last years can't have been easy for him. Still, he had at least been able to take refuge on the battlefield.

'Why are you smiling?' she asked sharply, the spoon poised half-way to her mouth.

'A sudden thought, that's all.'

'May I perhaps share it?'

'I don't see why not.' Henryk grinned. 'If I can be anything like as successful with women, bought or otherwise, when I'm his age I've got an instructive and enjoyable old age ahead of me.'

Amande gave an angry snort. 'He's got a filthy skin disease,' she said. 'Nothing but a laughing stock with all his potions and drugs. That's something you've never needed, darling,' she added with a giggle.

Henryk saw the two servants standing behind her, quite still and gazing impassively before them. In the old days, before the Tuntsevs and the Navy, he would not have noticed them any more than he would have noticed a dull piece of furniture, but now he saw them as men and wondered what they thought. Noticing his glance, Amande said over her shoulder, 'You can put the wine on the table and go.'

They placed the wine before her, snuffed out the candles on the sideboards and the walls, leaving only those on the table.

'Will Madame be requiring anything else tonight?' Henryk heard a trace of insolence in the man's tone but she did not appear to notice.

'No, nothing else. You may go.'

They bowed and went. As soon as the door closed behind them

she leant forward resting her bosom on the table.

'Tonight you're young. Do you have to wait for old age before you enjoy your pleasures—*our* pleasures,' she added, reaching across and putting her hand on his. A heavy strand of hair had come loose and hung down, clinging to the curve of her neck; her breathing had quickened.

'It's late. I must go.' But he did not move. 'I've been bad company tonight,' he said. 'You must excuse me but—' He rubbed a hand across his eyes. 'I'm very tired—the wine—all your excellent food—' He shook his head as if to clear it.

'There's something about you,' said Amande, softly stroking his hand, 'You've changed. More reserved somehow, or shy. You're not shy of me, darling—are you?'

He shook his head again.

'If I didn't know this was impossible,' she said with a laugh, 'I'd say you'd grown unused to a woman's company.'

He looked up, surprised. 'My secret is out.' Henryk glanced quickly round the room as if to make certain no one lurked in the shadows beyond the candlelight. 'Have I your word? Nothing of what I say to go outside these walls?'

She nodded, uncertain whether or not he was joking.

'For the last four years I've been in a monastery,' he declared.

For a moment she did not say anything and then her eyes softened and she burst out laughing. 'A monastery! Henryk Barinski in a monastery! Oh, that's good. And did they make you wear a hairy shirt and sandals?'

'Bare feet,' he said. 'You'll never believe it but I've got leather soles to my feet. I wouldn't even feel the *bastinado*.'

'No women?'

'No women.'

'And this didn't worry you?'

'No. Why should it? Life was very peaceful.'

'I see. But would you agree that when a man leaves his monastery he will be ready to enjoy a woman's' —she hesitated— 'a woman's company even more fully?' Her eyes had grown hot.

'I'd think that very likely,' he said gravely and got to his feet. 'Now I must go.'

'You won't be going anywhere tonight,' she said. 'Except to bed upstairs.'

Henryk knew he'd drunk too much; the wine hit him as soon as he stood up. His head was spinning, his eyes had difficulty in focusing; he steadied himself against the table as the house rolled and pitched to the storm.

'I came to see Louis,' he mumbled.

'You came to see me. You know it.'

Yes, he knew it. But now all he wanted was sleep—sleep; to lie down before his legs gave way or his head floated away from his shoulders.

' . . . comfortable bed . . . keep for our guests—. . .' Her voice came to him from far off. Damn her for a bitch and a whore but it was not only her fault; he was the one who'd come back. The candle-flames were red pin-points in the smoke, dancing like the muzzle flashes at Quiberon.

'I feel awful—must lie down—I—'

Amande stood looking down on his crumpled form, on her face a mixture of anger and disappointment; then she rang for the servants to help Monsieur to his room.

*   *   *

'Assist Monsieur, indeed! We had to lug him all the way up the stairs.' The first footman helped himself to the remains of the roast duckling sent down from the dining-room.

'Well, you should be used to that by now,' said the second footman, picking bits of creamed truffle from his teeth. 'We're always carrying the drunken bastards up those stairs.'

'What's this one like?' asked the cook. 'But different to most of 'em, eh, Jean?'

'I've never seen such a scar on any face before,' said Jean. He was busy running his finger round the silver dishes and licking off the gravies and sauces.

'Likely he got it in the war.'

'Maybe.'

'Wonder how long he'll last.' The man chuckled coarsely, inspecting his thick, greasy finger. 'The whore'd not be satisfied with this.' He dipped it into the congealing fat.

'You've no call to speak like that, Jean-Pierre,' snapped a thin, middle-aged woman in the doorway.

'Heh, listen to Mademoiselle Faggot there. Just because you dress and undress her—'

'It's not Marie who does the undressing,' put in the other man.

'Shut up, the two of you. You ought to be ashamed of yourselves. You take Madame's money quite happily.' The maid's dried-up skin flushed darkly, her little, black, peasant eyes glittered. 'I'll not have you speaking about her like this. I won't have it, d'you hear?'

The first footman clucked loudly like a hen; the other one belched; both broke into roars of laughter.

'And where does she get all this money of hers? We all know that, *don't* we? She and her fancy boys and dirty old men. Cartloads of silver and furniture and God knows what else besides arriving here every other day—'

'Well, and what of it? You two get enough pickings out of it.'

'Ah, get on with you, you scrawny old thing. It's you that ought to be tumbling round in that damned great bed up there night after night, not her, then you'd learn to be like the rest of us. You need unbuttoning, that's what's wrong with you.'

'What Madame chooses to do with her life is no concern of ours, you—you filthy oafs,' cried Marie and ran from the room.

'There, now look what you've done,' said the cook sadly. 'You've upset the poor soul again. You've no loyalty you two, I've told you that before.'

'Loyalty?' exploded Jean. 'Loyalty? To that!' He jerked his head at the ceiling, then spat on the floor. 'Monsieur away with his soldiers and sprouting the biggest pair of horns since Satan was born and you talk to me of loyalty. Pah!'

They bickered on about the habits of their mistress as they were wont to do every day at some time or other, enjoying themselves immensely.

*   *   *

Amande stood beside the bed, holding the candle above the pillow so that she could look at Henryk as he lay dead to the world, snoring lightly through his open mouth. In his sleep his face was not so taut, more relaxed, younger-looking. Since the servants had come down and reported with their usual servile brand of insolence that Monsieur was safely in bed, she had sat drinking heavily so that now she swayed on her feet and the shadows danced crazily about the walls as the candle gyrated in her hand. He had wanted her; she'd seen the look in his eyes. And, by Christ, she wanted him. Above the sheet his neck and shoulders were strong and brown. Her lips parted slightly as her eyes travelled slowly down the shape of his hidden body. He would hurt her, leave her darkly stained with bruises; she would bleed. That had always been the way between them.

He did not love her, she knew that; he never had. It was that other one he loved, the Polish woman he had once spoken of years ago, but only once. And even in those days he spoke of her in the past as if she were dead. Tears suddenly filled Amande's eyes and trickled slowly down her cheeks; maudlin, self-pitying tears. Would any man ever love *her* in this way? So that when she died he'd never forget her?

Unsteadily she put down the candlestick on a little table by the bed, fumbling at the fastening of her dress. One by one the skirts and petticoats fell to her ankles till she stood almost naked. Then she leant over and shook Henryk gently by the shoulder. He stirred and shifted, muttering thickly, his eyes still closed.

'Get away. It's not my watch—let me sleep—not my watch.'

'Henryk—darling. Look at me.'

He opened his eyes. The last garment fell slowly down her body. Without a word Amande pulled back the bedclothes and climbed in beside him; without a word she put her arms round him and pulled him to her and he felt her hand on his skin, urgent as a soft, white animal.

'Come on, Henryk. Darling, come on!' But he needed no urging and turned on her in a savage fury of pent-up lust.

That first time he did not keep her waiting long. She moaned and gasped and uttered one long-drawn cry that trembled on the edge of a scream and carried to the attic room where Marie, her maid, heard it in her cold, lonely bed and buried her face in the pillow with a little groan of anguish.

'My God, I needed that,' Henryk exclaimed as they rolled apart. He let out his breath in a great sigh of relief.

'You're brutal, Henryk, and I love it. I love it.' She was panting, brushing back the damp hair from her face. 'Oh, lord, it was wonderful,' she repeated, over and over again. He was even stronger than she remembered: hard, lean, marvellously exciting compared to her pale, Parisian lovers.

But it wouldn't last, he told himself. For a week she'd want him—at night, in the daytime, it didn't matter; for a week they'd satisfy each other and then?—Without love or tenderness there'd be nothing but scenes growing ever more bitter and then a final all-consuming boredom.

A fresh gust of wind rattled the windows; rain drummed on the roof and hissed in the red ashes of the fire. Any moment now and they'd be called to shorten sail. He grinned, feeling quite sober again and snuggled deeper beneath the bedclothes, revelling in the feel of the soft mattress, the smooth warmth of the woman beside him. When he needed her again he knew he had only to wake her.

'Henryk?'

'Yes.'

'Why didn't we stay together?'

'You know why. We fight like cat and dog; we get on each others nerves; we—'

'Isn't it worth all that—for this?'

He did not answer.

'Well, isn't it, darling?'

'Go to sleep, my sweet,' he said more gently. That was the only term of endearment he had ever used to her.

'Don't let's sleep too long,' she said sleepily. She also felt quite sober.

He laughed. 'Very well. Do I wake you then—?'

'We'll wait and see, shall we? That way it's more fun. Much, much more fun.'

'You're made for love,' he said. 'You're really made for love.' He felt her move against him.

'Your hands are straying,' she whispered after a minute or two. 'Let them—I like it.' With his hand on her breasts and his mouth parting her hair, searching for her ear, he said, 'You were right about the monastery. But it's not your company I want at the moment.' Her laughter was excited.

Dawn was near before they finally knew they must sleep.

'Darling?'

'Mm.' Henryk was hovering on the edge of sleep, sated, spent, utterly relaxed.

'There's no need to worry about Louis,' she said. 'We haven't slept together for years.'

Louis, he thought drowsily. He'd tried not to think of Louis Damn her. Why bring up something neither of them could do anything about, least of all now, at this particular moment. One day he'd see his friend; if he did, perhaps he'd tell him, perhaps not. Why hurt him? But would it hurt him? Would anything to do with Amande hurt him any more? A wife whose infidelities were the talk of a society well accustomed to wanton and vicious behaviour.

'The fact is,' she added, 'he's not a man who needs a wife at all. He's got what he wants in the army. His regiment takes the place of a woman in his heart; it's all he can talk about, think about. When he used to make love to me it was a poor business that brought no joy to either of us—' She talked on, excusing herself, while the early-morning carts rumbled below and the grey light of a cold, grey day seeped between the curtains. 'So you see, it really hasn't been *all* my fault.'

But Henryk was asleep.

*   *   *

The situation deteriorated even more swiftly than he had anticipated.

When the first hot flood of desire had cooled he found, as in the old days, there was nothing to take its place: no affection, no trust, no tolerance—nothing but two people who could not even take refuge in conversation.

Her demands on his body had at one point soared beyond all reason so that, at some moments, he really feared her lust had sent her mad. Her tastes, to his mounting disgust, had become viciously depraved and the sweating struggles in the large, curtained bed grew ever more animal in their frenzy until finally they came to leave a bad taste in his mouth, gall in his soul.

He knew he would soon have to leave her before the descent into Hell had grown so deep he would not be able to climb out. For the sake of his self-respect he must get away and, besides, he

admitted to himself with a rueful smile, he was becoming utterly
exhausted.

*　　*　　*

Then, in the second week after his arrival in Paris, things boiled
to a head. Insults, sneers and back-street language; screaming,
flouncing, throwing things, her voice shrill and venomous with
abuse. The women who shrieked and fought on the lower deck
had been no worse—and at least they did not pretend to be anything but what they were. Henryk answered her with silence,
remembering from his previous experience of her tantrums how
it drove her to further frenzies of rage.

'You aren't the only bloody pebble on the beach, Christ, you
aren't,' she spat at him.

'I'm sure the beach is grossly overcrowded,' he interrupted on
his way to the door.

'Where are you going?'

'Out.'

'Well don't come back, d'you hear, don't bother to come back.
I don't need you. I don't know why in hell's name I bother
with you.' But he had closed the door behind him.

He returned in the late evening, having, among other ploys,
visited his bank. 'Ah, yes, Monsieur, the money has been paid
regularly from Warsaw. Monsieur will be pleased to know there
is a large sum credited to him here.' The manager's expression,
at first openly suspicious, then scornful of Henryk's clothes,
had now altered to a sort of fixed, oily smile. 'Perhaps Monsieur
can tell us what he wants us to do with—'

'I'm sorry but at the moment I don't quite know. My future
plans are uncertain.'

'Monsieur will doubtless realise that we are here to serve him
to the best of our humble ability.'

'Monsieur appreciates your concern for his well-being.'

Bowing and washing his fat white hands, the bank manager saw
Henryk from the premises. 'Look at that fellow,' he said scornfully
to his senior assistant. 'With enough money lying here to fit him-

207

self out for Versailles and he goes about dressed like a merchant's clerk.' He spread out his hands, palm up. 'But take Count Ponia-towski now, he's a Pole too but always dressed in the height of fashion.'

'Ah,' put in the assistant, who considered himself a student of human nature, 'but then the Count is a *true* gentleman.'

Henryk strolled along the Rue St Honoré, enjoying the after-noon sunshine. The street was crowded with carriages, waiting their turn head to tail to draw up at number 372. Through the coach windows Henryk could see the flicker of the fans, the powdered hair, the wigs and the shine of expensive cloth. Beggar-boys ran past him, raising their hands to the windows; passers-by loitered to watch the arrival of the famous at Madame Geof-frin's *salon*. Today was Wednesday; today she mixed the aristoc-racy with the men of letters; today the watchers would be dazzled by the brilliant plumage.

He came level with the doorway. Two young men, gorgeous as golden pheasants, were mincing up the steps on high red heels. They gave him a careless glance, noting his dusty buckled shoes and thick white stockings; one of them said something, they both laughed. After they had gone inside he took a few steps towards the door, hesitated, then, with a little shrug and a smile he turned on his heel and threaded his way quickly among the gathering crowd. Madame G., as he always called her to himself, would surely be surprised to see him after all these years. But she'd recognise him all right; she never forgot a face and besides—his hand went to the scar. He'd like to see Toinon again; he had always got on well with Madame G's daughter ever since the evening she'd come home with Amande; the evening when Louis was there and they'd played *quadrille* till four in the morning.

He frowned at the thought of Amande, wondering what to do. Why not leave her as he had done once before? He knew other women in Paris; when he needed them they'd be only too pleased to see him, he knew that without boasting. The accumulated lust of years which had risen in his body at the sight of her was as-suaged; pride was reasserting itself. Why should he go on dancing to her ugly little tune for the sake of a few hours' sweating pleas-ure?

Henryk stopped in the street and stood trying to work out his immediate future while indignant citizens pushed their way round him, grumbling and cursing.

'That's it!' He slapped his thigh with relief at having reached a decision. 'By God, that's what I'll do.' A couple of apprentices tapped their foreheads and grinned derisively as they passed him. He smiled back and gave them a cheerful greeting.

For a month after recovering from the wound he got at Rossbach, before his return to St Petersburg for the second time, Henryk had rented an apartment in the Rue St Honoré, within a hundred paces of where he now stood; the three top rooms of a house owned by a Madame de Mirabon, an elderly widow who had fallen on hard times and was forced to augment her dwindling supply of money by taking in a lodger, naturally of only the very highest social standing.

'Yes,' she said after her first happy surprise was over. 'As luck would have it, or should I say, ill-luck, for poor Monsieur de Vevay is but lately dead of the pox, the rooms are vacant. You're sure it doesn't worry you?' She was small and round and must once have been very pretty.

'No.'

'Naturally all the bed linen—nothing that was used by the poor man, so very tragic, the whole affair—' Her eyes threatened tears.

'Don't upset yourself, Madame de Mirabon. For all we know he may be very happy where he is.' Arrangements were finalised, then he left saying he would take up residence next day.

She watched him vanish along the crowded street. She was delighted to have him back; for one thing she found him most *sympathique*, so understanding and considerate—and so romantic with those dark good looks, almost swarthy, like a gipsy, she always thought. And that *barbaric* scar and the grey eyes that used to laugh so much but now looked far wiser and more serious. She sighed, deciding what he needed was mothering.

Though it was still broad daylight when Henryk reached Amande's drawing-room he found the curtains closely drawn and the place reeking with a thick, scented fug. The heat was intolerable and he grimaced as he came in.

'Oh, so you're back, are you?' Amande's tone was unfriendly; she had obviously been drinking and was spoiling for trouble. The three men seated with her at the card table stared at Henryk apprehensively. Well, he thought with a sort of wry admiration, it hadn't taken her long to go back to her accustomed admirers. Two were youthful nonentities with languid, good-looking faces;

one was an elderly painted *roué* dressed in a coat of orange silk and one of the huge bag-wigs just coming into fashion.

'Are you not going to introduce us to your friend, my dear?' His teeth were almost black.

She did not bother to answer him but merely snapped at Henryk, 'As you're here you can put some wood on the fire.' The two young men suppressed amazed giggles. No gentleman would soil his hands when there were lackeys tumbling over themselves to put logs on the fire. They waited with interest for Henryk's reaction.

'Surely it's warm enough in here,' he said mildly.

'It's my room,' she flung at him. 'I shall have it as I like.'

'As you wish,' he said with a thin smile. 'But to me it stinks like the gun-deck. You need some fresh air.'

Amande flushed with anger. 'How dare you—' she began, but was interrupted by one of the young men upsetting his chair as he leapt to his feet, scarlet in the face with indignation.

'I must ask you to apologise to Madame for your remark and the tone in which it was made.' His hand had gone to his golden sword-hilt.

Henryk looked him up and down in silence. 'Sit down,' he said in a hard voice. 'And pour Madame some more wine.' For a moment the other held his ground. Henryk could see the sweat springing to his forehead. He looks like an angry sheep, he thought.

'Go on, Gustave,' urged Amande shrilly. 'It's time he was taught a lesson.' She must very much want to get rid of Gustave, Henryk thought with grim amusement.

'Sit down,' he said more kindly. He saw the gleam of steel as the boy pulled irresolutely at the hilt then, muttering something, he hurried from the room. They heard the clack of his heels on the stairs; a door banged; there was silence.

'Well then,' said Henryk equably. 'I'll leave you to your game.' He made a polite little bow towards the table and turned on his heel.

When he returned to the room half an hour later it was empty and the footman, Jean, was tidying away the cards and the glasses.

'Madame has gone out with her friends,' he said in answer to Henryk's uninterested query. 'She does not know when she'll be back.' He picked up the tray. 'Will Monsieur be dining in to-night?'

'Yes,' said Henryk. 'Monsieur will.'

For the last time, he thought, as he ate his way through the courses, watched by the silent portraits and the silent servants. And he experienced no feeling of regret, no sadness—except, he realised with sudden surprise, for Amande herself. God knows what would become of her. But she no longer wanted him; if he stayed it would end in violence. And yet, if it had not been for her he would never have come to Paris the first time and, if he hadn't come to Paris then he wouldn't have gone to Russia. No Russia; no Rossbach; no wonderful year with Kasia, no Siberia, no years at sea.... This sort of reasoning would get him nowhere. He left the table.

Next morning, before Amande came home, he left the house.

*　　*　　*

The days and the nights of the next week slipped by, each one devoted to pleasure. After so long without needing money, Henryk rediscovered the joy of spending. He bought himself expensive clothes and a good sword in place of the plain blade he had got himself in London; he allowed himself the luxury of being shaved after lying late in bed following nights of dice and cards and heavy drinking at the fashionable gambling-hall kept by the Comte Jean du Barry.

Day after day Madame de Mirabon heard him returning in the small hours, often after dawn had broken, and shook her head sadly.

'Your health is bound to suffer,' she said one day, finding him still in bed at three in the afternoon. He was unshaved, and his eyes had a red look to them; he had wrapped a wet towel round his head.

'Should you not try and get to bed early—well, at least once a week.'

He laughed, then groaned aloud with his hand pressed to his forehead.

'My God, why does anyone drink?' He ran his tongue along his front teeth, grimacing at the taste in his mouth.

'Stay there,' she urged. 'Just for today. I'll have something sent up.'

'You're very kind,' he said. 'But I'm going to Madame Geoffrin's this evening. I'll be all right.'

When she had gone, tut-tutting to herself like a worried hen, he lay back on the pillows. One thing: no one could order him from his bed; no bellowed curses could drive him out into the rain pattering on the window. He lay back in the semi-darkness of the curtained room; he could afford another two hours, then he would have to face the disagreeable business of preparing himself for going out. But after a glass or two of wine the world would seem a rosier place; he had that to look forward to.

Tomorrow he would go and bathe at Poitevin's floating baths near the Pont Royal. Who knows, there might be another story to be enjoyed like the one he heard last week about the Duc de Richelieu peeping through a hole in the cubicle and having the unexpected pleasure of seeing an eminent Bishop joining Madame de Mazarin in her bath. Just at the *moment critique* Richelieu had burst into a ribald little song so upsetting the noble cleric that he jumped from the bath unfulfilled.

Henryk was so tickled at the picture conjured up that he laughed aloud and Madame de Mirabon, listening on the landing outside, shook her head even more sadly. Such a shame, she thought as she went slowly down the stairs, to see a man like this debauching himself into an early grave—and who should know more about the subject than a woman whose husband had died of drink and what he quite inaccurately termed love before his twenty-ninth birthday? But then poor Eugène, for all his charm, had been weak as the water he so heartily despised. Monsieur Barinski though, he was a different story; he was—she stood in the hall searching for the words to describe him in her mind. He was more—more worth-while . . . yes, worth-while. She felt he was letting himself fall apart on purpose and longed once again to know the secrets that lay behind his eyes, which reflected changes of mood more certainly than did his face or words; now dark with experience, when he seemed lost in a private world of his own, now dancing, shining, more expressive than a woman's.

He never spoke to her of serious matters, never mentioned his immediate past, though once when she asked him how long he might be staying he had answered, 'I wish I knew. I feel I'm caught up by Paris. I'm doing nothing, getting nowhere—and yet I'm enjoying every moment of it, so why worry?' With a gay laugh he kissed her hand and was away, running down the steps to the street, away on another round of pleasure.

But was he enjoying it? Henryk lay staring with open eyes at the ceiling; cracks ran across the plaster, reminding him for some reason of ship's biscuits. The room smelt frowsty, stale; a fly buzzed monotonously round the walls, now and then swooping at his face. Since they dragged him into Shuvalov's dungeons, had there been a moment when he had not been trapped? Tuntser's tiny hut; the mildewed timbers of *Huntress*; and now, when he had thought himself free, the frothy whirl of Paris: the *bals masqués*, festivals, masquerades; the fencing—at least Primrose could not say he was neglecting his fitness, he thought wrily— long hours at the card tables. Soon, when the summer came, there'd be the gondolas on the Grand Canal, champagne as the fireworks burst above Versailles; picnics in the woods until autumn stripped the oak trees and Society came streaming back to Paris for yet another winter of mindless entertainment.

The rain pattered drearily on the panes, the fly buzzed its hopeless way round the walls and Henryk lay staring with open eyes, unable to make the effort to kill it or open the door and let it free.

*   *   *

Marble statues regarded Henryk coldly with blind eyes as he went up the wide staircase towards Madame Geoffrin's *salon*, towards the hum of conversation growing louder at every step.

He stood in the doorway regarding the scene in her Grand Salon. Nothing had changed; everything was as he remembered it: groups of people stood about the large room or sat round the small, frail tables, reflected in the long wall-mirrors so that the numbers were doubled and redoubled. The Beauvais tapestries still hung in their accustomed place, glowing in the light of the glittering chandeliers. In contrast to Amande's overcrowded rooms, everything was in perfect taste; from the pictures on the brocaded walls to the subdued colours of the Aubusson carpet, all made a worthy background to the distinguished talk and argument which rose on every side. No one so much as glanced in his direction; no footman came to demand his name for, much to the annoyance of her grander guests, Madame Geoffrin preferred that those who graced her *salon* on Mondays, which day she reserved for the *philosophes*, were allowed to enter unannounced. She said it upset their trains of thought to have a man bawling out names all the time.

From the acrimonious sounds coming from a group gathered by the fireplace, the distinguished argument was getting out of hand, Henryk thought with quiet amusement.

'But no, Monsieur Montesquieu, by no means do I agree with that supposition. It would seem to me to be so much arrant nonsense.'

'So. You are saying in fact that just because the King chooses to—' Another voice, one he recognised as if he had heard it yesterday, drowned the angry words.

'*Soyons aimable, messieurs, soyons aimable.*' Madame Geoffrin was soothing as honey. The pitch of the argument sank to normal levels and, turning to locate other raised voices, she noticed Henryk.

The same dumpy figure he remembered so well, in the same lavender and grey with the same mob cap on her white hair, hurried across to him, holding out her hands in welcome. A little more lined, a little more bent, but as bustling and busy as ever.

'Henryk!'

'Yes, it's me. I've come back.' He kissed her on both cheeks.

For a moment they regarded each other in smiling silence, then she broke into a torrent of questions. Where had he been? When did he get back? How? When? Why? And now he must come and sit down and tell her everything. For a moment heads were turned towards them, women whispered behind their fans, frequently glancing in Henryk's direction; a ripple of conjecture ran round the room, answered by those who remembered the scarred Pole. Well aware they were discussing him, Henryk let nothing show on his face but his pleasure in talking to Madame Geoffrin.

'And how is Toinon?' he asked, looking round the room for her tall, straight figure, listening for the clear, carrying laugh.

'My daughter is her usual energetic self, rushing here, there and everywhere, never sitting still for a moment—'

'It's amazing how closely she takes after her mother.'

'How you've always liked to tease me.' Her eyes strayed to one of the tables where a smallish man in a stained black coat

214

was holding forth to four or five spellbound listeners. 'Monsieur Diderot knows well how to hold an audience,' she said proudly, as if she were personally responsible for his very existence. Which perhaps in a way she almost was, Henryk thought.

'Toinon,' he repeated quietly. 'Is she here tonight?'

'No. I'm afraid she's away on one of her spring visits, staying at Dampierre with the Duc and Duchess de Luynes—you remember the Duchess, of course, from your time at court ... By the way, have you paid your respects to Her Majesty since your return to Paris? Not yet? Oh, I know, you must be terribly busy, so many things to do, so many friends to see, not a moment for anything.' Her tone was gently ironical.

'Will Toinon be back soon?'

'Not till the end of May.' She saw the look of disappointment on his face. 'You always got on well together, you two, didn't you?'

'Very, yes.'

Madame Geoffrin had always wondered whether Toinon had ever taken Henryk to her bed. She must have been mad if she hadn't, she thought firmly. Perhaps this time? Her daughter swore she'd never marry again but—Madame Geoffrin tried to visualise him as her son-in-law, and did not find it difficult. Though of course he must be a good twelve years younger than Toinon. Still, he had the look of one who would cope with her strong-willed intelligence.

'Now what's going on?' Her sharp gaze settled on a table in the far corner of the room where hands were waving violently and voices were raised. 'It seems I must—' She half-rose, but the angry argument subsided and changed to laughter.

'Monsieur D'Alembert has poured oil with one of his jokes. Disaster has been averted.' She waved with her fan. 'They're all here tonight. Montesquieu. Piron. Diderot. Monsieur le Cardinal de Polignac. The *Philosphes*, *les beaux esprits*. They still gather. Brilliant moths round a very old and very ordinary candle-flame.'

'Are you fishing for compliments, Maman?' He was among the small, select band allowed to address her by this title. He had always thought that Madame G. had more common sense in her plump little finger than all these great intellects put together. 'The flower of French intellect,' he said drily. 'The Republic of Letters.' With a sudden little flash of malicious pleasure he imagined Jem Pike and his Mates laying about them with their switchers, driving

215

these precious gentlemen to the masthead in a t'gallant gale.

'You're like Toinon,' she said sadly. 'You don't approve of their ideas, do you?'

'As you ask me, no, I don't. Even less now than before.'

In the old days, she remembered, Henryk had listened open-mouthed to ideas which, in his view, aimed at the very foundations of established custom, tilted at the idols of faith and tradition, threatened to poison the very bloodstream of France like some filthy, debilitating disease. In those days he had said little, content to listen in a sort of angry amazement, but now—Madame Geoffrin saw his mouth tighten, the arrogant tilt to his head, the cold contempt in his eyes as they swept the room and hoped he'd make no trouble.

'Surely you can't really—' he began, but she cut him off briskly.

'Who d'you think appeared the other day? Stanislas. You re-member Stanislas—I absolutely refuse to call him Stas—Poniatow-ski. What a charmer.' Smiling, gay, attentive, she thought, very unlike Henryk, who sat looking so grim.

'Yes,' he said softly, 'I remember him well.' His eyes were bleak. 'Did he stay in Paris long?' he asked in an effort to be polite.

'No. A week, ten days, no more, then away he went back to Warsaw.' She lowered her voice. 'I can tell you something, Hen-ryk, as one who has known Stanislas since you were boys together, but it's for your ears alone you understand.' He nodded. 'There's likely to be a brilliant future for him. Ah—hah, I can say no more than that, but you mark my words, before too long the name Poniatowski will ring through Europe.'

'I'll take your word for it, Maman.' This time he did smile with more like his old spirit. 'Is there anything you *don't* know?'

'I like to compare myself to a small round tree with branches on all sides. I share a little of everything and know a little of everything and in that way I hope to keep everyone happy. You are happy, are you?' she added unexpectedly. 'Forgive an old woman's inquisitiveness but you've surely seen and suffered much on these travels of yours.'

'No more than lots of others.' Elmquist screaming on the amputating table; Mendel, Croaker, Gammon going over the side for the last time. 'Less than many.' Brittle laughter rose above the drone of conversation, the delicate clink of china as Madame Geoffrin's distinguished guests drank their little cups of hot choco-late.

She leant forward and patted his arm. 'If I can be of any help —you know you can always talk to me.' Her voice was warm with sympathy.

'I know, and thank you. Perhaps one day I'll bore you with my adventures.'

Her small, lively eyes regained their twinkle. 'You shall dine with me next week. And now I have monopolised you for long enough. There are certain ladies in this room bursting themselves with curiosity.'

She took him slowly round the room, introducing him here and there. Polite little bows from the men, smiles from the women. 'You remember the Comte de Barinski?' 'But of course.' '*Enchanté.*' More bows, more smiles. 'How nice to see you back?' 'Where have you been hiding yourself, *monsieur*?' 'Paris has been quite dead without you.' Laughter, eyes appraising above picture fans of gilt and mother-of-pearl, the discreet lowering of dark lashes.

'Excuse me a moment. I must see to the new arrivals.' Maman bustled off, leaving Henryk standing among others by a table where Monsieur Diderot was holding court.

'The effect of colonies,' the philosopher was saying, 'is merely to weaken the country from which the settlers are drawn without adding to the strength of the country in which they make their new home.' He paused to take snuff noisily while his admiring audience waited attentively for what he might say next. 'No, my friends, men should remain where they are.' Much of the snuff, Henryk noticed, had remained on his dingy cravat.

'Colonies are not worth having anyway,' said a man with badly powdered hair and candle-grease on his cuffs.

'This last war must have pleased you then,' remarked Henryk. Faces were turned towards him in surprise and annoyance at his firm tone. 'For hasn't England stripped the French apple tree of all its fruit?' He was rather pleased with that. Kasia would have laughed fondly at him—'We're quite the *philosophe* tonight, aren't we, darling?'

An agitated sound rose from round the table. 'By no means all, *monsieur*. ... France retains the fishing rights off the Newfoundland banks ... England has blundered by leaving us a means of building a new fleet ... a nucleus of trained seamen from the fishing boats ... We still have the sugar islands of the West Indies ...' Not all of them, it appeared, took the same contemptuous delight in their defeat.

217

"*Messieurs, mesdames*, please.' Diderot waved his hand for silence. 'This gentleman here—' he stabbed at Henryk with his long, pointed nose, pinning him with cold, clever eyes—'spoke of war.' He paused until the attention of the table was complete. 'War,' he declaimed, 'is the recreation of kings and nobles with nothing better to do. It is waged by brutes under the leadership of idiots.' Henryk felt his anger rising. Dick Gammon had been no brute; Primrose was no idiot. 'It is a plague,' Diderot went on, thumping the table in time with his words. 'And any thinking man must abhor it as such.' A ripple of sycophantic applause echoed the stirring words. 'Do you not agree, *monsieur*?' A cold smile played along Diderot's thin lips.

'No, I don't.' Heads turned again, eyebrows were raised. 'It would seem to me,' Henryk continued, 'that with men as they are, and always will be, war has a part to play in the natural scheme of things every bit as important as, for instance, abstract thinking.' They gazed at him in amazement. Diderot was frowning.

'Before you say anything in reply, *monsieur*,' added Henryk quickly, 'I think I should say that I know a little of war and, by God, I hate it. Not because, as you said, it's the recreation of kings but because I've seen what it can do to men's bodies and—

'And their minds,' interrupted Diderot, flashing a glance of triumph round his audience.

'And their minds,' Henryk agreed. 'But always remember this: for every man brutalised by war there's—he searched for the right phrase—another who has been—well, if you like, ennobled in spirit. And now, *monsieur*, if you'll excuse me—' Henryk made a polite little bow. If there was one thing the discipline of the Navy had taught him it was to control his temper—but now the training was beginning to wear thin.

He left the group sitting in silence as he went to search for his hostess, feeling he could stand no more of this hot-house atmosphere where so much nonsense was talked by so many who had experienced little of life beyond their immediate, rarefied circle. They sipped their chocolate, exchanged their barbed witticisms, capping each others epigrams with others so polished and perfect that he could not help the thought that they had been practised and repractised before a glass. Sometimes they contented themselves with short, pithy statements:

' ... I myself have always considered it grossly bad form for husbands and wives to love each other.'

'My dear *monsieur*, almost as deadly a sin as believing anything you read in the Bible. As Monsieur Voltaire so rightly says, it will indeed be awkward if religion is quite exploded. We shall have nothing left to laugh at.'

What manner of men were these, Henryk wondered, who seemed to have no purpose in their conversation but a destruction every bit as deadly as that inflicted by *Huntress's* guns?

He was looking for Madame Geoffrin. 'Oh, but you mustn't leave yet,' she begged him, when at last he ran her to earth in a far corner uttering another of her favourite sayings to calm an argument about the Court and the Jesuits: '*Voilà qui est bien, messieurs*. Really, I think that's enough.'

'Monsieur Rameau is just about to give us a recital on the harpsichord—'

'I hope you've asked Black Bob to play his fiddle in accompaniment.' He laughed, quite restored to good humour by her expression of bewilderment, imagining the fiddler playing to this gathering in his torn leather jerkin and shaking the gold rings in his ears as he scraped away at 'Drops of Brandy' while the ship weighed anchor. 'Don't worry, Maman. I'll tell you all about him next week. A rough fellow, with the sea—and a strange sort of music —in his blood.' He bent over her hand and left the room.

In the street he drew in deep lungfuls of air. As he stood pondering how to spend the remainder of the evening before it was time to make his way to the card-tables at Du Barry's, a sedan chair stopped at the door. The two bearers lowered the conveyance from their shoulders and a man stepped out.

Even as he was getting out and Henryk could only see the crown of his new broad-brimmed hat, he knew it was D'Eon. The small, slim figure of the Chevalier hurried up the steps. He was dressed in plum-coloured velvet and dark green stockings; his well-curled wig showed the small neat ears of which he had always been so proud. But his once smooth, rather girlish face was now pitted with scars of the pox. The hand he held out to Henryk with a delighted smile still had the same steel grip that Henryk remembered.

They shook hands with many expressions of joy, laughing and clapping each other on the shoulder.

'I had heard you were in Paris,' said D'Eon. 'I'm but lately back from London and one of the first things I heard was of your return.'

'How—?'

'Conti,' said D'Eon in a lower voice. 'You were brave to come back, Henryk. Or mad. Or both—as you have always been. Now listen. I haven't time to tell you much at this moment. I promised Madame Geoffrin I'd be here in time to hear her new *protégé*, a Monsieur Ramy—'

'Rameau,' corrected Henryk. So Conti knew he was in Paris.

'Ramy, Rameau, it's of little importance. Anyway, he is to play one of Monsieur Haydn's latest compositions and as I have a taste for the German's music I really must hurry, but I'll tell you this: Monsieur le Prince knows of your arrest in Petersburg; he knows of your escape en route to Siberia—and that's all; that's all any of us know. What you've been doing these last years and how or why you came back to Paris—all these things you must tell me at our leisure. Shall we say the Bois, our usual place, tomorrow at three o'clock? Good.'

'But Conti, Charles—'

'Set your mind at rest. Five years have passed. It's unlikely you could tell him any Russian secrets he does not already know. While grateful for what you achieved during your time in the Empress's bed—how was it, by the way? Is she as ardent as one was always led to suppose?' He gave his little feminine chuckle. 'No, he doesn't want to see you. Now! I really must go, Henryk. *A demain.*'

Henryk strolled through the deepening dusk, his head bowed in thought. So Conti had known he was in Paris all the time. The man was like a spider, sitting there in the Temple, spinning a web which stretched to the farthest corners of Europe. I've been lucky; many men have died for failing the King's Secret. His mind jumped to D'Eon's other remark. The Empress? He had never been near Elizabeth's bed; D'Eon must have known that. What the devil had he meant?

Linkmen went by, the glare of their torches flickering along the walls, dying in the deeper darkness of the narrow alleyways, lighting up the faces of the passers-by so that for an instant they turned from grey shadows to red flesh and blood. The Chevalier would know the latest news from Russia; he would have seen Kasia, spoken to her, heard her laugh. Tomorrow, Henryk realised with a hot spasm of excitement, he would hear first-hand news of her, but tomorrow was many long hours away. Tonight he must contain his impatience as best he could.

He tried to put thoughts of her from his mind as he made his way to Du Barry's gaming-hall.

*   *   *

In the days before Henryk had gone to Russia for the first time he and D'Eon used to meet here, beside the lake in the Bois de Boulogne, safe from inquisitive ears, to discuss secret details.

The trees were taller now and threw more shade across the gravel walk, which was as well, for the afternoon sun was very warm. A number of people were promenading slowly up and down and every so often the Chevalier would pause in his stride, sweep off his hat, bow, smile, make some gallant sally and then, after a brief interchange of compliments with his acquaintances, would continue on their way.

Henryk was impatient of these interruptions; there was so much he wanted to learn from his friend.

'Tell me, Charles, why did you credit me with having reached the Empress's bed? I can assure you—' he added with a laugh— 'Elizabeth was not at all my type.'

'Elizabeth?' D'Eon stopped in his tracks, gazing at Henryk in astonishment. 'But—' Comprehension dawned. 'D'you mean you don't know? My dear friend, where have you been this last year?' Henryk looked at him quite blankly.

'Since last September, when she was crowned in the Uspensky Cathedral, Catherine has been Empress of Russia.' D'Eon was amused by the stupefaction on Henryk's face. 'So you really had no idea?'

Henryk shook his head. 'How did it happen? What about Elizabeth—and Peter? Was there revolution?' A sharp stab of fear sickened him. Kasia! What had happened to Kasia? His mind filled with visions of shots, the flash of blades in the gilded corridors of the Winter Palace; screaming women crouching behind flimsy barricades, awaiting the thrust of swords and pikes.

'Good gracious, no, there was no revolt. Not on the part of the country. No, no, the whole affair quite bloodless. Very like the *coup* that brought Elizabeth to the throne. The Guards, of course. They carried Catherine in triumph to Petersburg among her cheering subjects. Beer flowed in the gutters, bells pealed, guns boomed, peasants wept with joy—it was all very Russian. Or so I've heard. Not that I was there, of course. I had been going back to Petersburg, as a matter of fact, but then Elizabeth was inconsiderate enough to have a stroke and die. Peter at once reversed Russian policy and made an alliance with Frederick and so I didn't go. There was an idea I might have gone to Poland but that fell through and I went to London instead, with Nivernais, to negotiate the Peace of Paris. In fact I have to return to England tomorrow and—'

Henryk hardly listened as D'Eon talked on about his own affairs, interspersed with sudden little reminiscences of their time together in Russia. His head was reeling with the impact of this news. He wanted to stop the flow of words and ask D'Eon what had happened to Kasia in this so-called bloodless *coup;* to shout at him, For God's sake, I'm not interested in London or George the Third or Milord Bute. Shut up and tell me about Kasia! But he controlled his mounting agitation and steered the conversation back to Russia.

'Elizabeth died, you say, but what about Peter?'

Rather unwillingly D'Eon broke off an account of how he had cleverly purloined and copied out some vital dispatch for transmission to Versailles.

'Officially he died of a severe colic. Unofficially he died of an accidental blow received during a drunken brawl at Ropsha where he was being held, I imagine, until Catherine made up her mind what on earth to do with him. Even more unofficially he was murdered ... They say Alexis Orlov—you remember him, don't you? The biggest of the five brothers, the one with the scar on his cheek.'

'I hardly knew him,' said Henryk shortly. Another little stab of fear, but this time for another reason. Alexie Orlov, the handsome giant who had loved Kasia, who probably loved her still —after all, what man could fail to love her?

'They say Alexie had a hand in Peter's death. As he, and all his brothers, especially Grigori, had a hand in placing Catherine on the throne. If it hadn't been for them Peter would now be Tsar.'

What more natural, thought Henryk, with deepening despair,

than for Alexie to marry Catherine's favourite lady-in-waiting. If, of course, she was still close to the new Empress.

'I suppose,' he asked casually, 'you haven't heard anything of Kasia Radienska, have you? I'm sure you met her in Petersburg in 'fifty-eight. One of Catherine's ladies-in-waiting.'

'Oh, I remember *la belle* Radienska very well. A lady as intelligent as she's beautiful.' He chuckled. 'Prascovia Bruce's *bête noire* and even more so now, I should think, now that she's completely ousted the unfortunate Bruce and installed herself as the Empress's first *confidante*.'

'You're certain of this?' Henryk asked after a pause.

'My spies told me so. I can't vouch for it personally. We're a long way from Russia here.'

'Yes,' agreed Henryk. 'We are.' Even a man only half as quick and sensitive as D'Eon would have noticed the sadness in Henryk's voice. Then he remembered: hadn't there been something between Henryk and his lovely countrywoman? The rumour had reached the French Embassy shortly before Henryk's disappearance and had upset the Ambassador quite considerably. 'We cannot have him transferring his attentions at this stage,' he had said, 'His arms are certainly not long enough to hold both the Grand Duchess *and* this Radienska woman at the same time. No, Monsieur D'Eon, this nonsense must be nipped in the bud.' But, before anything could be done Henryk had vanished into the wastes of Siberia.

'There's no reason to suppose any harm has befallen Countess Radienska,' said D'Eon. 'I'm sure that by now she must know Catherine well enough to avoid anything likely to cause—ah—unpleasantness. Besides, it's thought that she too played an important part in the palace revolution.' He drew a small, jewelled watch from his fob pocket. 'Oh, dear,' he exclaimed, 'how annoying it is, Henryk. As soon as we meet it seems I have to hurry away. The fact is I've a mass of things to attend to before leaving for London. But you'll still be in Paris when I get back. Then we shall meet and you'll tell me how you managed to get from Siberia to the Bois de Boulogne.' His face lit up in one of his impish little smiles. 'We'll go to the *salle d'armes* and you'll show me if your swordsmanship has become even better since we last met.'

'I don't know,' said Henryk. 'I may still be in Paris. Tomorrow I'm meant to be going to Versailles, to pay my respects to the

Queen. After that—I honestly don't know.' He needed time to think; to sort out the urgent new thoughts chasing through his mind like the ducks skittering along the water of the lake in a flurry of white spray.

D'Eon held out his hand.

'*Au revoir*, Henryk. I can't tell you how much I've enjoyed seeing you again, and I look forward to our next meeting.'

'Goodbye, Charles. Enjoy yourself in London.' He watched the small figure hurrying off, very erect, very purposeful. When he was about thirty yards away D'Eon stopped and called out, 'Why don't you write to her?' With a cheerful wave he disappeared among the trees.

Until long after dusk had dulled the waters of the lake and silenced the birds in the trees and emptied the paths of the fashionable strollers, Henryk walked in the park, trying to bring some order to his confused mind. Kasia, Catherine, Orlov: Orlov, Catherine, Kasia, why not write to her? How could he, without implicating her? At the moment, if Charles was to be believed, she was not only safe but in a position of considerable power. Why risk dragging her down? Orlov. Would she not be better off with him?

But never to see her again ... Henryk stood looking down into the silent water. 'Oh, Rasulka,' he whispered. Never to see her again. No. That he could not bear. Catherine. Little Figgy. So now she was Empress, her boundless ambition satisfied. Had she ordered the slaying of her husband? Had her own small hand struck the blow? Had Kasia been present to see the miserable creature die? Side by side with Orlov? Henryk scooped water from the lake and cooled his burning head.

Kasia. Catherine. Orlov. Why not write? Why not write? The words thudded in his brain as he walked for hours beside the dark and silent lake.

* * *

Henryk did not go to Versailles.

After a near sleepless night and a day spent wandering the streets of Paris wrestling with the problem of how he could write to Kasia without giving her away to Shuvalov's spies, he sat, shirt-sleeved and ink-stained, at the table in his room.

For the fifth time he threw down the quill. He ran his fingers through his tousled hair, spreading a smear of ink across his forehead; then, with a shrug of exhausted irritation, he shoved back the chair and began to pace the room with short, angry strides. His shoes scuffed in the snowstorm of torn paper that littered the carpet; he poured himself a glass of wine and drank it in one swift gulp as he would vodka, but it did not help; his brain remained obstinately frozen.

How in hell's name could he write to her at all? He must have been crazy to think there was any way he could outwit the ferrets of the Secret Chancellery. He paused by the window. A coach came down the street; the horses were a spirited pair and the coachman was obviously having trouble for Henryk could hear his voice raised angrily above the heavy clatter of hooves and iron rims. Horses! By God, that was it, that was the answer. He hurried to the table, grabbed fresh paper and began to write.

He wrote slowly and steadily in his large, round hand, pausing now and then to chew the ragged end of the quill, his forehead wrinkled in thought, then once more bent over the paper, and the only sound in the room was the the scratch and squeak of the pen.

' ... and my father left the Ukraine upon the death of my mother in 1732 and, after various adventures with which I need not bother you now, I came to Paris and thence to England where I became very—' Henryk scored out the word 'very' and substituted 'passionately'. It would be better to write a flowery letter, full of feeling: an exiled Pole writing to a countrywoman in Poland. He would not be cold and matter-of-fact, not the character he was imagining. ' ... passionately interested in horses.

'I am deeply involved in the buying and selling of bloodstock. Your name having been mentioned to me by a noted Russian breeder, I have taken the liberty, madame, of writing direct to you as I have heard of your noted interest in and love for thoroughbred animals. I myself am travelling constantly in Europe and Arabia and, at this very moment, find myself in possession of an Arab mare of quite exceptional qualities. Not to put too fine a point upon it, madame, this mare (I call her Rasulka) ...'
The sound of the pen ceased. He sat with his eyes far away, far beyond the confines of that small Paris room, seeing a girl in a dark red riding-skirt and dusty, wrinkled boots, astride a pure

white mare; behind the black fall of her hair a little birch tree rustled its golden leaves. Surely she would remember the name Rasulka? He fought back the wave of memory that threatened to engulf him and went on writing.

' ... is for sale and, should you be interested, I could either bring her to St Petersburg (now that this terrible war, which has affected us all in some degree, is safely over) or, should you not find that convenient, a letter containing your wishes could be sent to ...' Here he stopped again. Where could it be sent? What address could he give without attracting suspicion. He lit the candles, drew the curtains, drank some more wine, trying to find an answer. Then a name came to mind, an echo from his youth in Warsaw. Polinski. He smiled at the recollection of how he had come to be Monsieur Polinski with the address of Novaya Pikova, an estate bordering on Lipno. Janek, his wild young friend of those days, had entered into the scheme with joy. Letters from various women, some old enough to be Henryk's mother, reached their destination via Polinski, Novaya Pikova. This was a happy arrangement for it obviated the inevitable inquisition from his father, who appeared to know everything that went on at Lipno, especially the frequent arrival of letters smelling strongly of a woman's touch. 'Am I paying all this money on your education at Konarski's, whom I don't approve of anyway with his lily-livered liberal clap-trap? By heaven, you've got to do something except hang about this place all day mooning over girls and drinking all the vodka. Why in God's name don't you make do with the peasant girls as I did at your age and leave those high-class whores in Warsaw to those who can afford 'em?' Then, having completely lost track of what he had set out to say in the first place, Count Barinski would finish on his usual roar of rage. 'I'll not have it, d'you hear. If Adam can work at learning to be a soldier then, by the Lord, you can work at—at whatever it is you're doing. Now get out of my sight.'

So Henryk became Polinski and rode over to Novaya Pikova to collect his love-letters. But this was before he had met the grown-up Kasia in the hollow by the birch tree.

Henryk sat down and finished the letter. ' ... to Monsieur Polinski at Novaya Pikova, Province of Podolia. An early reply would be much appreciated lest the matter be delayed a moment longer than is necessary. I remain, madame, your most faithful and devoted servant, H. Polinski.'

He added a postscript: 'I hope very shortly to return to our native country for I am becoming suddenly desperate to see the snows again, the birches in bloom, to hear the hunting-horns echoing in the forests and the music of the wild geese.... Forgive this rustic eulogoy but the truth is, madame, I have been too long away.'

And that was indeed the truth. He was filled with a great longing to feel the earth of Poland beneath his feet and once again to speak his own language.

He stretched his arms above his head in a massive yawn. Then he read through what he had written, altered some words and copied out the letter in its final form. Satisfied at last that nothing he had written could possibly incriminate her, he sealed the first letter he had ever written to Kasia in their lives.

When he went to bed he lay thinking for a while. So now the die was cast: he would not be seeing the Queen, nor Toinon, nor Ewen Cameron. This last made him sad and he tried not to think of his friend but of all the arrangements he would need to make before he could set off for Poland.

First, to arrange for the letter to travel ahead of him in the diplomatic bag to the French Embassy with a covering note asking that it be delivered into the hands of Countess Radienska at the Court of her Imperial Majesty, Empress Catherine of all the Russias. Second—what next? He was very sleepy—ah, yes, a letter to Madame G. saying goodbye and thank you! 'You shall dine with me next week ... ' Next week he would be on the road.

He must see about a horse; money; riding clothes. Tomorrow promised to be a busy day, a thing he had almost forgotten, and the next, and then, with any luck within a week from now he'd leave Paris on his long ride across Europe, for he must follow swiftly on the heels of his letter; get back to Lipno so as to be on hand for her answer, should it come. Of course it would come; of that he was certain. But what then? First get back to Poland. From there he would see more clearly what was to be done. Once at Lipno only a ten days' ride would lie between them.

With the thud of the hooves already in his mind as the miles fell away behind him and the domes of Petersburg rose above the northern forests, Henryk fell asleep on a long, contented sigh.

*   *   *

227

Two days later Madame de Mirabon was up well before dawn to supervise the final arrangements for Henryk's departure. Sleepy servants prepared breakfast in the kitchen and filled his saddle-bags with cold meats, bread, cheese and pastries.

'Well,' she said when he had eaten and stood ready in the hall, 'so you're really leaving.'

'Yes.' Outside he could hear the rattle of the bit, the stamp of hooves on the cobbles as the horse, a big, strong bay, fretted impatiently in the gathering daylight. 'I'm going home,' he added quietly.

'What will you do when you get home?'

'Just lead a peaceful life,' he said. 'I've grown tired of wandering.'

'And you think you'll get that in Poland?' She shook her head with a little quizzical smile. 'I'm afraid you weren't born for a peaceful life.' She looked at the long green riding-coat, the whip in his hand, striking lightly against a high boot, the sword scabbard, the scar that disfigured yet did not mar his face, and thought, This is how he should be dressed, not in velvet or brocade. He's more at ease, prouder somehow.

He nodded with a smile. 'Perhaps not. Now I must go,' he said abruptly, for he hated farewells.

Henryk kissed her on the forehead and went to his horse. He looked down at her from the saddle.

'Thank you,' he said simply. 'Thank you for all your help and kindness.'

She found she could not answer but she fluttered her handkerchief as he rode away. Half-way along the street he turned and waved his hat then vanished behind a cart of vegetables leaving her to go back into her lonely house.

As the sun came up beyond France, Germany, Poland, beyond Siberia, Henryk rode from the East Port and set his eager horse to a canter down the white, dusty road that led into the eye of the rising sun.

*   *   *

On the evening of the thirteenth day after leaving Paris Henryk sat in the taproom of a dirty little inn hard by the village of

Mosciska, on the northern fringes of the Carpathian Mountains. He had ridden some thousand miles already; he was tired and the great muscles of his thighs ached cruelly. Four years at sea, he thought ruefully, was no sort of training for long, hard riding.

The vodka he drank was warm and raw but at least it brought renewed strength to his limbs; the room was low and dark for the sun had dropped behind the mountains. The inn-keeper lighted a few thick tallow candles which added their rank smell to the general stink of the place. Though, he reflected with quiet amusement, compared with the gun-deck, this mixture of dirt, stale food, leather and smoke smelt sweeter than any flower garden.

'Heh, you there, another jug of mead.' The only other visitor to the inn, a young man in a plain brown riding-coat and long, dusty boots, banged his fist impatiently on the table.

'Yes, Your Honour, at once.' The inn-keeper shuffled out.

'God, what a filthy hovel,' observed the young man sourly. He had a sullen look to his freckled face and he often frowned as if seized by a sudden worry. His reddish hair was powdered with the dust of the road and his very blue eyes were slightly bloodshot from the effort of squinting into the summer glare.

'Have you ridden far?' Henryk asked politely.

'Too far for this damned heat.' His voice rose to a shout, 'Heh, hurry up, out there!' He fell to tapping his short, strong fingers on the table, his square chin sunk into his cravat, obviously not wanting to talk. Also feeling disinclined for conversation with strangers, especially bad-tempered ones, Henryk finished his vodka. 'If you'll excuse me,' he said, 'I think I'll try and get what sleep the bugs will allow me.' But his smile was not returned, the stranger merely nodding curtly before returning to his own pre-occupation.

The night was hot and sultry and Henryk stood for a while by the open window. Lightning flickered beyond the dark mountains and, mingled with the distant mutter of thunder, he heard the eerie cry of a wolf. A girl's stifled laughter rose through a darkness rich with the scent of pine trees and lilac.

He lay down on the hard pallet bed in his shirt and breeches, listening drowsily to the little scufflings in the thatch above his head and the throaty purring of a nightjar. A vivid flash of lightning lit up the squalid little room, scaring a rat back to its hole; Henryk imagined the crackling straw mattress beneath him to be alive with scurrying things thirsty for his blood; the bed was

229

tilted at an angle on the crooked floor—like a ship frozen forever in the middle of a roll. But, at that moment, with the howl
of the wolves in his ears, and the sound of Polish voices from
somewhere below, the taste of the cheap vodka in his throat, he
would not have exchanged the room for the greatest hall in Versailles.

For this was Poland. This was his country, his home. He was
tired of wandering, so very tired. He felt himself slipping into
sleep ... Kasia would write ... she would write and then she
would come to him. They'd marry ... there'd be children. ...
They'd grow old together and die and be buried together in the
Polish earth ... Never be apart again ... never. ...

Henryk woke at dawn with a hand on his shoulder and a voice
urgent in his ear.

'Wake up, Your Honour! Wake up!'

'What is it? What the devil's the matter?'

'Your horse,' the inn-keeper stuttered. 'The big bay—'

'Yes, that's my horse.'

'Well, the other gentleman's saddling him. When I said it was
not his horse he threatened to cut me down. I tell you, Your
Honour, he means to ride him away. He—' But Henryk had gone,
already half-way down the rickety stairs in his stockinged feet.
He'd ridden that horse from Paris and had grown fond of him;
he was damned if he'd see him stolen by some surly young lout.

As he reached the yard he saw the red-haired man leading the
horse through the gateway. Running forward, Henryk grabbed the
man's leg as he was throwing the other one over the saddle. With
a powerful heave he dragged the stranger from the horse, and
the two men fell to the ground in a tumbled heap. After a short
struggle in the dust of the yard the young man tore himself
loose from Henryk's grip and jumped to his feet, reaching for the
long pistol in his belt.

'Put it down, you young fool!' Henryk was on his feet facing
the levelled barrel in a half crouch, his eyes never leaving those
of the stranger.

'I'm taking this horse,' said the man in a low voice, conscious
of faces watching the scene round-eyed from the kitchen door.
'If I had any money I'd pay you for him, but I haven't so—stay
where you are!' He noticed Henryk inching forward, saw him
tensed like a cat about to jump. 'Move another step and I'll fire.'
Henryk heard the snarl in his voice, saw the desperation in his

230

eyes, and knew the man would not hesitate to kill.

'Is this a very dignified way of going about the matter,' he asked quietly. 'Brawling like a couple of coachmen in front of a crowd of inquisitive peasants. Can't we discuss things reasonably? Firstly, you must need a horse very badly to go to all this trouble —*behind you, look out!*'

Just for an instant the man's eyes left Henryk, the pistol wavered as he half-turned his head, caught by the oldest trick there is, and in that instant Henryk sprang at him. He took the man across his throat, striking with the edge of his hand as he had once seen it done by Matthew Swaine. As the stranger fell with a sort of dreadful croak, the pistol went off. Henryk felt the wind of the ball along the side of his cheek, heard the smash of broken glass, a woman's frightened cry.

He stood over the writhing figure, watching without much sympathy as the man jerked his head from side to side in choking agony and clutched at his bruised windpipe. After a moment or two Henryk turned and shouted at the gaping faces in the doorway.

'Bring some water—and vodka.'

He went on his knees beside the groaning man, loosened his cravat, holding the mug to the twisted lips. 'Drink this.'

With difficulty the man forced the liquid down his throat.

'Now this.'

He choked violently on the spirits, his eyes rolling in his head. Quite a crowd had gathered, standing in silence goggling at the two gentlemen, one of them in his stockings, the other spitting and hawking into the dust. Fine goings-on indeed there'd be to tell the village about: gentlemen—nobles like as not— fighting with their hands for all the world like ordinary folk, pistols banging, windows broken—and all before the sun was a finger high.

'Haven't you any work to do?' Henryk swept them with angry eyes. They vanished, chattering excitedly among themselves. 'Now, supposing you tell me what this is all about.' Henryk helped the other to his feet.

'I must get to Lvov,' said the young man, his eyes averted from Henryk's steady gaze. His voice was thin and strangled.

'And to get there you're prepared to kill me and steal my horse,' said Henryk slowly and clearly. 'Your business must be of some importance,' he added drily.

'It is. For God's sake, you've got to help me.' The words gathered strength as he spoke, though in a low voice, glancing round to see they were not overheard. 'You're a Pole, aren't you?'

'Yes.'

'You love Poland?'

Henryk nodded.

'Then I'll tell you this: I ride to Lvov on my—our—country's business and it's imperative I reach the city by nightfall.' He studied Henryk's expression as he spoke but it gave away nothing. After a silence the man shrugged. 'There's no reason why you should believe the word of a would-be thief and murderer.' He met Henryk's look defiantly. Take it or leave it, his expression said; I tried and failed, but at least I tried and better luck next time, should the contingency arise.

The obvious sincerity in the young man's voice when he spoke of his mission had impressed Henryk and, besides, there was something in the bearing of this man that appealed to him.

'I believe you,' he said. 'But tell me one thing. Why didn't you ask me direct for the loan of my horse when you found yours was lame? Were you afraid to disturb my sleep or what?' Amusement gleamed in his eyes.

'No,' said the young man with an answering grin that gave his face the look of a mischievous child. 'You see, if you'd refused me then, I'd have had to kill you in bed, and I wouldn't have enjoyed that.'

For a moment Henryk regarded this strange young man in silence, then he burst out laughing.

'Well, by God, that's the most original excuse for taking someone else's horse I've ever heard.'

The stranger joined in the laughter as much as the pain in his throat would allow, and through various cracks in walls and shutters eyes watched curiously as the two gentlemen held out their hands to each other, then brushed the dust from themselves, all the while talking cheerfully as though they were the very oldest friends.

And a keen disappointment was felt at the tame ending of what, at one moment, had promised to be a diverting and possibly bloody spectacle.

*   *   *

They rode in silence for the first few miles, the hooves muffled in the thick summer dust. On their right hand the thickly wooded mountains shone very green in the sunshine; here and there patches of silver mist still hung in the hollows and smoke rose lazily from the little timber villages and foresters' huts.

Before them the road stretched into the shimmering, hazy distance, leading across the plain to Lvov. They passed few travellers. Now and then a creaking cart with a peasant dozing over the greasy reins; an occasional figure trudging stolidly to somewhere.

Henryk enjoyed the sun on his face, upturned to watch the slow, majestic circling of an eagle.

'I'm sorry about what happened.' The stranger blurted out the words in a tone that showed Henryk he was a man who found it hard to apologise. 'I hope—' he paused, searching for words— 'I hope you don't bear me too much ill-will.'

'Ill-will? No. I expect in similar circumstances I might have done the same.' Though, he thought grimly, I'd have made certain of the business. 'Not knowing the circumstances however, it's a little difficult to be sure.' But the stranger was not to be drawn and sat bowed forward in the saddle of the sorry-looking beast Henryk had managed to purchase in the village.

'What's your name, friend?' he asked.

'Dombrowski. Jan Dombrowski.'

'And mine is Barinski. Henryk Barinski.'

Dombrowski straightened up with a look of keen interest on his face. 'Are you anything to do with Adam Barinski?'

'He's my brother. You know him?'

'Very well, yes. We meet often in Warsaw at the Diet. Sometimes I stay at Lipno.' Strange, Jan thought, he had never heard either Adam or his father speak of this brother. He knew he himself had never set eyes on him; you'd not forget a scar like that in a hurry.

'How is my father?'

'In good health. At least he was when we met about four months ago at the last Diet. You should hear him speak.' Dombrowski's voice grew enthusiastic. 'By heavens, he'll stand no nonsense from anyone. Why, he told Keyserling to his face that if the Russian troops were not withdrawn from Polish soil at once he personally would ride to Moscow—at the head of a Polish army. Oh, I tell you, your father's a great man, a true patriot.' So they'd taken to politics, Henryk thought, and left the running of Lipno to the agent, Walenski, he supposed; if he was still alive.

'Keyserling?' he queried. 'Who—?'

'The Russian Ambassador. Or so he calls himself. In reality he's Catherine's personal mouth-piece sent here to see that Poniatowski becomes the next King of Poland—'

'Poniatowski? King of Poland? Have you gone mad?'

Dombrowski gazed at Henryk in amazement. 'How long have you been away from Poland?'

'About thirteen years. I've no idea what's going on.' He watched an approaching cart, the little foal kicking up the dust behind it. 'But Poniatowski—*King*! No, I don't believe you.'

'Catherine wants him on the throne. The whore of Petersburg intends her paramour to wear the crown of the Piasts and the Jagiellos, the crown that Sobieski wore.' Dombrowski's voice trembled with anger. 'But, by God, he won't get it, not while there are men like your father alive—and many, many others who think like him. They're the men who *are* Poland, not the damned Czartoryskis and their toadies who want to see this country in the arms of Russia.'

He broke off as the long cart went slowly by, piled high with mown grass. A man with a grey beard and wrinkled, weather-beaten face flicked the mare with a curling lash; the girl beside him threw a quick sidelong glance at the two riders from her long blue eyes; she was barefoot and her strong brown legs gleamed with the sheen of polished wood. These people were Poland too, Henryk thought, raising his whip in greeting. Give them a leader, the right leader and, like the Dark People of Russia, they would fight. It was not only the nobles who should have the right and privilege to draw their swords for Poland. 'One never sees a smiling peasant in Poland.' That's what he had heard said. But she had smiled all right. He turned in his saddle and saw her craning round the grass for another peep at the fine gentleman who had called out 'Good day' so politely.

As they rode through the mounting heat of the day, through the little straggly villages full of geese, scrawny chickens, curly-coated pigs and dirty, brown children, Jan Dombrowski told Henryk of the shame that was threatening their country.

'Ever since the beginning of the war, when Russian troops marched through Poland to fight the Prussians, we've fallen more and more under Russian influence. And now that Catherine's

Empress, her ambition's so swollen she won't rest until this country's part of her Empire.' That was true, she had always been ambitious, even as a little girl. Henryk remembered her at Volochisk; the firm resolve in her childish words, 'I want to *be* someone. And some day I *shall* be.' He remembered the gipsy woman who told fortunes and how she had looked at Stanislas and little Figgy and refused to say anything, shaking her gaunt head in stubborn silence. Had she really all those years ago looked and seen crowns on both their heads?

He shook off his memories and concentrated on what his companion was saying.

'They're back on Polish soil again, ten thousand of 'em. Of course the pretence is they're merely marching from Courland to the Ukraine, though God knows why—'

'Are they causing damage or molesting people?'

'Not as far as we know. But—well, Christ alive, it's a damnable insult.' Dombrowski's face set in a pugnacious frown. 'But I tell you this much, at the first hint of trouble we'll rise and wipe them out and to hell with bloody Catherine. I tell you—' Dombrowski stopped suddenly and taking out his handkerchief wiped the sweat from his face. Careful, what did he know of this man? Just because the other Barinskis—how often in these dangerous days were families split? But he'd given away no names and the views of the old Barinski were common knowledge.

Henryk was wondering with a certain amusement what this fiery young man would say if he knew that his companion had once shared 'bloody Catherine's' bed; that her first Lady-in-Waiting was half a Czartoryski, and cousin to the man who might soon live as King in the royal castle of Wavel.

'Cavalry's what we need,' said Henryk after they had left another village behind. 'Light cavalry under a man like Lisowski.'

'Or Debolecki,' put in Dombrowski eagerly. These were men who had led Poland's cavalry the century before when she stretched from the Baltic to the Black Sea. 'The days of the Winged Hussars are over,' he went on. 'The modern musket has seen to that, and the guns.'

'Swarms of light cavalry,' said Henryk. 'That can strike fast and be away, back into the forests if necessary, before the enemy has time to realise what hit him.'

'We'd have the Tatars with us.'

'And the Cossacks?'

'I don't know.' Dombrowski shook his head. 'They're treacherous devils.'

As they rode and talked in this fashion Henryk thought of his words to Madame de Mirabon and her answer: 'Just lead a peaceful life.' . . . 'I'm afraid you weren't born for a peaceful life.'

For, as he listened to Dombrowski, heard the passionate fervour in his voice, Henryk's imagination took fire. His mind filled with phrases from the past that kindled a new vision of the future; hazy as yet, hazy as the distant spires of Lvov rising from the shimmering horizon. 'One day Poland will be great again.' . . . And Josef Pulawski, another patriot and one with a wise head on his shoulders, saying, 'The time will come when Poland will need men like you.' The memory of how his own grandfather had brought the green standard of Mahomet to Sobieski outside Vienna.

'When Augustus was proposed for King,' said Dombrowski, 'some Polish nobles were dragged to Warsaw in chains by the Russians to vote for him. Nothing's altered. If we don't act we'll all be in chains. Poniatowski talks of bringing a new era of learning and culture to Poland. What use is culture to slaves?'

'I can promise you one thing,' said Henryk slowly. 'I am no friend of King Poniatowski's.'

'Would you support the election of Prince Radziwill?'

'Anyone rather than Poniatowski.'

The sun was low behind them as they came within close view of Lvov.

'I shall be here for a week at least,' said Dombrowski. He hesitated for a moment before his next words. Henryk, noticing the pause, said quietly, 'You can trust me.'

'Whilst I'm in Lvov I have to see certain men who think as I do—'

'As *we* do,' Henryk corrected him with a smile.

'May I tell them you would join us?'

'Yes.' The answer came with no hint of hesitation. 'But first I must see my home.'

'You'll be at Lipno for some time?'

'Yes, you can find me there.'

The evening sun struck glowing brown from the walls. The sunset was behind him, he thought, with a sudden lifting of the heart. Ahead lay the sunrise, tomorrow, the next day, the next week, month, year, that way lay the dawn.

Spurring his horse, Henryk rode fast towards the city gates.

Turning his head, he shouted back to Dombrowski, 'It seems I've chosen a good time to come back.'

And Dombrowski followed his lead, thinking: This may be the man we need, the man that Poland needs.

*   *   *

A cloud of pigeons, descendants of Kasia's white fantails, flew with a clatter of wings from the ruins of Volochisk as the horseman coaxed his horse carefully across the rotting drawbridge and into the courtyard.

They circled for a while above the roofless, gutted house then swooped back to their nesting-places in the blackened walls.

Henryk sat hunched in the saddle, thick with dust, gazing at the spot where he had been cut down fourteen years before. His hand crept to the top of the scar where it divided his forehead and he felt again the shock of the slashing scimitar, expecting the hot blood to pour across his mutilated face.

Slowly his eyes took in the courtyard: the jumble of charred beams, stone, plaster and splintered glass visible among the grass and plaited briars. Remains of the wooden balcony hung from the wall—where Kasia had stood with a smoking pistol in her hand. In his mind he heard the high-pitched yells of triumph as the Turks burst through the gates, '*Allah akbar!* God is great!' God had surely been Turkish that day. The voice of Kasia's father, raised above the demented bedlam of battle—the rasping clash of steel, the screams of pain and fear—shouting for everyone to get to the chapel.

He heard the terrible sounds, trapped in the courtyard, rising with the flames to the peerless summer sky—it had been a day such as this until the smoke had rolled across the sun to bring the darkness of night to the great white house.

Now there was nothing but a little breeze stirring the long grass, cool on his heated skin; the placid murmur of the pigeons, and the ghosts who would haunt this place even when the last stone had vanished beneath the earth.

Henryk rode away from the Volochisk, past the overgrown remnants of the serfs' cottages and up the narrow, winding path that led to the ridge above the river running between the lands of Radienski and Barinski. Now and then he bent low in the saddle below the oak branches hanging across the path. The last time he had ridden this track it had been at full gallop behind the flying hooves of Kinga, the little white Arab, with death yelling at his heels. The woods were alive with birds, the soft sigh of the breeze, the hum of insects; the path was untrodden, for few ventured into the haunted valley of Volochisk.

But, up on the ridge, the hollow was still there, where he and Kasia had flattened the thick grass beneath their bodies; and, beside it, the birch tree.

He dismounted and, after tethering his weary horse in the shade of the oaks, Henryk lay down in the hollow, his arms under his head, a piece of grass between his teeth. Swallows flew high against a background of small clouds, promising more fine weather; a cuckoo called from the woods beyond the river, from his own lands, and another answered from near by; the horse rattled his bridle once then drooped his head with closed eyes, now and then flickering his ears lazily at the flies.

The birch tree thrust its branches over one side of the hollow. When he had first discovered her sleeping here, that little tree had been no more than six feet tall. Well, he thought, we're all thirteen years older now. But the small round leaves still flickered and rustled in the sunlit breeze as they had done that summer of long ago.

The insistent call of the wood-doves brought an overwhelming desire for sleep, but he raised himself on his elbows, glancing sideways to where Kasia had lain unashamed, her splendid body tawny gold in the sun. He heard his voice from the past, 'You'll always be my woman, Kasia.'

And hers in answer: 'Say it again, my darling. Say it.' Her head thrown back, lips parted in a smile of pure joy.

'You'll always be my woman.'

He felt again the same overpowering surge of tenderness that had filled his heart to bursting then.

'Will you wait, Rasulka? Whatever happens, will you wait?'

And she had replied, 'Yes, Henryk, I'll wait.'

But this time, would she have waited? The image of Alexie appeared before his eyes, unbidden and unwanted. And, if it came to war with Russia, on which side would her loyalties lie? With

Catherine, her friend and benefactoress, or with those Poles who wanted freedom for their country? Would she leave the Empress her friend—little Figgy—and come home to fight beside him? For, at that moment, the die was cast irrevocably and Henryk knew where his own future lay; he knew that for him a life of peace was no more than a wistful dream.

But Kasia? She was a member of the most powerful family in Poland; a family which, through jealousy, envy and its own misguided wish for friendship with Russia, was bringing upon itself the scorn and hatred of all her countrymen who preferred death to life under the Russian yoke.

He pulled a clump of grass from the ground; black earth clung to a length of root. He crumbled it between his finger and thumb, holding the rich, dark powder to his nose. Catherine's armies would trample this Polish earth; the Cossacks, seeing their chance to turn on the Poles, would swarm over the rolling Ukrainian hills which they always coveted for themselves. No birds would sing in the forests; the corn would stand neglected in the fields and at nights the skies would be red with the flames of burning villages, the sickly stench of the dead. He knew war and hated it but if it came then they must be prepared. As Dombrowski had said, 'If you stick your head in the sand, then the enemy can cut your body from it.'

There was work to be done, and every day would count. The days of waiting for orders, of mindless obedience were past. Now he would lead: not on his feet or on the splintering deck of a ship but in the saddle, with a sabre in his hand and the thunder of hooves behind him.

And when he returned from the charge Kasia would be waiting —somehow, though God knows how it would be done, she must be told what was at stake for the country she loved as he did.

Consumed with a sudden tearing impatience, Henryk leapt to his feet. Even now her letter might be waiting for him.

Mounting quickly, he rode down towards the river, towards the lands of Lipno, his home.

THE BANNERS OF WAR

(following *The Banners of Love*)

is the second of a sequence of novels

having the collective title of

DESTINY OF EAGLES